I0630958

TALES
FROM THE
LAZARETTO

BY THOM CARNELL

Secord turned to face his adversary. He was ready now. He had his gun, and he had a plan. He'd been in worse situations. And so... Secord unceremoniously kicked the big Italian in the chest, knocking him backward. Giordano's arms wheeled about wildly as he stumbled back a few steps.

The big man's back struck the window, his body weight sending cracks careening across the glass. He bounced off the damaged pane like a pool ball rebounding off a bumper and dropped to his knees. Secord was amazed at how fast he got up, especially for a guy his size. But then, just as he was coming to his feet and raising the .38 for a second shot, Secord beat him to the draw, rapidly shooting him a time or two in the center of his chest with the Smith & Wesson.

The force of the heavy bullets hit Giordano in the sternum like a kick from a pissed-off mule. The first bullet struck meat, lifting his body upward. Secord heard him grunt aloud as the slug dug deep. The Italian's eyes caught Secord's for a micro-instant. He blinked, and then the second bullet blew him through the damaged window. His heavy carcass arched back, crashing through the glass, and tumbling out of the shattered window like a thrown die. And the last thing Secord saw of the Italian as he disappeared into the night, were the soles of his polished shoes

Copyright ©2023 by Thom Carnell
ISBN 978-1-63789-713-3
Macabre Ink is an imprint of Crossroad Press Publishing
All rights reserved. No part of this book may be used or reproduced in any manner whatso-
ever without written permission except in the case of
brief quotations embodied in critical articles and reviews
For information address Crossroad Press at 141 Brayden Dr., Hertford, NC 27944
www.crossroadpress.com

First Edition

CONTENTS

FOREWORD

Back when I first started working on this collection of stories, The Coronavirus Pandemic had only just started ramping up (i.e., not a lot of people had yet died), and some folks were already beginning to isolate themselves. A few were even wearing masks. And so, with my wife and I having a background in (and an understanding of) science, we hunkered down: isolating, social distancing, masking up, not going out, etc.

I finally decided that it might be a good idea for me to gather all of the stories I wrote between then and a) when the whole thing was—for want of a better word—over, and b) I arrived at a word count that would signal I'd done enough (I was shooting for roughly 80,000 words or so). The idea was to write a bunch of stories on a variety of spooky subjects (i.e., whatever piqued my admittedly jaded interest) while in containment. Then, I would edit them, and gather them together into a volume in the order that they were completed.

Y'know, to show a little diversity.

I remember thinking, 'Well, well, well... aren't you just so clever, Thom?'

Since then, a year or three has come and gone, and far too many people have died. During that time, I've seen that a few writers have had the same idea as I did. But never being one who cared about what other people were doing, I kept on writing. Finally, I had (more than) enough tales to bind them all between the two covers you now hold in your hot, little, readerly hands.

The stories contained herein are, in this writer's humble opinion, fantastical, at times poignant, and written with an eye toward the reader signing on, buckling in, and having a bit of fun for a brief period of time. Like a dance... or something far more intimate. It's funny, I often think of my stories as brief interactions between you, the reader, and myself. A connection, if you will, that makes it possible for us to join together and to become a single imagining unit. Writer... and Reader.

Bound, albeit momentarily (or for as long as it takes you to read the story) for a brief interlude where it is my job to try and tickle your fancy, charm your intellect, and hopefully, frighten you a little.

It is a fantastic thing when it all comes together and works… and I think it does here. So, join me, for a brief dance, an intermezzo, a whirl or two around the dance floor. I'll try not to step on your toes.

ADVENT

This story came about as the result of a recent discussion I had with a good friend of mine about Death. Having worked in funeral homes for a bit, I have these discussions a lot; probably more than I should. I was saying how I'd grown tired over the years of seeing a preponderance of frightening, malevolent depictions of Death (and, by extension of that, of Dying) and I wanted to try something sometime that was a little less, well... intimidating. Y'know, take the idea of a non-threatening—almost reassuring—demise out for a spin and see what I might come up with. The story below is the result of that train of thought. The layout of the hospital, by the way, like most of the hospitals in my stories, is based on a real place at which I once worked: The Clinical Research Center at UCSD. It's my hope that this tale will make you think; maybe even reconsider your position on the topic. And, hopefully, it can blunt the edge of what is, let's face it, inevitable. As always, I leave it to you to decide...

The tired day's sun was just setting over the low-slung hills that surrounded the small coastal city of San Julio. Orange twilight splashed across the landscape, painting the sides of the downtown buildings in a Halloween-like glow as shadows, once firm and fixed, now grew long and rubbery.

At this time of the day, traffic from the city's evening commute had slowed noticeably on the one highway that cut like an artery through the center of town. Meaning that most of the people who worked in downtown San Julio had by now gotten themselves out of the city and safely home, where they were currently busy preparing their dinners and settling in for the night. Even the usually hectic pedestrian traffic around the city's main hospital had petered out by now, the physicians and administrative staff having departed their posts, and leaving the healing of the sick for another day.

Along the wards of the infirmary, as the dark of night loomed ominously overhead, silence settled over the corridors like the falling of an autumn leaf. Now, only the plaintive whimpering of the very ill and infirmed could be heard echoing through the halls as each pled their case before their respective gods, begging for some of that old-time salvation. But up on the ninth floor, in what was known as the Comprehensive Long-term Care Unit, it was quiet.

It was always quiet up there.

It was a place meant for quiet.

The Ninth Floor, as it was referred to by the staff, was a part of the facility that had been left unused for years. It had initially been built as a pediatric ward, but things changed over the years as each incoming Administration shuffled things around to serve their own agendas. Now, the entire floor housed but two things: a small two-bed sleep lab run by a doctor no one ever saw and a few polysomnographic technicians, and the multiple bed 'continuous care facility' which saw to patients who had suffered illness or trauma and were now in extended comas, left to dwell in the twilight of their own kind of medical purgatory.

Abigail Johansson had worked at San Julio General for more years than she'd like to remember, and she'd arrived every day that she was scheduled at this exact same time, walking these exact same streets. As usual, she went in through the E.R., taking the elevator near the gift shop, and making her way down the already darkening halls to her spot on the CCU ward. Most of the day shift had already left for home by now, and since she was the only staff scheduled on the floor that night, it was as quiet as a library. She knew that tonight it would be her and maybe one of the sleep techs—if they bothered to show up at all—working at the other end of the building. But that was about it.

When she'd arrived at the Nurse's Station, she greeted, and then said goodbye to, Cecily, the Charge Nurse who was waiting at the main reception desk to be relieved. Abigail said hello to her and smiled as she saw her pick up her backpack and head toward the elevator without saying much of anything. She saw Cecily wave back at her from over her shoulder as she got into the elevator.

After that, Abigail was all alone.

Her nights here on the CCU were usually pretty quiet and, for the most part, uneventful; exactly the way she liked them. Take tonight, for example. Tonight was a Thursday, so she knew that the most she'd have to do on her shift was to update a few patient charts after she'd made her rounds, and to try and make sure no one died.

Just like she had the night before.

Just like she did every night.

World without end, amen.

If something like that ever did happen, though, she knew to first log the time of death in the patient chart, and then contact the hospital's morgue. They'd have someone come to clean up everything and the body would be gone by dawn. In the morning, to any incoming eye, it would be as if that person had never existed; even their names would be gone from the Patient Whiteboard. Things were kept orderly here in the CCU, and Abigail was just one of the many people who worked hard to make sure that standards were maintained.

She hung her coat and purse up on a peg in the Break Room, stowing her usual 'egg salad sandwich and Ziploc bag of potato chips' lunch in the fridge. Several years ago, the wife of a patient who'd passed had given her the firetruck-red lunch bag she always used when she'd come to collect her husband's things. The front of it had a cartoon image of a nurse dressed like a superhero, her cape fluttering in an imaginary breeze. Abby cherished it and had used it on every one of her shifts ever since. The fact that it had been given to her by a patient's family... well, it made it all the more special, didn't it?

As she was leaving the Break Room, Abigail caught a quick glimpse of her reflection in the metal paper towel dispenser by the sink, her features pulled like saltwater taffy into something out of a fun house mirror. She took a second to stop to appraise what she could see of her appearance, tucking a lock of her brown and gray hair behind her ear before heading out onto the ward to get to work.

In the reflective surface, she'd noticed that there were more lines on her face—there, just around the eyes—than there had been back when she'd first started working here. Where there had once been smooth, supple skin, now there remained only weathered parchment. She idly marked it as an all too real reminder of the slow, but ardent, passage of time.

She'd been at San Julio General for several decades now and had continued to work here even during the terrible time of her James' passing. She'd always known that her retirement would come one day, but the notion that the majority of her time had already passed her by—and so quickly—still saddened her.

Some of the best years of her life had been spent working here at the hospital, most of her friends had come from the relationships she'd found and formed here. These days though, most of those folks had either retired, died, or moved on to other jobs, in other hospitals, in other cities. Gone, having left their friends behind.

It wasn't like anyone could be expected to work at one place forever, though, right?

At one point, about midway through her career as a Neo-Natal Nurse, the hospital administrators came to her and asked if she might consider a transfer here to the CCU, asking her to help care for those who could no longer care for themselves. The notion seemed like a good fit, like a good place for her to contribute and make a difference until it came time for her to one day move on, too.

So, she'd agreed.

And she'd been here ever since.

Not that she was looking forward to it, retiring. She'd just always been one of those people who defined themselves by what they did for a living. Being a nurse gave her an identity and a sense of purpose. She loved her job. She loved helping people, being there for them, and wasn't quite sure what she'd do with herself once she was forced to leave. She was sure she'd figure it out—she always did. But the idea of one day not being able to come here to help people filled her heart with an empty sense of impending misfortune.

Before getting to her daily tasks, she decided to first check the large Whiteboard mounted along one wall of the Nurse's Station for any updates on her patients. She was not surprised to see that none of the names or prognoses had changed, and luckily no new ones had been added. Which meant... that, while the majority of the CCU's patients were moribund, none of them were actively dying.

Not tonight anyway. No, these folks were content to merely idle here as they made up their minds whether to return to Life.... or to follow the light that kept catching their eye at the end of their long, dark tunnel.

"No new arrivals. No last-minute, or impending, departures," she whispered to herself, thankful for the promise of an uneventful shift.

Abigail did a quick walk-through of the empty hallways along the ninth floor to check for anyone working late. The last thing she needed was for someone to pop up and surprise her in the middle of the night. It had happened before, and she'd nearly soiled her britches each and every time. Thankfully, she found the corridors all deserted—even the sleep lab at the other end of the building was dark and unattended. She was all alone up here on the Ninth Floor tonight with no one to talk to and no one to bother her with their idle chit-chat.

"As it should be," she mumbled quietly to herself.

Returning to the Nurse's Station, she checked the clipboard for any general notes from the Medical Director, restocked the Pyxis station—an automated vending machine that verified prescriptions and dispensed medication to medical staff that had been granted the proper pass key—and she was ready to get started with her day.

Abby was responsible for making rounds twice every shift—once at the beginning, and once at the end—to chart on the condition of those in her care. For each, it was her job to document their individual vital signs, check them for anything out of the ordinary (like new bruising, bed sores, or sub-dermal bleeding), and then write all her observations into the patient's medical chart. Once her second round was completed at around five a.m., she had only but to wait until the first of her morning relief arrived at six.

Without feeling much of a sense of hurry, she walked out onto the ward, noticing with pride the precise way the bunks were all lined up along either side of the room. Curtain dividers separated each bed and looked like the bodies of ghosts that were hung out to dry. All but two of the beds were occupied, the slumbering patients all laying on their backs under thin, cotton blankets; quiet and still.

Each patient had their own individual configurations of machines, all gathered around them in their orderly fashion, attending them, betraying each of their biological secrets. Lights blinked on and off like Christmas strands, and the low thrum from the chorus of concentrators and ventilators that provided each bed's occupant with their required oxygen kept time.

Hhhhk-kah. Hhhhk-kah.

Hhhhk-kah. Hhhhk-kah.

All of which served as a counterpoint to the rhythm section of EKG monitors that steadily, albeit quietly, counted out time, beeping like metronomes.

Abigail approached the first bed on the left, knowing that she'd eventually work her way down the row, and back up the other side of the room. She observed the body of a small boy of about eight lying motionless in the bed. His thin arms were by his side, secured to the bed frame by thick, canvas straps. Leather mittens protectively covered his hands. They did that to keep the patients from hurting themselves with their flailing hands and fingernails. She watched him for a second as he lay there. She expertly checked the array of tubes and wires going in and out of the boy like supply lines.

He lay quietly in the bed as he had for weeks now, sometimes staring wide-eyed up at the ceiling, other times with eyes closed as if he were merely sleeping. By all appearances, he looked fine, even healthy; again, like he was only asleep. But the fact of the matter was that he was quite the opposite and was by no means well.

The boy had been catatonic like this since the day he was first admitted, and the doctors were beginning to fear something called "cerebromedullospinal disconnection" or "locked-in syndrome." That is to say, that they suspected he'd developed a neurological disorder characterized by complete paralysis (with the sometime exception of the eyes) wherein the patient remained awake and aware, but unable to answer. In other words, his mind could well be conscious, it's just that it was buried inside a body that had been left unresponsive.

She picked up the kid's chart from its hook on the foot of the bed. Flipping the metal cover up, she inspected the first page on the stack of paper clipped into the folder at the top. Even though she knew him from having been one of his attending nurses since he'd come in, she still checked the name at the top of the first page—Gordon, Franklyn—and then verified it against the thin plastic band wrapped around his wrist as per protocol.

She grabbed a pen from a small pocket in her scrubs shirt and began notating the boy's vitals: his blood pressure, his oxygen saturation, and heart rate. Everything looked fine, given that he was comatose, but she made note of them, nonetheless. With a click, she put her pen away and rehung the chart back on its hook. But then, just as she was planning to move on to the next bed, she noticed something move out of the corner of her eye, something—or someone—milling about the hallway over by the Nurse's Station.

The someone... was an older, Asian man, not too tall, with short-cropped, gray hair and a wide, friendly appearance. By the look of his face and complexion, he was one of the many Filipino workers that were employed by the hospital. He had on one of the gray jumpsuit uniforms that the maintenance people wore, and he was carrying a small, orange case about the size of a tackle box in his one hand. A thick pair of glasses connected by a length of chain hung around his neck to presumably prevent him from losing them. He was standing there looking up and down the hallway; first in one direction, and then the other. Like he was waiting for a cab.

"Can I help you?" Abigail called out to him, her voice bouncing like a ball down the empty, tiled corridor.

"He-hello?" he responded, as he continued to look around him, searching for the source of the voice. The man's tone sounded kind of confused, and a little lost.

Abigail stepped away from the boy's bed and walked into the

hallway that led out to where the man was waiting. She passed the Nurse's Station, checking the time on the wall clock out of reflex: 11:47. Rounding the corner, she caught up to the man near the fire extinguisher that was mounted on the wall by the elevator.

"You look a little lost," Abigail said, smiling and crossing her arms over her chest. For a moment, she thought that she recognized the man, thinking she'd seen him around the building sometime in the past. The when and the why of which eluded her, though. But she was sure she'd seen him before.

The short man smiled at her as he ran his hand through his thick, dark hair and looked embarrassed. He set his toolkit onto the ground, and pulled a dull, orange work cloth from his back pocket. Wiping his hands off on it, he extended one of them—his right—to her in introduction.

"Sorry, Ma'am," he said congenially. "My name is… Nathaniel. Nathaniel Pangilinan. I'm with Maintenance. I'm here about a Service Request we got regarding a dripping faucet." He grinned cordially. "Sound familiar?"

She smiled back at him as she hesitantly took his hand with the tips of her fingers. It didn't surprise her to feel how rough his skin felt against her own. "Oh dear, yes… it's in the Break Room. Darn thing's been leaking for ages." She let go of his grip and directed him down the hallway. "It's just over here. Y'know, I was about to make some coffee. Would you care for some?"

"Well, I wouldn't say no," he replied as he chuckled softly, picking his toolkit back up and following along after her.

Together, they walked down the long hallway to where the Break Room lay. An empty wheelchair had been left in the middle of the hallway, so Abigail moved it aside, making a mental note to call the switchboard after her break and have someone come and take it back to the E.R. where it belonged. As the two of them entered the small break room, Abigail pointed to the sink in question.

"That's it there… Nathaniel, was it?"

The Filipino man smiled at her and nodded but remained where he was in the doorway.

"Let me just grab the water I need for the coffee," she said cordially, "and she's all yours."

He nodded again, setting his toolkit onto one of the two folding chairs set at the small table where everyone ate. She took the pot out from under the coffee maker and filled it with cold water from the tap. The clear liquid swirled happily around the inside of the glass in a small whirlpool as it filled.

When she was done, she poured the liquid into the top of the machine and set the pot back where she'd gotten it. Reaching down, she retrieved a paper filter and a silver foil packet of pre-ground coffee from the drawer. With a practiced hand, she then loaded the screen into its basket, and broke open the bag of grounds, dumping them in.

"I've seen you around here before, haven't I?" Abigail asked nonchalantly as she busied herself with replacing the basket and switching on the coffeemaker. "I mean, you've been here on the ward before, haven't you? Maybe fixing something?"

He shook his head. "You very well might have. I mean, I've been up here on jobs a few times, but... I don't think we've ever officially met." He smiled. "I'd remember. I have a way with names and faces."

"Hmmm," she responded, her voice sounding like she was unsure.

No matter what he said, she was convinced she'd seen him someplace around the hospital. She, too, never forgot a face. And how could she ever forget a name like Pangilinan?

The thought nagged at her. And she'd learned long ago that, when her intuition tapped her on the shoulder—like when it told her that she'd seen someone somewhere at some point before—then, she could—and should—always bet the rent that she had indeed seen them. Finally, she was through cleaning up, and she presented the sink to him like she'd just performed a magic trick.

"All yours."

Nathaniel picked his toolkit up and walked over to the sink, setting the orange case onto the counter. He opened the cabinet door underneath and bent down to take a look. Poking around inside for a second, he fussed with something he saw there, before finally standing back up and opening his toolkit. He pulled a heavy pair of channel-locks from inside of the case and returned to whatever he was looking at under the counter.

"So, have you been with Maintenance long?" Abigail asked politely. Her mother had always impressed upon her the need to show interest in others, especially if there was even the slightest chance that you'd be working around them again in the future. "You said that you'd been here for a little while. Did you transfer from another hospital?"

"Not... really," he said from under the sink, his voice sounding hollow within the cabinet. "I mostly worked, uh... freelance before I came here."

Abigail smiled and nodded as she pulled the other chair out from the table and sat down. Once she was settled, she rubbed her hands together to try and warm them. It had gotten cold in the small room all of a sudden, and she eyed the air conditioning control on the wall suspiciously before glancing over to see how their coffee was doing. The steaming black water had filled the pot to about halfway, so she knew it wouldn't be long. Its rich aroma was already filling the air like incense.

"Well, I think you'll like it here," she said, her eyes drifting up to a small corkboard mounted next to the fridge. There were a few flyers for upcoming nursing seminars push-pinned there as well as a signup sheet for Cecily's son's baseball team's fundraiser. "I know I do. They're fair here and the benefits are excellent."

There was some muffled clanking from where Nathaniel was working, but all too soon, he was back on his feet, putting his wrench back into his case, and setting its latch.

"See, that didn't take long at all," he said, carefully shutting the cabinet door. "You just had a little somethin' under there that needed a bit of tightening."

"Job well done then," Abigail replied, getting back to her feet. "And perfect timing, too. The coffee looks just about done. Do you still have time?"

Nathaniel nodded eagerly and stepped aside so that she could pour them their drinks. Abigail plucked two small Styrofoam cups from a plastic sleeve that was set to the right of the shiny, metal coffeemaker. She quickly poured out a bit of the black liquid from the pot into the Styrofoam and handed one of the steaming cups to her guest.

"Be careful! It's hot," she warned with a grin, raising her cup to salute him over the rim.

Nathaniel accepted the drink and casually leaned up against the counter. He blew a stream of air over the rim, spinning the vapor coming off the cup into nothingness. He took a short sip and smiled. "Mmmm, that's good. If there is one thing I love here, it's the coffee."

Abigail wasn't sure what he meant by the remark, but she smiled anyway. Here? Did he mean at the hospital? Or in San Julio, or someplace else? She finally let it go, thinking that he seemed nice; not threatening or too officious. He seemed like the kind of person who enjoyed his work and was, judging by how quick he was with the sink, good at it. In the moment, she decided that she liked him… and was somehow even more convinced that she'd met him somewhere before. And besides… it might have been something as simple as a slip of the tongue.

"So, tell me," Nathaniel asked her conversationally. "Do you like working here in the CCU?" He took another hesitant sip of his hot beverage as he eyed her over the cup's edge.

Abigail nodded as she took a sip of her own beverage. The coffee was hot and rich, and she felt it quickly warm her insides as it cascaded down to her stomach. And yet, even with the temperature of the drink, she still felt oddly cold. The hair on her forearms was standing up, and she suddenly felt like something icy had just trickled down the back of her neck.

"I do," she answered after swallowing her mouthful of the bitter fluid. "You see, I'd been a nurse for a long time, and, while it was always rewarding, there was still a piece that I felt was missing." She smiled at him warmly as she shrugged her shoulders. "I found that piece—and peace, I guess—here. See, these," and she looked back toward the room where the patient beds lay, "are the people who Science and Medicine have more or less given up on. The ones who they've been unable to fix. So, they put them all up here on The Ninth to pass on unobserved." She looked up at him earnestly. "And I don't think that's right. I don't think anyone should die alone. Someone should be there to properly send them off, y'know?"

Nathaniel nodded thoughtfully in agreement. "And I don't doubt that that kind of thinking has helped ease the suffering for quite a lot of people, Abigail. But I don't know..." He thought a second, silently letting his gaze drift around the room. Then, "Don't you ever get tired of being around such hopelessness, so much, you know... death?"

She thought his question over for a second before answering. She wanted to properly compose her thoughts. But then, she shook her head and took another sip of her coffee. "You know, Nathaniel, right after I got my nursing license, I worked for some time in a Neonatal Ward. My goodness, I saw so many babies born..." Her expression softened at the memory and an almost angelic smile lit up her time-lined face.

Then, that very same smile lit up the room.

Nathaniel sipped his coffee but said nothing.

"And over the years," she continued reflectively, "I saw so much life come into the world. And yes, there was death and there was oftentimes pain... and plenty of tears. But overall, there was just so much life. Being there, much like being here, felt like an honor for me just to be in the room." She looked up at him earnestly. "It just made sense for me to eventually want to see the other side of things. Especially once my James passed. I guess this place ended up taking on a great import for me."

Nathaniel nodded. "It's been a long time, hasn't it?"

"Well, I've worked here for many years, yes."

The old man nodded almost knowingly. Then, he softly said, almost as if he were speaking to himself, "She's earned herself her rest."

Abigail glanced at him from the corner of her eye, her mind suddenly suspicious. She'd not really understood what he'd meant by his last few comments, but she sensed that something had subtly changed in the room. And in him. She wasn't quite sure what it was, but... she sensed something. Then, it came to her.

"May I ask you a rather direct question, Nathaniel?"

He nodded indulgently.

She eyed him with suspicion. "You didn't come here to fix the sink, did you?"

He smiled and cocked his head at her, impressed. He gently shook his head. "No."

"What are you here for?"

"I told you, I'm with... Maintenance."

"And Nathaniel... is that your real name?"

"Got me again."

She stared into her cup. "May I ask... what it is?"

The small man smiled at her, like a parent pleased by the cleverness of their child. "There have been many names, Abigail. Over the years. Hel, Dullahan, Shinigami, Ankou, Magere Hein, Astwihad, Mot, Mictēcacihuātl... that one's a mouthful, ain't it?"

She grinned along with him despite a growing sense of fear. But then, she stopped and looked up at him sadly. "Is there any I would recognize?"

"There might be a few."

The small man once again smiled warmly as he looked deep into her eyes. Abigail felt herself begin to fall into the blackness of his dark gaze. She felt the floor beneath her feet suddenly slip a little. Then, everything snapped back to normal.

"Is one of them... what I think it is?" she asked hesitantly.

Nathaniel's grin grew wider, and his eyes never left hers.

"Say it," he softly whispered through his closed teeth.

Tears began to well up in Abigail's eyes as she whispered her reply, "Death."

"Got it in one."

She looked deep into the eyes of the old man. "And you're here for someone?"

"I'm afraid so."

"For one of the patients?"

Nathaniel stared into the whirlpools in his coffee in lieu of responding.

Abigail set her jaw and nodded silently. "For me then?"

He looked down at the floor solemnly. "I am sorry."

Now it was her turn to smile, even as she was wiping away the first of her tears. "I told you…" She chuckled softly into her cup as she took another sip of coffee. "I've worked here at this hospital for a long time. When I first saw you tonight, I thought to myself that I recognized you from… somewhere, but I couldn't place from where. Then, as we were walking down the hallway, I remembered seeing a man here at the hospital when James, my husband, my James… died, what, ten years ago now?" She looked up at him, her wet eyes shimmering brightly in the bright, fluorescent light. "And then, I realized… that man looked like you. He looked exactly like you."

Nathaniel smiled and nodded his head, whispering. "I remember James."

"And then, there was that day, here on the ward, not more than a few years ago," she continued with a wet sniff. "When I saw that very same man—you—standing over by one of the patient beds." She looked back into her cup; her gaze fixed. She took another nervous sip, savoring the warm flavor for what she guessed was her last time. "A short time later, that patient coded and died."

"It happens," Nathaniel said, and his voice sounded genuinely remorseful. "People… people who are sensitive, people who are what they once called adept, will catch sight of me every once in a while. It's unavoidable, I guess. Others…" He looked at her with affection, like she was a child. "Others, I reveal myself to."

Abigail continued to stare down into her Styrofoam cup, adrift in her own thoughts. Memories wafted passed before her mind's eye like the pages of a child's flipbook. Then, she abruptly sat up a little straighter in her chair, as if she'd come to some kind of internal decision. She took a deep breath and looked up at him defiantly. "I'm not afraid."

Nathaniel chuckled indulgently. "And there's no reason why you should be."

She cocked her head to one side and stared at him with wary eyes. "There isn't?"

Nathaniel's grin grew wider as he picked up his glasses from the chain around his neck and place them onto his broad nose. "Not at all. See, Abigail, the pain, the fear, all the uncertainty… comes not from the act of dying, but from people trying to hold onto this world. Death…" He paused again in thought. "I… am not a thing to be feared, Abigail. But rather, just another moment, in a lifetime of moments, to be experienced." He smiled again. "Like all of the rest of Life."

Abigail sat back in her chair and thought it over. She'd never been one much for religion, but she'd always considered herself to at least be spiritual. Even as her James lay dying, she'd prayed every night that he might be spared. Instead, he only became thinner and thinner, his body getting weaker and weaker. Until, in the end, he closed his eyes that last time and never opened them again.

No muss. No fuss. No heralding of trumpets.

Since that day, her life had been one repetitive cycle of work, home with the cat and the television, falling asleep on the sofa, and then coming back to do it all over again the following day. Yes, her job was rewarding, and she did indeed love it, but she had also, if she were being completely honest, grown tired. Bone tired at times, it seemed. And, to hear Nathaniel talk of it, well... he didn't make it seem so bad, now did he? She stopped and looked over at the small Filipino man standing a short distance away, his smile already starting to warm the chill from the room.

Abigail looked up at him. "Can we at least finish our coffee?"

"I'd like that," Nathaniel said fondly as he raised his cup in silent toast. "It's darn good coffee."

Abigail nodded and let her gaze drift around the Break Room like a child's lost balloon. She chuckled silently. God, the memories she'd formed here. The friendships. She drew a breath and sighed. She was really going to miss this place.

"Is it okay if we just sit here and continue to talk for just a little bit longer?"

"Sure," Nathaniel said as he drew another hissing sip of his coffee. "I'd like that."

"So would I."

And in that small, silent Break Room, these two new friends 'clinked' Styrofoam glasses, and continued talking until just before the dawn.

I DOUBLE-DOG DARE YA

Recently, I realized that I had never done an out-and-out Halloween tale. I know, it seems weird, right? So... back when I worked in funeral homes, we used to get a lot of people snooping around the mortuary on the Halloween holiday. Lookie-loos mostly, but it was enough of a problem that we had to start scheduling people to be in the building so that they could keep an eye on things. I mean, the last thing anybody wanted was to have a bunch of kids break into the place in order to try and prove their bravery to one another. This story takes that idea and runs with it.

"Chicken! You're a chicken," Sam taunted as he and the group of boys he was with all stood out on the cold, October sidewalk on Norton Ave. He was holding court with a couple of the younger kids from school and feeling like a big shot. The chubby Asian boy brushed an unruly sprig of coal-black hair out of his eyes with the back of his hand. He loomed over the two smaller kids standing before him like a ghoul.

Sam was dressed like a pirate—sort of. His costume of a bandana over his head and eye patch were obviously homemade and had been undoubtedly scrounged from items he'd found in his basement or garage. At any other time, on any other day, he would have looked like he'd suffered a recent head injury dressed like that. Tonight... there wasn't a person who saw him that would have batted an eye at his appearance. He leaned in, towering over the smaller boys, self-satisfaction dripping like cream from his pursed lips. "Well," he grinned at them, "aintcha?"

Sam was older than his two companions by a year. And so, of course, they were paying him the strictest of attention. Him being older was a key factor in their social dynamic. But the fact that he was a lot bigger than they were was even more of a consideration. Sam stood, hands on his hips, glaring at the two boys like they'd somehow wronged him. Sneering, he looked them over, sizing them up.

What a sorry state.

What a sorry state indeed. His dad always said that when he saw something that failed to meet his standards: 'What a sorry state.' Sam wasn't sure if he completely understood what the phrase meant exactly, but he had the general idea that it was bad. Not as bad as 'piss poor,' but bad.

The two smaller boys were Ryan Forster and Jordan Brown. They'd both been circling Sam and his friend's periphery independent of one another for a while now during lunch at school; looking for a way in. Looking for a chance to be seen out hanging with the 'cool crowd.' Sam got a lot of that: the younger kids poking around and trying to hang out with the older ones. He guessed he understood them wanting to be a part of the group. Lord knows, he'd done pretty much the same thing when he was their age, once upon a time. On any other day, he would just send them cryin' back to the kiddie playground.

Not today though. Not tonight.

Tonight, things were different.

Tonight, it was Halloween, and Sam really, really wanted to do some Halloween stuff. It sucked that his friends were all off at some boring 'trunk or treat' party over at the Methodist church. But not him. He had plans. Big plans. He'd tried to talk a few of them into coming out with him instead, but all they wanted to do was to go load up on cake and punch. They kept saying that they 'had to' go, but Sam knew the real reason: they were all pussies.

So, he was out all alone instead, prowling the neighborhood streets by himself. A lone wolf. He'd given his parents a bit of hooey about how he was going to go to the party, and then out with his pals to trick or treat. But really, he was planning on going where he'd heard all the grownup kids were on this special day: out under the Halloween moon, young, and free, and making a little mischief for himself.

With the ghost of a sneer still lingering on his lips, Sam continued to look the two younger kids over. He didn't know either of them particularly well, but he'd seen them hanging around his brother, and he figured he must know their older siblings from school. He grinned at them malevolently. The two boys looked up at him awestruck, like he'd just discovered electricity or something.

Ryan Forster was a white kid who lived just down the street from Sam's aunt. He'd dressed himself up as a farmer in a pair of his dad's overalls that were rolled up at the cuff, a red gingham shirt, and a dopey straw hat. Sam dimly recalled hearing something about him having transferred here from someplace out East called New Jersey.

He guessed it was true as the kid still had this weird nasally accent to prove it. Under his hat, short-cropped blonde hair crowned his head, and his eyes were frosted an icy blue.

The other kid, Jordan Brown, was taller than Ryan, but not by much. He was dressed like a baseball player in his Little League uniform and hat. Tall for his age and thin, he was a stringy whip of a kid. His Black skin and hair caught the streetlight and shimmered in the moonlight like something wet.

Together, they were perfect for what Sam had in mind for the night: young, impressionable, and just small enough to get themselves in and out of tight places.

You know, if necessary.

See, Sam's idea on this cold, cloud-filled Halloween night was a notion born out of his own spontaneous invention, it having only just occurred to him when he'd seen these two dopes walking by themselves, coming up the street.

Coming up this street, in particular.

Sam had been strolling along, minding his own business, tossing sticker-balls at the windows of the houses he passed, when, he'd seen them coming. Then, by pure happenstance, he looked up and saw that they were standing in front of what was undoubtedly the scariest place he might have imagined on a Halloween night: the town's only funeral home. It was almost like the whole thing had been preordained.

After seeing all of the pieces spread out before him like that, it hadn't taken much for a guy like him to put them all together. His plan... was to get these two little kids to help him get into the funeral home somehow, so that they could have a look around. Then, once they were back outside and away clean, they'd all have quite the tale to tell at school tomorrow.

He grinned wider when he thought of all the kid's faces back at school—even the really older one's –when he told them what he'd done. And just imagine what they'd say if he showed them something that he'd taken from the place. Yeah, that was even better. What could be more Halloween than breaking into a funeral home and stealing something to prove that he'd been there? He shook his head at the idea's obviousness.

I mean, there were actual dead people in there!

The trio stood on the chilly sidewalk out in front of the large, gated property on which the funeral home stood, just a few blocks off the main drag of Downtown. The lot had three surprisingly verdant, albeit small, copses of apple trees that surrounded the large, plantation-style main house. The surrounding lawns were lush and green. The building itself was Gothic in its architecture, and therefore all the more spooky-looking at night. It had been one of the first homes built back when the town was first founded, and it was turned into a funeral parlor back in the early Sixties. Sam knew that there was a multi-car garage in the back that housed a stable of hearses and limousines, you just couldn't see it from the street.

The mortuary sat like a castle on the top of a small hill that rose like an abscess from the otherwise flat landscape of the town. Out front, facing the street, was a large sign made of manicured pinewood. Painted white with gold-colored lettering, the billboard was illuminated by a single floodlight set in the grass in front of it. Across its face was the name of the firm: Johnson, Levitt, and Hull. Below it, in smaller print, was more: Funeral Home and Mortuary. At the very bottom, a telephone number for perspective clients to call... should the need arise.

Sam looked up at the building towering over them, its peaks silhouetted against the harvest moon's pumpkin-colored glow. He smiled. It was all just too perfect; like something right out of a monster movie. Like the one he'd seen on TV a few nights ago when he'd stayed up late... with that Tall Man and them flying balls.

He grinned malevolently as he turned back toward the two younger boys.

"That's right, you big babies," he said snidely. "So, where's all that tough talk I was hearing back at school now, eh?" He pushed the blonde kid's shoulder and watched him stumble back a step. "Didn't you both say that nothing could scare you, that you wouldn't be scared to do anything, not even on Hallow-ween. Well," he looked back over his shoulder at the big, dark house on the hill. "Here we are!"

The two younger boys gazed over at one another, both of their faces looking like they did the moment just before a balloon was popped, bracing themselves for some imagined impact. The two of them had been heading back from the school's Halloween festivities and just sort of ended up walking together down the same street. They knew one another from both having gone to the same school for a few years, but they weren't what anyone would call friends. It was like, they knew each other, but... they didn't know each other. In fact, Jordan had been planning on heading off in the direction of home; a direction he knew wasn't compatible with the one that led to Ryan's house, at the next corner.

But then, they'd seen Sam up ahead, walking toward them like he had the devil himself in his back pocket. Sam was one of the few older kids who would sometimes acknowledge the younger ones' existence. Mostly, it was to push them around, or to help himself to portions of their lunch when he felt like it, but still... Sam had a little brother who was their age, so the older boy would still run into them every once in a while, either in the halls or at the bus stop. Everyone else was always trying to act older... and that meant that they never seemed to have time for the younger kids.

Unless they wanted something. Like now.

"So, listen," Sam said, "You guys wanna get in on this or what?"

Jordan looked down at his scuffed sneakers but said nothing. He didn't want to 'get in on' anything with Sam... especially if it was to go skulking around some dumb old funeral home in the middle of the night. Jordan reminded himself of how Sam often acted like a dick, and Jordan didn't want to be a part of anything that Sam thought was a good idea.

And for what, so that some of the other kids at school would think they were cool for a day? No thanks. Jordan knew what a funeral home was, and what went on there, and he wanted no part of it. His grandmother died last winter, and he'd spent a long and uncomfortable weekend here for what his parents had called, 'her service.'

Afterward, his dad had taken him aside and they'd had a very somber conversation about some things that made him feel pretty uncomfortable, conversations about Death and Dying, and the inevitability of both. He had the feeling at the time that the interaction was more for his father's benefit than his, but... It had all been weird and a little creepy, to be honest.

"I'll go," Ryan offered, but it didn't exactly sound like his heart was in it by the tone of his voice. His eyes wandered hopefully between the other two boys, searching their faces for approval. "You guys have to come with me, though..."

Sam laughed. "Of course, we will, ya dope... that's what I was sayin'," He turned to glare at Jordan. "Welp, I guess that just leaves you? Are you gonna help us do this or what?"

Jordan let his gaze wander from one boy to the other, and he felt the crushing pressure of their gaze. He didn't really want to do anything other than to just go home, especially not with these guys. But then, unbelievably, he heard a voice that sounded remarkably similar to his own say, "Okay."

The next thing they knew, they were all standing in the short grass outside the funeral home, near a small ditch by the south side of the building. The place was dark inside, with only a single, small electric light of a plastic candle visible in one of the front windows. The boys had circled the structure a few times, and were just about to give up, when Ryan spotted the small window that looked like it led down into the basement.

Jordan got down on his knees in the wet grass and, after wiping some mud from the pane, peered through the dirty glass. Inside, he saw what appeared to be a room with a couple of clothes washers that rocked gently in the dark as they chugged their loads clean. The small red lights of the control panels glowed like demon's eyes in the dark.

"It looks like this is where they do their laundry," Jordan suggested.

Sam nodded as he bobbed back and forth behind him, trying to see what he could of what was inside the building over the younger boy's shoulder. "We can get in through there though, right?"

"I'm not sure," Jordan replied doubtfully, getting up to let him in. He was tired of feeling someone looming over him, tired of smelling his bad breath and body odor.

The bigger boy readily took his place, bending down as if he were about to play marbles. He leaned in, pressing his nose against the glass, squinting to see in the sparse light. After a second or two, he put his hand up to shield his eyes from the moonlight overhead.

"I can't see shit," Sam muttered angrily under his breath.

Ryan, who was standing behind them, giggled brightly at the other boy's use of forbidden profanity. Ryan came from a family that went to church a lot, and any such utterance he heard was usually met with giggles and the feeling that he was involved in something sinful or naughty.

"Hey, wait a second," Sam suddenly said, more to himself than the other two. "I don't think this thing's all the way locked."

He jimmied the window in the frame by pressing the palms of his hands against the glass and pushing back and forth laterally. The wooden frame wiggled a little, and then, the whole thing moved slightly to the right on the sill. There was a rough, grating sound from its bottom, and then, the window just sort of popped out of its track. The pane slowly swung inward and a rush of air that smelled strongly of bleach came pouring out.

"That's got it!" Sam pronounced triumphantly.

He cautiously pushed the window the rest of the way open with one hand and stuck his head inside. Soft moonlight shone through the window's opening, and it cast what could be seen in the room in a soft bluish tint. A small sliver of light coming in from under the closed door slashed across the dark of the ground. The only other lights visible were the ones on the washing machine. Otherwise, the room was painted in nothing but darkness and shadow.

Sam pulled his head back from the window and turned to face the other two boys. "Okay, Forster..." he finally said to the young, blonde boy, "you're going in first. You're smaller than the rest of us and you won't make as much noise."

"Wha'?" Ryan asked, his voice now trembling involuntarily.

"We just need you to go in and make sure the coast is clear, okay?"

"Wh-what if someone comes?"

"It's okay. If they do, we'll just pull you back up. It's really no big deal."

But Jordan knew that what they were doing was a very big deal. In fact, it was a deal so big that it could land them all in Juvenile Hall if they were caught. And nobody needed that.

So, why was he here? he silently asked himself.

Ryan turned to look at Jordan and his face showed the fear that was slowly catching fire behind his eyes. His lower lip trembled slightly as he nodded his head to show his reluctant agreement. Forster had a reputation in school for being like that, always agreeing to whatever any bigger kid would tell him to do. He was an only child and he had this weird need to be liked—even if it sometimes cost him a little of his dignity.

Sam got up and moved out of the way of the window, still holding the portal open with one hand, but making enough room for little Ryan. He cast a quick glance up at the rest of the house to see if whatever noise they'd already made had alerted anyone, but the place remained dark and seemed genuinely deserted.

Ryan reluctantly moved closer to the opening and slid his legs in first. He angled his hips through the window, rolling over onto his belly, and shimmying in. The belt of his pants got momentarily hung up on the windowsill, and he had to shift his weight a bit to unhook himself. But finally, he hung in the window by just his arms, supported by Sam. He grinned up at them like a jack-o-lantern before nervously letting go. His surprised face disappeared like a ghost into the blackness of the laundry room. They both heard him land with a grunt a second later.

"You okay?" Sam hissed into the shadows.

There was a soft groan from within the inky black, but then they heard Ryan's voice whisper, "Yeah, I'm okay. It's just higher than I thought it was going to be."

Sam turned toward Jordan. "You go next. Make sure he doesn't make any more noise and get us caught."

Jordan stood silently for a second, weighing out his options like they were his last few coins. What was he doing? The last thing on Earth he wanted to do was to break into, well… anyplace… with these idiots. In fact, he couldn't think of a single good reason to have followed them anywhere, much less here into a funeral home … and on Halloween no less!

But he also didn't want to hear it from Sam, didn't want to be called a coward again. Or worse…. He didn't need to have him tell all the kids at school that he'd chickened out. School was bad enough as it was. He didn't need that kind of grief heaped on top of the usual crap sundae it was every other day. And so, not feeling exactly confident in his decision, he did what he was told, and climbed in through the window.

Jordan's feet hit the concrete floor without much of a sound. He made sure to bend his knees when he landed to absorb the impact, and to hopefully minimize the noise. It was a trick his brother had shown him once when they were playing Hide-n-Seek during the summer.

As he took in his surroundings, he noticed the washer cycling through its load while the dryer spun another one dry. The air smelled even more of bleach now that he was inside. He felt the acrid fumes coat his tongue, and the taste of it made him want to spit.

He cautiously moved deeper into the room, moving toward the door that Ryan was standing close to. Jordan pressed his ear against the flat wood but heard nothing. He looked back up at Sam whose face was framed, shining like the moon, in the window.

"Seems okay," Jordan whispered, his voice sounding like a gloved hand moving over silk.

"Okay, cool," Sam replied, pulling off his eye patch and stuffing it into his pants pocket. Immediately, he started to climb down into the laundry room. Due to his size, Sam wasn't the most agile kid, but he soon managed to make it through the window.

When the three of them were all inside, Sam rechecked the door, pressing his ear to the wood as he'd seen Jordan do. He tried to listen for the sound of any movement outside, but all he heard was the ticking of a clock somewhere not too far off. He listened intently for what seemed like a long time. Then, he shrugged, slowly turning the handle, and unceremoniously pulled the door open.

On the other side, there was a long flight of wooden stairs that led up to the main floor of the building. The steps were worn; their paint having been rubbed off long ago by years and years of heavy objects either being pulled up or dragged down the staircase, and the aesthetic had paid the price.

At the top of the flight of stairs, there was a landing that looked like it was a part of a longer hallway, leading to the main part of the building. The stairwell door hung open, inviting the boys to come up and have a look around. There, against the wall, was the old grandfather clock they'd heard. Its face had ornate numbers on it, surrounded by drawings of vines, leaves, and little, ornate flowers. Its looping chains and counterweights glimmered in the hallway's low light.

"Remember, go slow," Jordan instructed the other two. "I remember this building being old and the floors are super creaky."

Sam stopped and turned to glare at him disbelievingly. "How do you know that?"

Jordan stared back at him and smiled indulgently, like he was talking to someone who was not as smart as he was. And, in a way, he was. "I've been here before, man. Remember when my Gramma died and me and my brothers missed school for nearly a week last Spring?"

"I don't remember shit," Sam replied as he shrugged his shoulders and stared back into the empty laundry room. It was as if, just for a second, he had some regrets about breaking in, and he was trying to decide whether to turn tail and leave the way they'd come. Shaking his head to expel his misgivings, he quickly returned his gaze to the two younger kids and the hallway that lay behind them.

Yeah, he remembered the boys being out of school a while back, not seeing them on the bus, but Sam had never known—much less cared—as to why. He hesitantly put his foot onto the first stair and was just about to start up the staircase to the first floor, when the wooden stair beneath his foot creaked like an old ship's mast. He turned and looked back down apologetically at the others.

"See," Jordan hissed. "I told you."

Sam's expression screwed itself up tight as he was forced to silently acknowledge that the younger boy had indeed been correct. Being more careful this time, he continued up the staircase on tiptoes, using the sides of the wood planks rather than their centers.

When they'd all gotten to the top, they stopped, and Sam cautiously poked his head out of the doorway into the hallway. As expected, the corridor was empty, save for the ticking clock, a low-lying credenza at one end, and some landscape paintings hung along the wall like afterthoughts.

"C'mon, let's go check it out..." Sam said, triumphantly. He paused and a snake's smile spread across his face. "Unless the two of you have gone and gotten scaaaared."

Ryan shook his head back and forth, and he looked like one of those bobble-head dolls you saw at the county fair. He was so happy to have been included in on some kind of adventure, even one as janky as this one, that he couldn't stop grinning. He knew that hanging out with an older kid like Sam could only boost his reputation with the other kids in his class. He liked that feeling, he silently decided: being included.

Jordan thought back to the still-open window in the laundry room behind them and decided that he probably wouldn't be able to climb back through it alone. So, like it or not, he felt like his only way to get out of this mess was to simply keep moving through it. No matter how scared he was.

He just hoped it all didn't end up with someone calling the cops.

"Ain't nobody scared of nothing," Ryan said firmly, but it was obvious by the way his voice trembled that he didn't really believe a word of what he was saying.

Because if the truth were to be told, they were all pretty terrified. This was supposed to have been nothing more than some low-key Halloween fun—just doing the school thing, maybe some trick or treating at a house or two on the way home, then hanging out and maybe watching a scary movie if Mom said it was okay.

But then, everything had changed, and on a whim, too. And now, here they were... having broken into a place of business, trespassing, and slinking through the building like cartoon burglars. And that didn't even call into question the kind of gruesome business being conducted somewhere within these walls. Right now, all any of them— even Sam—wanted to do was to get this all over with so that they could get out of here and go home with a little pride.

"Good," Sam whispered, "You go first, then."

Ryan's face suddenly went pale as the implication of what he'd inadvertently agreed to fully sunk in. He looked down the hall, first one way, and then the other, as he nervously tried to gulp down his rising sense of dread. The boy wasn't so concerned with what might be said back at school any longer. Now, he was more worried that these two boys would suddenly decide to leave him alone and terrified in this spooky place to fend for himself. And so, screwing his bravery to its sticking point, the little blonde farmer chose a direction—to the right— and proceeded down the hall. The others followed along cautiously behind him.

The way ahead was dark, and the walnut paneling on the walls only made it seem that much darker. There was flat industrial-grade carpeting that ran along the floor, and while it looked nice, it was there mostly for its durability. It gave the appearance of class, but it could still take the beating that the mortuary's regular foot traffic inflicted upon it. There were three doors total along the hallway—two on the left, one on the right—and their doors were all closed. The boys continued forward guardedly, all three too scared to say anything.

"So, hey... what are we looking for anyway?" Jordan whispered from between clenched teeth.

Sam waved the comment away. His heart was racing and the idea that all of this wasn't such a hot idea anymore kept pounding in his head like a drum. "We just need something small, something they won't miss. It only has to prove we were here, right? It doesn't have to be much; not much of anything at all."

This is so dumb, Jordan thought to himself miserably. What the heck were they even doing here? They could all get into really serious trouble over this stupid shit. If they got caught, he was convinced that, whoever found them would surely call the cops. Or worse, call their parents. Despite this inner conflict though, he continued moving down the hall.

The first room they came to, the one on the left, was a small cube of a space. And, from the look of what was inside, it was used solely as some sort of filing room. Row after row of tall metal filing cabinets encircled the room like tin soldiers awaiting inspection. On top of each were stacks of assorted folders and papers waiting to be collated and filed. Disappointed, the boys shut the door and continued down the hall.

They next came to the room on the right, and it was mostly empty. There were a few piles of stackable chairs along the back wall, with a velvet blanket casually thrown over them like camouflage netting. Nearby, two large candles, like the ones you saw in church, sat next to one another in tall decorative holders. The room had a quiet air of expectancy to it, like it had been patiently waiting, waiting for something to happen. The feeling was sad and impossibly lonely, and all of the boys felt it, even if they couldn't put a name to it. Without any of them saying anything, they shut the door and moved on.

In the last room, the one on the left, they found only darkness. The lights were out, and the drapes had been pulled tightly shut, so there was nothing much for the boys to see. The sound of the clock tolling the hour struck abruptly, and they had to physically stop Ryan from crying out and running for the nearest door. Feeling more and more fearful, the boys stepped hesitantly inside the small room, closing the door behind them.

"Feel around for a light," Sam ordered quietly as he took a few steps a little deeper into the center of the room.

"Hey, guys... I can't see anything," Ryan whined sadly, and it sounded like he was about to cry. "I... I really don't like the dark, okay, so..."

"Wait a second," Jordan hissed, even as he was running his hand along the wall near the door frame, searching for the light switch. "Got it!"

There was a soft click and the room suddenly exploded into brightly flickering fluorescent light from overhead. There was a flash of illumination that revealed essentially the same setup as the other room. In this one though, the chairs had been separated and setup in two columns, and the candles were placed about six feet apart at the head of the room. There was something that looked like a long wooden box set between them. Arrangements of flowers flanked the crate.

And then, everything was gone as darkness fell with a chilling finality.

"Crap," Jordan cursed as his voice abruptly quivered in fear. "We blew the damn light bulb."

"What?" Sam replied, sounding truly scared for the first time.

"Yeah... what?" repeated Ryan plaintively.

Jordan cracked open the door and the meager light spilling in from the hallway made it a little easier for them all to see. Now, in this new light, the room just looked cold and unused. "I said, we blew the light bulb." He shook his head. "We should really go."

"Okay, okay," Sam huffed as he crossed his arms over his chest. "Shit."

Jordan looked the room over. "Wait a second... I remember this place. And I remember what they used it for when I was here for my Gram," he explained. "They called this a Visitation Room."

"And?" Sam.

"Yeah... and?" Ryan.

"If I'm not wrong, then..." Jordan said nervously as he raised his arm and pointed grimly at the box at the head of the room. "That box isn't just a box."

"It's not?" Sam again, now sounding like he was going to cry.

"It's not? What is it then? What's in the box, man?" Ryan again, sounding like he was back on the edge of tears. "C'mon... I'm really getting scared."

"I think..." Jordan whispered. "I think it's a casket."

Sam's expression fell to ruin and its collapse was evident to them all in the dim light. "A wh... a what?"

"A casket," Jordan said. "You know, a coffin."

"Do you m-mean?" Sam blubbered.

Jordan nodded as he quickly sidled out of the room and back into the hallway. His eyes had gone wide, his breath coming in little pants, and his expression had taken on a plaintive aspect. "There's a... a dead body in there."

Now, Ryan did start to cry. Not out and out bawling, but tears were pretty openly falling from his eyes, and he didn't care who saw them. He knew now that this entire adventure was a gigantic mistake; that this whole thing was just too... just too scary, man. Scary and getting really, really serious. Dead people, the small blonde boy thought. No thanks... He wanted to go home.

The other boys came stumbling out into the hallway, falling over one another's limbs, and bumping into the walls like pinballs suddenly set free. And, all the while, the more they tried to be quiet, the more noise they made.

"Shhh," Jordan reiterated insistently. "Shhh! Shhh!"

They stopped a second, clutching at one another for support, and listened for any sound of movement coming from the other parts of the funeral home. The air hung heavy with malevolent anticipation, each boy's heart beating like a tympani in his ears. Luckily, there was nothing, only the quiet metronome of the hallway's clock and the soft clicking of the far-off furnace. Separating themselves from one another, they tried to regain their bearings, and to make a plan for their escape in hushed whispers.

"This is getting creepy," Sam suggested with a nervous laugh. He looked toward the front of the building. "We should go this way."

"Seriously?" Jordan asked incredulously. He'd had more than enough of all of this, and he had no intention of 'going that way' or any other way except maybe out the front door and straight home. He'd had bad feelings about this whole stupid thing back on the sidewalk outside, and no matter what anyone else might think, it had only gotten worse from there. "We need to frickin' leave, man! Like right now! How could someone not have heard that?"

Sam stepped up to Jordan and stared down at him. He was nearly a head taller and had at least ten or fifteen pounds on the smaller boy, but it didn't matter. In his short life, Jordan had never been in a real fight, and, as he looked the current potential opposition over, he didn't exactly feel the need to suddenly start doing so right now.

And not over this.

"C'mon, man..." Sam finally said, trying a different approach.

"We're already here. Let's just grab what we came for, and then we'll leave, okay?"

Not feeling any real desire to argue the subject out there in the hallway, Jordan raised his hands in mock surrender. Better that they get this all over with and get going as quickly as possible rather than standing around bickering about it, thereby increasing the risk of them getting caught.

The hall emptied out into the building's foyer which was decorated like an old person's living room. Primrose wallpaper did what it could to make the space cheerier, but there was only so much it could do. There was a high-backed chair and end table set just to the right of the front door. A few side tables and lamps were littered about the entryway as well. A metal rack of prayer cards and church pamphlets was positioned on the other side of the entryway. Directly across from the front door was a set of double doors that led to a small chapel.

Sam walked over to one of the double doors and pushed it open with the palm of his hand. Inside a surprisingly large room, church pews were lined up in that familiar two-column configuration that they'd seen earlier. The place smelled faintly of old flowers and some kind of spice. At the far end, a raised dais had been built that served as an altar. There was another one of the long wooden boxes set on a pedestal in the middle.

Jordan peered over Sam's shoulder and took the scene in. "That's the chapel. It's where my Gramma was when the Reverend came and they had her funeral," he explained.

"A chapel, huh?"

"Yup."

The three boys all stuck their heads into the room, one by one, and looked around until their curiosity was sated. They then proceeded across the vestibule to the hallway that ran along the other side of the building, back around to where the stairway that led to the laundry room was.

Before heading out, Jordan went over to the rack of prayer cards and pulled a few out at random. He quickly organized them in his hands like he would a deck of playing cards, and then he handed the stack to Sam.

"Here, put these in your pocket," Jordan said as he set them into his hand. "They're your proof we were here. You don't just get those anywhere. See," he pointed to the back of the top card in the deck. "This has the name of each person who died, when they were born, when they died, and the name of the funeral home. They make them here, I guess. Or, they have them printed. Either way, you can't get them anyplace else."

Sam nodded and a wide grin slowly spread across his face. He tucked the cards into one of the back pockets of his pants with a palpable sense of satisfaction. "Cool. We can leave now. Let's keep going and we can find a way out."

Jordan cast an exasperated glance over his shoulder toward the front entrance. "But the door is right here!"

Sam glared at him again. "And it's probably hooked up to their alarm system or something, okay? We'll just keep going and, if we don't find anything better, we'll go out the way we came in, through the laundry room window. But, hey… at least, we'll be able to say we saw everything, right?" He looked at Jordan, whose irritation was plain on his face. "C'mon… don't be a puss. We haven't run into anyone so far. There may not even be anyone here?"

Jordan looked over at Ryan for some back-up, but the kid had the same kind of look a dog has when it's around its owner. He was staring at the older boy like he'd just performed a magic trick, so Jordan knew he wouldn't find any help there. He let his eyes wander back to the older boy, whom he looked at skeptically.

"Okay, but we need to stop fartin' around and hurry, that's all."

The case decided, the group stalked their way down the next hallway, moving carefully again so as to not make any more noise. Along the way, they found only a few small offices; arrangement offices, mostly, and a small storage cabinet with a vacuum cleaner and some cleaning supplies inside. The boys all peeked inside each of the rooms, the light from the hallway once again making it so that they could see. When they'd ascertained there was nothing of particular worth here, they moved on.

At the end of the hallway, they came to a single, swinging door that looked like it led into the very back of the building. A small window had been cut into the center of the wood about head high. There was no visible handle, just a silver panel of metal secured into place by small screws. The ghosts of a dozen smudged fingerprints dotted the surface like acne.

"We should try in there," Sam suggested, his eyes lighting up again with mischief. "There's probably a quicker way out in there, like a back door or something."

Normally, Jordan would have said no way, that they should all stick to the plan and go back the way they'd come… and they should do it now. But the truth was, that he was scared, more scared than he'd ever been in his whole entire life. And he was tired, and he wanted to go home. So, if someone had suggested that they chew their way out of this creepy place through the walls with their teeth, he would have probably signed onto it.

"Okay," Jordan agreed, "but we go straight out of here. We don't stop until we're outside. Okay? Just keep moving."

Sensing that the tide of power had suddenly shifted, Ryan looked over at Sam balefully. "Yeah... just keep moving?"

Sam held up his hands. "Okay, okay... sheesh." He pressed his palm onto the metal plate. "We'll go now, okay? We'll go..."

Just then, an unexpected metallic clanking sound came from another room, one that was behind the still-closed door. It sounded like someone had dropped an aluminum baseball bat or something made out of steel. The metallic sound rang out suddenly and its brittle tone echoed through the bones of the quiet mortuary.

The boys immediately dropped down onto their haunches. Jordan wasn't sure, but he thought he suddenly smelled the odor of urine coming off of Ryan. He briefly wondered if the kid had peed his pants, but he wasn't about to check. If he had, he could just well deal with it himself. Jordan angrily turned to look at Sam.

"Okay, Smart Guy," he hissed at him. "What do you suggest we do now?"

Sam ignored him and thought it over for a minute before answering. He finally nodded to himself like he'd made up his mind about something and rose to his feet. He quickly shot a glance through the small pane of glass in the door, swaying back and forth as he tried to get the best overall view. Then, when he thought he had a pretty good idea of the next room's layout, he got back down onto his haunches to confer with the others.

"Okay, so..." the Asian boy paused until he had everybody's attention. "No one's there. Also, there's a door that looks like it leads to the outside. You go in and turn to your left and it's right there. I mean, I think it leads outside. It must, right? Given the way the building is."

Jordan looked puzzled, shaking his head. "So, what are you saying?"

Sam looked at him in that indulgent way older kids look at younger ones. "We push open this door, go in, turn left, and we head straight out of the other one, the one that leads outside."

"What if it's locked?"

Sam sighed and once again swatted the concern away. "It won't be..."

Ryan nodded his agreement, now fully back on Team Sam. "Yeah, it won't be."

"I'll even go first if it'll make you feel any better," Sam offered as he got to his feet and turned, resting his hand back onto the door.

"Okay, okay," Jordan agreed, even though, once again, he didn't really feel good about the idea. "You go first. Then you go, Ryan. But don't make any noise, okay?" He stopped and thought about it. Then, he raised a finger in warning. "And, whatever happens, don't wait. Nobody stops. Just keep running."

"Why?" Ryan asked, and concern twisted his face in on itself.

"Because I'll be right behind you."

Sam took in a deep breath, and then gently pushed open the door. He poked his head in between it and the door frame and looked around. Ahead of him was a small open space that looked like it might have once been a garage or loading bay. Metal racks stuffed full of boxes lined the walls, and there were also these long shipping crates stacked in a corner. To the left was the presumed door to freedom. Across the room, he noticed a door that led to some other—smaller—area. All he could tell of what was inside was that it was blindingly bright, and it gave off this weird chemical odor.

He didn't see anyone around though, so he cautiously moved on through to the other side of the door. Ryan followed silently along behind him, taking the weight of the swinging door with his one shoulder. Once he was also through, Jordan was supposed to go next. He stood just inside the doorway, waiting for the other boys to clear the way.

By now, Sam was at the door that everyone hoped led outside. He reached out and put his hand on the doorknob, gripping it tightly. The handle spun freely in its lock, opening. He looked back at Jordan like, 'I told you so,' and then, he was outside; frigid air flooding in to take up the space where he'd only just stood. He held the door open for Ryan from the outside, waiting there at least so that the door wouldn't slam.

As Ryan got to the door and turned around to look back at him, Jordan started running toward the exit. About halfway there, another metallic crashing sound came from inside the small white room that was across the open workspace from them. It was followed by the sound of someone cursing harshly under their breath. The small room's door stood partly open, and Jordan could smell the acrid, medicinal odor that was coming from it. This close, it was even stronger than it had been.

Terrified to the point of panic, Jordan paused, unsure which way he should run: ahead to the door to the outside, or back into the concealing dark of the funeral home. He waited with his heart beating a mile a minute, mouth now gone desert dry, his head pounding from fear.

"Oh, crap," Jordan heard Ryan hiss.

He turned and watched as the kid did the one thing no one wanted—or expected—him to do: he let go of the door. Jordan heard himself gasp aloud as he watched his one way out disappear like mist right in front of his eyes. Worse, he knew—he just knew—that the sound of the door slamming would bring whoever it was that was working in the white room. And that person would find him standing there, gape-mouthed and looking as guilty as sin. The boy knew beyond all doubt that they'd surely call the cops. His heart clenched when he thought of the look that would end up on his mother's face when he was finally brought home... under arrest.

Just like his brothers...

Ke-blam!

The door slammed shut with a heartbreaking finality. And that, Jordan thought sadly to himself, was his ass. He paused, and in that time, he quickly decided that the best thing for him to do was to continue on and make that run for the door, to hell with the repercussions.

But then, a deep male voice suddenly called out from the white room, freezing him to the spot. "Hey," and the man's tone echoed in the empty room. "Who's there?"

And then, there was the awful sound of footsteps rapidly moving across tile.

Jordan spun on his heels, resorting to Plan B, and ran toward the still-swinging door that led back into the funeral home. He figured going back into the mortuary and racing for the front door was his best shot now. Or maybe he could hide someplace and somehow find a way to haul himself out of the laundry room window later.

He skidded to a stop when he abruptly spied what looked like the perfect place for him to hide, back behind some boxes where he was sure no one could see him. He figured he'd let this guy come out, take his look around, and see that there was nothing wrong. He'd hopefully go back to whatever it was he was doing in there, thinking the whole thing had been nothing more than his imagination. Then, once the coast was clear, Jordan would be able to slink out of here and head straight home.

Easy-peasy, right?

A man came striding out of the small brightly lit room, stopping in the middle of the open work area. He was tall, with dark hair gelled back, and he was dressed in a pair of dark slacks and a white button-up shirt. He had on a clear plastic apron that was tied in the back and his hands were covered by rubber doctor's gloves. His manner was an agitated cocktail of anger, fear, and annoyance. He stopped, looking around the open room suspiciously.

Slowly, he walked over to the door that led outside.

"I fuckin' hate this shit. Every god damn year..." the man grumbled to himself. He shook the doorknob to make sure the door was good and shut, and then he locked it with a click. The sound of the mechanism falling into place echoed ominously in the small room. "Fuckin' kids..."

Jordan felt himself relax a little when he saw the man start to walk back in the direction from which he'd come, back toward the mysterious white room. Jordan set his head down against the floor, feeling the soothing cold of the cement on his brow. He closed his eyes and waited, not daring to move a muscle, not even breathing. Once again, his mind was dominated by thoughts of home, and he swore—he swore—he'd never do anything this stupid again. Not ever again.

"Hey!" the man's deep voice suddenly shouted from directly over Jordan's head. "How'd you get in here?"

Jordan opened his eyes and looked up fearfully, his heart feeling as if it were going to explode in his chest. Fear poured adrenaline into his bloodstream like hot oil. Somehow, when Jordan wasn't looking, the man doubled back and had seen him in his hiding place. He was now standing over the boy angrily with his hands placed firmly on his hips.

Jordan sprang to his feet and did the only thing he could think to do, and that was to run. He wasn't exactly sure where he was running to, but fear had roughly taken control of his muscles and he felt like, if he didn't at least try to run, he'd shatter into a million pieces where he was.

He crashed into the door with the small window, the one that led back into the mortuary, with an audible grunt. Bouncing off, he careened away from the wall and made straight for the door to the outside. The man in the apron moved sideways like a hockey player to block his way, deftly angling his body so that he was between the child and the door to his potential freedom. Spreading out his arms, he slowly moved toward the boy to try and box him in, like he was herding a bunch of cats or something.

"Just relax, kid. I just need to know how you got in, okay? You're not supposed to be back here is all... It's like, super illegal, man."

Jordan stared at him with eyes now gone glassy with terror. Everything he'd ever been told by his friends, by his siblings, or even in his talks with his dad about Death and Dying, God and Heaven... it all came rushing back at him now in a horrifyingly twisted mythology.

The boy knew down deep in his soul that Death had come for him here in this place of mourning, and He'd brought all of the horrors of Hell along with Him. The boy's fear acted like kindling for the deeper dread he now felt coursing through his body. Soon, an inferno raged. Movies, TV, storybooks… every account he had ever heard about the dead and those that tended them, now came flooding back in a terrifying torrent.

Jordan quickly realized that he wasn't going to make it past the man, so he abruptly stopped; juking first left, then right. Then, just as suddenly, he reversed his course, heading toward the back of the building. He knew there had to be another way out and he'd tried everywhere else. There just had to be. If not, he'd try the door with the window again… or the front goddam door like he'd initially wanted. But he swore to himself he wasn't going to get caught. He wasn't going to disappoint his mom.

An electric buzzing coursed through his legs and his stomach felt like it was full of helium as he launched into this one last desperate action. And as he ran, he could hear the man coming up fast behind him. Too scared to think of anything else to save himself, he did the only thing he felt like he had left to him, he ran on. Jordan looked up and noticed the small, bright room that the man had come out of; the one that smelled of antiseptic and of copper.

There had to be a door in there, right? Jordan thought wildly to himself.

There had to be.

The boy's legs pumped like pistons, driving him forward and on toward the open room door. He saw a lot of white linoleum and cabinetry in front of him, and that chemical smell had increased to the point that it made him want to gag. As he rounded the threshold, he could still hear the man moving up quickly behind him.

"Wait!" the man shouted and there was a frantic desperation in his voice. "Not that room! Not that room!"

Jordan stumbled into the all-white room, falling to his knees. Time seemed to suddenly slow for him. He clearly saw the bone white walls, the clean alabaster floors. Saw the bleached cabinets and counters with their silver trays of shiny metal instruments. Even the weird-looking machine sitting on the counter, the one that looked like a large coffee pot. Its tank—a wide glass bowl essentially—was three-quarter filled with a foamy, pink solution. Thin rubber tubes came off of the pot like the tentacles of an octopus. His eye caught the word 'Sawyer' emblazoned across its front.

Jordan's gaze frantically searched for the other door, the one that would lead him outside and to home. It was then that he noticed the large porcelain table sitting in the middle of the room. The bench was rectangular, and it looked like an extremely shallow bathtub, with a wide recessed groove that ran around the interior of its circumference. The flat white surface was a little longer than a man, and just a little wider. Its bulk was supported in the middle by a heavy pedestal on wide metal wheels. Another set of rubber hoses ran from the foot of the slab into a small, porcelain drain tiled into the floor.

Jordan looked up from his vantage point on the floor and saw the man in the apron now filling the doorway, looking really upset. The boy's heart was still racing like a sprung rabbit as he climbed to his feet and continued to madly look for some other way to escape. Instead, though, his gaze fell onto the object that lay stretched across the tabletop's surface. And as his eyes took in everything he was seeing; his once galloping heart came to a sickening stop.

For there, lying flat on her back like she was sleeping, was the body of an older woman. She was about Jordan's mother's age, maybe a little older. Her hair was wet and colored dark brown, and it was spread like seaweed across the white of the table. She was big, with bread loaf-sized rolls of fat that encircled her abdomen like an innertube.

She was also very, very naked.

Jordan's eyes couldn't help but trace the curves of her body and his natural curiosity quickly took over. He'd never seen a naked lady before, other than his mom, and well, that was different. He let his gaze drift down her body, and it took a minute for him to process it all.

But then, he saw the first splash of crimson on the white of the porcelain under her arm. His eyes quickly moved along the contours of her round figure, until he saw the thick red line that ran down the center of her belly, from one end to the other. In a flash, he realized that someone—the man in the apron?—had taken something really sharp and cut from her ample breasts down to where the thick tuft of hair lay between her legs. His attention was momentarily fascinated by the bright yellow globules of fat that were poking out from the incision.

As he gazed in horror at the tableau before him, gravity began to exert its ever-insistent pull on one of the heavy flaps of the woman's skin, causing the flesh of her entire right side to tumble out onto the table. The image was like something out of a slaughterhouse. Jordan definitely saw ribs, and thick strips of what looked like meat. And as the slab of the dead woman's belly settled like a steaming pot roast onto the table, Jordan felt the heavy hand of the man in the apron fall onto his shoulder.

Terror roughly embraced the boy's mind and assumed full control of it, shutting it down like an electrical grid. The boy did his best to try and call out, but he found himself unable as the fire of madness raged within his small brain. His mind, finding no outlet from which to vent his white-hot dread, simply crashed. Like a computer that had been overloaded and needed to reboot, his intellect was instantly reduced to a single white dot on his mind's blank television screen.

After that, for the boy, there was only silence.

Silence, and an eternal emptiness.

LEALTÀ

This is a story pretty firmly rooted in the aforementioned world of 'tough guy' fiction. What can I say? I'm a fan and I've been reading a lot of that kind of thing lately. It's really been terrific. Pantheonic names like Don Hamilton, Erle Stanley Gardner (specifically the 'Cool & Lam' mysteries), Jim Thompson, Spillane, Chandler… just good stuff, Maynard. Do yourself a favor and seek out any and all books by these guys. They're really great and I promise you're gonna love 'em. There's an economy of words at play that I'm sure you're gonna dig. Their work excites me in a way similar to how I imagine a watchmaker feels when he sees a really well-made Swiss watch. And, on top of all that… there's a level of violence on display that can oftentimes rival any 'horror story.' So, what's not to like? That said, I like the voice of this one and hope the cinematic aspects of the narrative do these influences justice.

Frank Wells leaned his fat ass up against the black Lincoln Town Car and sighed to himself like he'd just missed a bus. They'd been waiting here in the North parking lot of some dump called the Stanford Brothers Sawmill for almost an hour now, off in the back where people rarely went, and the guy they were supposed to meet up with was late.

Wells looked around him angrily. The lot was an open and exposed patch of asphalt that was surrounded on all sides by a dense forest. Tall Redwood trees rose up like Roman columns, and the brush around their base was so dense that it was hard to see anything other than a wall of green foliage. Overhead, there were a few birds in the trees singing, but since their song was drowned out by the continuous rattle and hum coming from inside the sawmill, most didn't bother.

Frank got up off the fender and began pacing back and forth in front of the car, his hands stuffed into his pockets like he was forever looking for the right change. His anger boiled inside of him like a caustic stew.

His face burned a hot red. Never in his twenty-plus years with the Organization had anyone ever been this late for a scheduled meet.

And with no word? Not even a phone call?

They wouldn't have dared. The idea that some arrogant shit-hook would be this ballsy made him furious. He looked at the windshield of the Towne Car and glared at his two companions on this run. They were both still sitting in the front seat, baking as they all were, under the late-afternoon sun.

Georgie Moore was a gigantic Samoan guy in a powder-blue Hawaiian shirt who had been brought along as Muscle. Frank didn't like having to hurt people, even when the time arose and the situation demanded it, and his bosses knew it. He could tool someone up in a pinch… but only if it were critical to forging a positive resolution to the given problem. Better to allow some underling who'd been hired to 'get his hands dirty' to get his hands dirty, doling out whatever punishment had been deemed necessary.

Moore was six and a half feet tall, weighed about two-seventy, and was big in the chest like a bull, with a shaved head that shined like a pool ball when he sweat. And he was sweating now. They all were. It was hot as fucking balls out here.

Frank had picked Georgie specifically to come along on this run because they'd worked together before, and they were cool. He knew that having a guy around as big as Moore helped ramp up the intimidation factor. And that made his job all that much easier. And if things ever went south, it also gave his enemies something big to shoot at while Frank got the hell out of there.

The other guy—some stick of a kid named Jarrod Kennedy—was another matter. Brand spanking new to the Organization and only a year or two older than Frank's youngest son, the kid exuded that weird mixture of green naïveté and red-hot brashness that made Frank think he wasn't going to last too long in this line of work.

Being impulsive made you rash, and being rash made you miss things.

Missing things… that made you dead.

But his bosses said that they wanted to have Frank check him out, to teach him some of the ropes, and that this Buy was as good a chance as any for that. So, here he was, sweating his dick off with these fuckin' guys… and being made to wait.

Frank mopped his forehead with his handkerchief and the cloth came away soaked through. He'd been using it a lot since coming out to this shithole. It was so bad now that he almost considered simply tossing it away and having done with it, but he stuffed it back into his pocket instead.

"This fuckin' sucks," Frank said aloud as he crossed his arms over his broad chest.

The passenger-side car door popped open, and Georgie pulled his massive bulk out of his seat to get some fresh air. The springs beneath the car sighed in relief, happy to be free of their great load. It took him a minute to remove himself completely from the cramped confines of the car's interior. And as Frank watched him do so, he suddenly thought of the time he saw a magician once who pulled a seemingly never-ending length of scarf out of his mouth. Georgie getting out of the car reminded him of that. He just kept comin' and comin', pouring himself out of the automobile like The Blob.

"What'd ya say there, Boss?" the big man asked, shielding his eyes from the oppressive overhead sun.

"Huh?" Frank growled. "Nothing."

"So, uh…" Georgie asked hesitantly. "How long ya think we gonna wait for this jag-off?"

Frank shook his head back and forth unhappily as he looked up into the boughs of the trees for some god damn strength. This fuckin' guy was fuckin' late, and Frank was getting pretty fuckin' pissed about it. And it wasn't even like they had any sort of long-standing relationship with the prick, much less the people he claimed to represent. Truth was… no one in the entire organization really knew dick about these people. All anyone knew about him was that he'd gotten an 'all's clear' from Giorgio Santoni in Philly.

Santoni said that he'd cleared him with some fellas, fellas who knew things about things like that. He said he was someone they'd worked with once upon a time and that they could all vouch for him; said he was legit. So, despite some reluctance on The Boss' part, the meet had been planned and arranged. Which, once again, left Frank sitting in this fuckin' parking lot under this hot fucking sun.

Frank thought it over, replaying what had been said, and he was sure that he'd been pretty fuckin' clear with the guy: come out to the Stanford Mill at four o'clock in the afternoon sharp. Not four-oh-one. Not three forty-five. F.O.U.R. in the P.M. Frank eyeballed his watch like it had cheated on him. 4:45.

Mother. Fucker.

He shot another annoyed glance back at Georgie. Georgie returned it, but with an added look of understanding. He knew how shit like this infuriated Frank. Everybody did. Frank liked prompt. Frank like precise. Frank liked professional. And even a man of Georgie's limited intellect knew… this wasn't professional.

Frank nodded to him, knowing Georgie got it. They'd talked about things like this in the past while they were sitting in cars and waiting for money drops. Good man, that Georgie. Not too smart, but bigger than a brick shithouse… and more loyal than a hound dog.

The kid suddenly got out of the driver's side and, walking around the open car door, went over to Frank. He had short-cut brown hair and was dressed in what could well have been someone else's suit. The pants were too big for him, and they hung from his waist like sheets set out to dry on a windless day. The jacket was a tad too small as well. Frank thought he looked ridiculous, and he made a mental note to say something when they got back. Maybe they could get him into something that fit. Or maybe just get him a suit that was already opened in the back.

Y'know, to save the boys at the funeral home some time and trouble.

"Jimmy's on the phone for ya there, Frank," the kid said. He had his hand extended and there was a cell phone clutched in it.

Frank took it from him, turning his back to the two of them, and pressing the phone to his ear like it was a kid's toy. "Yeah?"

Frank listened for a minute, not saying anything, just nodding and looking more and more pissed off. He looked over at Jarrod for a second, watching him as he walked back to his side of the car. Then, he looked over at Georgie. He nodded his head a few more times to the voice whispering in his ear, mumbled a quick 'okay,' and then hung up. He tossed the phone casually back to the kid from across the hood of the car.

"Change of plans, boys," Frank said, discreetly pulling his Nine out from the holster under his arm. He quietly chambered a round, set the safety, and put it back where he'd gotten it. For later. "Looks like our delayed guest just had his invite revoked."

Georgie looked across the bonnet of the car at Frank like a dog who'd just heard a funny sound. "Meanin'?"

Frank grinned malevolently back at him. "Meanin'… Word is that Santoni got himself pinched a few weeks ago by the Feds. They've been monitoring his house and…" he paused for effect, "his cellphones ever since. From what we hear now, they even intercepted our call. And it turns out that the guy who vouched for our tardy friend wasn't Santoni after all."

"No shit?" Georgie responded incredulously.

"No shit."

All of a sudden, the kid whistled, having seen something coming up the road. Frank and Georgie looked over at him. The kid nodded his head in the direction of the gate at the far side of the lot and the long dirt road that lay beyond it. Far off, they could all see the figure of a man walking casually up the road toward them, carrying some kind of case in his hand. He was still too far away for anybody to get a clear look him, but as he got closer, it became easier to make out his details through the waves of heat coming up off of the road.

The man approaching was tall, rail-thin, and wearing a white linen suit and a pair of red alligator shoes. For a second, Frank was reminded of that writer fella, Thomas Wolfe, and the way he dressed in the latter part of his life; like he was some kind of southern gentleman. This guy looked a lot like that, only his hair was darker, and he wore a pair of thin glasses—spectacles—that clung to the front of his face like a mountain climber. As he got closer, casually moving through the gate, and entering the lot, you could see that he had a pencil-thin moustache perched above his upper lip.

"How you wanna handle this?" Georgie quietly asked Frank from out of the side of his mouth.

Frank thought a minute, letting the weight of the moment unspool in his head, and feeling the pressure in the air increase exponentially against his skin. He knew what he'd been told on the phone, the orders he'd been given, but he was also aware of the fact that things weren't always as simple as that. They were standing in the middle of a parking lot of a fairly populated place of business. He couldn't just 'handle' the situation like they wanted and not consider the possibility of fallout, right?

Then again, his bosses had been clear. There was no telling what they would say—or, worse, what they might do—if he failed to deliver on what he'd been told to accomplish. Because, as everybody knew... Frankie Wells always delivered.

"Let's hear what he has to say first, try and see if he has any friends waiting around someplace to surprise us. Try 'n' figure out what his game is," Frank said softly. "If I decide he needs dealin' wit', I'll decide and I'll do it. You both," and he looked at the kid to emphasize his point, and to make sure he was making himself crystal clear, "keep your shit where it is until you see me make a move. Got it?"

The kid nodded, and Frank was genuinely surprised he didn't hear maracas.

"And then," Frank continued as he looked back over at Georgie, "only cover each other. We don't need to get no kind of Gunfight at the OK Corral goin' up in here. Got it?"

Georgie nodded grimly to both his request as well as his reasoning.

The approaching man in the suit raised his right arm and waved it in greeting once he was thirty or so yards away from them. He pulled a handkerchief from his back pants pocket and mopped the back of his neck with it. Nonchalantly strolling toward them, he balled the cloth square into his fist and put it back where he'd gotten it. When he was closer to the car, he stopped, and set the briefcase he was carrying onto the ground.

Frank walked to the front of the Lincoln, and he motioned for the other two men to stay where they were. He leaned his ass against the grill and crossed his arms, once again resting his forearms across his belly like it was a shelf. A smile crept like a viper across his broad face. "How ya doin'?" Frank called out as he smiled.

"I am a-okay, my friend; absolutely a-okay." The man looked up to the sun overhead and shielded his eyes with one hand. "Sure is a hot one out here, eh?"

"Yup," Frank responded. "Can I, uh... help you, friend?"

The man in the white suit smiled and his eyes met Frank's as he nodded. He started to reach into his jacket, but Georgie tapped something heavy and metal against the roof of the car, and everybody froze. The sound of the Samoan suddenly clearing his throat in the quiet afternoon sounded exactly like the threat it was meant to be. The guy in the suit slowly removed his hand as if in reverse.

"My cell," he said and smiled like a car salesman. "May I retrieve it?"

Frank smiled back like a cat granting a mouse a last bit of cheese. "Slow."

"But of course," the man replied, completing his task deliberately. He flipped through a few things on his screen. And then, finding what he needed, he looked back up at Frank. "Wells?"

"That's me," Frank said. He eyed the man suspiciously. "You're Gaudreau, then?"

The man gracefully bowed his head to him.

Frank nodded to Georgie and the big guy ambled over to where the man in the white suit was standing. The big Samoan smiled at him and motioned with his pistol for him to raise his arms.

"Georgie here is gonna pat you down, Mr. Gaudreau. I hope you don't have any objections to that?"

Gaudreau opened his arms as if he were inviting Georgie in for a hug. "I assure you, Mr. Wells," he said gently, looking at him over Georgie's mountainous shoulder. "I come to you completely unarmed."

Georgie holstered his piece and started patting the man's chest, back, and belly. Then, he slid his hands up and down both legs. Standing back up, he turned to Frank and shrugged. "He ain't lyin'."

Frank chuckled to himself. "Not exactly a smart thing, is it, Mr. Gaudreau?"

Gaudreau furrowed his brow in genuine confusion as he straightened his jacket and tie. "What do you mean?"

"I mean, you coming all the way out here with no support, no real back up." He paused. Then, "Defensively-speaking, I mean, it sucks. After all, we could be some very bad people." He smiled again. "We could be some very bad people indeed."

Georgie ambled back over to his side of the car, side-eyeing Frank as if to say, 'Ain't that the damnedest thing you've ever fuckin' seen?' He shot a quick glance at the kid but saw that he wasn't gonna be of any help. He had this wide-eyed look on his face like he was at the top of a rollercoaster and just about to go down the scary other side. His eyes were open so wide you could see the whites around his irises and his mouth hung open, presumably waiting to catch passing flies. The big man chuckled to himself as he returned to his spot, leaning casually on the roof of the car.

This kid'll be dead in a week, he idly thought. Shit, maybe sooner.

Gaudreau continued with the adjustment of his suit coat, showing no bother over it; like he'd been expecting to be searched, and putting himself back to together was merely a small part of that. When he was done, he looked back up at Frank amiably.

"Well, yes, I could see how one might think that. But you see, Mr. Wells," Gaudreau said, bringing his hands up in front of him like he was about to say his prayers. "I'm a man who has lived his life relying on the better instincts of folks."

"How so?" Frank said, looking amused, like a child playing with a bug.

"Well, Mr. Wells, I'm one of those people who believe that he has someone watching over him wherever he goes, doing whatever he does. A guardian angel if you will. Someone who looks down from on high and watches over them, protecting them from danger. I know it sounds silly but… that's the way I've always approached life. And, as a result, I tend to embark on relationships with people trusting them to do the right thing. That way, I don't spend much of my time living in fear. Some have said that I am an extremely lucky man."

Frank shrugged and chuckled darkly, thinking how quickly things like luck could change, how fast they could run out. "Well, I'm happy to see that that's been working for ya."

"Well, thank you. You know The Good Book says, 'No evil shall befall you, nor shall affliction come near your tent, for His Angels God has given command about you, that they guard you in all your ways.' I've always liked the way that sounds. And so, I count on it in my daily life." He smiled broadly and clapped his hands together. "But... to our bit of business, eh?"

Frank smugly leaned more of his weight against the car, keeping his arms crossed over his belly. The springs protested the additional weight by briefly squeaking out their displeasure. He took a moment to admire this guy's brass. He was pushy, that's for sure. Kinda prissy, and sorta off-putting in his all-too-tailored suit. It was a goddamn miracle this cop—and make no mistake, that's exactly what this fuckin' guy was, Frank could see that quite clearly now—had ever made it away from pounding a beat.

Frank took another look around, taking in his surroundings. He was pleased to see that there wasn't anybody out lurking around; no one deciding to leave work early or driving in from outside the gate. If it kept up like that, there would be no witnesses to what was about to happen next.

Because, after all, orders were orders.

"Yeah, well, see... about that," Frank started to explain as he took a step away from the car. Surreptitiously, he'd slid his hand into his coat, shaking hands with the grip of his coal black, Beretta 92F. He allowed his hand to rest there as he made his point. "See, we just heard... there's been a problem with our friend Santoni."

Gaudreau looked genuinely unconcerned as he took another casual glance around the parking lot. His gaze lingered on a tricked-out Buick sitting at the far end of the lot, but then, it finally came back around to Wells. "Santoni?" His eyes held Frank's for a moment, then they drifted away again. "What problem?"

Frank stuck out his lower lip as if in concentration and rolled his eyes skyward. Then, he smiled at Gaudreau. "Well... from what we hear, Santoni has had himself a bit of trouble."

Gaudreau looked back at him, concern only now starting to pull at the corners of his eyes. "I don't understand."

"You know, trouble... as in, legal trouble."

The man in the suit rocked from one foot to the other but said nothing.

"But first," Frank said coolly as he drew the Beretta from under his arm, and, to everyone's surprise, he leveled it at the kid. Jarrod went as white as a Klansman's robe, ducking his head slightly and holding his hands up in surrender.

"C-c'mon, Frank," the kid stammered, looking first at Georgie, then at Gaudreau for some reason. His gaze was pulled back to Frank though as if by magnets. After all, he was the one pointing the gun. "Quit... quit fooling around, man."

Frank glared at him over the sight of the pistol. "Did you really think we wouldn't find out? They told me everything." He sighed in exasperation. "A Fed? A fucking Fed... You rat piece of shit."

The kid looked like he would have shit his pants if he thought it might have helped, and it was hard to blame him. Frank had been in The Life for a long time, and everybody knew how hard as nails he was. So, if he were to ever point a gun at you, you knew you were in some pretty deep shit. If it was possible, Jarrod's complexion abruptly went even paler.

"L-look, Frank," he said, "I don't know what you think you think you know, but... I'm square. I swear I'm on the lev..."

Frank unceremoniously shot Jarrod twice without even a hint of warning. The bullets hit the kid in the chest like a couple of fists, smashing bone and rending his muscle tissue to hash. And, while his body may have slowed the bullets down, they ultimately failed to stop them. Frank noticed as they hit the dirt in two little puffs of dust several yards behind the traitorous fuck.

The kid? Well, he crumpled into a wet heap right where he'd stood.

Then, without hesitation, Frank turned his gun back to Gaudreau.

Georgie had by now, gotten clumsily back to his feet. He wasn't sure what the hell had just gone down, but he knew that Frank for sure had his back, so he was ready for anything. He'd retrieved his gun from its shoulder holster more out of habit than anything else, and he waved it around in the air now, unsure of what he was supposed to be aiming at.

"Christ, Frank," the big guy finally mumbled.

"Whoa, whoa, whoa," Gaudreau said soothingly, even as he took an involuntary step backward. He raised his arms into the air like he was being held up, but still managed to take another small, barely noticeable, step to his right. His face though, even while trying to appear calm, still showed a certain amount of concern. There was, after all, a gun now in play.

Frank pointed his pistol at the stranger, the barrel aimed squarely at the center of the man's forehead. "And now, you..."

Suddenly, there was the sound of a loud whip-crack from somewhere far away. The snap echoed across the landscape in a brittle, repeating staccato. Birds took to the air from the safety of their hiding places and began circling in the sky above them. Immediately afterward, there was a frozen heartbeat in time when everything was calm, silent, and peaceful.

Then, just as Frank was turning his head to tell Georgie to grab ahold of this fuck, to explain to him everything he'd been told on the telephone, he saw the Samoan's head jerk violently back, like he'd been slapped in the face by an invisible giant's hand. The big man's body was roughly slammed to the ground, his corpse striking the dirt like an immense sack of meat. Dark blood immediately started pooling beneath what was left of his bald head.

Sniper, Frank thought instantly, recognizing the whip-crack sound from having done some time in the military when he was younger. Angry at himself for not seeing this whole thing for the setup that it was, Frank turned to kill the effete man in front of him. But the world had suddenly gone to jelly, like someone somewhere had hit a switch and set reality to slow-motion. His arm felt as heavy as lead and, before he could bring his gun online, he saw Gaudreau standing there, smugly smiling at him.

His arm was extended toward Frank, like he had something in his hand that he wanted to give him. It took a second for Frank to be able to focus, but when he did, he saw the Derringer now pointing at him that Gaudreau held in some kind of slick forearm rig. The damn thing had slid right out of his goddam sleeve.

Georgie never was as thorough as he should have been, Frank thought as gun smoke abruptly appeared, expanding to fill the space between them. An instant later, Frank felt punched in the throat as the .38 bullet found its target.

The heavy slug tore away a sizable portion of the muscle on one side of Frank's neck, spinning him like a top. Blood splashed like spilled paint across the asphalt and the chrome grill of the black Town car. From somewhere seemingly far off, Frank felt a couple of his ribs cave as his chest struck against the bumper. And the last thing he remembered before the eternal black came and ushered him away was the sensation of hitting the parking lot pavement, and of the gravel pressing into the soft skin of his face like shark's teeth... and how warm his own blood felt.

HITTING THE SPOT

This is an admittedly sordid tale. To tell you the truth, I'm not even really sure where this idea came from. It just sort of happened one afternoon as I was noodling around with some ideas while staring out the window (something I do a lot of). The idle mind truly is the Devil's workshop, I guess. All of which makes me remember a conversation I had the first time I met Clive Barker. I asked him if he'd ever noticed that the feeling one gets in the pit of their stomach when they are deeply afraid is very similar to the one that happens when they're really turned on. I remember him looking at me for a second and then asking, 'Do you know what the French call the moment right after orgasm?' I said that I didn't. 'They call it Le Petit Mort. The little death.' He waited a second, and then he said, 'Sex and Death have always been inextricably linked. The beginning of life, the end.'

So, with that in mind….

When dawn broke on Trafalgar Street, it found those that lived there in the peaceful little neighborhood fast asleep. The residents along the lonely little stretch of road had not yet rose from their beds to start their day on this sunny, Saturday morning in July. Most of them still lay sleeping and blissfully dreaming their middle-class suburban cares away. Those few who were awake had only just brushed their teeth and were beginning to think about the day's breakfast and first cup of coffee.

The neighborhood was peacefully serene as no one was out in their yards yet. Not to mow lawns, or to do their gardening. Not to wash their cars or even to do a bit of painting on the eaves that got missed when they did the trim last Spring. No, you could hear a pin drop along the quiet street as the morning's sun came up over the trees and soaked the tableau in its glimmering rays.

The early morning's light came pouring into Alyssa Baxter's bedroom window like floodwater, soaking everything it touched with its warmth. Bits of dust spiraled like swarms of fairies within the eddies of its golden brilliance. Slowly, the room began to shake off the chill from the dying night.

Clothes, in various degrees of cleanliness, were piled in stacks like hay bales around the cluttered pasture of the flat bed. Next to the foot were more stacks of laundry in plastic baskets, foothills next to the mountainous bedstead.

Off to one side, a low dresser flanked the room, its drawers pulled randomly out. There were more clothes and a stack of men's shirts still on their hangers lying across its top in a jumble. A Tetris puzzle of cardboard boxes was stacked to one side of the bureau, several hardcover books poking out from the top like cement pilings submerged in sand.

Suddenly, something stirred from beneath the clothing on the bed. The movement was barely noticeable at first. But then, its motion increased enough to topple over one of the piles of clothes. From beneath, a groan rattled in the stillness. There was more movement from beneath the bedding. Another of the mounds of laundry toppled over, its articles of clothing falling like clumps of wet leaves to the unvacuumed floor.

"Ugh," Alyssa Baker groaned from within her warm, blankety womb. "Shit."

She rolled over onto her back, pushing the comforter from over her head. A deep breath. Christ she was tired. Still. After what, eight, nine hours of uninterrupted sleep? Sleep so deep, in fact, that she didn't even remember ever dreaming, much less going to bed in the first place. Seems like these days though, all she wanted to do was sleep. Seems like, these days, even the act of opening her eyes and having to deal with the world was a struggle not worth undertaking.

Seems these days...

Say it.

Seems these days...

Say it!

... ever since Don died.

Seems these days, ever since Don died, it was all she could do just to cope. All she could do to keep her feet moving forward, to keep her mind focused on the next task on her never-ending list of things to do. Her list. She'd have been lost this past week... since... since Don died... without that damn list.

She sighed and let her body relax into the bedding. As she felt her muscles unwind, she noticed, as she usually did when she first woke up, that her thoughts wandered. And as usual, they ended up in one place. The same place.

In the past… with the man she loved. With Don.

Don Baker had been a Man's man. One of those big guys whose father had instilled in him an overwrought and exuberant sense of masculinity. Not only was he physically big at six-two, two-eighty, but he lived big. He ate big, drank big, fought big, and he loved big. Much like his father and his father had before him though, Don was also a drinker. He was known to polish off a twelve pack of beer with his dinner, and that was before the real drinking even got started for the night. He was the kind of guy who'd tell his friends—male or female—that it was time for them to 'man up'—or worse, 'cowboy up'—if he thought that they ought to do something. And then, he'd call them a 'bitch' if they didn't do as he'd demanded.

Alyssa stared up at the lines in the ceiling numbly.

Like suck his dick in the cab of his pickup truck at the drive-in when they were in high school. But he was strong and, God help her, he took care of her. He paid for things and promised that he'd always be there. And he was. Sort of.

But the biggest—and most important—factor in their relationship was that he'd been able to find her Spot pretty early on, during one of those truck / drive-in make-out sessions right after they graduated. She remembered the night that he found it. Well… she'd never felt anything like it. She'd cummed so hard that her legs were spongy for most of the next day. And the day after.

After that, she couldn't quit him. And heavens knew, she'd tried, time and time again. But then, he'd find her when she'd had an exhausting day, when her defenses were low, and he'd stroke her hair, and tell her how it was gonna all be different this time. And he'd start kissing the back of her hand. Then the back of her neck. Then he kissed her a few other places. So, by the time his probing fingers had picked her locks and had begun stroking the spot that drove her so goddamn crazy, she'd already started to forget what his transgressions had been.

It was as a result of such one of these encounters that she'd, in the heat of her passion, agreed to marry the big dope. His proposal had been given somewhere between her blowing him and him sinking in to his full length, right as his pace was going redline into his Danger Zone. She remembered him grumbling something romantic like, 'I wanna marry you so frickin' bad, babe' as he shot his wad deep within her belly, and the deal had been sealed.

They'd gotten married by the judge at the courthouse a month later.

Once they'd moved in together as husband and wife, not much changed between them. Don would still go out with his friends—The

Boys, he called them—and he'd still come home whenever he damn well felt like it, usually hammered.

Alyssa hugged herself and remembered those nights when he'd climb into bed, all Roman hands, and Russian fingers, with the smell of stale beer and tobacco on his breath. She'd hated them at first, wished he'd stop a minute and take his time a little. But soon… the barbarity of his attentions, the simplemindedness of his lovemaking, sorta grew on her. She was happy just as long as he paid attention to her.

And visited her Spot on the reg.

She blinked her eyes. God, there was a time when she would have followed that man to the ends of the earth just as long as he kept hitting it and making her feel that way again and again. The orgasms he'd given her… every time, she swore she was going to tear a ligament or something.

But then he started staying out later, past the time when the bars close. At first, Alyssa suspected that he had a side piece, but… she'd checked with a few of his friends on the q.t.—the ones she knew she could trust—and they all swore he hadn't. It was just 'boys being boys,' they'd said. 'Guy shit.' So, she'd done her best to forget about it, deciding to just let things play out. And as long as he continued to come home to her every night, and kept true to their marital vows, she didn't see any harm in him going out and hanging with his buddies.

So, she hadn't thought a thing the night that he walked past her, grabbed her ass, and announced he and the boys were going out to the bar for a few beers. He'd pressed her against the wall lustily, pushing one hand up under her shirt. He roughly cupped one of her breasts in his calloused hand, pinching her nipple between his thumb and index finger roughly. He ground his hips against hers, pushing his wet tongue between her lips and into her mouth. She thought to herself idly how he tasted like cigarettes and toothpaste.

"You like that, doncha dirty girl?" he'd moaned into the well of her neck as he ground his Levi-denimed crotch against her.

She was about to respond, to tell him, yes… yes, she liked it. She liked it an awful lot, and to please, by all means, continue… when he abruptly shoved his other hand down the front of her pants. Alyssa remembered gasping in both surprise and breathless lust as she felt his fingers push aside the cotton of her panties and touch her… there.

"Oh, yeah," she moaned throatily as she bit the lobe of his ear.

Her breathing caught as the tips of his fingers repeatedly did this woodpecker-pattern on her Spot, like an overeager door to door salesman ringing the house bell. She remembered warmth cascading down her legs in a numbing fog and her knees suddenly going all rubbery.

Then, he was gone. Walking out the door.

She'd been left leaning against the wall, her clothes in a state of crumpled disarray, her legs spread brazenly. She could still remember how wet she'd been. And how furiously she'd masturbated on the couch later that night while watching TV and waiting for him to come home. But it wasn't the same.

It just wasn't the same.

Alyssa pulled the covers back up over her head, rolling over onto her side. Sighing deeply, she quietly decided to hit the snooze bar on the day and go back to the sanctuary of her sleep. She had no place to go, just a few errands that had to be done later in the afternoon. So, she closed her eyes, and, in a few minutes, her breathing became more and more regular.

Soon, she was dreaming...

The thing that had once been Don Baker awoke with no recollection of its previous life. The first thing it could recall was waking up in the dark of the grave and clawing its way toward the promise of the Light. He wasn't able to remember much of anything about how he'd lived, or how he'd died. He definitely didn't remember going out and getting drunk with the guys that final night, didn't remember telling everybody how he was 'okay to drive' and getting behind the wheel. But he mostly didn't remember taking that curve on Marcelo Road a little too fast and rolling his 1995 Chrysler LeBaron four or five times. Nor did he have any memory of being pitched out of the front windshield midway through them rolls and having the car roll over him, killing him deader than a dead dog's dick.

No, the only thing he could remember was waking up in that field with all the statuary and rolling hills and feeling a deep compulsion to come where he was now.

To come home.

Baker looked down from seemingly far away and watched as his muddy Wingtip shoe planted itself on the landing of the stairs that led up to where he knew the bedrooms would be. Muddy grave water pooled into the carpeting with each of his steps leaving a trail of wet cartoon footprints in his wake. His gait was a sort of stiff-limbed stagger as he tottered forward, pitching his weight from one leg to the other, making his way up the staircase.

Most of his bones had been broken in the accident that killed him, so even beyond the fact that he was a dead man yesterday, his being up and walking around was something of a miracle. But still he came forward, lurching his way inexorably down the empty hallway.

Something from deep within the folds of his corrupted brain kept whispering to him. Like a conspirator, it told him that the thing he sought, the thing he desired most of all, could be found here on the second floor of this house. And so, he'd come. And all through the house, there wasn't a sound, nor did anything dare to stir, save for the ticking of a far-off clock.

Don continued moving down the corridor, shambling slowly. Finally, he came to a door that looked familiar to him, a place of import. He stood silently in the doorway for a moment, resting his forehead against the door's painted surface, before gently pushing it open.

His cloudy eyes searched the room for the thing, the thing that he desired, the thing the voice in his head kept promising him. Everything laid out before him seemed so familiar: the room, the dresser, the bed—like he should remember them and their significance, but just wasn't able. In the stillness, the sound of his hungry stomach suddenly growling sounded like a series of low, muffled gun reports.

He shuffled his way over to one side of the bed—his side?—staring dumbly down at the mounds of sheets, blankets, and laundry spread out spilled cargo before him. His eyes wandered the multicolored hills and shadowed valleys but saw nothing that sparked any primal interest.

Then, he noticed something… a foot sticking out from under the blankets, the thin bones of its ankle fully exposed. His eyes locked onto the uncovered flesh like a predator, and he slowly began to peel back the rumpled bedding for his prize.

In Alyssa's dream… Don and she are back at the drive-in. A retro-horror movie is playing on the giant screen in front of them (something about a team of scientists finding giant insects in the desert), but neither of them are really paying it much attention. Don has his mouth pressed over hers again and she can feel him running his hands over her body like there was a paycheck in it.

Roman hands… and Russian fingers.

By the flickering light from the drive-in screen, she can see him move over her to my god finally mount her. Alyssa is sopping wet again down there and more than ready for him. She can feel her vag pulsating with its need, dribbling out its desire in thick, syrupy strands of mucous.

Her attention is pulled out of the moment by the sudden smell of something rotting, but Don pokes his middle finger in deep and makes her forget all about it. Makes her forget all about everything. She sighs contentedly as she feels him touch her... touch her there... on her spot, and she groans like an animal with lust. She knows what's coming, and how good it was going to be... like a junkie in the moment just before pushing the dope into their vein. Wanting it. Needing it.

Once again, she is yanked out of the moment by that same fetid smell, like forgotten week old fish that was left out. She tries to find her groove again, to let the sensations Dream Don is causing to flow over her like waves at the beach, but then, she can't help but notice something else.

She thinks of how it suddenly seems like there are too many hands touching her. She concentrates on them each individually as she lets Don continue to do his stuff. She can feel the one on her tit, kneading her breast like it was bread dough. Then, there's the one lightly gripping her throat and slightly choking her. She didn't mind letting Don do that now and again because she knew how much he liked doing it; said it made him feel powerful. Whatever, Don... if he just kept doing what he was doing, he could do whatever he damn well pleased.

But then... she felt the other hand, the cold one on her outer thigh, and that just didn't make sense. In fact, it failed to make enough sense that the incongruity of it rattled her dream logic enough to cause her to abruptly awaken.

As Alyssa came to consciousness, the first thing she felt was the crushing weight on top of her. The sensation was quickly followed by the feeling of wet hands holding her down and moving over her body. She tried to get up but felt herself pressed roughly back down onto the bed instead. There was something on top of her, she knew that now, something heavy, and it was making it difficult for her to breathe.

But then she managed to wriggle her head free of the bedding, blinking her eyes into focus against the growing daylight coming in through the window. Her vision took a second to clear, and as it did, she continued to feel the hands pressing against her flesh, the sharp frigid fingers probing the clefts of her anatomy.

When she could better see, she wrestled her head around, clearing the last of the bedding from her face. It was then that she got her first look at the thing that was hovering over her like a parade balloon. And what she saw shook her down to the fibers of her soul. For there, leaning over her, laying on top of her—just like in her dream—was Don.

Her Don.

Alyssa could see that he was wearing the same clothes they'd buried him in; muddier than she'd last seen them for sure, but it was the same outfit, nonetheless. At first, she thought that she might still be dreaming, her dream-narrative somehow changing setting, as dreams can so often do. But then, she felt the wetness on her skin again, smelled the mold and earth on him... and she knew.

She knew.

Alyssa struggled beneath him, pushing his weight off as she did what she could to get a breath. As she fought, a clammy hand roughly grabbed her breast under her shirt. Then, his other hand was sliding, as if guided by some deep muscle memory, down her belly, to the place between her legs. She pushed against him, trying to wriggle her hips out of his reach, but then she felt a familiar hot flash of nerve endings spark as his cold fingers entered her.

God, no!

Abruptly, the thing that used to be Don stopped his aggression. He continued holding her down onto the bed with one powerful hand as the other discovered the moistness that remained from her dream. His fingers suddenly dove deep, locating her Spot as if by homing beacon.

His fingertips brushed up against it, and she felt a hot fire course through her; like too much electricity pushed through too little wire. And to her horror, she felt her body respond as it always had to Don's touch, a touch now gone icy cold.

Alyssa finally found her voice and began screaming.

Then, Don surprised her by quickly letting his head drop and pushing his face between her bare legs. Alyssa only had time to recall the night she and Don saw a show on TV about lions that lived on the Serengeti, and how they ate, before it no longer mattered. Soon, the sound of her wailing joined the chorus of voices coming from other houses, in other homes, all along Trafalgar Street.

SECUESTRADOS

Once I figured out what this story was, and what it was about (which, I'll admit, took a minute), the writing of it came together pretty quickly. It's inspired by more crime fiction; except I added the 'rope-a-dope' ending. Hopefully, I didn't mess any of the cultural particulars up.

The van door opened suddenly, and it clattered on its rails like a rollercoaster car click-clacking its way up its first hill. The door slammed against its chucks, rattling the rest of the van to its chassis. Doroteia Alves, who was sitting behind the wheel, jumped in her seat despite knowing that her man, Tito, and his friend Gaspar, were due back at any minute.

Back with their little golden goose.

Back with the kid.

The child in question was Otavio, only son of international financier, Renaldo Araujo, and sole heir to the vast Araujo fortune. The three of them—Tito, Gaspar, and Doroteia—had read about him in an article in the newspaper with the headline, 'Disabled Son of Banker Offers Shiny Outlook for the Future.' A puff piece, really, planted in the newspapers to bolster the public's perception of the senior Araujo to make him appear as if he were a good and decent man.

Truth be told though; Araujo was anything but. In reality, he was a lot of things (thief, racketeer, embezzler, fraud...), and not one of them was anything close to good or decent. The article, however, did bring the boy to the trio's predatory attention. And it hadn't taken them more than a couple bottles of wine and a cutting board of Lamb al Asador to decide that it could well be in their best interests to snatch the kid up, take him someplace safe, and ransom him for a sliver of that Araujo fortune. Crafting the plan of how to pull it off took them less time than it did to eat their Torta Envinada dessert.

This moment right here was the culmination of that preparation.

Doroteia turned around in her seat and saw her companions standing side by side in the street. They were both out of breath and huddled around the van's now open door.

Tito was carrying something in his arms that was maybe three or four feet in length, and from the way he was carrying it, the parcel looked heavy. He had the bulk of it draped over his shoulder. She saw that they'd wrapped the upper portion of the bundle in the brown blanket they'd purchased at a department store yesterday. Just like they'd planned, both still had their face masks on.

Tito was wearing jeans and a worn leather motorcycle jacket, with an old black, Rolling Stones tee underneath. The red of the logo's lips shone brightly in the shadow of the jacket's interior. Gaspar had on a pair of khaki pants, a wrinkled green button-up shirt, and a black baseball jacket with an American team logo (a large yellow letter P) on the back. The two men were both out of breath from their run back to the car.

Tito set the weight in his arms down as gently as he could onto the floorboards of the van. The package hit the carpeting with a muted whump. Two rail-thin legs wearing jeans and a pair of bone-white Jordans slipped out from beneath the blanket. Doroteia noticed that both of the limbs were encased in some kind of medical leg braces, like the ones they used to make patients with Polio wear.

"Make sure he can breathe, okay?" Doroteia prompted, the tone of her voice sounding genuinely concerned.

Tito nodded as he gently pulled the blanket back to reveal the face of a small boy, about seven or eight years old. He had on a T-shirt that had the words 'Xavier's School for Gifted Youngsters' in bold letters etched into a granite plaque on the front. On his head, sitting slightly askew from all of the jostling he'd suffered on the way here, was a green, knitted octopus hat with tentacles sticking up like palm fronds from the crown of his head. At the end of each of the eight woven arms were wide-eyed, bloodshot eyeballs. His black, curly hair stuck out from beneath the cap like crabgrass.

Once the kid was loaded into the car and sufficiently hidden from view, Tito climbed up into the front seat of the van, tearing his mask off the lower part of his face once he was inside and the door was closed. Gaspar quickly followed him into the car by getting into the opened side, climbing over the kid, and pulling the sliding door closed behind him. He crab-walked, bent over to accommodate the low ceiling, and finally sat down onto the bench in the very back. Doroteia quickly turned back around in her seat and, throwing the car into gear, she hit the gas. The van leapt forward like a jackrabbit, and they drove off down the quiet darkened road.

Circling the block, they proceeded up the interstate on-ramp, injecting themselves into the flow of traffic like a virus. The van accelerated and carefully moved over until they were driving in the fast lane. Once the van had gotten a few miles away, Doroteia eased up off the gas and slowed down in order to blend in. And soon, within just a few minutes of them meeting back up at the van, they'd done just that, disappearing into the sprawl of the city like a specter.

The small warehouse they'd rented was in a lonely part of the old meat packing district of the city. It wasn't used as much as it once was. There had been a few attempts at nightclubs and 'artist compounds' that had tried to make a go of it over the years here, but they'd all either been busted up by the cops or closed down due to lack of interest and the inevitable inertia of club kids' interest. Now, the few blocks surrounding the place were mostly just empty cement boxes that were being used as storage or as squatting space by the homeless.

The metal door to the warehouse clattered open noisily, its steel sections rattling like ghost chains as they disappeared into the upper part of the garage door frame. Inside, there was a large open room, probably forty by thirty feet with a few cement support columns sprinkled about. The place was empty. There was an obvious spot for the van along one wall, directly in front of the roll-up door. A small impromptu living area with a couple of couches and a kitchen had been set up in the back by the sink.

Doroteia angled the van inside, carefully steering around one of the cement columns to park the car in its grease spot-designated location. The passenger side door popped open immediately. Tito got out and ran back to close the roll-up. When he was done, he returned to the car, and pulled the latch on the sliding side door. He reached inside the instant it was open and came back out carrying the still-unconscious boy cradled like a baby in his arms. They'd used a mild sedative on the kid, something a doctor friend of Tito's had helped them with. And now, he was out like a light.

"Check to make sure he's still doing okay and breathing easily," Doroteia ordered as she got out of the driver's side and came around the front of the van. "I read that too much of that stuff can suppress his ability to take in oxygen."

Tito nodded as he gave the child the once-over. "It should be okay. I only gave him what the doctora told me to give him, enough to make him lose consciousness." He looked up at her. "See, he's breathing fine."

He carried the kid over to one of the couches and gently set him down onto it. The boy roused slightly, but quickly slipped back into sleep with a grunt and the smacking of his lips. Tito carefully removed the blanket from around the boy's small, almost fragile, frame, but then covered him up to make sure he kept warm.

Doroteia came over and stood next to Tito. They both looked the boy over for a few minutes. By now, Gaspar had followed them out of the van, finally pulling his mask from his face, and joining them by the couch.

"El parece estar bien," Gaspar said, keeping his voice low. He walked over to the kitchen area and pulled a beer out of the mini fridge they'd picked up on the same trip they'd grabbed the blanket. Once he had one of the cold bottles in his hand, he popped its cap, and drank most of its contents in one long gulp. When he was done, he swallowed, wiped the moisture from his mouth, and burped under his breath. "I think we're good."

Tito silently shushed him and indicated that they should all go over by the van where they could talk away from the kid. Gaspar took another drink of his beer, nodded, and walked back across the room to the van without saying anything more. Doroteia turned to follow him but stopped to tuck a loose flap of the blanket around the boy's feet before she did.

She took a second to get a better look at the metal struts of the kid's braces. Man, they looked like they'd be painful to wear. A chrome frame encased each of his legs like scaffolding and the metal glimmered in the low light. Velcro bands held the contraption in place. It looks so... medieval.

Shaking her head, she hurried to join Tito and Gaspar by the van. The three of them were soon huddled around the vehicle's still-open side door, speaking to one another in hushed tones.

"Okay, so," Gaspar said as he set his now empty beer bottle on the ground at his feet. "I think that went okay, don't you? I mean, I think it's safe to say that it went way better than we'd expected, right?"

Tito shook his head. "I don't know, man. Didn't that seem easy to you? Like it was too easy," he replied. He looked over at Doroteia, and concern tainted his expression. "We were expecting someone to be there, man; to put up some kind of fight. Not much, but some. But..." he paused, and his gaze drifted from Doroteia back to Gaspar, "we ran into zero resistance, man. Zip."

Gaspar shook his head. "What are you complainin' about?" He shrugged Tito's concerns away. "We hit it at the exact perfect time, that's all. The bodyguard was having his smoke and didn't even see us. So, as unbelievable as it may sound to you, maybe he was the only one watching the brat."

Tito shook his head in quiet dismay. The kid's father was one of the richest and most influential bankers in this part of the world. He had to be smarter than that, right? At the rate people got kidnapped in this fuckin' country... you'd think he'd have had more than one guy watching his one and only son and heir.

Right? I mean, the kid's disabled, fer chrissakes.

Tito paused and looked over at the frail child lying asleep on the couch. His attention was drawn as if by magnetism to the chromed metal of his leg braces. God, he thought, wearing something like that must just suck. And that didn't even factor in how cruel other children could be.

Tito continued to silently consider the puzzle for another minute, before finally giving up and deciding that none of it lined up right. It just didn't make sense that the kid had been so lightly protected. It just didn't. And he'd refuse to believe it was 'all cool' no matter what Gaspar said. This fuckin' country was known for how many and how often people got themselves snatched. The boy's parents had to know that someone would eventually try and make a grab for the kid.

So, why not have more muscle watching over him?

Doroteia looked up at Tito intently. He was worried, she could tell. Good, she thought to herself. She was worried. It seemed smart to be worried. They both had a lot riding on this job. She drew in a cold breath and sighed. This was supposed to have been a fast and easy score. A 'snatch-n-grab' is what Tito had called it: grab the kid, get the money, and return him unharmed... all within a day or two. And, of course, the all-important 'get away without any complications.' But now, with the odd way the job was falling together, Tito had developed a lot of seemingly well-founded trepidations.

Doroteia looked away from the men for a second to clear her head. This was getting out of hand, she mused. Just then, she noticed that the kid had woken up and was now sitting up on the couch. He still had the blanket wrapped around his shoulders, and it made him look like some kind of Munchkin holy man. He was sitting with his girdled legs in front of him, staring at the trio by the van. And he had this weird little smile on his face, like he'd been listening to them the whole time, and was amused by what he'd heard.

"Psst..." Doroteia hissed to the other two from out of the side of her mouth. "We have company."

"Shit!" Gaspar whispered under his breath so that only the three of them heard. "Shouldn't we blindfold him? Or... or fuckin' tie him up?"

"Don't be stupid," Tito chided him. "He's only a little kid, man."

"Yeah, but still..." Gaspar mumbled under his breath.

The boy was sitting in the middle of the couch. At first, he didn't say anything. He just continued to stare at the three of them from across the room like they were specimens in some kind of laboratory experiment. Remarkably, he showed no outward signs of being afraid. In fact, his blank, open-mouthed expression gave him the appearance of having a deep, Zen-like calm.

Doroteia went over to where the kid was sitting, approaching him slowly so as to not spook him. The boy looked up at her and smiled, but otherwise didn't move. She gingerly sat down on the arm of the couch, making sure to not make any sudden motions, and to always keep smiling.

Again, she didn't want to scare him. She knew instinctively that the next few days were going to go a lot easier if everyone remained calm and unafraid. Especially the kid. Calm led to compliance. At least, that's what Tito always said. Besides, if they played their cards right, he'd only be here for a little while. And so, again, the calmer everyone was, the better.

"Hey, Champ, how are ya doin'? My name's Sylvia," Doroteia explained, pouring on the maternal charm.

The kid grinned up at her dopily. His two brown eyes flashed like jewels beneath all of the other eyes that were knitted into his hat. His gaze took a languid tour around the room, sleepily taking it all in. He then opened his mouth and drew a breath.

"Are we..." he said, his voice scratchy from slumber. "Are we playing a game?"

Doroteia shot a quick glance over at Tito who nodded for her to go along with it. She looked casually back at the kid. "Kind of," she said brightly. "It's like a hide-n-seek game."

The boy nodded, a knowing smile slowly spreading across his face. "I know those games. Nanny and I like to play them. She taught me how to hide really well." He paused for a moment and a dark shadow passed over his gaze. "She was always worried that someone might one day come and try and take me." His gaze floated over to Tito and Gaspar suspiciously. He leaned closer to Doroteia. "That's what I thought when I saw them in the garden," he whispered conspiratorially.

Doroteia shook her head as if what he'd said was the most ridiculous thing she'd ever heard. "No..." she chuckled. "These guys are my friends. We're just hiding here until they call 'olly olly oxen free.' Then we can take you home, take you back to your parents."

The boy thought about what she'd said for a second, and then, he finally grinned. "Like you said, Sylvia: Hide-n-Seek. I like playing that game," he said as he looked at Doroteia, extending his hand in a put-on, grown-up fashion. "My name is Otavio."

Doroteia smiled for real. She couldn't help herself. The kid was just so cute.

"Hello, Otavio," she said, bowing slightly and shaking his hand. "It may be though, that we might have to be here for a little while. Until the game finally comes to an end."

The boy nodded. "Until they call 'olly olly oxen free,' right?"

"Right. Hey," she said suddenly, clapping her hands together. "You want something to eat? I don't know about you, but I'm getting kind of hungry."

The kid nodded shyly, watching her as she got up off the arm of the couch. He continued sitting silently, his eyes following her intently, like a scolded puppy. Every once in a while though, he'd suspiciously look over at the two men still standing by the van. And through it all, the kid said nothing. What he did do, was watch Doroteia like a hawk as she walked to the kitchen area to microwave them something to eat.

Several hours later…

Gaspar and Tito were stretched out on the floor. There was a pot of coins laid out randomly on the cement between them, and they each held a fan of playing cards in their hands. Doroteia was over on the couch with the kid. She'd been talking to him—well, listening, really—about some game he was playing at home on his computer.

At least that's what they all thought he was talking about.

The kid had become quite the chatterbox since she'd fed him and had been able to get him to relax. She'd been listening to him for a while now, pretending to give a shit, and nodding her head in all the right places. The two of them seemed to be getting along swimmingly. Which was good.

Finally, Tito checked his watch and saw that it was about time to make the call to the kid's parents. They'd wanted to give them enough time to notice that the kid was gone, and to start panicking. Now, all they had to do was to set the hook, and coordinate the exchange of the money, and the boy. Doroteia caught Tito's signal and nodded.

She then turned and smiled at the kid.

"Hey buddy, I have to go outside for a few minutes. I'm gonna go give your parents a call, okay?"

"To see if they've called all the ox in free yet?" the boy responded like a quiz show contestant who was sure his answer was the correct one.

"That's right! And we wanna get you back home as fast as we can, right?" She motioned toward Gaspar who was still sitting on the floor shuffling cards. "He will stay here with you until we get back. Sound cool?"

"And then I can go home?"

Doroteia smiled at him warmly. "Just as quickly as we can."

"K..."

Tito was pacing back and forth on the pavement in front of the warehouse roll-up door. Doroteia nervously stood nearby, nibbling her fingernails, and spitting them out onto the pavement. Tito had his cellphone pressed tightly to his ear, his manner now sorely agitated. He sneered angrily as he listened to the voice on the other end of the line.

"Look, man," Tito growled into the phone, the knuckles of his hand as he gripped the phone now gone white. "Make no mistake, Puto! I will personally put a bullet through your son's eye if you don't do exactly what the fuck I tell you."

There was a long pause on the line and Tito could have sworn that he heard someone sigh on the other end. He looked over at Doroteia and, for the first time, his face showed a real concern.

"I don't think you quite understand," said the boy's father, his voice sounding tinny and far away, his manner unnervingly calm. "My son... is an incredibly special child and has had a lot of health issues. Please... for your own safety and wellbeing, return him immediately. If you do, there will be no questions asked... and no repercussions. You have my word on that. But make no mistake... my son will return to his home and there's absolutely nothing you can do to stop that." The voice paused. "Believe it or not, son... I'm trying to help you. I'm trying to save your life. Comprende?"

Tito stood on the pavement incredulous. An angry red tide rose within him. Time to turn up the heat, he thought. "Well, maybe I'll just dump his corpse in the fuckin' river inst..."

"You heard me, please..." the father interrupted. "Return my son immediately. Otherwise, the consequences will be yours to bear."

And then, unbelievably, the guy hung up.

Tito and Doroteia stared at one another with dumbfounded expressions on their faces. Tito glared at the screen of the cell phone in his hand like he was expecting it to explode.

"What happened?" Doroteia asked, her eyes now gone wide with alarm.

"He fuckin' hung up," Tito said softly, and the tone of his voice was unbelieving.

"He what?"

Tito looked at her, his brown eyes taking on a steely tone. "He said that we should just return him," and he sounded like he was more trying to explain it to himself than to her. "Said it like he would have been doing us a favor by letting us bring him back."

Doroteia's brow furrowed tightly, betraying her confusion. "You told him what we would do to the kid, right?"

Tito nodded solemnly, sliding his phone back into his pocket. "You heard me tell him. You heard what I said." He shook his head. "That's why none of it makes any goddamn sense."

Doroteia didn't know what to do to calm him down, so she just stood there, looking at him wide-eyed, with her arms crossed tightly over her chest. Neither of them said anything for a few minutes as they each processed this new—and pretty substantial—wrinkle in their plan. She noticed that Tito's lips were moving slightly, talking to himself, as he sorted through their options and thought things through. It was like when someone moved their lips when they read something. In Tito's case though, he did it whenever he thought.

He finally looked up at her, his expression stern. "Okay, so..." he began. "Daddy doesn't think we're serious. I'll show him fuckin' serious..."

"Tito?"

"Maybe it's time we show him exactly how serious we can be, eh?" he replied, and his gaze grew hard. He looked at her out of the corner of his eye.

Doroteia narrowed her eyes suspiciously. Was he suggesting what she thought he was? She stared at him unbelievingly for another couple of seconds and did a little thinking of her own. They'd been together for a few years now. And during that time, they'd had a lot of laughs together, and the sex was great.

But she wanted no part in hurting this little kid.

"Let's not be rash, okay baby?" Doroteia finally said coolly. She knew how hot-headed Tito could get, especially when someone pissed him off by not doing what he wanted. She reached up and traced the back of her index finger across his warm cheek. "Let's just go back inside and we'll take us a little while to think this through. Baby, relax, okay? We're still in control. We still got the kid. We got all the time in the world. Everything's gonna be okay."

Tito closed his eyes and nodded. She was right. This was just some kind of misguided power play on the part of the father. An attempt to gain the upper hand. But there was no way he wasn't going to pay them what they wanted. It was his kid, after all. Maybe it was best for them to fall back and take a minute to consider their options.

No need for anybody to start jumping to any conclusions... or to be making any half-baked pronouncements. They'd give the kid's father a little more time to think it over and to fully come to terms with the gravity of the situation. And to consider all of what was at stake. Then, if the old man balked, they could send him something to show him just how serious the situation was. Something wet.

And if that failed, well...

Without saying anything more, Doroteia took her lover's hand and held it to her lips. She lightly kissed the flat of his palm and smiled at him through his fingers. She gently led him back inside. "We'll figure it out, baby. We'll figure it out."

The moment Tito and Doroteia bent under the roll-up door, they both sensed that something was wrong. A palpable tension hung in the air like the body of a corpse, and there was the rich taste of copper in every breath. Tito searched the room quickly for Gaspar, but he couldn't find him anywhere. What could have happened? They were only outside for a few minutes.

Doroteia noticed the kid sitting on the couch, wrapped in his blanket again like a guru. His empty soup bowl and spoon were sitting abandoned on the cushion next to him.

"Gaspar?" Tito called out as he went over to look around the van. "You asleep in there, man?"

Doroteia walked over to the couch to check on the boy. As she got closer, she saw that he was sitting with his head completely covered by the blanket. It was like he was hiding or something, making these soft, whimpering sounds and rocking back and forth ever so slightly on the cushion. She got down onto her haunches so that she could look him in the eye, but couldn't see much, since he kept the blanket pressed so tightly against his face.

"Heeey, Otavio," she asked softly. "You okay, buddy?" She reached out to gently stroke the top of his covered head. He retracted from her touch as if her hand were hot. "Did you see where our friend went?"

The boy made another soft, pitiful sound, like a cat stuck up in a tree, and shook his head beneath the blanket. He shivered, groaned, and drew the material even tighter around his shoulders. Then...

"Jesus fucking Christ!" Tito shouted from where he was on the other side of the van.

Doroteia got up, leaving the kid sitting where he was on the sofa, and strode over to him. When she rounded the front corner of the vehicle, she found Tito down on his knees, vomiting onto the concrete floor. She recognized the McMuffins they'd had for breakfast swimming amidst the coke, coffee, and bile.

Rushing over to him, she put her hand onto his back. "Tito, baby. What is it?"

In lieu of responding, Tito shook his head. His complexion had gone nearly white, and he looked like he'd seen a ghost. The only thing he could manage was to point at the far wall, balefully shaking his finger at whatever it was he thought he saw there. She looked where he was pointing, but saw nothing, only the bare cement wall.

Then, she looked up.

There, pressed into the cement up near the ceiling, was what looked like a wad of gum. At first, Doroteia thought it was a wasp's hive or a hornet's nest that she'd failed to see previously. But then, she noticed how wet everything was, how its slick surface glistened in the dim light. She was about to ask Tito what the hell it was, when she noticed the familiar green, button-up shirt enmeshed in the gore.

Doroteia recoiled as if she'd been slapped. But before she could do or say anything, Tito was pushing passed her and moving toward where the kid was. He came at the kid forcefully, a fire burning in his eyes, and unceremoniously ripped the blanket from his shoulders. He threw the cloth onto the floor as he towered over the kid.

"What the fuck happened?" he raged.

Surprisingly, the boy didn't seem overly concerned with the threat. He never even blinked. He just stared back at his attacker blank-faced and unafraid. Doroteia ran across the room, catching up to Tito and putting herself between him and the boy. She gently pushed him back with the palm of her hand.

"Let me handle this, okay, Tito?" she begged. "You're scaring the shit out of him."

"Scaring the shit out of him?" Tito threw up his hands and turned, stepping away. He pointed angrily back toward the van. "Did you not fucking see?"

Doroteia slowly approached the couch. She sat down onto the seat next to the kid and tried to act casual; like everything was fine. She put her hand onto the boy's skeletal shoulder and stroked him like a cat. "Did... something happen here, Otavio?" She looked over toward the van. "Did something happen to our friend?"

The boy shook his head and hugged himself. "You'll be mad," he said pitifully.

"No. No, I won't," she calmly assured him, even as she looked over her shoulder at Tito. "I promise. I just want to know..."

The kid didn't say much of anything; he just stared into the palms of his hands.

"Hey, she's fuckin' talking to you, you crippled brat!" shouted Tito as he came roaring back over to the couch. Shaking with rage, he reached out and snatched the knitted octopus cap off of the boy's head and threw it across the room. "What the fuck happened to Gaspar, you little shit!"

Silence fell like a hammer over the room, but none of the trio stirred. Somewhere in the wall, steam pipes groaned in a stuttering bass staccato. Then, the boy got up from his seat, climbing to his feet with great difficulty. He took a few teetering steps away from the couch, his braces softly squeaking in the silence. The kid glared at Tito, raising his right hand in a languid fashion, and pointing his open palm at him.

Tito chuckled at the kid's impotency.

"I want to go home," the kid said quietly, and his tone was labored, like he was holding something immense back from suddenly breaking loose.

Closing one eye, the boy squinted with the other, looking down his arm like he was sighting down the barrel of a rifle. The moment expanded and everyone gathered in the room felt compelled to hold their breath. Finally, the boy made a clenching motion with his fingers like he was grabbing something, grabbing onto Tito.

Tito's body went stiff, his back arching like he'd been touched by a powerline. His arms were pressed tightly against his sides. His fingers twitched in pain as they searched for something to grab onto, something he could tear away to make the pain stop. The leather of his jacket squealed as it was being compressed in a vice.

Tito's face went flush, and he tried to scream, but the pressure being exerted around his chest was too great. He finally managed to groan something unintelligible as his head lolled lifelessly to one side. Blood trickled out of one of his ears and ran in a thick crimson rivulet down his neck.

The kid glared at the nearly dead man teetering before him with open curiosity, like a chimp with a Rubik's Cube. He looked into Tito's reddening eyes and sadly said, "I thought you wanted to be my friends. I thought you wanted to play... to play the hiding game."

Tito managed to burble something, as if the pressure around his chest was slowly increasing and causing him new and unbearable pain. The boy stared at him, and his mouth abruptly broke into a wide grin. He sighed, then without ceremony, he closed his fingers into a fist.

Tito made a sudden croaking sound, and his chest just sort of collapsed in on itself, like an aluminum can being crushed for recycling. Hot blood, so red as to be almost black, spurted from his open mouth and nose in thick syrupy glops. Drops of crimson splattered wetly across the floor, like spilled pigment from a painter's palette. His ribs made a sharp cr-crunching sound, and then the cage of his chest twisted, his back snapping like a branch.

The kid unclenched his fist regrettably, releasing him, and lowering his arm. Tito's ruined body hung suspended in the air for another heartbeat. And then, it dropped to the floor like a wet rag.

Doroteia felt her legs go weak, and she couldn't help but drop to her knees and scream. Not only was what happened to Gaspar the most stomach-turning thing she'd ever seen, but this… this was Tito. Her Tito. Tito, whose strong arms had only so recently held her and told her everything was going to be okay. Tito, against whose chest she'd so often found her one true comfort in this world… now squished like a bug right in front of her eyes.

But how?

"And you…" she heard the boy suddenly say from someplace far off. "You acted nice as well, but… I can see that you're just as bad as they are."

All Doroteia could do was shake her head in a desperate disbelief. She had no idea how any of this was happening, but something inside of her told her that it was indeed occurring, and it was all very, very real. Tito and Gaspar were dead. And now, somehow, she felt in a great and terrible danger.

The boy glared at her, and he slowly raised his hand, pointing at her with the same finger he'd pointed at Tito, pointing as if in accusation. "I don't think I like this game anymore. I don't think I like you," he said solemnly. "And I think… I want to go home. Now, please."

Doroteia drew a quick breath—like when she jumped into the icy water of the pond at her parent's house in the country this past winter— and she felt something wrap itself around her chest like a vice. She tried to speak, to say something, tried to plead her case, to tell him that he was never in any real danger. That they were always going to bring him back home safely. But then she felt the grip that was enveloping her slowly start to squeeze, and Doroteia's world went cold and red forever.

THE MUMBLE

This is another one of those tales that came to me out of the blue. It's just a sad, sad story that regrettably happens all too often in the world. Word of warning on this one though, kids: the tale has to do with child abuse, so… trigger warning.

The boys' bedroom was small in size, only slightly bigger than a walk-in closet. Sparsely decorated, it had only the one dresser and a shared bed as furniture. The initial idea had been for the boys to bunk up, their parents thinking it'd save them some space as well as help the kids to bond as brothers. Now, though… now that Mom was gone, the room had become not only the place where the boys slept, but it had also become their prison.

Gordon was the elder of the two at nine years old. Little Jody was three years younger. The two of them were in the bed, cozily buried beneath the thin blanket they shared. Both boys had their knees drawn up as far as they could so that their toes wouldn't poke out from under the covers and be bitten by the frost. They lay like two spoons facing one another, heads submerged beneath the blanket. Their foreheads were nearly touching, and they lay looking intently into one another's eyes, like survivors of war who were waiting for the next bomb to drop.

"It's good that we got all of the chores done, right, Gordy?" Jody asked his brother in a soft whisper, his blue eyes flashing like sapphires in the darkness beneath the covers.

Jody was one of the few people who still called Gordon by his nickname; the one Mom had given him when he was just a baby. Gordon was about to correct him but didn't. He knew it was kind of a thing with the younger boy, something that reminded him he'd said of their mother. He'd promised that he'd only use the name in private though, so Gordon let it go.

It still bugged him, but… he let it go.

"I just don't want…" Jody looked around the small room nervously, as if searching the shadows for something malevolent lurking in the room. After a moment of breath-holding silence, he finally finished his sentence. "Well, you know…" he dropped his voice down to the quietest of whispers. "The Mumble."

The Mumble was a monster Jody had made up. He'd told Gordon about it right around the time that their mom had left. He'd said that The Mumble came when you least expected it. That it was there to punish you whenever you did something bad. He'd even gone as far as to say that he'd actually seen the creature once. Gordon hadn't been sure what he'd meant by that, dismissing the whole thing as just another product of the younger boy's fertile imagination.

But then, one day, Gordon saw it as well.

They'd been playing in the garden when he'd gotten his first glimpse of the beast. It was hot out that day and Dad had been cutting the grass in the backyard. He'd gone into the shed to put the lawnmower away. Jordy and Gordon were playing with their Matchbox cars in the flower bed where Mom once kept her roses, when the creature finally decided to show itself. There had been a loud bang from inside the shed right before it appeared out of the shadows. The thing was a hulking mass of anger and violence with huge red eyes and these gigantic, reaching arms. And its hands… more like claws really, claws that grabbed and clawed and clutched. Gordon remembered the thing as it came roaring into the backyard from near the shed where Dad had gone.

Gordon dimly recalled grabbing Jody and trying to protect him, but that only meant that he'd wound up taking the brunt of the beating the snarling beast doled out instead. His back and legs had been badly bruised, and he'd cried for days about it afterward.

Soon though, the monster had gone, and Dad came back out of the shed, acting like nothing had happened. Later, after silently dressing Gordon's wounds, he'd taken them all out for pizza. He'd even let them play a few videogames and had splurged on an Extra Large just for the three of them. And through it all, Dad had a look on his face like he'd done something he was sorry for.

"Well," Gordon softly replied under the blanket. He smiled warmly at his brother. "At least we got 'em all done, so there's no need to worry."

Jody nodded back at him and smiled happily. "Good." A pause. "I love you, Gordy."

Gordon grinned. "And I love you, too, Short Stuff."

Once again, the house settled into quiet, silence lying heavily upon the wood and mortar of the cold, empty rooms. Gordy closed his eyes and thought about how their mother used to sing them to sleep at night.

She's tuck them in after giving them each their baths, then she'd read them a story until they got tired. Then, she'd softly sing to them as they drifted off to slumber. It was one of Gordon's favorite memories, and one he thought about a lot—especially at night.

The boys suddenly heard the door to the front of the house burst open. The door bounced off of the wall, hitting it hard, and making the bones of the entire house shake. Everything was still for a heartbeat, even the furniture and fixtures seemed to be holding their breath, and then, the door was slammed violently shut.

There was the sound of heavy boots clomping around the living room, then you could hear them moving in the kitchen. Cupboards were thrown open and then forcibly slammed shut. The refrigerator immediately followed suit.

Then, it was once again quiet in the house.

Somehow, it all seemed worse now that it was quiet.

The boys waited expectantly, huddling even closer in the bed. The world paused for them as they tried to determine who it was that was out there, loose in the house. Both of them hoped it was Dad.

"You know," Jody suddenly whispered out of nowhere, sounding almost conspiratorial. "I bet it was The Mumble that got Mom."

Gordon closed his eyes and shook his head sadly. "No, Jody. Don't be dumb. Mom just had to go away. Dad told us, right? Remember? He said she'd be coming back to us soon. Ya know, Dad wouldn't lie about something like that."

Gordon sighed. He hadn't meant to respond so harshly to what Jody had said about their mother, but… here they were. The kid just got crazy ideas like this in his head sometimes. The younger boy's eyes slowly started welling up, and Gordon put his arm around him to comfort him.

Suddenly, from right outside their door, they heard the boots clomping slowly down the hallway. The footfalls fell in a seemingly random pattern. First, a couple of steps, then silence. Then, a few more in a pattern that never seemed to repeat itself. And through it all, a muffled voice could be heard through the door as whatever it was that was there softly whispered to itself.

"Dammkitz," the thing muttered, its mouth sounding like it was full of marbles… or eyeballs. "Dammbish."

Now, even though he had been trying hard not to, Jody was crying in earnest. Tears were visible running down his cheeks even in the low light beneath the blanket. Viscous snot flowed freely, wetting his upper lip. His eyes were open so wide that Gordon could see white all around his irises.

Jody's mouth fell open as he silently stared at his brother; terrified. Slowly, his lips moved, mouthing the words: The Mumble. Gordon couldn't think of anything to say, so he just pulled him closer and tried to focus his attention on the sounds and where they were coming from outside the door... and, most importantly what they were doing.

The house had gone silent again. Nothing stirred in any of the rooms and not a sound could be heard anywhere, except for the heavy breathing and whispering coming from the hallway. Suddenly, something bumped against the door. Then, it happened again, harder this time. The creature outside drew a long, ragged breath and let it out in a hiss. The boys could smell its breath's fetid odor through the shut door.

"Gordy? I'm scared," Jody whined plaintively in a voice that, for some reason, had gone even higher than what it was normally. "God, Gordy... it's The Mumble, isn't it?" His eyes furtively darted toward the door, tears spilling from them like rainwater. "It is The Mumble! And it's right outside."

Gordon did his best to try and calm his little brother, but the truth was that he himself was every bit as petrified. By now, he'd come to understand all of things of which The Mumble was capable; knew how much—and how badly—it could hurt them both. Gordon felt the first of his tears come unbidden when he heard the monster outside the door once again grumble, and the boy wasn't sure if the door would be enough to hold him back this time.

"Dammkitz," it was mumbling to itself again. "Fuggenbish."

And that's how things were for what seemed like the longest time, seemingly the whole of the night: the two boys huddled in their bed, and the horrible monster lurking just outside their door. And, all the while, the creature could be heard moving up and down in the hall, huffing and puffing, and quietly talking to himself. Every once in a while, they'd hear it crashing into something, hammering its frightening fists against the walls and doorframes, and growling menacingly as it patrolled the length of the corridor.

But then, all of a sudden, The Mumble was back at the bedroom door. Its mighty fists pounded against the plane of wood angrily, and its fury shook the wood to its frame. Gordon drew Jody closer to his chest, covering his little brother's head with his arms, and not allowing him to look. Despite telling himself not to, Gordon closed his eyes. It was then that the door burst open, and The Mumble came roaring into the room.

"Dammbish," the creature roared, its temper now in a full rage, its words slurring together drunkenly. The beast raised its hand into the air, a length of leather belt help poised like it was an executioner's ax within its fist. He held it there for a moment, ready to strike. "Lef' me here… wi' dese dammkitz."

Gordon pulled his brother even tighter, lowering his head, and prepared himself for what he knew would come next.

REAL ESTATE

This is a story that's based on something that actually happened to me when I was working in the funeral industry in San Diego, CA. See, back when I first got out of mortuary college, I worked as a Family Service Counselor for a major chain of funeral homes / mortuaries / memorial parks. Which meant that I was expected to "work services" (to act as an usher / funeral director) as needed and to sell funeral / burial packages to folks both "at-need" (aka at the time of death) and "pre-need" (sometime before the death actually occurred).

A big part of selling burial property was that—legally—you had to show any potential buyer the parcel of land you were selling to them before they could actually purchase it. It has to do with Federal Trade Commission / Better Business Bureau edicts, and it all gets very 'official' and 'legally.' But it is within that idea that this story's genesis lies.

One thing about this tale: I remember this gentleman's face to this day, although... his name has faded from my memory over the years.

It's funny how that can happen sometimes ...

"Hey, Bob, you're eleven-thirty's here," Melanie Simmons said brightly, poking her head into the door of Bob Douglas' closet of an office. Melanie was one of the firm's apprentices, a pretty little thing who'd come from Oklahoma and was enrolled in her second semester at mortuary college. She was a nice kid, worked hard, and was never someone who let the grimness of the job affect her. Supposedly, she had family in The Business. "I think it's that Pre-Need that called earlier this morning. The, uh... Jorgensens. Fred and Connie, remember? They mentioned looking for property, services; the whole nine for the both of them."

Bob glanced up from the pile of paperwork he was looking over and smiled at her in greeting. He did indeed remember the Jorgensens.

They'd been referred by The Fischers who attended the same Rotary that Bob did. From all accounts, they were cut from the same cloth that most of the people in this town were, good simple folks just trying to get by.

Bob shot a quick look over at the whiteboard mounted on the wall. The large, erasable surface was how the firm kept track of how busy they were. It tracked client names, dates of death, contact name and number, and the date and time of services. Bob noted that things were slower than usual given the time of year, and he secretly hoped he'd be able to help these people. The funeral home could use the revenue.

He got up from his chair with a small groan and stretched his back.

"Thanks, Melanie. I'll come out to meet them in just a second."

The girl nodded and disappeared from view.

Bob picked his suit coat up off the back of his chair and pulled it on. Looking over at the small mirror he kept on the wall for just such occasions, he straightened his tie and made sure he looked presentable. He stared at his reflection and noticed a few more gray hairs in his beard. Ah well, he thought, even the Mona Lisa is fallin' apart. When he felt like everything was in its proper place, he took a moment to mentally prepare himself for this next appointment.

Pre-Needs could be challenging things. They weren't like when there was a death in the family. That was sudden; unexpected and tragic, albeit unavoidable (at some point). Pre-Needs were more of a tactical financial move: they essentially froze all of the mortuary's services at the time of sale. So, no matter how much prices went up in the future, the client was covered. Often, they were also the first time the person across the desk from him ever really had to think about their own mortality, and of the inevitability of themselves one day getting sick and dying. For many, it was like watching them confront their own deaths in real time.

He plucked a file folder out from the metal rack on the right side of his desk, making sure that it had the name 'Jorgensen' written on it. The wife—Connie, Bob reminded himself—had called to make the appointment at first light, and he'd already prepped the file with the forms he knew he'd need. He also had his preliminary notes, the ones he'd taken over the phone, so he wouldn't have to ask the same questions twice.

Bob Douglas had worked in what was often euphemistically called "the aftercare industry" for nearly twenty years now, so he was content to let muscle memory gather the rest of the paperwork he'd need to make whatever arrangements these folks had in mind. Bob never judged. As

long as what they wanted wasn't illegal or immoral, it was all okay
with him. How someone wished to be interred—or be remembered by
their loved ones—was none of his concern. Bob always felt that that was
something best left between the dead, their family, and their respective
makers.

But he was a stickler for the paperwork. See, Bob believed that
when it came to funerals and the remembrance of the dead, you had
'one shot, one kill.' One chance to get it absolutely right. One chance
for everything to be perfect. Get it wrong... and there were people
who would be scarred for life. People will usually forget when a bride
stumbles as she's coming down the aisle.

But, put Mom in the wrong casket...

Bob left his office and slowly made his way down the hallway toward
the lobby. He made a mental note to ask Melanie if she'd vacuum the
carpeting when she had a chance. It was important that things always
be kept tidy. He'd just finished straightening his tie when he entered
the vestibule of the mortuary.

The lobby wasn't particularly large, maybe twenty-by-thirty, but it
was warmly decorated; almost like the living room of someone's home.
There was an ornately carved desk made of dark oak wood immediately
in front of the door. It greeted people as they came in, and it was where
the firm took all incoming calls. Behind it, Melanie was sitting in an
office chair, printing up prayer cards for the service that was scheduled
for later this afternoon.

A small waiting area sat just to the right of the door. There were
two faux leather couches and a coffee table there, over near the big front
window. Copies of today's newspaper lay fanned like playing cards
across a low tabletop. An end table with a clear, blown glass lamp was
against the other wall and it completed the cozy scene. By design, the
space was made to feel warm and familiar, comforting and womb-like.

Over by the big window, Bob noticed an older couple standing close
together, looking out at the flowers and foliage in the garden outside.
They weren't elderly, per se... but they were definitely on the far side of
middle age. She wore a simple outfit of a pair of slacks and a blazingly
white tennis blouse. He was distinguished looking, dressed 'golf
casual.' They didn't look rich, but they definitely looked rich-adjacent.
Bob approached them respectfully, with a warm, welcoming smile.

"Mister and Missus Jorgensen?"

The woman turned around first, looking about as anguished as
Bob had expected. She slowly nodded her head as she let go of the
man's hand and took a step forward. The man continued to stare out

of the window, saying nothing. It wasn't until she touched his arm that he snapped out of it. Slowly, he turned toward her, and she gently redirected him toward Bob.

Bob couldn't help but notice how thin the man was, like rail thin, and impossibly tired-looking. His eyes were red and looked wet, like he'd been crying very recently. His face was worn and lined from worry, his skin a washed-out, ashen gray color. They looked positively drained, 'exhausted' being a point on the emotional map they'd both passed a long time ago.

Well, now that we know who everybody is…

"Hello there, folks," Bob began, projecting a respectful charm. "I'm Bob Douglas. I'm one of the owners here at Gibson, Nodden, and Douglas." He looked at the woman and smiled again warmly. "Mrs. Jorgensen, I believe that we spoke on the phone earlier, so I have a pretty good idea of how it is that we can help you. But if you wouldn't mind…, would you both please follow me to one of our Arrangement Offices where we can sit and talk more comfortably?"

He extended his hand, directing the couple back toward the hallway from where he'd just come. Connie Jorgensen nodded and looked relieved, gently taking her husband by the hand. Fred nodded at her and did his best to smile, his eyes never leaving hers. And without any further conversation, the two of them dutifully followed Bob down the hallway.

The trio passed Bob's office, and jogging to the right, they continued on to one of the small Arrangement Offices at the end of the hallway. The corridor was austerely decorated with a few paintings of sunsets and waves crashing on the beach done by local artists. They were all hung on the wall like afterthoughts. Their imagery set a somber, but necessary tone. When they arrived at the Arrangement Office door, Bob held it open for the couple, and invited them inside.

It took a minute for them all to get settled and pick their seats at the conference table. Melanie popped her head in and asked if anybody needed coffee, but the Jorgensens said they'd stopped for breakfast at the IHOP on the way over, so she excused herself and left the room, shutting the door carefully behind her.

As Bob was setting his folder onto the table, he once again noticed how frail Fred Jorgensen was, how he very nearly collapsed into the chair when he went to sit down. Connie hovered over him like a protective mother bear, doing everything she could to make him comfortable. Finally, she took the seat next to him. Bob sat across from the couple; his paperwork now laid out methodically in front of him.

"So, Mr. and Mrs. Jorgensen, I understand that the two of you have expressed interest in one of our Pre-Need packages?" Bob said, beginning what he'd come to think of as 'his spiel.'

Fred Jorgensen dropped his chin to his chest suddenly, his manner seeming despondent; deflated. His shirt sagged like a sail on his shoulders and Bob noticed that the skin on his face had gone even paler that it had been in the lobby. He surreptitiously glanced down at his notes to check Fred's birthdate: 57.

Christ, he looked ten years older than that, at least.

"I... I can't do this," Fred abruptly sighed as he went to try and get up.

Connie set her hand onto her husband's shoulder, gently pressing him back into his seat. He readily complied to her touch, the fight draining out of him pretty fast due to him being too weak to put up much of a protest. She leaned over and whispered something to him, and he resignedly calmed down.

"I'm sorry..." Fred said quietly once he'd gotten control over himself again. He looked up at Bob sheepishly. "This has all just been so hard."

Bob nodded solemnly, knowing the sentiment well. After all, hadn't he'd heard it time and time again, year after year, since signing on to this job? He searched his brain for just the right thing to say. In the end, he went with the tried and true.

"I can only imagine how difficult it's been." Bob turned his head to look at Connie. "On the both of you." He paused. "Look, I'll try to make this all as brief and as uncomplicated as I can, but... I have to be honest, it's going to take some time, maybe an hour or so. I hope that's okay."

Connie Jorgensen looked to her husband, checking in with him. He nodded to her ever so slightly, and she returned her gaze back to Bob. After a second, she smiled gratefully and nodded to him.

The two of them sat there, holding hands, and putting on their brave faces as Bob went through the paperwork. Fred was as still as marble in his chair, never really responding to any of Bob's inquiries, and staring holes into the woodgrain of the tabletop. Connie just stared at Bob like she was bracing for some sort of impact. Bob picked up his pen and slid the first piece of the paperwork that needed to be signed toward them.

Sure enough, the Arrangement intake ended up taking a little over an hour as expected. Fred Jorgensen continued to say little throughout, and as their story unfolded, Bob could see why.

Fred and Connie had been married to one another for over thirty-five years. They'd raised two kids together and were just getting ready to retire and enjoy a bit of the good life. Connie said they'd had plans to take their RV and travel around the country 'like hippies. Y'know, seeing the sights, and 'doin' old people stuff.'

One day though, out of nowhere, Fred mentioned how he'd started feeling tired as of late. He said he felt like he just kept running out of gas after any kind of exertion, even just walking up and down the stairs. Connie said she'd kept an eye on him, but, after a little while, she noticed his loss of appetite, his shortness of breath, and some pretty significant weight loss.

Then, one day as he was getting out of the shower, Connie noticed some weird lumps under his arm and on his neck, and she'd made an appointment for him to see Doctor Blanchard.

Long story short… after a lot of tests and far too many office visits, the doctor finally gave them his diagnoses: lymphoma. Worse than that, the disease had already progressed to such a state that they figured Fred really only had a short time left to live. He'd been told in no uncertain terms to get his affairs in order, and this visit to the funeral home was the first painful step in all of that.

Over the years, Bob had seen similar situations play out like this too many times to mention. Good people living their lives, doing what they thought was right, when Life came along—as it does to all of us— and slapped them right into the dirt. In a heartbeat, their realities were tossed into the air like the contents of an overturned card table. Fred looked perpetually shell-shocked. And Connie… well, she looked as if her entire world was collapsing around her ears.

And, in many ways, it was.

"Well, that looks like that's finally about it," Bob said, shuffling all of the now-completed paperwork into a loose pile in front of him. He slid the bundle into the file folder marked with Fred's name in black Sharpie. "The only thing left to do is to take you out into the park to inspect the property."

Fred looked over at his wife anxiously. His expression was one of panic. He shook his head at her, and the motion was nearly imperceptible. Connie stroked his forearm and looked back across the table at Bob, distraught.

"Is that really necessary?" she asked, holding Fred's hand in both of hers for reassurance. "This has been very hard on my husband."

Bob nodded and he looked genuinely regretful about having to insist. There were laws in place that were rigidly enforced in this business of Death. State laws, Federal, OSHA, all the way down to governmental entities like the Better Business Bureau and the Federal Trade Commission who oversaw how business was conducted here, how liquids were cleaned up, and, most importantly, where the money came from, and where it went.

The sad reality was... that, in the days just after someone dear to them dies, people were vulnerable. And there had been many folks over the years who'd taken advantage of that—not at this mortuary, but at others. As a result, laws were passed that governed exactly how business was conducted. It wasn't that Bob wanted to show these people the property they were buying and run the risk of upsetting them. But rather, he was legally obligated to do so.

"I'm afraid I must insist. I need to take you out to see the land in order to be compliant with some governmental rules and regulations. But I assure you, it'll only take a few minutes," Bob gently explained. He got to his feet, tucking the manila folder under his arm, as an invitation for the couple to join him. They both responded reflexively and stood as well. "I'll even drive," he said with his winningest smile.

Bob escorted the couple back down the hallway and out the front door through the lobby. As they walked by the front desk, he dropped the folder off to Melanie who was still at her post. She'd take it and get the ball rolling on getting everything filed for when the time eventually came when they needed it again.

He had the Jorgensens wait on the curb of the circular driveway in front of the building while he went and got the Town Car to escort them into the park. As he was driving back, he noticed that the couple was now deeply involved in some kind of conversation as they waited. And as he rolled the car to a stop, he saw Connie wipe something away from her husband's cheek with her index finger.

Bob put the car into Park and got out, leaving the engine softly idling. He opened the back door chauffeur-style, and indicated for the Jorgensens to get in. Fred hesitated, but then his wife sort of eased him into the car by taking his hand and drawing him along. Soon, they were in their seats, and Bob shut the door, getting back into the driver's side.

"This won't take but a minute," Bob reassured them as he put the car into Drive, and they started to move slowly forward. "Just need to run up and take a peek. We'll have ya back and on your way before you know it."

The drive through the cemetery was a silent affair. They usually were. Fred stared out his window at the passing landscape, and it was evident from his expression how far away his mind was. Connie sat looking out the window on her side and gently stroking the back of Fred's hand with her thumb. Every once in a while, she'd look over at him and smile lovingly.

"You doin' okay?" she asked him at one point.

Bob saw Fred in the rearview mirror turn toward her and smile back weakly, his eyes already welling up with fresh tears. He rested his head on her shoulder, and then he looked down to stare at their intertwined hands. Fred closed his eyes, seemingly overwhelmed by the maelstrom of emotions currently raging within him. And even though Bob had seen this same scenario play out so many times before, it still succeeded in breaking his heart. Somehow, he knew it always would.

The Town Car circled around an area of the park that was known as the Garden of Remembrance, and then it drove passed the Sanctuary of Roses. The park was empty this time of morning with only a few of the gardeners and a couple of small clusters of visitors visible. The sun was climbing in the sky, already starting to warm up the grass, and it was beginning to look like a beautiful day. Bob eased the car to a stop on the side of the road, next to the Garden of Devotion, and they all got out.

"The property is just this way, at the top of this hill," Bob said as he led the couple across the immaculately manicured grass. "It's a nice set of lots. They're both under a tree."

The lawn was a flat expanse of closely cropped grass interrupted by a matrix of evenly spaced rows of low, metal and concrete grave markers. Most of the headstones were flat, gray slabs of stone; made of marble, granite, slate, and sandstone. Littered amidst those, were the standardized copper gravestones that were issued to veterans by the military. Several clusters of young Alder trees and Japanese Andromeda bushes topped the hills like leafy toupees. Bob led the Jorgensens up the grassy knoll to the top of the hill. They followed along after him like ducklings after their mother.

As they walked, Bob covertly kept track of the small metal tabs on the ground that designated the gridlines where each grave was located in correlation to the main map back at the funeral home's office. The map was basically a print-out of the entire park where each plot was designated by a small rectangle. Each space had been assigned a letter and a number that not only told the staff who owned it, but whether the space was occupied. It was how they kept track of who was where and what spaces were empty. When they finally reached the spot where the property in question was located, Bob stepped to the side of it, and showed it off like he was Vanna White.

"Here we go," he said. "Garden of Inspiration, Lots B-17 and 18."

The couple stared under the tree at the blank area of grass in front of them. Neither knew how they were supposed to feel about it. Connie looked around the hilltop, gazing at the foliage and the panoramic view.

A large blackbird flew down from one of the trees and lit upon the ground. It poked its beak into the soft sod near one of the headstones as a gentle breeze came rushing up and over the crest of the hill.

"This is nice," Connie finally declared aloud. "I like these trees." She turned toward her husband, trying to read his face for a glimpse of where he was at emotionally. No one knew better than she how hard all of this was on him. "It's so peaceful. Don't you think so, dear?"

Fred stood behind her, a pillar of anguish, saying nothing but wringing his hands as if he were strangling something. He looked distressed and anxious as he rocked from one foot to the other, hugging himself, and looking around them nervously. His eyes finally landed on Bob, who had been keeping an eye on him, and he slowly shook his head.

"I… I can't do this. I thought I could, but I can't," Fred said quietly as he leaned against Connie once again for support. His voice sounded pulled, as taught as piano wires, and all the color had drained from his face. He looked back at Bob and his desperation was there for all to see. "It's all just… well, it's just a little surreal, y'know?"

Bob smiled sympathetically and did his best to understand, even though he wasn't exactly sure what the man meant. He surreptitiously glanced over to Connie to see if she thought her husband would be okay, as he continued smiling and nodding his head.

"Now, Dear…" Connie said soothingly, stepping up to support him.

"I mean," Fred continued, "it just feels weird to stand here and…"

"It's okay, Fred. It's okay," she cooed sympathetically.

"It's just…" he chuckled darkly. "It's just not every day that you get to see, much less stand over, your own grave, right?" Fred wiped away another tear from his eye with the back of his hand. "It still just doesn't seem real."

Connie hugged him closer and slid an arm around his waist. Fred leaned into her, and she hugged him back tightly. She looked up at him and her eyes were so full of love for her husband that Bob felt suddenly odd, like an intruder observing a moment of intimacy between two longtime friends, lovers, and spouses. All he could think of to do was to silently count the blades of grass at his feet.

"So, whatcha think, Freddy Spaghetti?" Connie asked him gently.

"About what, this?" Fred responded quietly so only she could hear. You could see that he was trying to get his emotions under control, but it was also pretty clear that it was being accomplished with no small amount of difficulty. "One's just as good as any other, I guess. It's not like either of us are ever really gonna know the goddamn difference."

"Oh, Fred," she chided him again, handling him now as if he were fragile and made of glass. She glanced over at Bob and her eyes were wet again with another fresh batch of tears. "I'm sure this will be fine, Mr. Douglas." She paused. "This has just been very difficult for us. We appreciate your understanding."

"Yes, thank you, Mr. Douglas," Fred replied perfunctorily, now standing a little bit straighter and showing a bit of what must have once been his normal demeanor. "We both do indeed appreciate all your help, but, as my wife has said... this was just a little too much for me today. It's all still rather mind-blowing if you can understand?"

"Of course," Bob replied.

"So, if there is anything else, could please send them to the house?"

Bob nodded. He could tell that Fred Jorgensen was a proud man and this new state of vulnerability wasn't easy for him to get used to. Bob smiled compassionately. "Yes. Yes, of course."

Weakened, Fred turned toward Connie. "Is it possible for us to go now? I'm feeling very, very tired."

Not waiting for an answer, Fred shook the funeral director's hand, and then started walking alone back to the car. A few yards away, he stopped, and looked back at his wife. His face was a billboard for the tumult of feelings he was experiencing: the sorrow, the frustration, the worry for his wife's future.

But mostly, there was fear.

Connie walked along after him, and Bob followed dutifully behind. Bob gave them their space and allowed the couple to go ahead, watching as they walked hand in hand across the field back to the car. The trio made their way down the hill at a leisurely pace. When they got to the car, Bob once again opened the door for the couple, and they got inside.

There wasn't a lot of talking on the ride back to the cemetery office and Bob knew to take the shortest route possible. The Jorgensens sat in the back, and, when the tears finally came, they came in great heaving sobs. Bob said nothing. He just kept driving.

Back at the office, Fred wrote out a check for his and Connie's services and burial lots on the hood of the Town Car, and nothing more was said about it. Bob silently walked them back out to their car and shook each of their hands in turn. He then wished them well, and watched reflectively, as they drove off. For some reason even Bob didn't understand, he waved goodbye to the both of them.

Postscript…

Bob was at home about a month or so later, when he got the call that Fred Jorgensen had passed. Mr. Jorgensen's decline had reportedly been fairly swift after their meeting, and he died like we all wish we could: surrounded by his family and cradled in the arms of his one true love.

His service was quite lovely and The Jorgensens had some of their church's singers come and lead the small group that had gathered in a hymn. The burial was held in the late afternoon and Bob made sure that he ordered doves and a piper at no charge. Mrs. Jorgensen thanked him profusely and even gave him a kiss on the cheek before she got into what Bob assumed was her daughter's car, and solemnly drove away from the graveside.

As is so often the case in couples that have been together for a long time, Connie passed about eighteen months later. Her health started failing her right after Fred's funeral, and her daughter said that it was like she'd just given up and lost her will to live. Eventually, she started talking about how she was looking forward to being back with Fred again soon. She said that she knew beyond a shadow of doubt that he was waiting for her on the road to Heaven. Bob made sure there was plenty of flowers at her service, some of which he purchased from the flower shop himself.

In the end, the couple was buried next to one another, in The Garden of Inspiration, Lots B-17 and 18. They were interred side by side—the way they had always been, the way they both always wanted to be.

PAW-FLY

My best friend these days, besides my wife of course, is my granddaughter, Ripley (aka The Rippah). We spend a lot of time together and we usually watch a bit of TV before going to the park to play on the slides. What we've been watching will be pretty apparent in just a second. Children's television can be an odd thing when you're me. You end up asking a lot of really problematic questions... and looking for a lot of answers that just aren't there. This story is the result of that type of thinking.

There was still a thin cloud of tobacco smoke from the night before hanging suspended in the bar as Mark Tomlinson came in through the front door. Tendrils of the fog swirled in the air like spiders' webs torn asunder, the smoky lace as much a part of the bar's esthetic as its stock of alcohol.

The joint itself was small and, not surprisingly, empty given the time of day. There had been a lopsided bamboo sign hung over the doorway when he came in that read The Blue Lagoon. At least he thought it had said The Blue Lagoon. He hadn't really bothered to look at it too closely when he came in. He knew it was something tropical... and painted marine-blue and green. Not that it mattered. His day had gone to shit early, and, in the mood he was in right now, one dingy watering hole was as good as another.

He honestly couldn't have cared less.

The aforementioned shit started right off the bat when he had a fight with the wife about their mounting bills. And, of course, that had led inexorably to his inability to find a job. He'd left without saying goodbye and had immediately stepped in a pile of dog shit that the neighbor's Collie left on the lawn. He made it to his bus, but only barely. Then, as they were halfway there, the bus broke down on the highway and they'd had to wait nearly an hour to change vehicles. He'd finally gotten downtown and ended up only just making it to his appointment.

Mark had been out of work for almost a year now, and this job interview was the one that was supposed to change everything. Or so he'd thought... He'd skidded into the lobby of the building where his appointment was like Kramer entering Jerry's apartment, with maybe a minute or two to spare. Of course, they'd made him wait another hour before seeing him, leaving him to chill his heels in their lobby.

Finally, some kid who looked like maybe he'd watched too many gangster movies growing up came out to greet him. He had this slicked-back hair and lantern jaw, but he was swimming in a suit that looked at least a couple of sizes too big. The kid strode up to Mark, smiling like a car salesman. Mark had only just started to introduce himself and hand the guy a copy of his resume, when the kid interrupted him. He thanked him for coming to see them but said something about how 'the job had already been filled, but they were keen to keep his application on file.'

Blah Blah Blabbity Blah.

The guy shook Mark's hand like he expected a gum ball to come out of his mouth. When one didn't, he turned on his heel and disappeared like a ghost back into the labyrinth of cubicles behind the front desk. Which left Mark standing there with his hand—the one with the resume—sticking straight out, looking like a dope.

Feeling more than a little humiliated and pretty goddamn miserable, Mark decided he'd try and salvage the day by grabbing a newspaper and looking through job prospects over a cup of coffee. But then, he saw the kitschy sign of the Blue Lagoon, and opted for a little day-drinking instead.

Shit, why not? Nothing was going right today, and he figured he deserved to take a little time to salve his bruised and battered ego. He wasn't looking forward to explaining any of this to his wife when he got home. And so, feeling extraordinarily little guilt, he'd pulled open the heavy metal door to the bar, and went inside.

The interior of the Blue Lagoon looked exactly like what you'd find if you searched for 'dingy bar' in a dictionary. Dark wood paneling made the walls appear like something out of a 1970's rumpus room. Red and white neon beer lights that blinked on and off were hung around the room like artwork. Near the back of the room brooded an unused pool table. Three balls sat like abandoned farm equipment upon the green felt pasture of its flat, slate surface. In the furthest corner, a beat-up old jukebox ground its way through an array of 70's and 80's rock music.

Mark took in the room, allowing his eyes a little time to adjust to the dimmer light inside. Once he was better able to see, he moved deeper into the room. At first glance, he didn't see anybody there. All the tables were empty, some of them even had their chairs still flipped upside down and sitting on the tabletop. No one appeared to be tending the bar, and he didn't see anyone sitting at it. The place looked empty.

Then, Mark caught a bit of movement out of the corner of his eye. A middle-aged guy in jeans and a green Pendleton shirt came out of the back carrying two industrial buckets full of ice. He nodded to Mark in greeting as he took his place behind the bar.

The bartender looked like he'd spent a lot of time on a motorcycle once upon a time, a real old school biker. His long gray hair was tied back into a rough ponytail, coal black strands punctuated the silvery plait. He immediately dumped the buckets' cold contents into the freezers under the counter.

Mark ambled up to the bar and took the first seat he came to. He got himself comfortable, settling the meat of his ass into the seat, and tucking the tips of his shoes under the metal bar at the bottom of his wobbly stool. He smiled at the biker bartender and idly watched him as he finished stowing the empty buckets on the floor behind him.

"Be with ya inna second, my friend," the old guy said.

"Not a problem," Mark replied. "I'm not in any real hurry."

Mark sat perched on the stool like a vulture, letting his day so far play out like a movie trailer across his mind's eye. It was like watching one of those 'funniest videos' where a guy gets kicked in the nuts over and over and over again. He rubbed his eyes and tried to relax.

Christ… he thought, as he pulled his hand across his still-freshly shaven face. It just fuckin' sucks. More and more, day after motherfuckin' day, it felt like someone had slapped a gigantic "kick me" sign onto his back and no one's told him.

How many resumes had he sent out? How many had been answered? More importantly, how many hadn't? He shook his head sadly. This shit was enough to start seriously messing with a man's sense of self-worth.

The bartender came over just then, interrupting his train of thought. "So, what are ya havin'?"

"Is it too early to get a Jameson?" Mark answered with a wry grin.

The old biker laughed. "Not at all. In fact,…" He jerked a thumb toward the other end of the bar, and he leaned in a little closer, "that guy's been drinking it since we opened at six this morning."

Mark squinted in the low light so that he could better see the guy in question. Sure enough, there was another person sitting where the bartender had indicated. The guy looked like he was in his late thirties with dark hair and a red and gray jacket. Even at this distance, Mark could see that the jacket had blue piping and white sleeves. It looked like it was made for snow. His face was shaded by beard stubble and his eyes were dark and brooding. He sat on the last stool, hunched over a trio of empty glasses, and looking intently at a handheld electronic tablet.

The bartender set a small tumbler of brown liquid onto the bar, snatching up the five-dollar bill that Mark had put there. Mark picked the glass up and swirled the heavy liquid amidst the ice cubes that were stacked inside. A woody, smoky odor rose like ether from the rim and Mark suddenly felt his mouth flood with water.

The biker shot a quick glance down the bar to check on his only other customer, and then went back to whatever he was doing in the backroom.

Mark took his first sip of his drink in silence, enjoying the warm, numbing feeling he felt radiating to his limbs from his belly. He could already feel the tension in the back of his neck, in the place where he'd been told he carried his stress, begin to relax, unspooling like a clock spring. He sighed and took another drink, feeling the coils of his shitty day fall off him like rope.

"Aaah," he breathed out with a palpable sense of relief, his mind already beginning to drift back to his mountain of problems.

He wasn't sure what else he could do to land a job. He had a lot of education. A degree... for all that was worth. He was physically able. Smart... quick to learn. Had a solid work history. He shook his head forlornly. It seemed as if nobody was hiring in this shit town. It may just come down to something as simple as that. He shook his head, trying to derail his morbid train of thought.

From down at the end of the bar, he suddenly heard the guy sitting there say something. Whatever it was, Mark was too far away to make it out. Not clearly anyway. But, with the old biker in the back, it could only have come from one place.

On a whim, Mark picked up his drink and made his way down the line of stools toward the end of the bar. It was stupid that they were the only two people in the entire place and they were sitting so far apart. He didn't know the guy from Adam, but it just felt like it would have been rude to not at least go over and introduce himself.

"I'm sorry, man," Mark said once he'd gotten closer. He smiled broadly and tried to appear friendly. "Were you talking to me?"

The guy looked up from his tablet, dark circles framing his eyes, but said nothing.

"I just thought I heard you say something," Mark explained. "I didn't want it to seem like I was being rude and ignoring you." He smiled congenially, suddenly feeling like it had all become weird and awkward.

The guy grunted something unintelligible but kept his eyes on the tablet laying in front of him. Mark shrugged his shoulders and sat down anyway on a stool a few spots away, setting his drink onto the bar top.

It was like that sometimes in bar culture, 'adversity making strange bedfellows,' and all of that. It was the same way with smokers... You know, the folks who gather together in clusters outside of buildings and strike up conversations with complete strangers as they puffed their drug of choice into their bloodstreams.

It was the same sort of thing with drinkers.

Mark settled into his seat and took another sip from his drink. Once more, the warm liquor felt good running down his throat. He grinned to himself, feeling his mood once again begin to lighten. After a minute, he set his glass down and looked back over at the guy sitting nearby. And suddenly, it struck him...

There was something about the guy that Mark was sure he recognized from somewhere. At first, he thought it might have been that they went to school together, but the difference in their ages made that impossible. They might have missed one another, him being in one grade, while Mark was in another, but no... he was pretty convinced it was from somewhere else. Maybe he'd been in the papers... or on local television? Did he once play on one of the local sports teams? Maybe... he was famous.

The questions were like a tickle at the back of Mark's brain.

After a second, his curiosity finally got the better of him and he had to ask.

"Hey, man," Mark said, his voice creaking a bit from nervousness. "You may get this a lot, but..." He paused, now feeling sort of stupid to have even brought it up. He finally decided 'what the heck,' and continued on, feeling just buzzed enough from the whiskey not to care. "I mean, you look super familiar to me, man. Like... did you go to school around here?"

The stranger chuckled darkly. He shut off his tablet, and gently slid it to the side. "School... no," he replied sadly. He picked up one of the glasses in front of him and drained the last of what was in it into his open mouth. "Not really from around here."

"Oh?" Mark replied with a nod of his head. "Where ya hail from?"

"Place up in Canada..." he said, and a dark shadow passed over his eyes. "I doubt you've ever heard of it."

"Try me," Mark replied, shifting in his seat. "My parents used to take us up there all the time on vacations."

The man looked at Mark solemnly. "Ever hear of a place called Adventure Bay?"

Just then, the bartender came out from the backroom, interrupting them. He made his way over to where the two men were sitting, wiping down the bar as he went. When he got close, he leaned over and grinned. "You guys good, or do you need something else?"

Mark checked the state of his glass, and then he glanced over at the one in front of his new bar pal. He nodded to the bartender deciding to splurge and held up two fingers. It's not like his wife could get mad at him twice, right?

The battle axe.

The bartender deftly reached behind him and retrieved the Jameson bottle from one of the shelves. He quickly poured them both their drinks, making sure to let a little extra splash over. He then grinned at them and winked as he put the bottle back in the rack.

He came back with a small wicker basket of shelled peanuts. He slid them down the counter like he was playing shuffleboard. Snatching up the ten-spot Mark held out—the one Shelly had left for him on the counter for his lunch—he went back to replenishing the bar's stockroom without another word.

"Adventure Bay, eh?" Mark shook his head. "No. Never heard of it. Nice?"

The man nodded and sipped his drink like it was medicine. "Yeah, I guess. It's a small fishing village up near Nova Scotia… Not a lot of people live there."

"Sorry," Mark said. Feeling rude, he got up and took a step over to him, extending his hand. "I'm Mark Tomlinson."

The man on the stool grinned wryly as he leaned over to shake it. "The name is Stark. Ryder Stark."

Mark narrowed his eyes and looked at him suspiciously. Wait a second, he thought. He knew that name. He was sure of it. He just couldn't for the life of him remember where from. He looked his new drinking partner over a bit more. He was clearly someone who had seen a bit of bad luck, someone who'd evidently decided that whatever answers he was looking for in the world could only be found at the bottom of a bottle. Who else started drinking like this at six in the morning?

Mark eyed Stark's jacket and noticed a small emblem on the coat's breast. It was a red badge of some sort with a white dog's paw on it. It looked official, like something given to professional dog handlers... or Search and Rescue. Once again, Mark felt his memory twitch, like it was something he'd seen before, something familiar.

Then, it struck him... a dog trainer, from Canada. He remembered reading about something like that, what... twenty, thirty years ago? There'd been something... some sort of accident... but that was as much as he could remember.

"Hey, man..." Mark asked gently, just in case he was wrong. "I don't want to embarrass you or anything, but... I think I remember where I might have heard of you." He pointed at the crest on his jacket. "I mean, you train dogs, right?"

Stark's face suddenly turned hard. His eyes narrowed as he looked over at Mark suspiciously. "I did... once upon a time."

"Yeah, okay," Mark said more to himself than to whom he was talking. He looked back at the guy grinning. "I, well... I knew I knew you from somewhere, man." He paused and took another sip from his drink to fill the silence. "You still doing that?"

Stark stared at the counter and seemed to get lost in the sea of his own memories for a second. He hated when things like this happened, when people made him remember, but... what could he do, other than address it on its face head-on? After a minute, he snapped out of his reverie and picked up his glass, looking at the light as it filtered through the ice.

"No," he finally answered gravely. "Not... anymore."

"No?" Mark said conversationally. "Why not?"

Stark emptied the rest of his drink into his mouth and drank the acrid liquid down in a single gulp. He set the glass back down onto the bar firmly and ran one of his hands over the surface of his tablet. Mark noticed that he let his fingers linger over the red and white badge—the same one that was on his jacket—that was mounted there. His fingertips slid over the insignia like he was reading something in Braille. His eyes suddenly grew glassy, and Mark saw his bottom lip quiver slightly.

Shit, was this guy gonna start to cry?

"Let me tell you something, man," Stark finally said, as quietly as if he'd talked in church. As he continued to speak, he stared at the blank face of the tablet intently, his eyes narrowing as he gave himself over to his memories. "I... I was only a kid... when I..."

Mark shook his head, not really understanding what the guy was talking about. "What do you mean?"

"I mean, it was all just so crazy, man," Stark said, finally looking over at him. A terrible emotion rose like mercury in his eyes. He shook his head, finally managing to get himself together. He looked back at Mark closely. "Do you like stories... Mark, was it?"

Mark clandestinely checked his watch. Then, he eyed his still half full glass. Deciding that he really had nowhere better to go, and just enough reason to stay, he nodded to his new friend. "Sure, man," he replied. "I'm all ears."

"Okay," Stark said with a deep sigh. "Well, I got a doozy for ya, then."

Mark raised his drink in silent salute, and Stark returned it even though his glass was empty.

"See, I was, like ten when," Stark began, setting his glass back down onto the counter. "No, wait... let me start over." He quietly composed himself. "When I was just a little kid, the teachers at my school said I showed a certain... ability for things like science from the time I first entered elementary school. My grades were good, and my teachers were always looking to enroll me into one program or another: science camps, computer camps, labs and seminars, and what used to be called 4H. My parents thought it would be good for me, so they agreed. There, I showed an aptitude for training animals—especially dogs—winning a ton of ribbons, trophies... a bunch of other shit."

"Okay," Mark replied as he took another sip from his glass, not knowing what else to say. He was a captive audience, and he knew it. At least the booze was good.

"One day," Stark continued, and his eyes took on a faraway look. "I get called to the school principal's office. They take me into a room and there's this lady there. She's older and dressed in a sort of 'business casual' pant suit. I remember her having this big purse that kept moving and making this weird noise as she clutched it to her chest."

Stark shook his head as he leaned closer to Mark. "Now, here's where I should have just said, no thank you, and kept to my normal, boring life." He leaned back on his stool. "Anyway, at one point, she opens her purse and, I shit you not..." He chuckled. "There was a chicken inside. A fuckin' chicken!" He shook his head in disbelief. "And the entire time we talked, she kept it in her lap and, well... seemed oddly focused on the damn thing.

"Anyway, she proceeds to tell me about how she's this mayor of this city up north and that they'd approved a new concept in civil maintenance that puts the power directly back where it belongs: in the people's hands. She spoke of computers, and equipment... and, ultimately, of a squadron of specially trained dogs that would help civil authorities keep the peace. It all sure sounded good, but again, I was ten." He held up a hand to stop Mark from saying anything and interrupting him. "I told you, it was crazy."

"So," Mark piped in incredulously, "this lady... gives a ten-year-old kid, what? Funding?" He laughed. He couldn't help himself. He'd heard some whoppers in bars in his time, but... this one was taking the cake. "Look, I'm happy to sit here and listen, but... you can't expect me to believe any of this bullshit."

"I know... I know," Stark shook his head despondently. "But it gets weirder."

Mark chuckled and picked up a small cube of ice from his glass with his fingers. He put it in his mouth and bit down on it, the cube fragmenting into smaller bits and pieces. Over the frigid mouthful, he asked, "How?"

Stark leaned in conspiratorially and looked him directly in the eye. "Those dogs... they could talk, man."

Mark barked out another laugh. "Get the fuck outta here!" he snickered and took another sip.

"Hey, believe it or not," Stark finally said, sounding a little hurt. "Makes no difference to me."

"Not!" Mark laughed and set his glass down.

Undaunted, Stark continued. "Adventure Bay was such a small, under-populated town that all the data they had, said it would work. And it did. It actually did work. For a while, anyway. They first brought me a German Shepherd, a police-trained pup. I named him Chase, after my old dog at home. When that seemed to go well, they brought in a Dalmatian, and a Bulldog." Stark shook his head. "Then, a Labrador, a Cockapoo, and a mutt."

Mark grinned. He was all for listening to some tall tale while drinking, just as long as whoever was telling the story kept it interesting and reasonably within the realm of possibility. But this whole thing was well on its way to sounding like Grade A, American-made bullshit. But okay... He mentally strapped himself in for the rest of it, sure that, whatever it was that he was about to hear, was going to be a doozy.

"Okay, okay," Mark capitulated, "so, go on."

"No, forget it," Stark said, sliding his tablet back in front of him.

"No, no..." Mark said apologetically. He smiled warmly. "C'mon, I was only fuckin' around. Really... I'm interested. Go ahead."

Stark acted reluctant, but he quickly picked his story back up exactly where he'd left off.

"Like I say, things went okay, for a while..." he said as that faraway look returned to his gaze. "But then, one of the dogs—the one that had been trained to fly a helicopter..."

"Wait, what?" Mark chuckled.

Stark glared back at him but kept on talking. "... crashed into the town square and some people were hurt. One was even killed. As a result, the story got out, and that brought a lot of media attention to the town. There was an inquest and, well... everything fell apart."

Mark shook his head, his amused interest now reignited. "What do you mean, fell apart?"

"Bro, questions were asked... about the governmental involvement, about my role—as a child—in all of it. I mean, I was ten, man. They asked about where the dogs had come from in the first place? Who'd actually trained them? The whole awful thing was all over the papers."

Mark nodded, realizing this was where he'd first heard about him.

Stark shrugged his shoulders and continued talking. "All I know is... that they carted the mayor away—the one who'd first come to my school, the lady in the pants suit."

"The one with the chicken," Mark interrupted emphatically.

"That very one. Carted her and her chicken away in handcuffs. Ended up indicting a bunch of people including a local ship's captain, a restaurant owner, and a couple of farmers. It was the kid who ran the town's pet salon who finally ended up turning state's evidence against all of them."

"Man," Mark sighed with a shake of his head. Despite himself, he was now interested in how this crazy story turned out. "So, what ended up happening?"

"The biggest charges were filed against the mayor," Stark replied almost casually. "Bribery, misappropriation of civic funds, endangerment of a child, the wanton endangerment of animals... you want a list? I mean, they'd programmed those damn things to actually drive and to talk, man. How does that even fuckin' happen?"

Mark stared a hole into the counter in front of him. "That's crazy" was about all he could manage in response to everything he'd just heard. He swirled the ice in his glass like he was shooting dice, all the while shaking his head in disbelief.

"Anyway," Stark finally said, waving his hand in the air as if to erase the bad memories. "After the accident happened and the inquest was over, the mayor—and her chicken for all I know—and the rest of them were taken away. Even the town's charter ended up being rescinded. All too soon, it just became easier for everyone in the area to just forget it ever happened. And in the end, only I was left to carry the memory of those pups."

They sat silently for a minute, each lost in their own thoughts. Mark had been leaning toward the idea that all of this was made up, or the delusions of a drunk, but… Stark was just so goddam earnest. If it didn't happen like he said it did, he definitely believed that it had. Either way, Mark decided that he'd go back to minding his own business from now on, to stop himself from striking up conversations with weird-looking strangers in the future.

"So, what happened to the dogs?" Mark finally asked. For some reason, he needed to know, to hear how Stark brought this shaggy dog tale in for a landing.

Stark looked over at him with a haunted look in his eyes. "What happened to them? You want to know what happened to them?"

Mark nodded. "Yeah, did they let you keep them?"

Stark shook his head grimly. "The court decided that they were all nothing more than 'medical experiments.' They said that something had to have been done to those animals even if they never found out what… or by whom."

Mark stared at him warily.

Stark went back to running his hand slowly over his tablet. "Do you know what they do to medical experiments once the experiment is over, Mark? Do ya?"

Mark shook his head. "Hey man, I didn't mean anything by it."

Stark hung his head and chuckled darkly. "I know… I know. I'm sorry." He looked up into the overhead light and the whites of his eyes were streaked with lightning bolts of red, like he'd once started crying and had never been able to stop. "It's just that," he wiped his runny nose onto the white sleeve of his jacket. "Those dogs… were my friends, man."

Mark finished the rest of his drink, suddenly feeling an awkwardness in the room, like he'd stumbled into someone else's intensely personal moment, and now, he couldn't figure a way to back himself out of it. He was starting to think that having that coffee was sounding surprisingly good right about now. He still had a little cash left, enough for a cup anyway.

Mark looked over at Stark, finally deciding that his story was just too 'out there' to be believed. Who knew, though? The guy could well have been just another drunk spinning the tallest tale he could think of in the hopes that someone might buy him his next drink. And it had worked. After all, hadn't Mark done that exact thing with the last money he had. Maybe Stark thought he needed to do something to balance the scales, to set things square between them… and this story was all he had? Maybe he thought Mark was good for a few more drinks? It didn't matter. In some weird way, the toll had been paid and the story shared, and somehow that was enough.

After a minute or two, long enough to not seem rude, Mark got up off his stool and threw a few dollars of tip money onto the counter. "Well, good to meet ya, man. I'm off to, uh… try and change my luck on the job front."

Stark smiled, like he'd been half-expecting Mark to get up and leave at some point. He'd seen the look that was on his face plenty of times before. It was the look that said they didn't believe you, that you were lying. That they thought you were crazy. No matter. Stark knew that he was telling the truth. He knew how things had been. He'd seen what had happened to those dogs—to his friends—when it all came crashing down around their ears. He reflexively reached for his tablet and turned it back on, never noticing when Mark finally got up, and walked out of the bar.

BURYING THE BONE

Sex and death… they can both be pretty frightening.

Summer, 1988

"Geez, this party is freakin' lame, man," Dennis complained to Teddy as they both leaned up against the wall in the kitchen of Sarah McGovern's house like gunslingers waiting for 'high noon.'

The two of them had only been here for less than an hour, but they knew a dead party when they saw one. And they were looking at one right now. The crowd that had gathered so far was a weird mix of jocks and their cheerleader girlfriends mixed with some of the more scholastic types in the school (in other words, 'dorks'). There were even a few stoners gathered out in the back doing what stoners did seemingly every minute of the day.

But Dennis and Teddy were none of those things, although they had elements of them all. Both were good at sports but had never really been defined by their involvement in them. They were good at school but weren't nerds. They even smoked weed, but it didn't rule their lives, not like some people.

Instead, the two of them were quite content to thread the line between any one of a number of social groups in their high school. Dennis always thought that it had been the thing that had—initially—brought them together as friends: that ability to be a lot of different things to a lot of different people, and to swim in the strangest of waters. The fact that they were both, like most boys their age, preoccupied with trying to get laid every single minute was simply icing on the cake. Together, they eyed the back door as they each started planning their escape.

"Well, Robby said there was going to be beer here, but…" Teddy replied sadly, shaking his head, and looking around the kitchen like he was at a funeral. "I haven't seen a drop yet." He paused. "We should bail."

Dennis disgustedly nodded. The party was a non-starter, and it didn't look like it was going to improve anytime soon. "Let's give it another minute, and if something interesting doesn't show, we'll go and score our own brewskis, even if that means drinking them in the car. Sound good?"

Teddy reluctantly expressed his agreement, but then said something about 'wanting to take a last lap' through the house. He said he wanted to, as he put it, 'scout out any local talent that may be hiding somewhere.' He walked away, disappearing like a specter into the sparse forest of people clogging the hallway.

Dennis took this time to scan the room. He recognized a bunch of people from school—Jordan, Phillip, and their meathead pals from the school's baseball team—huddled around a worn pool table that had been set up in the living room. There was a trio of cackling girls watching them, standing in the doorway between the living room and the kitchen. He'd seen the girls prowling the halls at school, like lionesses in search of a mate... or for prey.

Conversely, standing near the back door so that they could presumably execute their escape at a moment's notice should the jocks decide to get rowdy and look for someone to pick on, were Jeff and Billy Thompson, the school's biggest science fiction geeks. In other words, the place was Loserville.

Dennis scanned the crowd looking for Teddy so that they could get the hell out of there. It was getting late, and he wanted a beer. Just then, an unfamiliar face of a girl appeared like a phantom out of the darkness of the backyard. One second, she wasn't there, and the next... she was coming in through the open back door like something out of a dream, this beautiful face slowly appearing over the Thompson boys' shoulder. Dennis watched her admiringly as she shouldered her way through the crowd and into the kitchen.

The girl had this long black hair, dark, mysterious eyes, and she was wearing a loose-fitting, olive-colored button-up shirt, tied into a knot just below her breasts. The outfit was completed by a leather motorcycle jacket that was slung over her shoulders and looked as old as dirt. But most notably though, to Dennis' eyes at least, she had on the tightest pair of shorts he'd ever seen. If someone would have told him that they were painted on, he would have easily believed them. He felt his heart skip a beat in his chest when he saw how the material struggled to cradle the cheeks of her ass.

Well, hello...

Dennis' eyes followed her like he was an eyewitness to a crime as she came into the kitchen, stopping a few steps in to look the crowd over. She ambled over to the Living Room doorway and poked her head in between the trio of lionesses. Not seeing anything of interest, she then disappeared into the shadows of the hallway. Dennis waited and kept an eye out for her in the small crowd. She was out of his sight for a minute or two, but then she came sauntering back into the kitchen, like a panther prowling a petting zoo.

Dennis discreetly followed her with his eyes—well, the important parts of her, anyway—and was happy when he saw her finally take notice of him. She gave the room another once over, and then she ambled over and took Teddy's spot next to him on the wall.

"Hey," she said, and her voice was like a silken ribbon twirling on the air.

"Hey."

"Name's Liz."

Dennis grinned as he looked down at his shoes. "Dennis."

She turned her body and looked at him, cocking her hip out seductively. "This party..." she made a scoffing sound, "is lame."

He chuckled. "We were just saying that."

Shit, Dennis couldn't help but think, this chick—this Liz—was so hot.

She looked him in the eye like she was daring him to look away. "We? You here with someone?"

Dennis laughed and shook his head. "Oh, I'm here with my boy, Teddy."

"Teddy, huh?" She looked around the kitchen disinterested. "Where's he?"

Dennis tried to look uncaring. "On the hunt for something to drink, I think."

Liz's eyes scanned the room again with a look of displeasure. "Is there even any beer here? I mean, what kind of a party doesn't at least have beer?"

Dennis shook his head. "They said there was some coming, but... I haven't seen any sign of it yet."

Liz shook her head in disgust. "Fuckin' lame."

Dennis nodded sagely in agreement.

After a few more minutes of crowd appraisal, Liz pulled her pager off her belt and started flipping through her messages. Dennis recognized some of the names and numbers on her screen, but she was scrolling through them so quickly that he couldn't see much more than that. After another minute, she shut it off and clipped it back onto her belt where she'd gotten it. Finally, she sighed dramatically, and looked up at Dennis.

"Hey, you wanna get out of here?" she asked, continuing to let her indifferent gaze drift over the room like it was a lost balloon. "This place is boring, and I know somewhere where we can go that's a lot cooler."

Dennis grinned. He tried to be cool about it, but his excitement at the idea of taking this girl, well... anywhere, was too much. He took another look around for Teddy so that he could tell him—okay, brag to him—about what was happening... and to tell him he'd need to find his own way home. Regrettably, Teddy was nowhere to be found.

Dennis turned back to Liz. "Sure," he said still grinning. "Where do you want to go?

Liz looked at him and smiled seductively. "How about my place? We can take my car. It's right outside."

"Shit," Liz said with a sad desperation. "Look, I'm sorry, okay? The gas gauge has always been unreliable. I really don't know how this happened."

Dennis shook his head and half-heartedly shrugged his shoulders as they continued walking down the dark country road. Trees loomed along the sides of the path like a phalanx of possible muggers. Wide shrubs and bushes looked poised to strike, and they were easily mistaken for predators. Overhead, a summer moon hung in the sky like a porch light.

"It's okay," he finally conceded, but it was pretty clear, it wasn't.

Liz's car had been an old red Chevy with a crumpled back passenger-side door and a cracked windshield. They'd found it parked on the street outside of the party, right after she'd pressed him up against the first tree they'd come to and given him a taste of what she had in mind for the rest of their evening. After a short but effective make-out session, she'd led him by the hand like he was a puppy to the car. The way she kept looking back at him and grinning made the front of his pants feel tighter.

Things escalated pretty quickly as she'd driven along with her furtive looks and knowing smiles. Finally, she reached over and unceremoniously set her free hand into his lap. He could feel her hand pressing firmly against the denim and caressing him with every bounce in the road.

Predictably, it had driven Dennis crazy.

And then, the car ran out of gas.

Dennis couldn't believe it at first. One second, he was leaning his head back against the headrest with Liz's hand taking his pulse through the coarse material of his jeans. And the next, he felt the car sputter and abruptly lose power, slowly drifting over to the side of the road. The next thing he knew, they were walking down the road. She said she'd seen them pass a small country store about a mile or so back. If they could just get there, they could call a tow truck.

That... had been half an hour ago.

"I know that store is around here somewhere," she finally said, trying to change the subject. "You saw it when we passed it, right?"

Dennis hadn't seen shit. He'd been too busy concentrating on the dance her hand was doing in his lap. But, as he was still holding out hope that he could salvage some small part of his evening, he nodded but didn't say anything. Truthfully though, he'd been pretty pissed off by the whole situation. Or rather, he had been at first. But the further they got away from the moment (and the softer his dick got), the better he felt about waiting until they could get to where they were going.

In other words, to her place.

But Liz was undeniably attractive, though. 'Hot as fuck,' as some of his classmates might say. There was no denying that. And he found that he sorta liked the way she was aggressive sexually. He didn't see too much of that in the girls he ran around with. Most, well... most dealt with your junk the same way they might deal with raw liver in their hands. So, he didn't want to blow it. Not now. Not when he was so close to sealing the deal and nailin' this girl.

He checked his watch—10:30 PM—and figured there was still plenty of time to get something going with her. No cause for concern. No need to panic... yet. He knew he could still pull the evening out of its tailspin. All he had to do was to just get them to this store (wherever the fuck that was) and get her back to her place. After that, everything would be as cool as ice. He'd find his way back to his car afterward (or tomorrow morning if he was lucky); maybe call a cab.

"Hey, look," Liz said, her voice suddenly sounding like a kid who'd just spotted a circus. "Is that a... cemetery?"

She pointed toward a fenced-in field up ahead. The moon bathed the morbid tableau in a silvery-blue light. Inside of the fence, an array of stone and granite headstones were laid out in precise rows, poking up out of the ground like discarded Mahjong tiles. Trees and small copses of shrubbery were sprinkled about, giving the scene a look like something out of an old horror movie.

In the middle of the lawn, on a small hill in the center of the lot, brooded a large white, stone mausoleum. Its pale walls reflected the moonlight, like the beacon of a lighthouse over a dark and desolate landscape. Overhead, billowy clouds started to roll in, infringing on the moon.

"Yeah," he said, sounding uninterested. "I think so. I mean, it sure looks like one."

Liz stopped walking, but took his hand, forcing him to stop. "Hey, let's go inside?"

Dennis blanched, pulling back from her. "Inside where? There?" He chuckled dismissively. "For what?"

She smiled up at him seductively, rising up onto her tiptoes to kiss him again on the mouth. Her tongue pushed passed his lips and he felt her ardently press that impossibly tight body of hers up against his. With her body pushing up against him, her breasts poking into his chest like that, Dennis found it hard to think straight.

Suddenly, she pulled away from him, and slowly untied the knot in her shirt. The blouse fell open and revealed a bit of the swelling in the middle of her breasts. Taking a small step back, she grinned at him mischievously.

"You know..." she said as she licked her lips like something out of a porn film. "I've always wanted to... do it in a graveyard."

"You... you have?" Dennis replied dumbly.

"Uh-huh," she moaned as she made her lips pout.

He felt his eyes suddenly open wider as his crotch stirred and his dick sat up to take notice. Was this it? Was this really where they were going to do this? The idea that it might happen now, rather than later at her place, made him more than a little willing to overlook a few things. Like her running out of gas for instance.

And the fact that she wanted to go fuck in a cemetery.

"So, what d'ya think?" she asked him, and her voice had gone husky with her ardor. Her fingers danced across the front of his shirt. "You wanna?"

Dennis wasn't sure which of her questions she wanted him to answer first. Yes, he wanted to go have sex with her. Desperately so. She was beautiful and the idea of her being naked had been dominating his thoughts since he first laid eyes on her back at the party. But no, he didn't want to go prowling around in a cemetery in the middle of the goddam night like some dope in a cheap-ass horror film. That shit was stupid, and it never worked out right... for anybody.

Making up his mind, he opened his mouth to tell her to forget it, when he heard someone that sounded a lot like him say, "Yeah, okay."

They managed to wedge themselves through between a small opening in the front gate. Dennis went in first. They figured, if he could make it through, then it would be no problem for Liz to follow him. He scraped his back up on the wrought iron metal of the fence, but otherwise got passed unscathed. She followed him and the sight of her still-open shirt and half-exposed breasts in the moonlight helped convince him of the wisdom of the adventure.

Once they were both inside the cemetery, she stopped in the middle of the road and turned back to look at him. She then sauntered toward him, and the way her hips moved back and forth, well… it was hypnotizing, like a metronome swinging in the moonlight. Placing her hand onto the center of his chest, she leaned in, and kissed him again. Her tongue ardently probed his mouth, and he could taste a faint hint of spearmint on her breath.

Then, in the middle of them kissing, she pressed something that had a harsh chemical odor, like gasoline, up against the underside of his nose. The fumes made his ears hot, and his head feel light like a balloon. Her hand on his chest suddenly felt like it was on fire, his skin awash in an unbelievably warm sensation that spread down his limbs like grass fire. He opened his eyes and saw her staring at him intently, a tiny bottle half-filled with a dark unknown liquid in her hands.

"It's Amyl Nitrate," she said, and she held it firmly against one of her nostrils. "They say that it makes sex even better."

Breathing in deep from the small brown bottle, Liz' eyes glassed over, and she leaned into him like she was suddenly drunk. After a second though, she roused, and kissed him again, this time using her hand on his crotch to make sure that she had his undivided attention. His skin felt like ice against the warmth of her roaming palm.

Dennis felt himself responding to her touch, pushing his hips forward to—if at all possible—incrementally increase the pressure on him. But then, just as he was sliding his hand up her torso and cupping one of her bare breasts in his hand, she let go of him, and pushed him away. He opened his eyes just in time to see her running off into the low forest of headstones, laughing.

"Hey," he called out after her into the dark night. "No fair."

The cemetery lay bathed in the kind of moonlight that made everything look otherworldly. More headstones poked up from the ground; bleached thumbs protruding from the soil, shimmering in the silver light. Memorial placards mounted on small concrete squares were littered across the open field like spilled playing cards. The whole scene was like something right out of a spooky Halloween cartoon.

Dennis followed along after Liz briskly, his eyes searching every shadow and under every tree for any sign of her. It was only when he passed a grave marked with a statue of a weeping angel that he saw Liz's shirt laying draped clownishly over the cherub's head. Not too far after that, he found her bra.

His pace increased. By this point, he wasn't exactly running, but he was certainly moving through the rows of gravestones at a good clip. He followed the trail of her discarded apparel like breadcrumbs, snatching them up as he went, until he finally came to the foot of the large mausoleum on the hill, the one he saw from the road. There, laying seductively across the steps of the crypt, naked as the day she was born, was Liz.

Her skin shone like mercury in the moonlight, highlighting the shadows of her curves, and making them appear all that much more erotic. She sat up, arching her back and cupping both of her full breasts in her hands. Her eyes looked up into Dennis' never breaking eye contact with him. Dumbfounded, he breathlessly watched as she slowly slid one hand down her belly, until her fingertips became entangled in the patch of dark hair that lay between her legs.

It was the hottest damn thing Dennis had ever seen.

He clenched his sphincter tightly and tried to relax, desperate not to ruin the moment by poppin' off too quickly in his pants. Without waiting for her invitation, he unceremoniously dropped the pile of Liz's clothes he'd been carrying, and then, stripped his shirt and pants off like they were on fire. When he was every bit as naked as she was, he stood brazenly at the base of the stairs, grinning at her as if she were now his prey.

"Come here, boy," she moaned to him, and her eyes flashed brightly in the moonlight. "I want to feel you so bad."

Dennis felt his erection bob in time with his gait as he quickly mounted the alabaster steps. He felt a sudden cool breeze blow over his exposed cock and balls and the chill temperature took his breath away a little. But then, Liz had her arms around him, pulling him in, and his world suddenly became very warm.

Her hand suddenly wrapped around the head of his dick, and he felt it envelope his length like a boa constrictor. She kissed his neck and began to pull on him, to tug at him, and he smiled to himself as he started laying out the story in his head that he was going to tell Teddy when he saw him next.

"I've always fantasized about doing something like this," Liz moaned into his ear. She bit down on the lobe, and he nodded, totally believing her.

Liz wrapped her legs around Dennis' waist, and he felt the warmth of his cock brush up against the cold expanse of her thigh. She groaned and bit him again, lifting her hips to make herself even more accessible to him. It was like she needed this, needed him. Dennis put his forehead against the nape of her neck and got to work.

Liz felt the hunger in the pit of her stomach abruptly coil and twist with its need. The feeling was like a knife sawing away at her insides. It had been a long time for her, too long. She stared down at the top of the boy's head and knew that was all about to change. A smile of satisfaction spread across her face when she felt his glans at the opening of her sex, knowing that her desire, her need, would soon be satisfied.

Dennis ran his fingertips over the lips of her vulva, and he felt them come away sopping wet. He was amazed that this girl, this beautiful, beautiful girl, was as excited as she was. He'd always heard that women usually took a bit of manipulation—some kissing, some cooing, a little fingering, going down on them, etc.—to get them this wet.

At first, he thought she'd peed herself. But then, he felt the fluid's slickness and knew it for what it was. Casting any remaining doubts away, he pushed himself into her and forgot all about the dumb party, forgot all about how cold he was, even forgot about them running out of gas. He forgot about everything. All he could focus on now was how good it felt as he started working his length back and forth inside her.

Liz locked her legs around his waist the instant she felt him enter her. She used the muscles in her legs to draw him in as deep as she could, holding him there and grinding up against him. They both groaned when he bottomed out, but everything soon settled down as they searched for, and eventually found, their mutual rhythm. Dennis was afraid he was too heavy, so he started to raise himself up off of her, but she yanked him back down with a strength that was surprising.

Liz bucked beneath him, her nails clawing at his back. To Dennis, it all felt fantastic; way better than he ever thought it could. Boy, he thought, they really undersold this shit. He couldn't wait to report back to Teddy and his other buddies, rub their noses in it.

Soon, he became lost in the intense sensations that were coursing like electricity through his body, he pressed his face against the side of Liz' neck and did what he could to hold off his rapidly approaching orgasm.

Liz settled into the boy's rhythm, feeling the connection being made the moment he was deep inside her. He was young, a boy with a fierce spirit. To her, though, now he was little more than a feast set out for her consumption. Holding him tightly to her chest, she relaxed and felt the necessary psychic channels slowly open. She moaned softly as she began drawing off the energy she sought from the boy.

At first, it was a challenge to keep the flow regulated and not be overwhelmed by it. She always thought it felt like trying to hold back a flood with a kitchen spatula. But soon, she was able to get a better handle on it and started feeding in earnest.

The boy fought a little toward the end, his body bucking and jerking aggressively, as he began to realize what was happening to him. Some deep part of his lizard brain must have kicked in with a primordial understanding that he was in a very real kind of mortal danger long before his intellect ever got involved. And when he finally expired, when he'd finally given up his last to her, she fed on the dregs until the moon began to wane in the summer sky.

Liz continued to lay beneath the boy, cradling him close to her bosom. She stared idly up at the setting moon as she lounged across the steps of the mausoleum, her thoughts adrift in a world of its own. Her bare chest had been splashed with a bit of the boy's blood and the thick liquid appeared black in the waning moonlight. He'd gotten a nosebleed as she'd drained the last of him and some of it had fallen onto her breasts.

Which happened sometimes, the succubus idly reminded herself.

The woman lay dozing; lovingly stroking the back of the now dead boy's head. Already, she was making plans for the things she needed to do once the afterglow of this feeding had passed. She still had a few things to do before the sun fully rose.

Deep inside, she suddenly felt an emotion that was akin to gratitude toward the boy. He'd been young and so very full of life. The tableau of his essence had been like walking up to a buffet to her deprived and woefully undernourished senses. And, despite the lateness of the hour, and the nearness of the sunrise, she couldn't help but to continue to sup on him until she was unable to draw any more.

Finally, the woman gently rolled the boy's body off of her. His desiccated corpse struck the marble steps like a bundle of hay and tumbled limply to the ground. She slowly got to her feet, using some of the boy's discarded clothing to wipe the blood from her skin. When she was done, she tossed the stained garments onto the boy's rapidly-cooling body. Once she'd dried herself sufficiently, she gathered up her own clothing a piece at a time and got herself dressed.

The creature looked to the Eastern horizon as she re-tied the corners of her blouse together. As she adjusted the shirt, she noticed that the sun was just starting to poke its head above the uppermost ridges of the surrounding mountains. Daylight spilled over the peaks like waves of seawater. And as she made her way back toward the front gates, she figured that, if she hurried, she could use the gallon of gas she had stowed in her trunk and still make it home before dawn.

ABLUTION

Someone emailed me recently and said that they really wanted to see more of the Detective John Secord character from the "Concrete Angels" story in Tuxedo Junction. Of course, I was only too happy to comply, as I enjoy working with the character. As usual, there are a number of cinematic references planted here and there to keep you kids on your toes. I'll leave it to you to find them all. Oh, and those last martial arts moves came from something I saw once while watching a guy play CALL OF DUTY: WARFARE on Twitch (an excellent source for gun play choreography, by the way). I deconstructed it, field-tested it, and voila! A nasty piece of business of which I'm actually sort of proud.

But first, a definition…

ab·lu·tion (əblo͞oSHən) noun

the washing of one's body or part of it (as in a religious rite)

Secord bumped open the door to his small, and let's face it, dingy apartment with the fat of his ass, stowing his keys in his front right pants pocket as he came in. He was still wearing the clothes he had on while he was at work—brown oxfords, matching slacks, and his one permanently-wrinkled button-up shirt. His sleeves were rolled up lazily to his elbows, like he'd spent the day trying not to get any of the city's filth on his cuffs. He carried a beige suit coat draped over his one arm like a limp rag. And as his six foot six, two-hundred-and-fifty-pound frame stepped through the entryway of his home, the door closed silently behind him. Looking back, he stopped to flip the lock.

The apartment laid out before him was plain, decorated like a motel room. There was a couch, a TV on a flimsy metal stand, a couple of chairs, and a small table immediately visible. The furniture was all old and there was little on display to show that anyone lived here: no personal photos hung on the walls, no pictures in frames on display anywhere. There was a sparseness to the place that seemed downright monastic.

Off to his immediate right lay the kitchenette with its small stove and even smaller fridge. There was a single sink with an empty dish rack on a mat set to one side. His coffee cup sat on the sideboard; small crumbs of his morning toast stuck to the rim like barnacles.

In the next room, on the same side of the apartment, was the Spartan living room with a wide window that looked out over the street far below. Further along, there was the hallway that led to the bath and on to his bedroom.

All in all, it was about seven hundred and fifty square feet of endurable squalor. The place had been his home for the last ten years, give or take. It wasn't a fashionable place to live, but it was all he could afford on a policeman's salary. Secord groaned, finally allowing himself to feel the exhaustion of his long shift; happy to be home.

Secord yawned and threw his coat over the wooden chair that was in the living room. It landed across its back and hung there, swaying like a drape in the dim light. He stretched his arms wide and couldn't help but yawn again. Fuck he was tired, he idly thought as he pulled his right arm out of the leather Shapeshift shoulder holster he wore. He sighed with relief, grateful to be free of the weight of his Smith & Wesson .40 caliber handgun.

This must be how women feel when they got home and could finally take off their bra.

After hanging his gun and shoulder rig on the chair, he stepped into the kitchen for a second and opened the refrigerator door. He looked around at the multitude of To-Go containers inside, but finally grabbed a Fuji apple from the fruit bin and a beer from the door. Biting into the flesh of the fruit, he felt a rush of sweet liquid splash across the flat of his tongue. He'd considered picking up some more Take-Out on the way home from the Indian joint on the corner, but he'd opted to come straight home instead. The only thing he wanted to do now was to take a long hot shower and go right to bed.

Secord left the kitchen and made his way across the living room, heading down the hall. He set the beer and what was left of the apple down on the counter in the bathroom and continued on into the bedroom. Piles of his clothes lay spread out over every available flat surface. Some of the piles, he knew were clean. Others, well… Let's just say that he wouldn't have been surprised to see a cloud of cartoon flies swirling above them.

Secord quickly stripped off his clothes and tossed them into the pile that looked the dirtiest. It had been a rough week and some things—like folding clothes and a few other of his household chores—had sort of fallen from his Priority List. He'd been assigned to a new case and his bosses were already needling him about showing results.

The case in question was a nasty affair involving a local wannabe gangster by the name of Gordon Valmont, and his main enforcer, a pseudo-tough guy known as Giordano. The particulars of the jacket were pretty standard as these things went: new tough guy rolls into town (Valmont), starts infringing on other people's territories (the city's already established criminal status quo), and the interloper gets himself spanked.

The only thing was, in this case, the spanked... spanked back.

Secord had learned from doing a bit of research that Valmont had, once upon a time, worked in Philly for a very undesirable group of people. Over the ensuing years, decades, he'd quickly become known as an 'earner' and all the right folks seemed to like him. As a result, he'd climbed the ranks in short order and made a good little life for himself.

Time passed and Valmont finally got to that age when people decide to start taking things a little bit slower, easier. You know, settling down. It was just that, now that he was getting on in his years, he wanted a small operation to retire to; someplace out of the way where he could continue to earn for the organization, but not have the pressure—or risk—of running a bigger, more complex operation. Anyway, as a result of all of this, he'd come to The City looking to setup his small bit of business and basically retire.

Then, this spanking business happened.

Like most tough guys, Valmont knew from experience that when one encountered a difficult problem such as this, it was best to address it early, and with the utmost speed and weight. Cut to present day, and Secord suddenly had mobsters showing up dead all over the goddamn place.

Normally, he wouldn't have given two shits about a snake pit of gangsters getting themselves murdered, except that their deaths created a series of vacancies in the criminal hierarchy of the city. Shook the organizational Etch-A-Sketch if you will. And of course, these sudden vacancies created a power vacuum... and, as we all know, Nature abhors a vacuum. So, between Valmont ordering the elimination of these key players, and the ensuing fighting for scraps between the newer—younger—talent, Secord hadn't slept much in the last 72 hours.

He tossed the last of his clothes—his underwear—onto the pile and walked back naked to the bathroom. The cool air felt good on his skin and the chill made him wake up a little as he entered the small, tiled room. He left the light off and the door open behind him in order to let the steam from his shower out. Standing in front of the mirror, munching on the rest of his apple, he gave his reflection the once over.

Jesus tap-dancing Christ, he thought dejectedly, he was looking old. There were more lines than ever on his face and a carpet of salt-n-pepper hair covered his chest and slightly bulging abdomen. Even his pubes had gray in them. He still had the muscle tone of a man ten years his junior, but he could tell that things were starting to head south. He reminded himself to double up at the gym. Like that was going to help.

"Getting old ain't for kids," he laughingly confided to his reflection through the appley mush in his mouth.

Turning to look up at the shower head, he felt the fatigue in his legs twinge and bark for mercy, so he opted for a hot bath instead. He bent over the tub and plugged the stopper into the drain. Then, he turned on the hot water. Once the water was flowing steady and steam started rising into the air, he added in a little cold.

He stood back up and returned his gaze to the mirror as he waited for the tub to fill. Leaning over the sink so that he could get a closer look, he pulled his lower eyelid down, closely inspecting the whites of his eyes. Blinking and rolling the orbs around in their sockets, it was impossible not to notice how red they were.

Man, I look like shit.

He shook his head in resignation as he ran his hand over the stubbly part of his face. Pulling on the flesh like taffy, he yawned again, and almost skipped the soak and just go straight to bed. But then, he felt a warm draft of steam coming up from the bathtub against his leg, and he figured, no... bath first. Poaching his muscles would do them—and him—a world of good. And it would also go a long way in getting him to relax enough so that he might actually get some sleep.

His bath was longer and wider than most normal tubs. It was one of those claw-foot jobs with a wide, stainless-steel spigot. It was the thing that first drew him to the place. He was a big guy, and he needed more space than normal people to do the things that normal people did. And even if the apartment was small, he liked that it was big in the places that counted.

Secord slipped his right foot into the water and winced as the liquid's warmth enveloped his toes. It felt like putting on a sock straight out of the dryer. When he'd put his other foot in, and was standing in the tub, he had to wait a second for his skin to get used to the temperature. The sharp pins and needles bark of his flesh soon subsided, though, and he sat down, easing his ass into the water. As he leaned back, he rested his torso against the back of the tub, immediately feeling big chunks of his shitty day begin to evaporate like phantoms into the steam coming off of the bathwater.

God, this feels good. Much better idea than the shower.

Secord leaned back, sliding his body down into the water, and letting it sink to the bottom of the tub like a submarine. The warm fluid rose to his chin as he set the back of his neck against the lip of the tub. His knees poked up from the surface of the water like pale islands rising out of a steaming sea.

Once immersed, he lay there quietly, relaxing, and doing his best not to think about anyone... or anything. But, as his eyes closed and he felt himself starting to unwind, his mind slowly drifted back to where it always went, to his work.

When Secord figured out that Valmont was the catalyst for all the uproar, he'd checked with some of his friends to find out what he could about the man. These friends... were not exactly the kind of people the police force's Internal Affairs department would have approved of, but sometimes you had to bend the pole to catch the fish, y'know? He just had to see to it that the rod never actually broke.

Once he'd learned all he could about the man, Secord decided that it might be best for all concerned if he went out to see him—face-to-face. Y'know, the direct approach. He just wanted to make sure that Valmont knew that the cops weren't stupid, that they knew what he was up to, and that they weren't going to just look away on something like this. He wanted to make it clear that they would prosecute each and every one of his people if they found blood on their hands.

And that meant everyone, including him.

Of course, the old gangster had claimed all kinds of innocence, saying that he was simply an honest businessman looking to retire and be left alone. Giordano had stood nearby as they talked, looking like a gargoyle come to stoic life. He was a big Italian guy in a greasy suit, who, by the looks of him, was more brawn than brains.

In the end though, Secord had left without getting much of anything, but not before he'd pointedly repeated his warning to them both. That... was yesterday. And so far, things had been almost sedate in The City, with no one who was connected to any of the city's criminal underworld being murdered.

The big man sat up in the bathtub and leaned out of the warm water just far enough to grab his bottle of beer. There was still a couple of swigs left in it, and his tongue was dry in the small room's humidity. With the bottle now in his hand, he slipped back beneath the surface of the warm water.

When he was once again warm and settled in his watery womb, he lifted the lip of the still-sweating bottle to his lips, draining what was left in one long pull. When the bottle had given up its last, he held it out over the side of the tub and blindly let it slip from his hand. He heard the clunk of it hitting the floor, thumping as it struck the bathmat and clattered on the tile. Luckily, it didn't break.

The apartment fell silent. Secord lay there beneath the water for a while, soaking his sore muscles and resting his rickety bones. He'd had a lot of injuries over the years—broken bones, contusions, a torn this, and a ripped that—and well... being him was getting rougher and rougher. These days, the pain was something he always carried around with him, like pocket change.

After a little while, he felt himself doze, his mind drifting like a kite in and out of consciousness. It was fantastic. His aggrieved body felt like it was suspended in a wet, soothing netherworld. His arms floated limply across the water's surface; hands suspended upon the fluid's surface tension. Soon, his troubled thoughts floated away, slowly cocooning themselves in a cottony salve of thermal contentment.

He roused abruptly and shook himself awake. He had been having one of those dreams in which he was falling, and he'd awoken with a start just before hitting bottom. He shook his head, finally deciding that it was probably for the best that he got out of the tub and went to bed. In a minute, he thought lazily. Laying here like this felt pretty terrific, and he saw no reason not to stay right where he was, for just a moment longer.

He turned his head and lethargically gazed down the length of the hallway. His field of vision was limited: just the shadow-enshrouded corridor and a small portion of the living room. He could still see the light coming from the kitchen and entryway though.

Then, to his surprise, one of the lights—the one in the entryway by the looks of it—abruptly went dark. At first, Secord thought that he must be tired, and that his eyes were simply playing tricks on him. But then, undeniably, the light in the kitchen also went out, and such thoughts evaporated like the steam coming off his rapidly cooling bathwater.

By now, Secord was already up and climbing out of the tub still wet. He planted his bare feet onto the tile, doing what he could to keep the sound of the splashing water to a minimum, but it was what it was. He stood to his full height, his body dripping water onto the floor. Moving his head around, he tried to use the mirror to get a better angle on what was happening in the rest of the apartment.

But of course, he couldn't see shit.

Then, a shadow suddenly passed in front of the living room lamp. There was no noise of movement heard anywhere in the apartment, just the sound of the traffic going by on the streets outside. But a second later, the living room light also went out and the apartment was plunged into darkness.

Secord crouched down onto the tile floor and waited for his eyes to become accustomed to the dark. From the Living Room, he could now make out someone moving around, slowly advancing across the carpeting toward the hall. The steps were hesitant, trying to be as silent as possible, but insistent.

Too bad it was a little too late for all of that.

Secord quickly looked around the bathroom, searching for something he might be able to use as a weapon with which to defend himself. Nothing. Whoever it was that was out there, it seemed pretty clear from the way they were moving around the apartment that their intentions weren't good ones.

Secord knew that he'd made sure to lock the door when he came in. He was sure of it. And he'd given the apartment the once-over when he'd first arrived. So, this person somehow either had gotten themselves a key, or they'd broken in. Any way you cut that up, it meant that they probably weren't here to tuck him into bed.

Not having much of a better choice, Secord snatched up the plunger from where it was sitting to the side of the toilet. He quickly tested the integrity of the wooden handle and was satisfied that it would hold for what he had in mind. He hoped.

In the dim light, his eye caught sight of his own naked reflection in the mirror, brandishing the toilet plunger like an ax, and he shook his head in dismay. Great, he thought, just great. If this intruder didn't laugh his ass off at the sight of him, Secord could beat him unconscious with his plumber's helper. Hefting the weapon like a hammer, he turned his attention toward the door, and to whoever might walk past the bathroom next.

After a second, Secord heard more hesitant footsteps on the carpet in the hallway. A heartbeat later, the snub-nosed barrel of a .38 revolver slid like a manta ray into view, its silver barrel glimmered in the faint light. Secord chose that moment to abruptly step out into the hallway, surprising the intruder. He then struck at the wrist holding the pistol, really putting his back into it. The flat of the plunger's wood struck bone and the .38 clattered to the ground, disappearing into the shadows on the floor behind them.

Secord immediately shoved the butt end of the plunger up and into the intruder's face. The wooden handle struck teeth and he heard the trespasser give a pained grunt in the dark. He felt the guy—and it was a guy, a very big guy, he could feel that now—go soft when he hit him, so he pushed him back down the hallway toward the main room of the apartment in order to give himself some room to work.

The two men spilled out into the living room like drunks. Secord shoved the big guy's bulk back toward the couch. Gun gone and now bleeding from his lip, the intruder quickly got up and turned to face Secord, his fists rising like hammers to defend himself.

"Giordano," Secord spat disgustedly as he suddenly recognized who it was.

The intruder's physicality immediately changed in response to hearing his own name. His back seemed to get a little straighter, and he stood there in that same greasy suit, rubbing his wrist, and glaring back at him. Through it all, the interloper didn't say a thing.

"Flip on the light," Secord ordered, pointing at the lamp with the plunger.

Giordano reached his unhurt arm out slowly and hit the switch on the wall with the flat of his hand. The room abruptly filled with light. The big Italian was standing near the far wall, to the left of the big window, by the television, holding his rapidly swelling wrist and glaring at Secord with contempt.

Secord knew how ridiculous he must have looked, standing there wet and naked in the middle of his living room, waving a toilet plunger in front of him like it was a machete, but he didn't much care. He'd put the pieces together for himself by now and the picture it showed wasn't one that the cop particularly liked.

It didn't take a genius to arrive at the conclusion that Valmont had sent this goon here to kill him... and that pissed him the fuck off. Giordano glared back at Secord defiantly, now standing with his hands on his hips. He sneered as he stared around the apartment.

"You live in a dump, cop," he finally said. "Christ, what a shithole."

Secord grinned. "Well, that just hurts my feelings, man. This is my home. I mean, is that anyway to talk?"

"Yeah, well, fuck your feelings."

"Speaking of being fucked... The way I look at it, you kinda fucked up here, Hoss," Secord said, smiling like an angry viper. Again, the Italian's presence here pretty much confirmed all of Secord's suspicions as to who was behind the growing pile of murder cases that were currently clogging his desk... and how far Valmont would go to keep things quiet. "I mean, what's your bougie boss gonna say?"

"About what?"

"About how much you suck at your job? Jesus Christ," he laughed and shook his head. "You'd think a guy with Valmont's backing could afford better. What, are you his nephew or something? I mean, look at that suit. What did you do, piss off your tailor? It's fuckin' pitiful."

Giordano looked down at his clothing and wiped at the corner of his mouth. Anger bubbled in his eyes when the back of his hand came away with a smear of blood on it. He glared at the naked man standing in front of him. He wanted to kick himself for losing the pistol. After all, he'd been sent here to do one simple job: cap the cop and get the hell out of Dodge. And somehow, it had all gone sour.

Giordano eyed the big cop standing in front of him, sizing him up. The Italian hadn't had to tune anyone up in a while, but he hated fuckin' cops, so… why the fuck not start with this one?

"Who says I've failed?" Giordano said menacingly, and he took a step forward.

"Buddy," Secord said with a wry grin, "you're about to make a gigantic mistake."

"Yeah, well…" the Italian replied dismissively, and then he was moving across the room.

Secord parried the first punch with his free hand as he struck Giordano in the leg with the meat of the plunger, hitting the tendon just behind the knee. The Italian's leg buckled, dropping him down onto one knee. For a second, Secord mused, he looked like he was about to propose. Somehow, he managed to counter with tight little hook punch that hit Secord in the floating ribs. Secord answered him with a back-fist to the jaw that sent the big guy sprawling onto the floor.

As he fell, the Italian suddenly scrambled away, obviously going for the gun in the hall. In response, Secord dove for the chair where he'd hung his jacket and holster and the .40 caliber Smith & Wesson. But just as he was grabbing ahold of the gun's grip, Giordano somehow managed to find the .38.

The Italian came up onto his feet, raising the pistol and circling the room. He grinned malevolently as he leveled the gun at Secord, and without hesitation, he fired. The gun going off in the small confines of the apartment was loud, incredibly loud. Both men winced as their ears immediately started ringing.

Secord only just managed to angle his body out of the way at the last second, turning the plane of his torso to one side. The bullet whizzed by, missing the meat of his shoulder by inches. It had been so close in fact, that he was sure he felt the wind from the bullet's passing as it went by.

Dumb fuckin' luck!

Secord turned to face his adversary. He was ready now. He had his gun, and he had a plan. He'd been in worse situations. And so… Secord unceremoniously kicked the big Italian in the chest, knocking him backward. Giordano's arms wheeled about wildly as he stumbled back a few steps.

The big man's back struck the window, his body weight sending cracks careening across the glass. He bounced off the damaged pane like a pool ball rebounding off a bumper and dropped to his knees. Secord was amazed at how fast he got up, especially for a guy his size. But then, just as he was coming to his feet and raising the .38 for a second shot, Secord beat him to the draw, rapidly shooting him a time or two in the center of his chest with the Smith & Wesson.

The force of the heavy bullets hit Giordano in the sternum like a kick from a pissed-off mule. The first bullet struck meat, lifting his body upward. Secord heard him grunt aloud as the slug dug deep. The Italian's eyes caught Secord's for a micro-instant. He blinked, and then the second bullet blew him through the damaged window. His heavy carcass arched back, crashing through the glass, and tumbling out of the shattered window like a thrown die. And the last thing Secord saw of the Italian as he disappeared into the night, were the soles of his polished shoes.

Secord stepped up to the shattered window and looked out over the shards that remained wedged in the frame. Down on the street far below, Giordano lay spread eagle down on the sidewalk, looking like he'd tried to leap into an Expressionist's painting. Almost immediately, the cop heard someone banging on the door.

"Secord!" a gruff, albeit familiar, voice shouted. "What the fuck is going on in there? Open up!"

Sawyer… the building's Super.

Sawyer was an old man who lived down the hall from Secord who lived on a military pension. He came over every now and then when the cop was at home to play chess. He was a good guy, but… bored. He had a habit—like a lot of older folks—of sticking his nose into everybody in the building's business. Again, good guy, well meaning, just kind of a mild pain in the ass.

Secord strode over and threw open the front door.

Sawyer was in the hall, his right hand raised as if he were about to knock on the door again. Seeing Secord standing in the doorway, the old codger suddenly got a dumbfounded look on his face. And that's when Secord realized that he was standing there still naked from the bath. Worse, he was naked and holding the smoking Smith & Wesson at his side.

Out of the corner of his eye, Secord noticed his neighbor, a broad-shouldered, middle-aged Latvian woman named Anastasia, brazenly staring at him… and his naked body.

"Call 911," the cop demanded as he slammed the door.

Secord sighed in annoyance. He needed to get dressed and he needed to get his ass down to the precinct. But what he really needed to do was to get his hands on this Valmont mutt. Like right now. And with the sounds of the commotion in the hall still echoing in his ears, he went to the bedroom to throw on some clothes.

STUCK

Another tale 'ripped from the headlines'… as something very similar to this incident actually did happen. I remember reading about it in an article in the local newspaper, and me being me, I made a few notes regarding the story's particulars, and moved on. I figured that I would one day return to it… or not. Apparently, I did.

And here we are…

As someone who suffers from a bit of claustrophobia, the idea of this story messed with me a little back when it was first coming together. I found myself having to stop periodically, so that I could take a step back to reclaim my writerly objectivity. Throughout though, the puzzle was, how to make the events work; both logistically and logically? It confounded me for a second, then I figured it out.

By the way, the main character's name in this is a riff on a pseudonym the great Italian genre actor, Giovanni Lombardo Radice (Lenzi's CANNIBAL FEROX, Fulci's CITY OF THE LIVING DEAD, Michele Soavi's THE CHURCH), once used: John Morghen. Why? I don't know. Like a lot of my narrative decisions, it just felt right at the time of its creation.

And so…

Jane Morghen came stumbling down the long flight of stairs that led to the basement of her college dorm, moving lazily, not in any obvious hurry. The hissing of her feet sliding on the unburnished concrete echoed throughout the industrial staircase, reverberating up and down the stairwell like whispers from a snake. It was Winter Break at the school and pretty late at night, so the building was virtually empty, most of the other students having gone off to spend the holidays with their families.

Not Jane, though. Her mom was gone, dead now five years, and Dad had decided that he and Shirley, the new wife, would be skipping the familial pleasantries this year and spending Thanksgiving in Switzerland instead of with her.

She… would be stuck here at school. Again.

It was okay, though. Jane and Shirley had never really gotten along. In truth, Jane saw the woman as a craven interloper and something of a bitch. And Dad, well… watching him kowtow to her was enough to put anybody off their holiday giblets.

Jane was here at the university studying for a degree in Biology, and she hadn't seen or heard much from dear old dad since, well… since he'd met Shirley and started his new franchise family. See, Dad worked for a pharmaceutical company and traveled a lot. He'd met Shirley in one of those Grief Therapy classes he'd gotten into after Mom passed. Shirley had lost a husband to cancer a few years back, and they just sort of gravitated toward one another, grief finding grief in an almost magnetic way.

A few months after they'd settled the last of Mom's affairs and Jane had returned to school, her father called to more or less let her know that he was making plans to remarry. While a little shocked at first by how quickly his plans for matrimony had come together, Jane had ultimately understood since she knew how lonely her father had been since Mom passed.

That all said, Jane was still not exactly willing to abdicate her mother's place in her heart—even though her father had given up her place in his bed—to this newer, and younger, model. Not now, and probably not ever.

Jane hopped down the last few stairs, carrying a wicker clothes basket in her arms. Inside, there was a small bottle of detergent sticking out of the crumpled laundry like a gravestone. She'd thrown in a Ziploc bag with a few dryer sheets tucked inside, along with her woefully out-of-date cell phone, and a tattered copy of Stephen King's 'SALEM'S LOT which lay tossed on top of the pile like the afterthought it was.

Jane came out of the stairwell and moved along the cold hallway that ran along the length of the building's basement. Her Vans shuffling on the concrete floor made the bottoms of her shoes sound like they were made of sandpaper. Every time she moved her feet, it was like the building itself was telling her to be quiet. And it was cold down here, and everything felt damp somehow. It was an atmosphere that made her feel even more lonely than she had in her apartment; like she was the only person left in the world.

These days, the building's basement was used almost exclusively for the storage of old furniture, cardboard boxes, and the other assorted things that people accumulated, but sometimes couldn't fit in their apartments. There was also a small room set aside as a laundry room with a single industrial washer and dryer installed as a convenience to the building's tenants. But the most important thing was that it was the only place on campus where a girl could do her laundry this late at night and feel safe.

Jane made her way down the hall and into the laundry room, her breath coming in short, ragged breaths. She'd hurried down from her apartment on the sixth floor and, due to her being a little overweight and not exactly the kind of person who did a lot of exercising, she was now out of breath.

It was a long way. At least it felt like it to her.

Without all the other students running around, the empty building had somehow grown infinitely creepier. Where there had once been hallways of bustling people, a dissonant soup of blaring music, and an almost constant commotion, now... there were only silent corridors and empty rooms, where it was all too easy to imagine any one of a number of frightening things reaching out from the shadows, reaching out... for you. As a result, she'd hustled to get down here as fast as she could.

Entering the small laundry room, she set her basket on a table that was pushed up against the far wall. Across the room, there was the single washer / dryer unit wedged into a small alcove. Both machines were large industrial models that were made of brushed metal and looked like they weighed a ton. A small trash bin sat on the floor nearby, empty save for an abandoned travel-sized bottle of fabric softener.

Setting the Ziploc, her phone, and the book onto the table, she went over and lifted the lid of the washer and began unceremoniously dumping her laundry into the machine's yawning opening. She fed six quarters into the coin slot, the coins disappearing from her fingers like a magic trick. Almost instantly, a stream of cold water started pouring into the washer's basin, slowly filling it.

Jane glanced down at her shirt, the black one—of course—with the Universal Studio's Halloween Horror Nights logo printed across the front. She had a tank top on underneath, and she briefly considered throwing the shirt into the churning water, but finally decided against it due to how cold the room was. She didn't bother to separate anything, since, with the state of her faded wardrobe, it didn't really matter. Everything she wore was a blend of faded black and tainted gray anyway, so what the hell?

When she had finished stuffing all of the basket's contents into the mouth of the washing machine, she grabbed the bottle of detergent from the table and free-poured a shot or two into the swirling bath. After that, she closed the lid.

Now that the laundry was going, she looked around the small room for someplace to sit while she waited. No sense walking all the way back up to her room, she thought, when she'd only have to change the wash load to the dryer in a few minutes. May as well just wait.

Since there were no chairs anywhere, she climbed up onto the table, grabbing her phone from where she'd set it. It wasn't easy for her to get up there as Jane was short and a little heavy-set, but she'd finally managed it. Once she'd gotten herself settled, wobbling from one butt cheek to the other, she dialed the number of her best friend in the world, Jordan.

She and Jordan had known one another for, well, ever, and had been more or less inseparable since junior high school. Over the years, they'd done just about everything together. Jordan still lived back home in Bakersfield, though, and was going to community college there, but they had plans for her to join Jane here in the city at the end of the semester. The two of them being apart like this was tough. On both of them. Luckily, they could still talk and text on the phone. The earpiece rang the number once, then twice, before someone finally picked up.

"Hey!" a tinny voice said from the phone's speaker.

"Hey, girl," Jane replied, happy to be talking to someone, happy to be talking to anyone, right now. As they spoke, her eyes drifted aimlessly around the room. And even though she was virtually alone in the building, she found that she reflexively kept her voice down to a hush for fear of being overheard. "Are you back home?"

The voice on the other end responded in a warm mezzo-soprano that made Jane immediately feel a little better about being stuck here at school. The voice was comfortable and warm, and it reminded her of home.

"Yeah, I got in about ten minutes ago."

"Anything exciting happening tonight?" Jane asked, surprised by how much she cared about the answer.

"Naw," Jordan replied lazily with a yawn. Her electronic voice curled up in Jane's ear and made itself comfortable. "We went to The Funhouse, but no one was really there. Barb got into a fight with Cliff and got drunk." She giggled a little. "Get this. She ended up getting sick all over Laura's car, and well… you know how Laura is about her ride."

They both laughed themselves to tears and it helped warm Jane's lonely heart, if only for a minute. Laura was another friend they'd both known forever. She'd worked all last summer at the Dairy Queen saving up to buy her cousin's beat-up, old Hyundai. Once it was hers, she took care of the damn thing like it was a museum piece. Jane could only imagine how pissed she must have been at someone puking in her baby. She'd undoubtedly been as mad as a wet cat.

"Was, uh… Phillip there?" Jane asked casually, trying hard not to sound like she was too interested.

Phillip was a guy Jane had had a crush on since they were all in school. Captain of the water polo team, B.M.O.C., Jane used to fantasize about their wedding while she was falling off to sleep in bed at night. She'd talked to him once at a school dance, but… so far, their great love affair was something of which only Jane remained aware.

"No," Jordan replied. "And you need to just get over yourself about that guy. You're at college now, kid. There must be nothing but hot guys just lining up to take you out."

Jane looked around the empty laundry room and had to rein in her sense of awe. "Oh, yeah… plenty. I'm having to swat them all off with a stick."

And that's how it went for the next half an hour or so, two lifelong friends just shooting the breeze and talking about nothing—and everything, and all things in between—while Jane's laundry chug-chugged its way through its wash cycle. Both girls were happy just to be reconnected with someone they cared about and had had in their lives forever. And just for a little while, Jane's despondency over feeling left behind by her dad was held at bay, and she didn't feel quite as lonely as she had before.

Finally, the washer's alarm went off, and Jane jumped a little in her skin.

"Oh, shoot," she said chuckling at her own nervousness. "That's my laundry."

"You're doing laundry?" Jordan asked incredulously. "This late?"

"Yeah, it's a ghost town here. Let me go switch this load to the dryer real quick and I'll call you right back."

"Okay, but give me a minute," Jordan replied, and it was easy to imagine her nodding her head. "I gotta go take Charley outside to pee. Stupid dog. He chewed up something of my dad's, and now he's in solitary confinement in the garage on Time Out."

They agreed to call one another back in ten minutes and hung up. Jane kept her phone in her hand as she jumped off the table. She grinned as she imagined the look on Laura's face as Barb started throwing-up her appetizers all over the Hyundai. She snickered and shook her head as she went over to move her clothes out of the washer.

There was a moment of awkward indecision as she realized that she would have to put the basket down before she could open the washer lid and get to her clothes. C'mon, Jane... get it together, she reprimanded herself as she leaned over and set the wicker onto the top of the dryer.

But then, just as she was setting the hamper down, she felt her phone suddenly slip from her grasp. She'd been holding the damn thing pinched between her thumb, index, and middle fingers while she gripped the rim of the basket with her ring finger and pinky. Suddenly, she felt it slip. All she could do was to watch impotently as the black rectangle struck the metal surface of the dryer and bounced off it like a rubber ball.

The phone arced into the air, turning on its axis, as if it were moving in slow motion. As the phone fell, tumbling end over end, it looked like something right out of a movie. Jane tried to reach for it as fast as she could but missed. And in the end, she could only groan and watch as it fell into the gap, disappearing into the shadows between the appliance and the wall.

"Damn it!" She banged her hand on the metal top of the dryer. "Shit! Shit! Shit!"

Jane immediately forgot all about her wet and waiting laundry. Forgot about her dad leaving her here alone to go to fuckin' Switzerland. Forgot about that bitch Shirley! She even forgot about Jordan and calling her back. This was her phone. This was her life! Without it, she had no way of calling out, no way to text, well... anybody! Shit, no way to get onto the fucking Internet! Not to mention that she didn't have the money to replace it.

"Damn it!"

She hastily put the empty laundry basket back onto the table. She was so angry that she had to stop herself from throwing the damn thing across the room. How stupid could she be?

Moving to the right side of the dryer, she looked deep into the darkness between the appliance and the wall. She squinted her eyes and searched for some small sign of her phone. All she saw there though was the endless blackness that ran along the baseboard.

She dropped down onto her knees on the floor like she was praying (and in a weird way she kind of was). She pushed her right arm into the shadows, waving it around frantically. She couldn't help but imagine all the creepy things—like bugs and spiders and worms and, ugh... even snakes—that could be waiting for her exposed hand as she foraged around in the dark for her phone.

Then, just for a second, she imagined what it would feel like if another hand were to suddenly reach out of the blackness and grip her own. Somehow, she just knew that it would be as cold as a corpse and probably wet. It took all she had not to retract her arm from the crevice.

However, just as she was about to give up, she heard a muffled buzzing coming from somewhere behind the dryer: Jordan... calling her back. With renewed vigor, she pushed her face into the thin, dark space, pressing her cheeks between the flat metal of the dryer and the drywall. Squinting and trying to focus, she was able to just see a sliver of light coming from the floor, over near the molding. She moved her arm toward it, momentarily catching sight of the dim illumination as it reflected off her fingernails.

Shit, it was so close.

She gave up suddenly and climbed back onto her feet exasperated. She used the stability of the heavy dryer to pull herself upright. Once she was standing, she leaned over the appliance again and repositioned herself, directing her arm back down into the open space where she knew her phone was. Looking down, she could just make out the fucking thing on the floor, just behind the dryer.

Pushing her body into the crack as far as it would comfortably go, she felt a rapidly growing sense of frustration when the tips of her fingers were only able to brush up against the polished glass of the phone's face. If she could only get a little bit closer, maybe a quarter of an inch at best, she could slap it back toward her, and she could get it.

"God damn it," she hissed. "Just another inch or so..."

Jane strained to reach that little bit further, wedging her torso even deeper into the gap. She felt the hard metal of the dryer push painfully into one of her boobs, so she wriggled a little to get it to stop. She stared down at the ghost of her phone, like she was lost at sea, and someone was about to toss it to her as a life preserver. She grunted from the effort.

Christ, she could almost get it... almost.

Her fingers bumped up against the case again and she could just feel the buttons on the side sticking up and pushing into the pads of her fingers like Braille. If she could only just get that little bit closer, she thought. Raising herself up onto her tiptoes, she gave it one last push.

Just then, just as she was getting a workable grip on the side of the phone and had begun to pull it up, she felt the toes of her worn shoes slip on the concrete floor. She remembered leaving her place and grabbing her old pair of Vans that were by the front door, their soles rubbed smooth by years of wear, and throwing them on as an afterthought. She hadn't wanted to go all the way to her bedroom to get a decent pair, and these were just handy. She remembered putting them on thinking she was only going down the laundry room for a minute. It wasn't like anything bad was going to happen.

Her feet came up and off the floor, like a quarterback diving the last few yards to make it over the goal line. Her body seemed to float there in the air for a second or two. And then, she felt her torso and hips become painfully pinched between the wall and the dryer.

Gravity immediately took hold of her, and she felt herself pulled inexorably toward the ground. Her increased weight worked against her, dragging her down deeper and deeper into the gap, and wedging her body into the confined space like a cork. Jane's breath was kicked out of her in a painful-sounding whoosh, and she made a guttural grunting noise as her body scooted down the wall to a stop. Then, there was nothing; just the disquieting silence of the dorm's basement, closing in around her like a tomb.

Jane groaned aloud, and her voice sounded labored and out of breath within the small space around her. She did what she could to reach down with her one arm. Somehow, she managed to touch the floor, supporting a little of her body weight on her one hand. Doing this relieved some of the pressure on her chest and it made it a little easier for her to breathe. Her ribs still felt like they were being pressed in a vice, though, and she knew she had to figure a way out of this fast. God forbid anyone coming in and finding her like this.

As she struggled to get some sort of foothold, the tips of her shoes scraped against the floor futilely, like the toes of a man being hanged. An abrupt wave of tears rose like a tide within her, but she managed to hold them off. Getting emotional wasn't going to help anything. The problem was that every time she tried to move and free herself, her body weight would pull down on her, wedging her even tighter into the gap.

"Fuck," she managed to grunt.

The whole thing felt like she'd fallen into some kind of quicksand and was slowly slipping deeper and deeper into its soup no matter what she did. And the longer she was stuck here, she noticed, the harder it was for her to catch her breath. She wasn't completely panicking quite yet, but... she could sense fear's fire slowly starting to catch in the dry brush of her brain.

But it was clear to her that her biggest concern was how much her chest hurt, and how hard it was for her to take in any air. She could feel the hard drywall pressing against her back, as well as the cold metal surface of the dryer pushing into her. Together, they were scissoring her ribcage and compressing her lungs. With both sides tightening around her chest, it felt like a giant snake constricting her, making it damn near impossible for her to move.

Okay, she thought, her panic rapidly intensifying, this was getting serious.

Her first instinct was to not call out. Christ, how embarrassing would that be, right? She knew, from the bullying bullshit she'd already had to deal with in this school, how cruel people could be. She thought back to how she'd recently told a classmate about a crush she'd had and how that person had instantly betrayed the confidence. The boy found out and, ugh... it was awful. But the more trapped she now felt, the more she figured, screw it. It didn't really matter. She really needed help.

"Lord, please don't let me die in such a stupid way," she whispered to herself, and her words echoed hollowly within the small laundry room. She took as big of a breath as she could and called out weakly. "Hello?"

Remaining still, she silently waited—prayed—for a response, any response, to come. But there was nothing; only the electric thrum coming from the fluorescent lights and air conditioning ducts overhead.

Jane finally decided to take a chance and tried to move a little, bending at her waist. She figured... if she could just get one leg underneath her, she could support more of her bodyweight, and that would make it at least easier for her to get a breath. She could sort out the rest of it once she felt more stable.

But as she drew her right leg up, her center of gravity radically shifted, causing her to pitch forward. As a result, her head was driven deeper into the crack, pushing her head down lower than her butt, leaving her ass well over her tea kettle. Once again, both of her feet began kicking wildly. She dropped unexpectedly, and as she did, her forehead slammed into the cement with enough force that it made the room spin for a second.

Then, the lights went out.

When Jane woke up and her bruised head finally started to clear, she groaned aloud and tried to calculate how long she'd been unconscious. She could feel a painful lump on her forehead, and she now had a splitting headache, so she knew she'd hit herself pretty hard.

Hard enough to knock herself out, apparently. But again, for how long?

She turned her torso a bit in an effort to relieve more of the strain, and felt her body slip another inch or two downward. Now, it was even more difficult for her to breathe. She felt like she was at the bottom of the ocean and trying to get a breath through a drinking straw. Feeling her panic rise like a firework into her mental sky, she drew as big of a breath as she could and tried calling out one again.

"Hellooooooo?" Another stuttering, feeble breath. "Pleeeeeease!?!"

She listened intently as the sound of her voice echoed down the empty hall outside. She waited, listening again for someone—anyone—to hear and answer her. But, just like the last time, there was nothing, only the low hum of the empty building.

She did what she could to draw another breath but found that it was getting progressively more and more difficult to do so; much harder than it had been before. Unable to help herself and barely able to breathe, Jane finally started to cry. Frustration welled up within her like the molten lava of a volcano and, well… she just couldn't stop it this time.

What was she going to do?

She tried to imagine what she must look like, wedged upside down between the dryer and the wall like this. She was essentially standing on her head, with her ass and her feet poking up in the air like the legs of an abandoned doll. It'd be funny if it weren't becoming so goddam serious.

Jane closed her eyes and suddenly realized how loud her heartbeat sounded in her ears. It was this intense squishing sound—like pssh, pssh, pssh—that started behind her eyes and coursed like battery acid throughout the throbbing meat of her brain.

When she opened her eyes once again, she sensed that time had passed, that she'd lost consciousness again. She couldn't be sure how long she'd been asleep, but it felt like it had been a while. Blinking her eyes, she struggled to call out again.

"Heee-eeelp!" she rasped, but with the way her chest was being squished, her voice came out of her mouth as only a hoarse croak. Silently, she wept and moaned, "He-he-heeeelp me, pleeease!"

Jane tried to calm her panic as she did what she could to take her next few breaths. Then, she slipped another inch. Alarmingly, she now discovered that, due to the increasing pressure on her torso, she was unable to expand her ribcage enough to get even a sip of air. She reflexively tried panting like a dog, drawing little cups of oxygen into her lungs to compensate for the gallons her body was currently demanding. Rapidly, she was learning that it wasn't enough. Her head was going light. And soon, the only thing she could focus on was the reverberating drumbeat going on deep within her skull.

She closed her eyes.

And things went black again.

When she awoke, she took a second and rested her head against the icy cool of the concrete. Her eyes fell closed sleepily. The cold surface felt good against the hot skin of her forehead, and she rested there for a minute in respite. Her breath was coming in shorter and shorter pants now as her weight continued to press down on her. The load was slowly, but effectively, crushing her lungs into accordions within the birdcage walls of her chest.

This was all so stupid, she thought. And it had all happened so fast. One minute she was just doing her laundry and talking on the phone. And the next…

She opened her eyes and found herself staring into the blackness that lay behind the dryer. Suddenly, she saw something laying on the ground just a few inches from her face, like a thin black sliver of hope. Her phone. She couldn't help but chuckle at the irony.

The screen suddenly lit up and she could see that the caller I.D. read 'Dad.' Her instinct was to do whatever she could to grab it, to cry to her father and plead for his help. But… her thinking had by grown as cloudy as cotton candy, and her dexterity was not what it had once been.

And besides, her limbs were more or less useless now, twisted behind her, and starved for the life-giving oxygen they so desperately needed to save her. The call rang twice, then the screen returned to black once again, and the only thing Jane was able to do was hang there as the darkness expanded, enveloping her, and claiming her for its own.

THE SOMNAMBULIST

For many years, I worked in what is known as Sleep Medicine after I left funeral service. It was a good gig, but a fairly odd one. If you've ever gone in for a sleep study, you can attest to just how awkward and invasive it can be with all the wires pasted to your head, the elastic belts around your chest, the hoses up your nose, and the uncomfortable intimacy of being tucked into bed and watched for the night by a complete stranger.

Now, imagine working there…

The long dark hallways of Our Lady of Benevolent Care Hospital were empty as Ford Meyer arrived for his overnight shift. Ford worked up on the ninth floor of the hospital in a small sleep lab as a Polysomnographic Technologist, or what most people just referred to as a Sleep Tech. There, his duties included the performance of diagnostic sleep studies, sleep latency tests, and narcolepsy protocols that helped physicians diagnose any parasomnias or sleep disturbances in the patient.

Ford had worked at the hospital for a good while now, a few years at least. He remembered first hearing about the gig from a Respiratory Therapist friend of his that he knew from surfing. This friend knew that Ford had his proper accreditation for the position, so he'd mentioned that the hospital was looking for a tech.

Ford applied, and he'd been here ever since.

The lab mostly took care of sleep apnea patients: people who repeatedly stopped breathing during the night. They also performed a number of studies for drug companies, for sleeping pills and other medications that had already been designated as safe for humans. For these studies, the administration office kept a roster of students, semi-homeless, and other civic-minded citizens who routinely acted as research subjects for a modest per diem.

There were four beds to the lab, but to be honest, they rarely needed all of them. The town they were in wasn't a big one, so there were only so many people that could potentially be scheduled; only so many fish in the barrel, so to speak. The work was steady though, and it wasn't particularly stressful. And again, the drug studies helped keep the lights turned on.

Take tonight for example…

Ford had been at home, chilling on his day off, when his phone started buzzing across the table like a mad hornet. He'd almost let the call go to voicemail, but then he saw that the call was from work and decided to pick it up. His boss, a neurologist named George Sylvester, was calling and he said that they needed Ford to come in for the night. A patient from Dr. Rollins' depression protocol had been scheduled for a Baseline Study and the other tech—a longtime friend of Ford's named Mary Gorshin—called in sick.

Normally, Ford would have said no, and as a union employee, that was his right. He liked his days off and usually defended them pretty ardently. However, he'd also made some plans for a little ski vacation in a couple of weeks, and well… the extra cash proved too tempting to pass up.

And so here he was, walking down a long, darkened corridor as he mentally prepared himself for the impending twelve-hour workday. The sleep techs here were scheduled for long, oftentimes boring, shifts that usually lasted ten to twelve hours. The lab's unstated policy was that the person caring for you when you got here, was the same person who was there when you got up and left. Dr. Sylvester said that it brought 'closure.' The nice thing about that was that techs only had to work three days a week to make 'full time' and get them all-important bennies.

He turned the corner and pushed through the set of double doors that led into the sleep lab. He had on his usual uniform of green hospital scrubs and a pair of slip-on boat shoes. As he entered the lab's Control Room, he dropped a black and neon green backpack that he had slung like a potato sack over his right shoulder onto one of the two office chairs

Closing the door behind him so that he could get to the light switches on the wall, he flicked all six of them up, and banks of fluorescent lights began coming on up and down the hallway. He pulled a set of keys from his front pants pocket and used them to open the File Room door.

In the small room, there was a long metal credenza and a bin for recycled paper. The cabinet had drawers that you pulled out. In each, there were an array of prepared patient files in manila Pendaflex folders. On top of the metal cabinet lay a single folder with the name

'Bose, Sylvia—F PN: 43910' written on it in Sharpie. Ford snatched it up and returned to the main part of the Control Room, casually tossing the folder onto the desk.

He took a minute and unloaded his lunch from his backpack, putting his sandwich and soda into the small mini fridge sitting under the long table on the far side of the room. While he was at it, he pulled the book he was reading out as well and put it next to the computer he'd be using that night. Pulling a chair over, he sat down and slapped the Space Bar on the keyboard. The computer screen in front of him flickered to stuttering life.

After he'd input all the patient's preliminary information into the computer, he set the girl's patient file on top of his book for later. He knew he had to 'chart' on her every thirty minutes, so he wanted to keep the file handy.

Normally, the Department didn't like male techs to do one patient study nights with a female patient. The idea of a lone male and a single woman in this admittedly intimate situation was too rife for accusation (and, by extension of that, litigation). As a result, they'd scheduled Mary Gorshin to conduct the girl's study.

But again... she'd called out sick.

"Hello?" a young woman's voice coming from the hallway abruptly broke his reverie.

Ford looked up and saw a young girl with really short hair standing in the doorway. She was maybe fifteen years or so younger than him, and she was wearing a worn black leather jacket, a dark tee, and a roughed-up pair of jeans. The hems of her pant legs were stuffed into a pair of worn Doc Martens. There was a small, stretched-to-bulging plastic bag, like the kind you got at the grocery store, hanging from her hand like a medieval mace.

"Hey," he said in his most friendly voice. "You Sylvia?"

The girl nodded shyly, but kept her eyes pointed down toward the ground instead of meeting his gaze. Her manner seemed wary, skittish, like she was uncomfortable in her own skin. As almost an afterthought, she began nervously swinging the bag in her hand back and forth, letting its bulk strike her thigh first, and then letting it swing around to bump her butt.

"Okay, cool," Ford said, standing up and walking into the hallway. "Follow me, then. I can take you to your room." He proceeded down the corridor, and she followed along obediently after him. "This sleep study... is not near as bad as you've probably imagined. It's super chill and, other than putting some goop in your hair, you'll hopefully just have a good night's sleep in this weird hotel room."

The girl nodded again shyly and continued to follow him down the hallway to the room. As they went, he noticed that she kept nervously twisting the plastic bag and its contents in her hands. It was like she was trying to wring water from a rag with a Lady Macbethian obsession.

Midway down the corridor, Ford stopped in front of a room with a small placard glued to the wall that read 'Room 614.' He pulled his keys out and used the Master to open it. He angled his hand around and flipped the light switch on, and they both entered the room.

What was revealed did indeed look like a motel room. There was a queen-sized bed, a small table and chair, and a flat screen TV mounted on one wall. The décor was intentionally nondescript, like it had been designed so as to not offend, well… anyone. Ford stepped aside to let the girl—Sylvia, he reminded himself—go in and make herself comfortable.

"So, we're running what's called a Baseline Study here tonight, Sylvia," Ford started to explain. "I'm sure your doctor has gone over it with you, but basically, I'll be attaching a bunch of wires and doodads to you and letting you try and, hopefully, sleep. It's all pretty straightforward."

The girl nodded and did her best to put on a brave, albeit nervous, smile. "O-okay."

"If you need to use the restroom at any point during the night, though, you're gonna need to callout for me to come unhook you as you'll pretty much be wired to the wall."

Sylvia looked a little horrified. "You're going to watch me as I sleep?"

Ford smiled. He'd heard the concern many times before and had an answer at the ready. "Sort of. See, we record audio and video of you so that the doctor can see or hear if you do anything of interest. I only really look at the video if something happens on the tracing, something I think the doc will ask about." He thought about it a minute and decided to be completely honest. "Or when I chart on you for your file."

"Like what would be of interest?" she asked as she slowly walked over to the bed and set her strangled bag onto it.

Ford laughed. "You'd be shocked by what some people do when they're asleep. Some talk. Some wave their arms around. I had a guy once conduct an orchestra while he was completely out. Some get up and try and go for walks. We do a PTSD protocol where folks get into fist fights with invisible opponents while they're completely asleep… which, as you might imagine, can be a problem for an unsuspecting bed partner."

Ford chuckled at his attempt to lighten the mood but stopped when he noticed the girl's blank expression as she gingerly sat down onto the bed. A lot of patients were nervous like this, having imagined all kinds of Torquemadian tortures being inflicted upon them when they were at their most vulnerable. Ford knew from his experience that the only way to get them to relax was to explain everything as best he could and try and make it seem like it was all not a big deal. Which, to be honest, it really wasn't.

Ford started off by taking the girl's heart rate and blood pressure, jotting the numbers down onto the palm of his hand with his pen. He then explained that she'd need to get ready for bed and try to relax. "I can get you an Ambien if you feel like you're gonna have trouble getting to sleep, but you need to let me know as soon as possible, so I can order it up from the Pharmacy."

The girl shook her head no. "I should be fine. Getting to sleep has never really been my problem."

"Cool, cool," Ford replied, staying on task. "Then, I'll be back to hook you up in, oh… about an hour. Lights out is planned for 10 PM for insurance reasons. At least that's the time I need to start the tracing. You can take however long you need to actually fall asleep."

Sylvia nodded her understanding as she continued to look around the room. "What am I supposed to do until you come back?"

Ford went over to the small table and picked up the room's TV remote control. He held it up and wagged it at her, smiling. Gently tossing it to her, he strolled back to the door. She caught it, but once again did everything she could to avoid his gaze.

"Any, uh… any other questions?" he asked as he took hold of the doorknob.

Sylvia shook her head, but she continued to stare only at the TV screen.

Ford thought that she looked nervous, sorta spacey, and he wondered if he shouldn't just go ahead and order that Ambien anyway. He could always return it in the morning if she didn't want it.

"Okay, cool," Ford finally replied. "See you in about an hour, then." When she didn't answer, he shrugged and left, gently closing the door behind him.

Walking back to the Control Room, he made a mental note to check the girl's file to see if there was anything in it that he should be concerned with. He hadn't seen any red flags when he first peeked at it, like a seizure disorder or night terrors. Things that were usually called out. She clearly had some social anxiety issues. He'd noticed the way she never seemed to look him in the eye when he talked to her, and the way she'd damn near strangled that plastic bag. But at least she was able to get around on her own, and at least she looked clean... which was a plus. A lot of the patients who came in here weren't.

Once he'd gotten back to his desk, he quickly inputted the rest of Sylvia's Vitals into the computer. He jotted down a note about how she appeared to be in good health and wasn't in any sort of visible distress or discomfort for his notes. Standard stuff.

When he was done doing all of that, he checked a metal clipboard that was hanging on the wall near the File Room door for any new memos or correspondence from his bosses. Day Shift and Night Shift rarely ever saw one another, and the clipboard was oftentimes their sole means of communication. For better or worse. Seeing nothing new, he sat back down at the computer and started writing up the beginning of his Daily Report.

The hour passed...

Ford looked away from the computer, rubbing his eyes and checking the clock. It read 7:55. He reached over and switched on the Room Intercom, so that he could speak with his patient—Sylvia, he needed to remember that—and not have to walk all the way back down to the room. The screen faded into view like a desert mirage, appearing in undulating shades of black and white. Things cleared, and he was finally able to see her sitting cross-legged on the bed, looking intently at the screen of her phone. He flicked the Talk button once in order to alert her that the Intercom had been turned on.

Then, he said gently, "Hey, Sylvia?"

He saw her jump on the monitor and immediately felt bad for startling her.

"Y-Yeah?" she responded as she looked around the room nervously.

"Up here," he said, and he tried to sound warm, or at least comforting. "In the ceiling... the camera."

She looked up in the direction from where the sound of his voice was coming and saw the lens of the camera that was mounted there. She visibly relaxed and returned to the multitude of mysteries to be found in her telephone.

"Yeah, sorry about that," Ford said. "Didn't mean to startle you."

She smiled up at him. "It's okay. You just surprised me."

"Yeah, again, sorry... but I'll be in to hook you up in a minute, so if you need to use the restroom or anything, go ahead and do it now. I'll be there in, let's say, ten minutes, okay?"

Sylvia nodded and began climbing off of the bed. "Okay. It should only take me a second." She went to the bathroom and walked inside, closing the door behind her.

Ten minutes or so later, Ford was headed back down the hallway toward his patient's room. When he left the Control Room, he'd grabbed the small plastic fishing-tackle box each tech kept full of replacement leads, Q-Tips, respiratory belts, EEG paste, and the gritty scrub they used to clean the surface of the patient's skin. The wires he needed were kept bundled together at the bottom of the case. There was also a computer interface there—called a headbox—and a few oximeter probes to document the patient's blood oxygen levels throughout the night. When he got back to Sylvia's room, he knocked on the door twice before gently opening it and poking his head inside.

Sylvia was back on the bed, sitting cross-legged in the middle of the mattress. She was wearing a pair of loose-fitting pajamas that looked like they were made for a kid. The outfit was black and had a never-ending conga line of bone-white skeletons dancing in circles on them. Small images of laughing orange pumpkins punctuated the fabric and green glowing eyes stared back at him with a malevolent intent out of the blackness of the fabric.

"Hey," Ford said.

"Hey," she replied softly.

"Okay if I come in?"

"Sure."

Ford entered the room, making sure to leave the door open for propriety's sake. He carefully pulled the chair over from the table for her to sit in. Immediately, he went to work, getting her to stand near the seat, and first running long pairs of wires into her shirt, then down into the legs of her pants, and out of the bottom hem near her feet. These, he'd later attached to her shins to document whether she moved her legs while she slept. He then carefully wrapped two elastic belts, one around her chest and the other around her abdomen, to monitor the effort of her breathing.

"Go ahead and sit down," he said, directing her to the chair.

She complied, fidgeting until she'd made herself more or less comfortable. It was the first time Ford got a real look at her. She was young, maybe in her early twenties, and attractive despite how short she'd chopped her hair. She had what his mom used to call 'good bone structure' with big eyes and full lips.

The first thing Ford did was to attach the leg wires to each of her shins with small adhesive pads that were usually used to measure EKG. He then connected two more of the wires to her chest, up near her collarbones, in the same way in order to measure her heart rate and electrocardiogram. That done, he moved on to her head.

He started by connecting a number of wires to her face using small strips of tape. For her scalp, across her skull, he used a compress of EEG paste and thin gauze that matted with the hair to help it stay in place. Once you got the hang of how to apply it, the wires stayed in place the whole night, believe it or not. All in all, there were a dozen or so wires placed in a very specific matrix across her head.

When he was finally done, he began carefully plugging each wire into its proscribed place in the headbox he pulled from his kit. Finally, he set a medical cannula and another small sensor underneath her nose, taping them into place by pinning it to her cheeks with more strips of tape. He plugged the last two sensors into the headbox and hung the entire contraption around the girl's neck like a giant medallion. A rat's nest of wires stuck out from it.

And through it all, Sylvia sat very still in her chair. She was responsive. She'd move when asked. But she managed to keep her vocal responses to mostly yes or no while doing so. Other than that, she was as quiet as a mouse.

When Ford felt like the hookup was not only done, but secure enough to last the night, he began cleaning up. Since patients were going to sleep in this get-up, he'd learned the hard way over the years that it was worth spending a few extra minutes during this part of the study to make sure things were secure, rather than trying to troubleshoot problems while the patient was already in bed and—hopefully—getting back to sleep.

"Okay, that's it," he finally said. "I'll be back at ten to plug you in and let you get to sleep. Take any medications you have now. Brush your teeth… whatever you need to do. Are there any questions?"

Sylvia looked up at him unhappily. "And I'm supposed to sleep with all this stuff on?"

Ford chuckled as he moved toward the door. "Everyone says that. And everyone gets to sleep—eventually."

"So, uh…" She thought about what she was going to ask for a moment. "Will this help them figure out what's wrong with me?"

Ford shrugged since he genuinely didn't know. "I'm sorry. They don't really fill us in on too much regarding you guys. You come for a test. I test you. That's it. I try not to dig any deeper than that, y'know?" He smiled warmly. "Besides, there are laws… and most things I don't need to know. Your doctor will go over your results with you though once he's had a chance to look at them." He clicked his tongue. "I'm afraid that's all I can really say."

Sylvia smiled but her gaze drifted off disappointedly. "That's okay," she said with a resigned shrug. "No one seems to know anything anyway. Nothing they do seems to help."

Ford nodded in sympathy. He'd heard things like this from a lot of patients, that tone of hopeless resignation. It was like they'd given themselves over to whatever was happening and were willing to do whatever it was that their doctors were telling them; trusting that they knew best.

"Okay, then... ten o'clock?"

Sylvia smiled and her wet eyes caught a sliver of light and held it for a heartbeat. "Ten o'clock."

Ford smiled, nodded, and walked out of the room, slowly closing the door behind him.

Back in the Control Room, Ford was sitting in his chair, taking a closer look at the girl's chart. Much to his surprise, there wasn't a lot here. She must have been one of Dr. Sylvester's new patients, he mused. What he did find in the file though told a pretty specific story.

Sylvia Bose had suffered from insomnia ever since she was a child. From the notes her General Practitioner left, it seemed clear that she simply did not sleep a lot as a kid. As a result, she grew up thin, frail, and prone to bouts of depression.

But then, just around the time she was entering puberty, things seemed to settle down and she began to experience long periods of nothing but somnolence, sleeping sometimes twelve to fourteen hours a day for weeks at a time. Not unexpectedly, more depression and social issues at school commenced not too soon after.

Ford picked up his phone and opened his Facebook application. Feeling a little like a stalker, he searched Sylvia's name and, after some poking around, found her personal page. Like her patient file, there wasn't much there, just some basic information and a few photos of her and some friends at a concert. Everything else was either YouTube links to videos by Goth or Metal bands, and pictures of cats.

In one of the concert photos, she was standing next to a boy, his arm draped possessively over her shoulder. She stood next to him indulgently, staring down the barrel of the camera with those eyes. Ford idly wondered to himself if she was happy when the photo was taken. Or was she just acting like it, playing a part?

He shook his head to clear it. Checking the clock, he saw that he still had thirty-five minutes before he needed to put her to bed. Not having anything else to do, he decided to do a little reading while he waited for the time to pass.

As he picked up his book—Aldous Huxley's THE DOORS TO PERCEPTION—he glanced up at the camera again to check on Sylvia. Unsurprisingly, she was still sitting where he left her, in the middle of the bed, focused on the phone she held like an oracle in her hands. He turned to where his bookmark was in the book and picked up reading where he'd left off.

The alarm on Ford's watch went off at 9:55, reminding him that it was time to put his patient to bed. He glanced up at the camera and saw that the girl hadn't moved since the last time he'd checked. She was still sitting in the exact same place he'd last seen her: cross-legged in the middle of the mattress, forever staring into her phone.

He hit the button on the Intercom. "Hey, Sylvia?"

"Yeah?" She looked directly up at the camera.

"It's almost ten," he said cordially. "I'll be in there inna second and we can get you horizontal. Sound good?"

She nodded her head, and drew in a deep, resigned breath. "Sure."

"Go ahead and try the bathroom one last time, okay? It'll keep you from needing to use it later."

"K."

He watched her on the monitor as she got up from the bed without a lot of hurry. She sort of ambled over to the bathroom, casually tossing her phone onto the bed as she carefully closed the door behind her.

Ford got up from his chair and stretched his back, setting his book onto the counter. Time to make the doughnuts, he thought to himself as he left the Control Room and walked into the hall. He took his time going down to Sylvia's room. He wanted to give the girl enough time to finish whatever she was doing in the bathroom before getting started for the night.

His hope was that he'd plug the headbox in, run through the necessary Bio-Calibrations with her, and be back to reading his book in no time. It'd be an easy night for him after that, until the girl left in the morning. As it turned out, watching people sleep wasn't the white-knuckle thrill ride everyone thought it was.

Ford chuckled to himself as he knocked on the door. He entered the patient room carefully, opening it slowly in order to give Sylvia time to get into bed. Thankfully, she was already under the covers, lying on her back, when he came in. She looked up at him, blankets pulled up under her chin, like a child waiting to be tucked in.

"Okay, pardon me," Ford said as he slowly reached out for the headbox that was still hanging around her neck. He gently lifted the lanyard over her head and hung the contraption on a hook on the nightstand. A thick computer cable hung like a corpse from the headboard. "I just need to plug this in, and we are good to go."

"Okay," she said, and the sound of her voice was muffled by the blankets pulled up over her mouth.

Ford extended the cable from where it was hanging and inserted its end into the headbox. He jiggled them both to make sure they were firmly connected. The last thing he needed was to have them become disconnected during the night. When he was sure everything was seated and secure, he rehung it on the nightstand, and looked down at the girl.

"Now remember," Ford explained as he pointed to the headbox. "This, and all the leads I put on you, means you're pretty much wired to the wall. So, don't go getting up without calling out and letting me know. I can hear you through the Intercom if you need anything or want to go the bathroom. Just holler and I'll get back in here as fast as I can. Cool?" He looked at her like he expected her to say something.

She nodded her head silently instead.

"Okay, so you just lie here still, and I'll be talking to you from the ceiling again in a second. I have a list of little things I need you to do, like look up and look down, blink, that sort of thing. It's to make sure everything is working properly."

Once again, Sylvia nodded her closely-shorn head without saying anything.

"Okay, talk to you inna second," and Ford walked out of the room, turning the lights off, and closing the door behind him.

Back in the Control Room, Ford used the mouse to click on the button that started the Study recording. Instantly, a matrix of scribbles appeared in a window on the screen. Squiggly black lines started slowly tracing their way across the graph. Soon, some of them—the ones that showed Sylvia's breathing—fell into slowly-undulating waves. The others—EEG and muscle tension channels primarily—continued to scratch their frenetic way onto the graph.

The documentation and diagnosis of Sleep was a funny thing. It utilized a combination of physical data that, when properly put together, brought to light a clear picture of what was going on with the patient as they slept. EEG tracked their brain function and helped show, by how the tracing looked, what stage of sleep the person was in. EKG, pulse oximetry, and heart rate all had their own channels and tracked Life. Muscle tension in the face and legs were documented as well. Each signal worked in concert to tell the tech (and, by extension of that, the doctor) a little bit more as to the patient's overall condition.

It took time to learn the science of it all, but, once you did, it was like looking at a snapshot.

Ford hit the button on the Intercom. "Okay Sylvia. Can you hear me?"

The girl in the bed on the monitor raised her hand into the air and gave a hearty thumbs-up. She lowered it, laying both arms to her side. "Shoot, sorry... Yes, I can hear you."

"That's okay," he chuckled. "Remember, I have a camera on you, so I can always see you. Ready to get started?"

Her flickering image gave another thumbs-up.

And for the next few minutes, Ford ran down his list of pre-prescribed physical actions that showed whoever it was that might access the record later that all the leads were connected and working. He had her look up, look down, left, right, bite down, wiggle her toes, breathe in, breathe out... all dictated by the study's protocol.

When he was done, he wished Sylvia a good night, marked 'Lights Out' on the computer, and shut off the microphone on the intercom. He waited for a few minutes, observing the monitor, until he saw the girl roll over onto her side. Marking her new body position in the computer, he looked the tracing over and, all too soon, recognized the rolling eye movements that told him that she was falling asleep.

Ford clapped his hands together. "Okey-doke, time for lunch," he pronounced to the empty room.

Now that his patient was in bed, Ford's night got a whole lot easier. From here, all he had to do was keep an eye on her (and the computer tracing), get her up should she need to use the bathroom, and then finally unhook her in the morning. Once she was showered, and on her way, he was done. After so many years of doing it, it was cake.

The next few hours passed without incident. Ford ate his lunch, read a little more of his book, and started in on the tech report he had to include in Sylvia's file at the end of his shift. Things were so slow that he even spent more time than he should have checking his social media and playing a game on his phone.

Every so often, though, he would raise his gaze to check on the camera monitor to see if the girl had moved or sat up. Thankfully, she stayed on her right side, her EEG moving effortlessly through long periods of Stage 2 sleep. He saw a multitude of tight, little scribbles called 'spindles' and the spiky 'k-complexes' that signaled deep sleep amidst the other thin black lines of her graph.

His watch alarm suddenly went off, reminding him that it was time for him to once again chart on his patient. Techs were responsible for making these small notes every half hour which gave an update on the patient's condition. The notes helped create a timeline for the doctors (and proved the tech wasn't himself sleeping) in case anything ever went wrong. They never did, but… you never knew.

He wrote in the file that the patient continued to be on her right side and was in Stage 2 sleep. He noted the rate of her respiration and her oximetry. Then, as he was looking at her brain activity, he noticed the familiar 'sawtooth' pattern that signaled that she was going into her first REM cycle.

REM (or 'rapid eye movement') is a stage of sleep when the brain sort of reboots, like a computer, as the person otherwise dreamed. Metaphorically, REM allows the brain to shift old information out of 'short term memory' and integrate it with the older, existing knowledge base. Any new information coming in could then take its place in the short-term memory database. Dreams, contrary to widely held belief, were nothing more than light shows people's brains created via a chemical called Dimethyltryptamine, to keep their intellect occupied while all of that was going on.

At least that's how Ford saw it.

Suddenly, a weird cracking sound, like a twig snapping, was heard over the intercom. Ford checked the monitor again to see if the girl had maybe moved or gotten up, but she hadn't. He scrunched his nose up and twisted his face in confusion as he stared deeper into the monitor.

Suddenly, something wide and blurry moved past the camera lens. It was hard to see exactly what the something was though, because of the grainy monitor. At first, he thought it was a speck of dust or maybe a moth, but then it moved again, covering the camera's field of vision.

"What the hell?" Ford whispered to himself.

He grabbed one of the heavy black Mag lights that were kept in a basket on the desk by the door. He then went out into the hall. Rather than going in and turning on the overhead lights in the room like a lot of techs did when they had to check on something, he found that it was easier on the patients if he went into the room with only a small handheld light. The trick was to go in, fix whatever you had to fix, and get the hell out without ever waking the patient.

He slowly made his way down the empty hallway, heading toward Sylvia's room. It was really late now; well after three in the morning. Around him, the entire hospital was still, and its corridors were as peaceful as a graveyard. This late, all the patients were fast asleep in their beds. And the staff? Well, they were all busy with their respective duties and daily chores. Other than that, the building was quiet.

When he got to the room, Ford waited for a second outside the door. He leaned in, pressing his ear carefully to the plane of wood, and listened. He was able to catch the soft sounds of muffled movement, and what seemed like the chirping of birds. He listened closer and was also able to just make out the sound of rustling, like wind gently moving through the boughs of trees.

"Hmmm," he mused softly to himself. "She must have left the TV on."

Reaching out hesitantly, Ford turned the doorknob while still pulling the door closed. It was a trick he had learned early on in his sleep career. The opening of a door made a lot more noise than one would think. By opening it this way, you disengaged the lock first, then you could just swing the door open without it making a sound.

"Paging Dr. Jacobs. Paging Dr. Jacobs," a woman's voice unexpectedly announced from the hospital's paging system overhead. Ford ignored it, being too focused on what it was that he was doing. The last thing he wanted to do was to wake the girl up. She might not get back to sleep. Keeping disruptions to a minimum was sort of the point of the job, he reminded himself.

The door slowly swung inward, pulled open by its own weight. A sudden gust of warm air came rushing out of the gap in the doorjamb toward Ford. Remarkably, the wind was rich with the scent of turned earth and verdant greenery. He hesitantly angled his head and peered inside the room.

Unexpectedly, a bright light assaulted his vision, blinding him and forcing him to take a few blinking seconds until he could better see. He idly wondered if he might have left the light on when he'd put Sylvia to bed. But then he remembered seeing them being off on the monitor when they'd done her Bio-Calibrations.

His sight finally cleared, but what he saw spread out before him defied any kind of rational explanation. The bed, the furniture, the room... were all gone, even the walls had seemingly disappeared. In their stead, there was a lush expanse of forest that stretched out across a broad valley for as far as the eye could see.

"What the hell?" Ford whispered as he leaned back into the hallway, and looked first to his left, then to his right.

None of this made any sense. On one side of the doorway was what he knew to be the normal world: the Control Room, the hospital, and, well... reality. On the other, lay a dense forest teeming with a variety of flora and fauna. It was the weirdest goddamn thing.

He looked back into the girl's room and felt another gust of warm wind reach out from the doorway to embrace him, drawing him inside. The warmth on his skin reminded him of the summers he'd spent on his grandparent's farm as a kid, of afternoons that seemed to stretch out in front of him like a highway to forever. He grinned affectionately at the memory, and without thinking too much more about it, he took his first step forward.

"Paging Dr. Jacob," the paging system's voice once again repeated over his shoulder. "Paging Dr. Jac..."

The ground was lush, and it felt soft when he pressed his foot down onto it. Once more, he shook his head in disbelief. It should have been firm, hard even, like the concrete floor that he knew it was. Instead, though, the soil felt pliant, as malleable as mud. He felt the soles of his boat shoes sink into the soft topsoil as he put his weight onto them. The ground was covered by a carpet of thick moss. Small white flowers punctuated the fuzzy blanket like flakes at the beginning of a snowfall.

"This doesn't..." he trailed off, his confusion now past the point of articulation.

Ford looked up and stared gape-mouthed into the trees above him. Leaves sparkled like sequins in the light. There, hanging high in an azure sky, just beyond the canopy of green, he saw the fiery ball of the sun overhead. His intellect told him that there had to be a ceiling no more than a few feet above his head, but he could see only what was in front of him. Just then, a large bird of some kind arced through the trees abruptly, taking off like a jet, and soaring into the blue high overhead.

Instinctively, Ford knew that this was all somehow connected to the girl. After all, hadn't she been in REM when he'd first seen whatever it was that he'd seen on the camera? Everything had been normal just prior to that. And, by the time he'd manage to walk to the room, she would have been deep into dream-mode. He looked around unbelievingly at the panorama of green around him. As far-fetched as it sounded, it was the only thing that made sense.

"This is her dream," he whispered softly to himself as if to drive the point home. He wasn't exactly sure how he knew that, but it felt like it was right somehow, so he decided to go with it. "And whatever it is that she's dreaming is spilling out into the room and..." He stared at the plants and trees around him, amazed. Absentmindedly, he reached out and let his fingertips glide over the broad surface of a Cutleaf Philodendron plant nearby. The leaf was smooth, like silk, and colored a vibrant green. "Into our reality."

He took a few more steps forward, moving further away from the doorway hesitantly. His feet nearly slipped from how wet the ground was, the soles of his shoes now slick with mud. Stopping to right himself, he looked back the way he'd come. There, in a cleft of one of the large trees, like it was growing out from within, was the doorway he'd just come through; the one that led back to the hospital.

Through the portal, he could see the hospital's familiar hallway—the pale walls, the industrial carpeting—just as he'd left it. The duality of the situation struck him like a bat to the back of the head. On one side was what he knew to be real, the tangible world. And on the other... was this place: a lush, verdant jungle, that, well... he wasn't sure even existed. On one side, it was the middle of the night. On the other, a warm and beautiful day.

It defied all reason.

Ford suddenly heard someone's voice coming from the brush ahead, a kind of singing that seemed to float on the wind. The sound was rich and full and most definitely feminine; like a fragile, beautiful thing that had suddenly been set free in the forest.

And it was coming from just up ahead of him.

For some reason even he didn't understand, Ford felt deeply compelled to stay as close as he could to the doorway just in case he wanted—or needed—to run back through it in a hurry. But the sound of the woman's voice pulled him inexorably further away from it, compelling him deeper and deeper into the tapestry of the forest.

He took another few steps, his eyes searching the wall of green in front of him for the source of the sound. It was hard for him to separate the voice from the variety of birdsong in the boughs of the trees, but he was finally able to home in on it. It seemed to be coming from a copse of trees off to his right. Without thought, another step was taken away from the portal.

Then, not too far off through the dense trees and shrubbery, he saw a flash of movement. Whoever it was, they were moving toward him, albeit slowly, aimlessly, as if they hadn't a care in the world. Ford leaned forward, craning his neck, in an effort to see as far as he could in that direction.

Suddenly the foliage directly in front of him parted and a girl stepped into view. At first, Ford failed to recognize her, but then he started slowly putting the pieces together. It was Sylvia, only she looked way different than she had when he put her to bed. Like, a lot different. Her hair was longer, for one thing... and it was this sort of sun-bleached blonde color. And she was wearing a dress. He almost didn't recognize her, but he looked into her eyes, and he knew. The two of them stared at one another like deer caught in headlights, both momentarily dumbfounded and confused for a second. And then, Sylvia's face contorted with a painful, raw emotion.

"Who are you?" she screamed at him, panic rising like a tide in her voice. "How did you get here?!?"

Ford started to try and talk to her, to explain what little he could about how he'd come to be there. He could tell from her reaction that she didn't recognize him. And from the way she was walking in circles, glaring at him, and rubbing her temples with her fingers, he got the feeling she never would. To her, he was an intruder, an interloper, someone who had somehow invaded her most treasured space, her Sanctum Sanctorum. And the incongruity of him being here created a contradiction in her mind, upsetting her.

Ford wasn't sure how he knew it, but he was suddenly convinced that he was in very real danger. Somehow, the more upset Sylvia got, the more excited and confused she became, the more the trees and shrubs around him seemed to flicker and become momentarily transparent, as if suddenly transformed into smoke. And the more everything flickered, Ford somehow knew, the greater the chance was that she would wake up. He'd seen people in REM rouse for the slightest reasons, a noise, a sudden light, hearing someone's voice. So, the only thing he could be sure of, the only place he knew to be real, was back through the doorway, back at the hospital.

Sylvia stopped her frantic pacing and stared at him angrily. Her lips moved silently as she tried to sort out how any other person could have found their way to her place, how something like that was even possible? She'd come here for as long as she could remember—longer— and had never before encountered another living soul. It was her retreat from her oftentimes cruel world. It was hers and hers alone. And she knew... that no matter how bad the waking world outside got, she could always return to this place of solitude to salve her wounds.

Ford turned without answering her, and sprinted headlong back the way he'd come, back toward where the doorway was hidden within the cleft of the tree. There, he knew he'd find his way back to the world that he knew, back to the world that made sense. He ran blindly forward, but as he did, his shoes once again slipped on the wet, moss-covered ground. He scrambled across the jungle floor bent over like a dog, using his hands to help him along, feeling as if he were moving in slow motion.

Behind him, he heard Sylvia call out, but he couldn't make out any of what she was saying. Her tone was shrilly pitched, and you could hear the mounting distress in her voice. Ford scrambled on, the trees and shrubs around him becoming more and more indistinct. And when he'd finally gotten close enough to the doorway that he felt like he could make it, he dove through the still open portal.

"…cobs. Paging Dr. Jacobs," the voice on the hospital paging system intoned from the hidden speakers overhead.

Ford landed heavily on the industrial carpeting, splattering mud everywhere. He rolled off his shoulder and came to a stop by slamming against the far wall. He sat up out of breath with his heart pounding like a kickdrum inside of the rigid framework of his chest. Still frightened, he turned to look unbelievingly back into the darkness inside Room 614.

The interior of the patient room had somehow returned to its previous state of appearance, being that of a normal patient room. Ford could see the girl lying on her side under the blankets in the bed. One of her arms hung off the edge and the position of her fingers made her hand look like a claw. From where he sat leaning up against the wall, he was able to hear her take a breath and sigh as she rolled over onto her back and settled back into sleep.

After that, the corridor returned to silence.

Ford got to his feet painfully, his shoulder already feeling bruised. He walked over and carefully shut the door to Room 614. He still wasn't sure what had happened as he slowly made his way back to the Control Room. He felt unsteady on his feet, so he used his hand on the wall for support. He was shaken, unsure if what he thought he had just experienced was real, or was it something else? Had he hallucinated the whole thing? Was something like that even possible?

But much like any dream, even as his mind was trying to piece all that he'd seen together, elements of the experience were already becoming hazy and dissolving within his memory, like cotton candy floating atop warm water. To him, it felt like when you woke up from a nightmare, and as you struggled to remember the particulars of the dream, the pieces of it were already slipping from your mental grasp.

And so, by the time the next morning rolled around, Ford had already chalked the whole bizarre experience up to him being overworked and undoubtedly too tired. It was the only thing that made sense to him, the only thing he'd let make sense.

Because, at one point in his considerations, he was confronted by only two plausible possibilities. The first was that he'd indeed been more exhausted from work than he'd suspected, and that fatigue had cause him to imagine the whole thing.

And the other, well…

The other was just too crazy to be considered. The other was that it had all really happened just as he thought it had; that the girl had actually created an alternative reality within the confines of the small hospital room. But, he reminded himself, it wasn't like that was possible, right? That was just bananas. It defied all logic and reason... and, most importantly, science.

Despite the mud and moss still clinging to his shoes.

So, that next morning, when he woke up Sylvia, Ford didn't say anything about what he'd thought had happened. He unhooked her from the bird's nest of wires, made a little innocuous small talk, and let her shower. While he was unhooking her, though, he noticed that she kept staring at him surreptitiously out of the corner of her eye, like she wanted to ask or tell him something, but couldn't. Maybe she was looking for some sign of recognition in him, in his face, like he, too, remembered their encounter from her dream, but he could never be sure. Neither of them would—or could—say anything about it. And then, when she was done getting herself cleaned up and dressed, she gathered her things and left without saying a word.

When Ford's relief—a young intern name Claudia—arrived, he said that he wasn't feeling well, and he left for home a little early. 'Maybe I got what Mary had,' he'd told her. In truth, he wasn't even sure why'd he said it, but the idea of coming back here later that night made him feel immediately anxious.

And not once—nor ever—did he mention what he'd seen that night in Sylvia Bose's hospital room to anyone. Not in his notes. Not on his next scheduled shift. Not even during his Performance Review a month or two later. Because much like how he knew he was in danger in the forest of Sylvia's dream, he knew that to dig too deeply into what he remembered was to start digging into something that could, and probably would, undermine the very foundation of his ideas on reality.

Ford quit working at the hospital not long after that. He got a new gig at another sleep lab across town, but he only lasted there a few months. His bosses would have said that his job performance suffered due to the fact that he'd grown reluctant to enter a patient's room.

Especially when they were asleep.

And still, every night as he himself got into bed, Ford would find himself thinking of Sylvia and of her beautiful forest. And as he'd drift off to sleep, sometimes, when the barrier between the Real and the Unreal was at its most fragile, he swore that he could hear her singing, and the sound would beckon him to return to the landscape of another person's dreams.

CARRION

Another minor trigger warning on this one… there's some fairly rough stuff here, kids. The crime is real. It was something that I saw on one of those forensic shows on television. The idea here—and admittedly most of my stories begin with me giving myself a challenge—was to take a horrific, isolated moment in time and slow that instant WAY down in order to give myself (and, by extension of that, you, dear reader) time to notice a few things of import. It was also a chance for me to maybe wax a little poetic.

And it all begins… with the ticking of a clock.

*T*ick!

It was quiet in the house at 247 Elm.

Tock!

Within its walls, everything was still, motionless. Noiseless, save for the sound of the small clock that was ticking on a nightstand in one of the darkened bedrooms at the back of the house.

Tick!

One might have said, if one were to be so morbidly inclined, that the place was 'as quiet as a tomb,' but that would have been a little too on the nose given the macabre circumstances.

Tock!

The main room, the largest in the house, had been used as the primary living area. The space looked very much like what you'd expect to find in most average suburban homes. Roughly ten by twelve foot, the room was sparsely decorated; the decor plain and unremarkable. The walls had been painted an off-white, eggshell color once upon a time, back when the tenant—a 35-year-old divorced woman by the name of Claudette Harris—had first moved in. But in the ensuing years, tobacco smoke and a lack of any real talent in the housekeeping department had tainted their surfaces and colored them all a pale, jaundiced sort of yellow.

Tick!

There was an old, tan sofa that had been rescued from one of the neighborhood's garage sales not long ago stretched out along the main wall. Its cushions appeared threadbare and as worn as burlap. Two modest end tables flanked the divan protectively. A wooden entertainment center took up most of the wall on the other side of the room, an old Motorola tube TV set sat like a Buddha in the middle of it. A shin-high, glass-topped coffee table, littered with stacks of yellowing magazines and a large glass ashtray that was filled to overflowing with butts and ash, separated the couch from the TV like a referee.

Tock!

The front door lay to the right if you were sitting on the sofa. A broad window took up the rest of the wall next to the entrance, the view outside obscured by dark polyester curtains. On the remaining wall, the door to the hallway that led to the bedroom completed the room.

Tick!

There wasn't much in the way of art or photos hung on any of the wall's surfaces. The majority of that stuff never made it here in the move over from the old house. Really, the only thing that did was the single framed photo that was sitting next to the TV of Claudette, her ex-husband George, and their two jug-eared kids.

Tock!

On the couch, Claudette was lying face down, her head buried deep between two of the seat cushions. Her prone body was nude. The white skin of her exposed back shone brightly in the dim light, its tone now gone an unnaturally pale. From her anguished position, it was clear that whatever clothing she'd had on had been removed by force. Their tattered material lay bunched up on the floor next to the coffee table in a blood-soaked wad.

Tick!

Claudette had been asleep, having drifted off while watching a late-night western on the TV, when someone had come into the house. This someone had found her fast asleep and oblivious, dreaming there on the couch. They'd hovered over her for God knew how long, smelling her hair, furtively touching her skin. Whoever it was ended up doing indescribable things as she lay there unaware.

Tock!

And when she'd awoken abruptly and began to protest, he'd hit her with his balled fist, splitting her lip. She'd heard him growl something unintelligible at her, and then, he was striking her again across the face repeatedly, using his open hand as punctuation. His blows clouded her vision, and they made it hard for her to think straight. She'd done what she could to fight back, but... he'd caught her in the midst of sleep and had quickly proven himself to be so much stronger than her.

Tick!

Finally, when he was done with his touching... and his sniffing... and his probing of her, he'd flipped her over onto her stomach, roughly holding her down by the back of her neck and taking her savagely. The pain of the attack was searing, and she'd cried out, begging for him to stop. Ignoring her pleas, he continued until his fury—and his lust—had exhausted themselves. In the aftermath, he'd used a length of rope he carried in one of his pockets as a garrote to throttle her.

Tock!

Of course, she'd done what she could to free herself from his grasp, did what she could to save her life, but he'd ended up putting his knee onto the middle of her back and holding her down like a roped calf. She'd felt his great weight and sharp knees bear down on her spine, driving her deeper and deeper into the blackness of the couch.

Then, cranking back as hard as he could, he'd pulled at the ligature, strangling her, and crushing her larynx like a tin can. Blood spilled to fill her collapsed airway and she'd quietly—and all too quickly—drowned in her own blood.

Tick!

And still, long after she was gone and all of the light had faded her eyes, he'd kept pulling on his length of rope, and continued doing so until the muscles in his arms were spent, hot with the fire of fatigue. And only when he'd finally let her go, and Claudette was gone from the world, did the room settle back into silence.

Tock!

Suddenly, off in the back bedroom, a phone that was destined to remain unanswered rang out and shattered the gathered stillness to brittle shards. Claudette had been waiting on a call from her coworker, Phyllis. But she'd fallen asleep... and that had, as they say, changed everything.

Tick!

Once the man had gone, he and his anger disappearing back into the blackened night like a ghost, Claudette found herself 'on the wrong side of the grass,' as her dad used to say. Her spirit, once as bright and warm as the light of a lamp, hung momentarily suspended in the air, swirling in the ether like a phantasm. Then, her specter reluctantly disappeared, echoing out of existence like a thunderclap in a cavernous hall.

Tock!

After that, there was nothing, only the silence as it held sway within the room.

Tick!

Another moment passed, maybe it was an hour. Then… another.

Tock!

Until the only thing to be heard in the house at 247 Elm was the soft, metronomic heartbeat of the clock.

Tick!

IJHYEOJIN

Boy, do I love a good ghost story. Books or movies, it really doesn't matter to me. And, over the years, I have fallen in love with the ghost story movies coming out of places like South Korea or Thailand. I mean, Songyos Sugmakanan's DORM has quickly become one of my favorite films of all time (find it and see it—trust me on this one). My enjoyment of the film has a lot to do with its pacing (narratives tend to be generally slower in Thailand which works well when it comes to these kinds of things). That and the fact that the stories themselves are all just so damn tragic. Anyway, "Ijhyeojin" (Korean for "forgotten") is my humble attempt at creating one of those very tales but set in a more Western location (sort of like what they did with Danny and Oxide Pang's THE EYE).

Oh, and for those of you who were wondering, the Hikikomori are a very real phenomenon in Japan, but there are variations in every country all around the world. You can find documentaries about them on YouTube. I'd also recommend Saito Tomaki's excellent book on the subject.

The morning sun rose slowly over the trees of the quiet neighborhood along San Salvador Street. Its fiery face shone down from the heavens, brightening the panorama of the pale June sky. Golden rays kissed the grass, warming the flora, and seemingly bringing everything to life. Colors seemed more vivid in the new day's light, shadows deepened and became full of mystery.

Nora Allen pulled up in her little red car and parked it outside of the large Victorian house at 4284. She'd learned of the apartment listing from something online called BookIt.com. The site was one of those rental assistance deals that helped match up needy renters with prospective property owners. She'd ended up speaking to a guy named Jordan on the phone, and they'd set up this meeting to see if she could have the place.

Nora was what people called, 'new in town,' and, well… if she were being honest, she needed this place to live pretty desperately. She'd had to leave her last place—and the memories she'd made there—in a bit of a hurry after her roommate (and then boyfriend, Paul) had gotten a little violent with her. It wasn't anything serious (he'd slapped her), but… Nora had had relationships that turned 'handsy' in the past. She knew the signs. The first time was the hardest. Things got easier after that. And she knew what 'that' always meant. So, she figured that the best thing for her to do was to get the hell out of Dodge—to get while the gettin' was good—before anyone got hurt… meaning her.

She parked her little red Hyundai on the street out front and got out. Walking along the pavement, she proceeded up the walkway that led to the large gray and black Victorian at 4284. She breathed deep of the cool morning air and felt a wave of optimism wash over her. Things were looking up, she thought.

Wearing a pair of faded blue jeans and a white peasant top, she was trying to look casual, but also not so casual that she looked like a 'security risk.' She'd pulled her blonde hair up into a bun and had on a pair of glasses instead of her usual contacts. An 'academic' vibe was what she was going for…

Y'know, 'student,' and not so much 'vagrant.'

The Victorian was a gray and black, two-story monstrosity that looked like it could have been designed by the Addams Family or the Munsters. It wasn't rundown or anything like that, far from it, but the structure as visibly old and had this look from another time with its high peaks and ornately gabled arches.

The house had a Mansard roof with fish-scale shingles, and a quaint wooden porch that had these beautifully carved Ionic columns that wrapped around the house like a winter scarf. A wrought iron table and some chairs sat out on a veranda in a spot by the door. It was easy for Nora to imagine people sitting there having tea and warming themselves with a bit of sun.

She strolled up the walkway that led up to the front door, taking it all in, and noticing in particular the flowers and bushes that decorated the front lawn. It was pretty evident by how well everything was kept that someone paid a lot of attention to the foliage. The bushes were trimmed and attended to with an obsessive attention to detail. The flowers were all blooming with big full buds that bowed their heads as if in mourning. The tableau was like something out of a nature magazine.

Not even close to what I'd imagined, she thought.

Nora had been sure the ad had been wrong when she first read the listing and its asking price on BookIt's website. She'd always heard that rents ran high in this part of town, much higher than she'd had to pay at her last place back home. And what she'd seen in her limited searching corroborated that. But this place... not only was it downright reasonable, but it was really lovely. Even the guy she'd talked to on the phone—Jordan—had been pleasant. Honestly, at the price they were asking, she'd expected the place to be a dump. But this... this was nice.

The whole thing seemed... off to her.

But then again, who was she to look a gift horse in the mouth?

She climbed the wooden steps and hesitantly approached the front door, the ornately carved spindle balustrade that complimented the porch momentarily catching her eye. And even though she knew she was expected, she still had the feeling that she was intruding, like she shouldn't be here.

Or like, maybe someone was watching her.

She shook her head to clear such idle thoughts and decided she was just being silly. After all, who cared? She needed a place to stay, and this seemed like a pretty darn good one. And now that she was here and had gotten a look at the house's accoutrements, the whole deal was looking even better. The only thing she had left to do was to charm whoever answered the door enough to get it.

She could do that, she told herself.

Right?

And so, with a shrug of her slim shoulders, she reached out and rang the bell.

"We'll just need to finish filling out this short application. Do you have time?" Jordan, the man who'd ended up answering the door, asked.

He'd introduced himself as the building owner and apartment manager and was every bit as nice in person as he had been on the phone. Tall and a lot more handsome than she'd expected him to be, he'd brought them iced tea to drink as they sat together on the porch. "I know we have your online thing, but..." He shrugged his shoulders as if to say, 'what are you gonna do?' Then, he pulled out a pen and started filling out the blanks in the application.

Jordan looked up at her inquisitively, like he was about to ask for help on a crossword puzzle. "Last address?"

Nora closed her eyes for a second. She knew this part was coming, the need for her to give some kind of rental history, but... it still made her nervous. She'd managed to cover her tracks away from there, away from him, away from Paul, really well. It seemed counterintuitive to start sharing anything now, especially to a stranger.

But sometimes in Life, there were things you just had to do.

"9298 Forrester Road," she said, reciting the address she remembered making up previously. "In Silver City."

Jordan smiled at her and dutifully wrote the information down. He next asked for her Social Security number as well as a few other things and she gave them to him with a hesitant air. Again, she wasn't happy about lying, but she went ahead and did it anyway. She knew she'd never get the place if she didn't show some kind of verifiable credit history... even if some of it was a little fudged. It was just the way the world worked.

As the man—Jordan, she reminded herself—continued filling out his paperwork, Nora took the time to look him over. Jordan was a good-looking guy in his early forties with short brown hair who was dressed in a pair of cargo shorts, this gaudy yellow Hawaiian shirt, and an old pair of Birkenstocks. He gave off the energy of someone who was either retired... or an artist.

"The apartment still has some stuff in it that was left by the last tenant: a TV, a few tables, a couch, I think," Jordan explained. "You're welcome to them if you want. But, if you want them out, just let me know. I can get my husband, Josh, to help bring them down. The apartment is on the second floor, Number 4. It's a nice place. Quiet. We're all pretty quiet around here."

Nora smiled happily. "Sounds great."

"Good." He smiled at her and returned to filling out his paperwork.

Up in one of the trees, a bird began singing a song that sounded like a lullaby.

When Jordan was done filling in all of the blanks, he pulled the paperwork together and slid them into their manila envelope. He wrote something on the back flap, then he set it and the pen to one side. When he was done, he folded his hands in front of him, and once again smiled at Nora.

"Look, Nora," he said gently. "I know it's not really any of my business, but... I need to talk with you about something. The address you gave me just now... it's different than the one you put on your online application. You said, 9298 Forrester Road... and the address you gave online was 4298. I bet neither of them really exist. So..." He looked down at the ground as if in thought. Then, his gaze drifted sympathetically back up to meet her eyes. "Are you in trouble, girl? I mean, are you trying to get away from someone?"

Despite her best intentions, Nora felt herself pout and her eyes start to well up. Then, she stared at Jordan intently and slowly nodded. She couldn't help it.

"A man?"

She nodded again, but remained quiet, knowing that she would start crying for real if she said any part of it out loud.

"Okay, look..." Jordan said with a warm and understanding smile. "We can sort all this paperwork stuff out later. I..." A pause. "Well, let's just say that I've been where I think you are—once. Hell, haven't most of us?" He patted the back of her hand gently. "I got lucky. I found Josh."

Nora smiled at him, sniffing back the worst of her emotions. "How long have you been together?"

"Oh, god," Jordan replied with a chuckle as he leaned back in his chair, "legally... whatever the fuck that means, we've been married for ten years. We got married as soon as the courts said that we could." He grinned at the memory, tucking the folder underneath his arm. "But really, well... we found each other more than twenty years ago." He paused and smiled again. "And not a minute too soon."

Nora returned a smile. "What does Josh do?"

"He's a lawyer at a firm downtown," Jordan said proudly. "You'll meet him, I'm sure... eventually." Jordan got to his feet and extended his hand to Nora. "Are you staying with anybody now?"

Nora stood up, feeling sort of dumbfounded, and shook his hand. "No, I don't really have, well, anyone. Paul..." she hesitated. "I mean, I just arrived in town yesterday. But I'm staying in a motel out by the airport for one more night." She paused. "What little I have is out in my car."

Jordan abruptly put his arm around her and hugged her protectively. He smiled and pulled a key from his pocket. "Well, I have a good feeling about you, Nora, and I'm usually a pretty good judge of people. Like I said, we can sort all this stuff out in due time. Let's get you someplace safe and we can figure out the rest of it later."

The tears that were brimming in Nora's eyes finally spilled over, rivulets running down her cheeks like rainwater. Life had not exactly been kind to her lately. Back home, she'd lost just about everything she had, including all her old friends who'd sided with Paul, when she left. She didn't really blame them, she guessed. She'd never said a word to them about what he'd done, about him hitting her, even though doing so would have changed a lot of their minds. No, for reasons even she didn't understand, she'd kept that part quiet, and had allowed herself to be painted as the 'crazy ex-girlfriend' instead.

It was all just so goddam embarrassing.

"Well, you can relax," Jordan said paternally as he pressed the key to the apartment into her hand. "You're home now." He smiled and patted her shoulder. "Let's go take a look at your new place."

The next morning, Nora arrived at the Victorian bright and early, dragging a heavy green leather suitcase and a black garbage bag bulging with the sum of her wardrobe behind her. She had on a pair of faded blue sweatpants and a red tee shirt that had the word "protagonist" printed on the front in a faded white Courier font. She lugged her stuff up the front stairs to the porch with some slight difficulty, opening the door with her key. The door swung slowly inward, and she hesitantly entered the house.

Inside, there was a large foyer that took up most of the center of the building. Lovely, flocked wallpaper colored a forest green which resembled Christmas wrapping lined the walls. Pine trim, stained a deep brown, completed the room, giving it a distinctly rustic flair. A wooden table with two carved chairs was set against the wall to one side of the entryway. There was a large bouquet of flowers from the garden in a crystal vase set on top for decoration. Branching off from the central room, several hallways expanded out in all directions, giving access to the other parts of the house. And dominating it all was the curving staircase that led to the apartments upstairs.

She had to admit it. The place was decorated with a keen, cultured eye. From the state of the antique furniture to the paintings that were all hung 'just so,' the place exuded the same attention to detail that the yard did.

"There she is!" Jordan's voice echoed to her from down the hallway on the right.

He entered the foyer like a breeze, dressed pretty much as he had been yesterday; only the color of his shirt had changed from yellow to a road worker orange. Trailing behind him like a reluctant guest walked a thin man of roughly the same age. Good-looking like Jordan, he was dressed better than the apartment manager wearing a pair of tan slacks, a white button-up, and a comfortable-looking pair of loafers. Nora immediately took him for the previously mentioned Josh, Jordan's husband.

"I'm happy to see that you survived your night by the airport," Jordan joked as he gave a little chuckle. "Honey," he said to his companion, "this is our new flat-mate, Nora. She's in from out of town…" He cleared his throat. "She's the kid I mentioned to you at dinner last night."

Josh's face brightened, then went dark, like a cloud floated across his consciousness. Then, just as suddenly, it gently drifted away. He smiled at Nora, his eyes staring at her warmly. Nora noticed how it made his carefully concealed crow's feet suddenly more noticeable.

"Oh, yes, of course," he said, stepping around Jordan and taking her hand in both of his. "You are most welcome, dear. I think you're gonna absolutely love living here."

Jordan brushed passed his husband, reclaiming his status as host. He took the heavy green suitcase from Nora's grasp. "Here, let me carry that up for you." He chuckled. "Lord knows you've carried it long enough."

Josh came up and gently took Nora's plastic bag of clothes and they both followed Jordan up the stairs. As they walked, Nora felt his protective hand on the small of her back.

"So, that was our place off to the right: Number 1," explained Jordan as they rounded the landing. His voice echoed in the large, open space. "Miss Aubrey," he stopped and looked at Nora. "You'll meet her as well, I'm sure. She lives in Number 2 off to the lower left. Number 3 is upstairs, and that's you on the right, Number 4."

As the three of them got to the second floor, the front door below them suddenly burst open and a young girl, maybe twenty or twenty-one, came stumbling in. She was an attractive blonde with a full figure wearing a USC sweatshirt and a pair of jeans that looked like they had been painted on. Bright white running shoes completed her complementary outfit.

"Hey, Aub!" Jordan called to her from upstairs.

"Hey, Jordan," she replied, looking up. "Hey, Josh."

Jordan smiled down at her from over the banister. "Honey, this is Nora. She's taking Number 4 up here. Be nice to her. She's new in town."

"Number 4, eh?" Aubrey asked, and then she laughed to herself, shaking her head, as she headed toward her place. She disappeared down the hall, with only her voice echoing back. "And, hey, I'm nice to everybody."

Jordan gazed over at Nora through his eyebrows as if to question the statement. Nora wasn't exactly sure why, but she thought that the look seemed out of character, and it surprised her. Setting that aside for the moment, she eagerly looked down the hall toward her new apartment. Lord knows… she didn't need to get off on a wrong foot with her landlord on the first day she was here.

Then, all at once, Nora felt an icy chill trickle down the length of her spine. It was like the air around her had grown suddenly cold. Jordan and Josh had only just gotten to her door and set their respective loads down when she felt it. And then it was gone, replaced by the feeling that someone, somewhere, was watching her. She looked over her shoulder, down into the lobby, to see if Aubrey might still be there, but found the foyer empty. Somewhere far off, she heard a clock ticking time.

She checked down the other hall to her right, but it, too, was vacant. The only thing of note was the door to Number 3 and the small window at the end of the hall. But still… A flock of gooseflesh suddenly migrated down her arm in a wave, and she felt the cold abruptly return, its frosty fingers coiling around her legs like a snake.

Then, just as she was looking away to go and open the door to her new place, she noticed that the door to Number 3 stood slightly ajar. At first, she thought it was just the shadows playing tricks on her. But then she noticed a subtle difference in shade at the crack of the door and saw that it was indeed standing open.

For some reason, the shadows inside the apartment seemed lonely and foreboding to her. Reflexively, her imagination quickly caught fire, making the gloom within the room appear far more frightening than it had just a second before. She shook her head, dismissing her thoughts as mere nervousness at the prospect of beginning this new life.

"You have the key, kid," Jordan interrupted her rumination.

"Right," she answered, sounding a little embarrassed as she walked to them. "I'm just amazed at how beautiful this place is."

She stepped between the two men and carefully inserted the key into the door. She smiled, feeling a warm sense of satisfaction wash over her when she heard the lock turn and disengage. This was her place now. Not Paul's. Not her parents. Not anyone else's. Hers.

She felt giddy with the possibilities of what her life could be like now, now that she was free of him. Him and his awful friends. And who knows? Maybe she'll make a group of her own friends and have them over for dinner parties. Maybe she'll meet another—better—guy and finally be happy.

"To new beginnings," she whispered as she gently pushed the door open.

Jordan and Josh helped Nora with her bags, setting them just inside the door. Jordan gave her the Grand Tour once again, making sure to point out all the changes they'd made to the apartment. And then, as if on an agreed upon cue, they left her alone to get settled in.

"If you need anything, just let us know, okay?" Josh told her as they headed out the door and back down to their own apartment. He patted her arm with affection as they left. "Honey, you've got this."

Nora felt silly and a little embarrassed by how paternally he and Jordan were treating her, but she had to admit that the support made her feel a little better about things. She thanked them both for their help, and then she watched from the doorway as they made their way back down the stairs.

After they had left and she was once again alone, Nora stood in the doorway of her apartment for a long time, awash in a pool of conflicting emotions. She was scared, she could at least admit that. Scared for her future, scared about being a woman alone in a new town, scared that she'd made all the wrong decisions, and that she'd not been thorough enough in her attempts to hide herself away from Paul and the danger he represented. She looked out over the open gallery of the foyer and smiled.

So far, though, she'd done okay.

"I'm really doing it, aren't I?" she asked the number pinned to her door, its hand posed coyly on its own hip. But since the Four said nothing to her in reply, Nora stepped back inside her new place and slowly began to shut the door.

The apartment itself was small, but tidy. She was grateful for the furniture Jordan had mentioned and made a mental note to go and get a bed from one of those furniture rental places she'd seen on the way here. It'd take a while, she thought, but I'll make this place a home.

But then, just as she was closing the door, she couldn't help but look over to the apartment next store—Number 3. She squinted in order to look closer at the blackness she'd seen at the crack of the door jamb. She couldn't help but feel that the blank space was staring back at her, daring her to delve deeper into its unfathomable depths. Not really knowing why, she closed her door the rest of the way and locked it, feeling somehow safer about the whole thing.

A few days later, Nora came rushing out of her apartment wearing her navy blue, business-casual suit, and matching low-slung heels. Her plan for the day was to hit a few of the employment agencies in town to get her search for a job started. She'd been able to hide a little money away from Paul in the weeks prior to her deciding to leave, but, well... it was running out fast. A lot faster than she thought it would. The deposit on this place, her first and last month's rent, getting utilities set up, and all the other little things she'd forgotten she needed had taken bigger bites than anticipated out of her savings.

And so, the need for a job.

She had a few leads from searching the recent newspapers—a secretary thing with an insurance agent, a possible court clerk position with the county—but nothing that was guaranteed. But she knew she was a good typist and had worked in offices for years, so she wasn't too worried. She knew she'd find something.

It was all a matter of timing.

And so, she'd made the decision to start at the agencies, maybe even splurge on a coffee and a bagel for breakfast while she did some more searching through the want ads. After that, who knew? She might have even landed a job by then.

Fingers crossed.

She slid her key into the lock and turned the tumblers. The click of the mechanism engaging sounded like the cocking of a gun in the secluded corridor. Removing the key, she gently jiggled the door in its frame to make sure everything was locked up tight. Sliding the key into her pocket, she felt a small rush of pride in herself and in the results of her recent decisive actions.

Never mind how lonely she'd been over the last few days. How scared. She'd expected—even anticipated—that... a little. She'd left behind her entire social structure, not to mention the man she was sure she would one day marry. It only stood to reason that she'd now feel isolated and alone. She knew that the depression that came with such drastic life changes could only be held at bay by keeping up her forward momentum and optimism. She also knew that if she let herself fall into despair, she might not ever find her way back out of it.

Nora turned to head down the stairs when her eye was once again caught by the cracked-open door to Number 3. The black space between it and its frame once again stared back at her blankly, daring her to come closer to its Cimmerian void.

But every time she looked, there was nothing.

Nora raised her hand and, already feeling a little foolish, hesitantly waved in the door's general direction. "Hello?" she quietly asked the empty hall.

Silence expanded in the corridor, and she felt the air surrounding her abruptly go thin. Suddenly, the hair moved on the back of her neck, the strands caressed by a gentle wind that came spiraling down the hallway. The breeze didn't feel cold nor was it particularly warm, but she still shivered as she felt it swirl around her and down the corridor. In the backdraft of the breeze, the door to Number 3 was slowly drawn closed as if a string were pulling it. Its worn hinges sighed softly as the flat panel of wood gently kissed the doorframe. After that, there was only silence.

Nora stared at it for a moment, then she shrugged, and chastised herself once again for being so silly. Her imagination had been getting away from her as of late—which, she guessed, was to be expected given the circumstances. She sighed softly before finally heading downstairs.

She crossed the foyer and went directly out through the front door without stopping. She didn't want to get stopped by Jordan or somebody else. She had a lot of things to get done today, and, as nice as they all were, she had to get going.

Outside, the sun had risen, and it was already warming the lawn and flowerbeds, drying the last of the morning's dew with its rays. Light reflected off the flowers and leaves making it seem as if the whole scene shimmered like something out of a child's fairy book. It was absolutely beautiful.

"Hey!" Jordan's voice suddenly called out from the flower beds by the fence. He was on his knees behind one of the bushes doing something in the dirt with the plants and small shrubs that were planted there. "You look great!"

Shit.

Nora pasted on a smile and sashayed a bit to show off her outfit. "Do you like it? I'm heading out job hunting. I found the names of a few agencies online, so..." She shrugged as she continued down the walkway toward the sidewalk in front of the house. "I decided to put on my best secretary outfit and give it a whirl."

Jordan chuckled and gave her an 'okay' sign with his thumb and forefinger. "You're gonna slay 'em, kid." He returned to his dirt. "You break a leg, okay?"

Nora waved as she got to the driver's side of her Hyundai and unlocked the door.

"Fingers crossed."

But just as she started to get into the car, and Jordan was going back to his gardening, her eyes slowly drifted like a lost balloon back to the house, and up to the window of Number 3. The morning's sun reflected off the panes of glass in a kaleidoscope of colors and glimmering white light. And as she sat down and slid her car key into the ignition, she was sure that she saw someone up in the apartment, a face looking out at her through the rainbow-colored haze.

Later that night...

Nora entered the house wearing a rumbled version of the blue suit she had on when she left. Her hair had been mussed by the wind and she carried her wrinkled suit coat over her arm like a used bath towel. She knew without looking at herself that she looked every bit as bad as her day had been.

She'd visited half a dozen agencies and not a single one had anything for her. They all made the same comments as to how qualified she was, how professional her resume looked. They just didn't have any openings—say it with me, kids—right now. Dejectedly, she'd already begun contemplating looking for a gig in retail.

No need to do anything rash, Nora, she thought. Not quite yet.

The Victorian was empty and lay as quiet as a library as she wearily made her way up the stairs to her apartment. She was tired and each step up took a seemingly Herculean effort on her part. She turned the corner on the second landing and was already pulling her key out from her pocket when she saw that the door to Number 3 was once again ajar. Even though she was exhausted and wanted nothing more than to go grab herself something to eat and get into bed, her curiosity got the better of her and she leaned in to try and get a peek at what may have been inside. But try as she might, only blackness and shadow returned her gaze.

But then, something, deep within the darkness, blinked.

"Oh!" she cried out reflexively, drawing back. She stood up and looked around the hallway embarrassed. "Um… H-Hello, is anybody there."

A small voice responded to her in a whisper from deep in the shadows. "I… I'm sorry." The voice was male, and it sounded like it was coming from someone who was maybe in their teens or early twenties. "I… hope I didn't scare you."

Nora smiled at the black sliver of darkness in the door and felt silly doing it.

"No, you didn't scare me. You just surprised me," she responded to the disembodied voice. And then, she laughed nervously. "I'm Nora. I just moved in a little while ago."

The numbered door creaked opened a little more. Peering in, Nora could just make out the pale face of a young boy staring back at her, like the moon shining in the sky on a starless night. He had black, bowl-cut hair and she could see that he was dressed in an old pair of sweats and a gray shirt with a faded Nintendo logo printed on the front. Dark circles raccooned a pair of piercing, deep brown eyes like matched bruises.

"Yes," he said softly. "I know. I heard you move in." He paused for a moment as his eyes shyly fell to the ground. He stared at a spot just outside the door for a second. Finally, he looked up, and without opening the door further, he softly said, "I'm Daniel."

Nora smiled warmly, wanting to appear friendly. The kid was clearly shy, and she didn't want to exacerbate that for fear of him shutting the door on her. If that happened, she knew that every interaction from here on in would be awkward, and she didn't want that to happen.

"Well, it's certainly nice to meet you, Daniel."

"Nice to meet you, too," he softly mumbled.

Nora took a curious step closer to the door until she was able to make out a little more of what was inside the boy's dimly lit apartment. She noticed several long bookcases that ran along the far wall, each shelf spilling over with books. Placed sporadically on the shelves were several ornately carved statues that looked like they were something out of a cartoon or a science fiction movie. Each one had a varying assemblage of tentacles and teeth and they all had long arms with razor-sharp claws that extended outward. The light of the computer screen illuminated the otherwise empty space.

"Have you, uh… lived here long?" Nora asked. She knew that people liked it when you asked them about themselves. She also knew how important it was to seem interested when meeting new people, especially if you wanted to look friendly.

The boy's brown eyes took on a faraway look. "Long enough for it to seem like forever." He chuckled to himself as he slowly raised his gaze to meet hers.

Nora grinned along with him, even though she wasn't exactly sure what it was that he found funny. "Well, I should probably go," she finally said. "It was nice meeting you, Daniel. As you can probably tell from the look of me, I've had sort of a long day." She laughed. "Right now, all I can think about is taking a long shower and putting my feet up for the night."

The boy smiled back at her, melancholy soiling the edges of his pale features. And, as he slowly drew back and shut the door, she heard him softly reply, "And it was nice meeting you… Nora."

Before she could say anything in response, the door clicked shut and Nora found herself again standing alone in the hallway.

The next night, Nora lay on the couch in her pajamas under a fluffy blanket she'd recently purchased at Target. She was watching one of those baking shows on television and continuing to pour over the employment listings in the day's paper whenever the mood struck her. The search was turning out to be, to put it mildly, slow going. There weren't a lot of listings for the jobs she was qualified for in this town, and the ones that were hiring, weren't paying enough for her to live on. She finally set the paper and her pen aside and reluctantly got up from the warmth of her couch cocoon.

Nora strolled over to the apartment's small, kitchen area which was mostly just the sink, a small refrigerator, and a single burner stovetop. But, hey… everything worked. For her, for now, it was enough.

She grabbed a packet of popcorn from the box in the cabinet and tore off the cellophane. Opening the microwave, she placed the packet of kernels onto the glass turntable flat on its back and shut the door. She then set the timer and hit Start.

Inside the appliance, a light came on and the turntable started slowly spinning. Nora stood back with her arms crossed, watching the bag heating up and inflating like a tiny hot air balloon. Soon, the kernels began popping and the smell of the warm butter in the bag started to permeate the room.

As she waited, a muffled sound came creeping to her ears from behind the living room wall, from what could only have been Daniel's apartment. The tone was low, secretive, and it sounded like there were two people talking, which surprised her. Daniel hadn't seemed like the kind of person who had a lot of friends, much less someone who entertained. In fact, she'd been of the opinion that he was a bit of a loner.

The conversation was difficult for her to hear much of what was being said, as the sound of her popcorn popping was so loud that it drowned a lot of it out. But all too soon, the staccato gunfire of the corn kernels bursting slowed, and she turned the microwave off before anything burnt inside. When it was once again quiet, the sounds of the conversation coming from next door were clearer and easier for her to hear.

Nora could now tell that there were two distinct voices. She recognized one of them as Daniel's soft male tenor, but the other one sounded female and definitely older. Who could he be talking to? She hadn't wanted to eavesdrop, but the volume of the conversation—now clearly more of an argument—had grown incrementally louder and it made it impossible for her—or anyone—to ignore.

"You have to understand," the older woman wailed, her voice sounding upset and near tears. "Since your Papa... died, well, it's been harder for me to pay all the bills, Daniel? If you could only help out..."

Daniel's response was short, and his tone sounded agitated. "I don't know what you want me to do, Mother?"

Mother? That threw Nora. For some reason, she hadn't expected that.

Despite feeling every bit like the nosy neighbor, Nora found herself leaning closer and putting her ear to the wall.

"Daniel..." the older woman paused for a second. "Daniel," she finally repeated, and her voice sounded pained and highly distressed. "I mean, how can you live like this? You need friends, maybe go back to school, and to learn how to provide for yourself."

Nora heard movement in the apartment, like someone was pacing.

"Mom," Daniel's voice said, and it was obvious by his tone that he was trying not to lose his temper. "You know what Doctor Hoffman told you. I..." he paused as his voice cracked with emotion. "I can't leave here. I... I just can't face... it."

"Face what, Danny?"

"The world... out there. I don't know how to explain it to you any better than I already have."

"But how am I to continue to pay for all this then? Papa is gone. It's only me now." She paused as if in thought. Then, "What am I to tell our friends?"

A leaden silence descended over the entirety of the second floor. For a moment, it felt like the entire world paused, and the only thing that could be heard in the house was the soft music coming from Nora's television program. It was as if reality held its breath for one small moment in anticipation of... what? Nora pressed her ear closer to the wall, feeling awful for being so nosy.

And for another instant, there was only silence.

But then Nora heard the older woman say something so quietly that she couldn't tell what it was. A palpable tension, like an electrical charge, could be felt coursing through the wall, and Nora drew a breath in anticipation of what might happen next.

"What did you just say?" Daniel said angrily.

Another leaden pause...

Then, she heard the woman softly reply, "I am embarrassed to call you son."

Nora held her breath and her eyes went wide.

Daaaamn... that one could only have hurt.

"And I... am ashamed that you are my mother," Daniel responded spitefully.

There was an abrupt slapping sound that was so loud that it made Nora jump. Then, she heard a thump, and something heavy struck the floor. Three more sharp, quick bumps rang out, and then the old house settled back into its austere silence.

Nora turned her head and firmly pressed her other ear to the wall. For a second, there was nothing; only the silence and a palpable feeling that something really bad had just taken place. Then, Nora could have sworn that she heard someone—Daniel?—softly weeping.

All too soon, even the sound of that fell away to nothing.

The next few minutes passed slowly for Nora, and each one of them were weighted with a dark feeling of dread. Then, just as she was once again chastising herself about being exactly the kind of neighbor she hated, just as she was about to go back to her popcorn and her television show, she heard something else fall in the room next door. Whatever it was, it wasn't as heavy as the last thing she'd heard dropped. This... this sounded like it had a lot less mass, like a chair got knocked over or something. After that, the only thing Nora could hear was a gentle creaking, like the rigging of a ship's mass. All too soon, even that receded into the night's lonely silence.

One week later...

Nora climbed out of her Hyundai wearing a pair of her favorite faded jeans, some sneakers, and a shirt she got on her and Paul's first date at an Eagles concert. She locked the car doors by hitting the button on her key fob as she walked around to the trunk. Once she'd popped the lid, she picked up the two bags of groceries she'd purchased at the local market and carried them inside.

She had to admit it. Over the past few weeks, she'd gotten kinda used to living here at the old gray and black Victorian. And by that, she meant that she knew where all the stores were in the area, and where the closest gas stations were located. And the best thing of all was that she hadn't heard anything from Paul or any of their stupid friends back home. Which was good, she finally decided. Fingers crossed that that situation would continue.

She carried her parcels into the house through the front door and walked across the foyer to the stairs. Halfheartedly, she looked for Jordan, Josh, or even Aubrey for a little conversation, but the house was, from all appearances, empty. She shivered, suddenly feeling like a small, insignificant baitfish having just been swallowed by something much bigger—and hungrier—than itself.

She chuckled and shook her head at her own childishness. She was being ridiculous, and she knew it. Going up the stairs, Nora shifted the grocery bags in her arms. Christ, they were getting heavy. There was a gallon of milk in one of them and the damn thing was making the bag's weight uneven in her arms.

Once she was on the second-floor landing, she proceeded down the hall toward her apartment. She pressed the bags against the wall with the flat of her body, fishing her keys out of her back pocket with her free hand, and unlocking the door. She left the keys hanging in the lock and went into the apartment, setting her armload onto the counter. Her hands now free, she went back to get her keys and shut the door.

But then, just as she was pushing the door closed, her eyes drifted back out into the hallway. She did it more out of habit than anything, like a reflex or an errant impulse. The empty corridor stretched out in front of her like a deserted airport runway. All she saw was the empty hallway that led back to the staircase and on to Number 3.

In that instant, her curiosity got the better of her, and she took another peek at the apartment next door. It took a second for her to recall the tenant's name, the kid: Daniel. But then, she remembered the argument she'd heard the other night and it all came back to her. She grinned to herself when she saw that the apartment's door once again stood ajar.

But then, as if someone had called him by name, the boy's face appeared in the crack, peeking out from between the door and its jamb. "Hello again."

"Oh, hey," she said sounding a little startled. "I... I didn't see you there."

He smiled and his pale skin blushed slightly, a red tide coloring a barren shore. "I heard you coming up the stairs and I wanted to say hello," he paused and let the door slowly open a little bit more as an invitation for them to chat. He looked toward the floor awkwardly. "I didn't want to startle you like I did last time." He chuckled softly. "I guess better luck next time, eh?"

Nora laughed and wandered a little further out into the hallway. She stepped closer toward where Daniel was but stopped a few feet away from his door. Once again, she wanted to appear friendly, but also... she was instinctively cautious. She'd had neighbors before who, while seemingly nice at first, had proven themselves to be anything but. Hell, who hadn't?

"It's okay. A little startle won't harm ya, now, will it?" she replied. "How are you?"

Daniel stared at her silently for a long time. Then, a smile trickled to his lips. "I am well. Thank you for asking."

"That's good."

"And you?"

"Oh, you know," she said, casually leaning against her door's frame. "I'm still out looking for that job, but I'm confident I'll find one soon. So, uh..." There was another pause as Nora tried to think of what to say next, and how she wanted to say it. She didn't want to blurt out anything about the argument she'd overheard, but she was also curious to see if everything was okay between the kid and his mom. "So, do you, uh... work from home?"

Daniel's smile faltered. "Sometimes. My parents help me pay for this place." He grinned at her, but a faraway look took over his eyes.

"They do it to keep me out of their hair, I think." He snickered. "As a result of being on my own, I don't really go much of anywhere." He paused, as he thought how best to put it. "I... I can't."

Nora looked at him clearly puzzled. "Can't?"

"I have something the doctors call agoraphobia. I even have an official diagnosis," and he chuckled darkly. "Literally, a note from my doctor."

Nora put on a sympathetic face. She'd heard the condition talked about once in a movie that had Sigourney Weaver in it.

"I'm sorry," was all she could manage though.

"I used to go to school," Daniel continued. "I was a student at the university. I even had a job at a comics store in town. But then, well..." Daniel ran his hand through the strands of his dark hair as he shook his head in dismay. "On the Internet, I saw a documentary about how there are people like me in Japan. Psychiatrists there call them 'the Hikikomori.' At least that's what the documentary said." He paused again, and then looked directly at her. "My doctor says it's an anxiety disorder. My parents... well, they've never really understood."

Nora did what she could to look empathetic. She knew what it was to have trouble with one's parents. No one knew better than her how difficult Family could be.

"Well, I should probably get back to it," she finally said with a sigh. "I just got back from shopping, and I should probably put my groceries away before they all melt. I'm going to be making dinner in a little while if you care to come and join me."

Daniel smiled, looking genuinely touched by the invitation, and just for a moment, the dark cloud he seemed to live under evaporated a little. But then, surprisingly, he shook his head as if he'd remembered something important that he had to do. He nervously stepped back into his apartment and started to close his door. "No... no, thank you. But it was nice seeing you again," he said softly, almost reluctantly, as the door clicked closed.

Nora couldn't help but feel that he sounded sad, almost melancholy. Not knowing what else to do, she turned to go back into her apartment. "Okay, well," she said to the empty hallway, raising her voice so as to be heard through Daniel's closed door. "Open invite then. Any time."

When no answer was forthcoming, she went back into her apartment and slowly closed the door behind her.

Later that night, after she'd eaten her dinner and finished with the dishes, Nora was back on the couch in her pajamas, watching another one of her baking shows. She wasn't being lazy. She was still pouring over the want ads in the day's newspaper like a biblical scholar, but a girl needed her distractions, right?

The search for employment had still not been going well. She'd applied at virtually every office in town but had so far heard nothing back from any of them. Add to that the fact that her money was rapidly running low, and it made for a pretty depressing picture. Nora remained confident though. She knew it was only a matter of time before something shook loose. It'll happen, she kept telling herself. It'll happen when you least expect it.

It was during one of her show's commercial breaks that she was shaken out of her reverie by the sound of more voices coming through the walls from Daniel's apartment. His mother must be back visiting, Nora thought to herself.

"You have to understand," the woman's voice said—his mother—the tone of her voice once again sounding frantic and a little distraught. "Since your Papa… died, well, it's been harder to pay all the bills, Daniel? If you could only help out…"

Nora heard Daniel's response pretty clearly, but it was clipped and panicky. "What am I supposed to do, Mother?"

Nora turned down her television with the remote. She didn't want to eavesdrop, but… come on! Her curiosity about whatever was going on next door between Daniel and his mother had been more than piqued. She almost felt like she had a vested interest in it now. So, in that moment, she felt perfectly willing to break a small social rule or two to get to the bottom of the mystery. She idly wondered if what they were discussing—money—was a common topic for them?

"Daniel…" his mother said, and her voice was upset and near tears. "How you live… like this. You need friends, and to learn how to provide for yourself."

There were some footsteps and then someone stamped their foot.

Whoa, Nora thought. Déjà vu.

"Mom," Daniel's voice said, "You know what Doctor Hoffman told you. I…" he paused as his voice became wracked with emotion. "I can't leave here. I… I just can't."

"How am I to pay for all of this then?? Papa is gone now and it's only me." Her voice paused as if she were deep in thought. Then, "What am I to say to our friends?"

Silence.

In her bedroom, down the hall, Nora could hear the sound of her alarm clock ticking, slowly meting out the time. She held her breath as she waited for someone in the other apartment to say, well… something, but there was only this heavy, anticipatory silence.

Finally, Daniel's mother mumbled something unintelligible.

"What did you just say?" Daniel asked incredulously.

More suffocating silence...

Then the woman said softly, "I am embarrassed to call you son."

"And I am ashamed to call you mother," Nora whispered as tears filled her eyes.

"And I..." Daniel shot back venomously from the other apartment. "...am ashamed to call you mother."

An abrupt slapping sound rang out sharply. There was a sudden thumping, and then something heavy struck the floor. Something—a door slamming, maybe?—made a bumping sound, and then everything slowly settled back into stillness.

A few minutes passed, but Nora heard nothing further. She shook her head as she aimed the remote at the television to switch off the sound on her show. Did they have the same argument every time she visited? She couldn't believe it. She made a mental note to ask Jordan or Josh about it the next time she saw them.

But then, she was suddenly interrupted by the sound of something falling and hitting the floor. Whatever it was clattered noisily, like it wasn't particularly heavy. After that, nothing; only the quiet of the house and the sound of the trees outside gently brushing up against the windows.

Nora waited a few more minutes for something else to happen, but from what she could tell—and what she could remember from the last time—the argument was more or less over. His mother may have left, she thought.

Turning her show back on, she silently considered everything she'd heard and once again wondered how common of an occurrence these fights were. It was pretty clear, she thought, that Daniel and his mom fought a lot. And, by the sounds of it, they fought about the same things. Nora had heard them before, and now here they were fighting again. She didn't like to pry, but... come on. The walls were so thin here; it was like she was in the same room with them anyway.

She curled up tighter on the couch, tucking her legs beneath her and wrapping the blanket she'd cocooned herself in even tighter. She tried to get back into her show, but that proved pointless. There were just too many wild ideas floating around in her head right now: finding work, her finances, and now this thing with Daniel. She finally gave up and turned it off.

As she headed toward bed, she thought about the lonely boy next store. She remembered the conversation they'd had when he told her some of his sad story. And about his inability to go out into the world. Learning that his father had only recently died only made the situation seem that much sadder. It wasn't like she could do anything about it, but still... he seemed like a nice kid. She hated to see things go so poorly for him.

Once in bed, she picked her pen and newspaper back up meaning to look for more prospects. She pulled her blanket around her, marking a few items of interest, but, in short order, she was fast asleep.

A few days later, Nora was once again leaving her apartment, locking the door behind her. She was wearing her same navy-blue business suit, and today, she was in a hurry. She'd finally landed a job interview with a medical insurance company, and she wanted to get there early enough so that she could grab a cup of coffee and get her head on straight. She hated rushing and wanted to allow herself enough time to chill out a little before she went to the appointment. She was coming down the stairs and heading for the door when she heard someone—a woman—call out to get her attention.

"Hey," the voice said. "Nora, right?"

Nora looked over the banister and saw the girl she'd met the first day she'd moved in: Aubrey. "Yeah, hey... hi," Nora answered back smiling.

"I don't know if you remember me, but..."

"Of course. Aubrey, right?" Nora asked.

The young, blonde woman smiled warmly and nodded her head as she came to meet Nora at the foot of the staircase. She was pretty, dressed casually again in a pair of jeans and a black and red striped baseball tee.

"Yeah, hey," she said. "How's it goin'? You doin' okay? Finding everything in the neighborhood all right?"

"Yeah," Nora responded. "Jordan and Josh have been really great. Thanks to them, I'm finally settled in—snug like a bug in a rug—and starting to look for work." She brushed a lock of her hair away from her eyes. "In fact, I'm on my way to a job interview now."

Aubrey smiled and pointed at Nora's suit. "I can see that. Oh, that's awesome."

"Yeah."

"Yeah..." Aubrey looked around the foyer, her manner clearly saying that she had something else on her mind, that she had something else she wanted to say, but wasn't sure exactly how—or where—to start. Finally, she just blurted it out. "I see they finally found someone to rent that apartment upstairs." She looked around the foyer again, like she was looking to betray a secret. "You know, Apartment 3."

Nora looked confused, cocking her head and squinting. Wait a minute, she thought, that was Daniel's apartment. Why would Jordan be renting it? Did Daniel move out during the last few days, and no one told her? How was it possible that she missed that? Was it because of the situation with his mother?

Nora furrowed her brow and looked at Aubrey. "What do you mean?"

"The apartment," Aubrey explained. "The empty one next to yours."

Nora shook her head. "No, there's somebody that already lives there: Daniel."

All of the color abruptly drained out of Aubrey's face. Her eyes grew wide and both corners of her mouth dipped sourly. She took a noticeable gulp as she gently shook her head from one side to the other. It took a second for her to formulate her next few words.

"What do you know about that?"

Nora pursed her lips in thought. "Well, I know that I spoke with him just a few days ago and he never mentioned anything about moving." She thought a minute before telling her the next bit, that she'd eavesdropped on him several times and she knew he and his mother were having some kind of trouble. "I don't mean to have listened, but I heard him talking kind of loudly with someone a few nights ago. I think it was his mom."

If it was at all possible, the already ashen color of Aubrey's face went even paler. She took a small, involuntary step back, then raised her hand and nervously touched her cheek.

"His m-mom?" Aubrey stammered. "But that's, that's impo…"

Nora stared at her, unsure as to what she meant. "Why?"

Aubrey gently took ahold of her arm and pulled her close. "Do you have a second to come down to my place?" She looked around them as if she were expecting to see something dangerous. "We shouldn't talk out here."

Nora laughed, gently, but firmly, pulling her arm away. "What are you talking about? Aubrey, you're kinda freaking me out here."

Aubrey replaced her hand on Nora's arm. "Just come here, okay? It'll only take a second."

Nora shook her head but checked her watch. "Okay but… I really need to get going in a second."

Once they were inside Aubrey's place—a lovely single-roomed apartment with a terrific view of the yard at the front of the house—they sat themselves onto the couch. Aubrey took Nora's hand and looked her keenly in the eye.

"Look," she began slowly, "I'm gonna tell you something and it's gonna sound crazy given what you just said to me in the hall. But I think it's important that you hear it…"

Nora wanted to laugh, but Aubrey was looking at her so ardently, her eyes burning with this weird intensity. "Okay," Nora said. "But I really do need to get to this appointment…"

Aubrey nodded, looking relieved, as she finally started to speak.

"So, a few years ago," she began, "it was right after I first moved in, that I heard that there was a guy who lived up in Number 3. Well, a young man, really. He was in like his late teens or early twenties. Sort of a shut in, a hermit, you know?"

Nora nodded. She knew.

"Well, apparently… after he'd lived here for a while," Aubrey continued, but stopped abruptly to interject. "And remember… this is all stuff I heard second-hand from Jordan. Anyway, Jordan said that this kid's parents were the ones who were paying all his rent, his utilities… his food. Everything. The kid supposedly once told Josh that he did some work online to help out with the finances, but…" She anxiously ran her hand through her blonde hair. "His parents basically took care of everything for him. And you know how much it costs to live in this town when you're out on your own."

Nora kept smiling but failed to see how any of this was applicable.

Or how it might answer any of her questions.

"Anyway," Aubrey settled into the cushion of the couch as she continued to tell her story. "According to Jordan…"

Daniel logged off from his computer with a weary sigh. He'd just turned in the last of his bug reports, and he was ready to start winding down for the day. The company where he was employed tested games and online gaming systems and it was his job to log on for a few hours every day to chase ghosts from within the framework of their coding. It wasn't a fantastic job, or one that gave him a lot of satisfaction, but it helped him with a portion of his monthly expenses, and it kept him busy.

The majority of his bills, though, were paid as a part of an agreement he had with his parents. Daniel had lived with them until the early part of his twenties. He'd moved out despite a pretty advanced case of social anxiety, needing a space of his own. The condition began presenting itself when he was in his teens, with an acute shortness of breath and a breakdown in his ability to function and communicate. It was a situation where, as he grew older and came closer to his full maturity, any and all social interaction became an immense source of stress and anxiety for him. So much so that, at one point, they started initiating powerful—in some cases, debilitating—panic attacks.

The very idea of talking to someone—to anyone—outside of his parents filled him with such anxiety that it all too soon became impossible for him to even leave the house. An overwhelming panic would set in, and he'd end up collapsed into a shivering, panting, angst-filled heap on the floor.

His parents thought he was just being dramatic. At least they did at first. They had said as much, out loud and in the open. Fainting solely for the attention, his father had declared. But after it happened at school a few too many times, he'd been referred to an actual doctor who diagnosed him with a condition predictably called 'acute social anxiety disorder.'

As a result, Daniel's parents were told that he would need to be homeschooled if he wanted to complete high school. His mother ended up having to leave a rather lucrative real estate career in order to be there for him, and that was something Daniel always thought made her resent him just a little.

But the thing was... Daniel was smart, and soon exceeded the limits of his parents' ability to teach him. And so, his instruction went online years before that sort of thing became popular. While this did do a lot to help decrease his anxiety levels, it did nothing for his burgeoning need to be alone. When he'd gotten his high school diploma early (and in the mail), he moved on to an online college where he got his Bachelor's in Game Design. All of which, he'd quickly found out once he got out into the workplace, counted for nothing if he were unable to leave his house.

This current game testing job only worked for him because he'd never been asked to go to an office someplace; to leave home. In fact, they asked little of him save for his daily 'bug reports' and making sure he clocked in and out correctly. Other than that, everyone more or less left him alone.

Which was a-okay with him.

As time passed, his parents got it into their heads that he'd be better off living on his own. That it would somehow benefit him—force him, more like—to leave the house and get a better paying job, to go shop for things, and to have to interact with people; to try and live, as they said, a 'normal life.' And so, they'd gotten him this small apartment in this old Victorian house where he'd been living in seclusion ever since.

As it turned out, the move didn't really change much for him. Not a damn thing, really. He still never left his room, still had no friends. And as far as going out for food and the like, he preferred to either have whatever he needed delivered… or he got his mom to bring it to him during one of her frequent visits.

Daniel slowly let his gaze drift around the small, one room flat. The place was okay, he guessed. He had a bathroom with a small shower, but… other than that, it was just this one room and a small closet to the place. His bed was an olive-green futon that, though now laid flat, doubled as a couch, and dominated most of the confined living area. The four walls were lined with bookshelves, each filled to capacity with his carefully curated assortment of books, comics, bound graphic novels, and Blu-Rays. He was a voracious reader as a result of his always being alone, and had, over the years, become something of a collector.

Daniel got up from his computer and moved toward the corner of the apartment he thought of as the kitchen. He was hungry and was just about to throw something into the microwave—the last of a pizza he'd had delivered last night—when there was an unexpected knock at his door. A sudden sense of panic rose within him in a blinding red wave. For him, such interruptions were a real and tangible threat. He paused before going to see who it was, using one of the breathing techniques his therapist had taught him to calm himself down. After a few deep breaths, he was able to get everything under control to a point where he could take a peek through the door's peephole.

"Shit," he whispered under his breath as he pulled back to let his visitor in.

He began unlocking the door almost reflexively, pulling away the door chain and unlocking the array of deadbolts with a practiced hand. His fingers moved quickly over the locks like a harpist at his instrument. He finally grabbed the knob and pulled the door open.

"Hello, Daniel," his mother said softly from the hall.

Out in the hallway, there stood an elderly woman wearing what Daniel knew was her 'city clothes:' that same faded grey dress and coal black overcoat, black loafers, and her 'big' purse which was slung like a water-skin over her right shoulder. In her arms were two large, brown paper bags from Dresden's, the nearby grocery store.

Of course, she had her own key, but this knocking was a dance they did every time she came over. And she came over a lot. A week didn't go by that she didn't drop by unannounced to, according to her, check on him. Daniel always thought though that it was to make him feel bad for the way his life had turned out, like a weekly shot of guilt. Potato… potahto, he guessed.

"Hello, Mother," Daniel said, stepping aside so that she could enter.

She slowly moved deeper into the room, looking around appraisingly. Her expression betrayed her recurring feeling of revulsion. Both she and Daniel's father had never approved of the way their son kept his room, and they'd never felt the need to be shy about expressing it. Now that his father was gone, though, dead now, what... nearly a year, she thought that it was a part of her job to double-up on the cliched parenting of the boy.

"Oh, Daniel," she said softly, almost as if she were talking to herself. She went over and set the bags onto the counter. "How do you continue to live like this?" She shook her head sadly. "I brought you some groceries and some of those vanilla cookies I know you like."

Knowing what came next in their shared script, Daniel threw himself down onto the futon dramatically. Here we go, he thought to himself.

"Mom, please," he moaned despondently.

This was an old argument between them and one they'd both grown tired of having. Lord knows... he'd heard it enough. And he certainly didn't want to go over it yet again. Not now. Not when he was this tired and this hungry.

His mother waved at the air as if swatting at a fly. "But I don't want to talk about that now, Daniel." Her manner suddenly became agitated, and as she stared back at him intently, her eyes brimmed with the promise of moisture. She wiped away a tear. "I need to talk to you about something else; something important."

Daniel sat up on the futon and sighed dramatically. As he sat there, he idly picked up one of the heavy, porcelain statues on the bookshelf, slowly turning it over in his hands. The sculpture was of a muscular man—or a demon of some sort—from a popular anime he liked. The creature displayed a pronounced wingspan that curled like a shroud around its formidable body. The weighty object measured almost twelve inches tall and had a real heft to it. The boy focused his attention on the character's angry face rather than on whatever it was that his mother was squalling about.

"Daniel, please," he heard her say under her breath, her voice thick with agitation. "This is serious. This is very important."

Daniel had always been a good boy, she thought; challenging because of how smart he was, but still well-behaved. This thing with him being unable to be around other people had begun right after he started puberty, and it had only gotten worse with time. Lord knows... She and her husband—God rest his soul—had tried to understand, but... it was all just so hard.

Daniel looked up at her, his expression annoyed, as he quietly said, "Okay, so what is it, Mother?"

"I know we've talked about it before, but..." she said haltingly, as if she were afraid to say aloud the very thing she'd come here to say. "I need you to understand... since your Papa died; it's been hard for me to pay all the bills. Both my bills and yours. I just need you to... well, if you could only just help out a bit more. Maybe pick up some extra hours at your job?"

Daniel's response was clipped and nearing panic. They had been over this too many times in the past. The idea that the only reason she'd come over now was just to bring it up all over again fueled the conflagration of his growing rage. He looked over at the sacks of groceries on the counter angrily.

"What am I supposed to do, Mother?" he finally spat out.

"Daniel... you don't understand," his mother cried, and her voice was twisted with shame and regret. She noticed that her voice had unconsciously risen in its volume, so she paused, reminding herself of the need for rationality. "It's just become too expensive, Daniel. Everything... is just so expensive now."

She walked the short distance to the wall on the other side of the room.

Abruptly, Daniel got to his feet from the futon and pounded his foot on the floor. He pointed at her with his left hand angrily, his right constrained by the weight of the sculpture.

"Mother," Daniel shouted back, yelling now in response to her having raised her voice. "You know what Doctor Hoffman told you. I..." he paused as his voice cracked like dried timber. "I can't leave here. I... I just... I just can't, okay? They'll make me go into their office if I ask to increase my hours. I just can't do that."

"But," she was pleading with him now. "How am I to continue to pay for all this then?? Papa is gone now and it's only me." She was openly crying, her voice crescendoing to a high-pitched whine. "What am I to tell our friends?"

The apartment abruptly went quiet, and stillness spread like a dense fog throughout the entire building. It was as if the house itself were holding its breath in anticipation of what might come next.

Finally, the woman sighed and mumbled something.

"What did you just say?" Daniel demanded incredulously. He took a hesitant step toward her; the room, the house, even the statuary he held in his hand, all but forgotten.

The two of them stood staring at one another for the longest time;

mother and son. The woman's eyes were wet with her tears. The boy's were set aflame by his anger.

More silence...

Then, the woman softly repeated, "I am embarrassed to call you son."

Daniel fumed; his fury now a raging inferno within him, fire burning out the last vestiges of his reason. He looked at his mother indignantly and took another step closer. His eyes tore a hole through her heart. There was another long pause.

"And I... am ashamed to call you mother," Daniel shot back.

The older woman reacted as if she'd been struck. She winced as if she were in some kind of sudden physical pain. Looking up at him, she glared at the boy. Finally, her anger broke free, and she reached out and slapped him across his face, the crack echoing sharply within the confines of the small room. Daniel reacted instinctively, without ever really thinking of the consequences of his actions, and his hand lashed out to stop her from striking him again.

Suddenly, Daniel saw the statue that he still held in his hand strike his mother across the brow with great force, roughly rocking her head back. Blood erupted from her scalp, blossoming like a red flower from the top of her head. She teetered where she stood for an instant, then her body fell forward and she struck the floor face-first. Blood began pooling like oil beneath her head.

Horrified by what he had done, Daniel stumbled backward, dropping the now-bloody statue from his hand. The heavy object fell to the floor with a thump, and it rolled, finally coming to rest beside the futon. After that, a hush returned to the house like the quiet after a death knell.

A few minutes passed as Daniel stood over the inert body of his mother with wide, terrified eyes. He watched over her as a growing puddle of blood beneath her head slowly spread across the bare floor. His mother—the woman who had given him birth—lay there on the floor like Humpty Dumpty after his great fall. Daniel knew instinctively that, much like the fabled egg man, there would be no putting any of this back together again. Nor was there any way to ever make this right.

He watched impotently as her breathing abruptly faltered. From the looks of it, she was able to draw air in, but not blow any of it out. He was about to touch her when her respiration sort of hiccupped, and then it stopped.

Daniel fell to his knees on the floor and began to weep.

"He hung himself from the ceiling almost immediately after he did it," Aubrey said, concluding her story. She sat back, satisfied she'd not forgotten any of the lurid details. "Jordan told me that the guy who came when they called 911, the one from the Medical Examiner's office, said that the kid used one of his own belts." She shivered in her seat. "Slung it over a beam and put it around his neck like a noose. Then, I guess he just stepped off the chair he was standing on, and bingo bango... next stop, the Pearly Gates."

Nora looked visibly rattled. What she'd just heard was simply impossible. She'd just spoken to Daniel, what... a few days ago? She'd been inside his apartment, for God's sake. Were Aubrey and Jordan pulling a joke on her? A prank? Fucking with her because she was new in the house? It seemed like such a weird and unnecessarily cruel thing to do. She adjusted her position on the couch.

"Everyone that's lived here since, well..." Aubrey continued, "has heard noises. I'm sure you've heard the arguing by now..."

Nora's eyes went wide.

"Yeah," Aubrey continued. "We've all heard it. The first time I did, I almost moved the fuck out. But The J's assured me that it was all harmless and the only thing that had ever manifested itself was some noise. I guess, at some point, they contacted a psychic or something, and, anyway, that's what she'd told them. Besides, living in a real haunted house is kind of cool, right?" She looked at Nora with a wide, almost innocent expression.

"Look, Aubrey," Nora replied. "I don't want to seem rude or anything, but... what you're telling me, it's just not possible." She got a faraway look in her eye, like her brain was so busy processing all this new, weird information that it couldn't think and stay focused on talking at the same time. Her eyes suddenly cleared, and she continued on as if nothing had happened. "I not only saw the kid, but I was inside his apartment. I saw his books, his bed... I saw his fucking computer." She looked at her new neighbor intently. "I mean, I spoke to him."

Aubrey looked genuinely surprised, like, in that instant, it all just got too real for her. It was one thing for people to hear thumps and bumps in the middle of the night, but... when they started seeing things, well... that's where she drew the line. But then, the blonde girl got a wicked expression on her face. Slowly, she smiled and took Nora by the hand. "Show me."

The two women left Aubrey's apartment together and nearly ran up the stairs to the second floor. At the landing, they turned left and strode up to the door of Number 3. This time, the door was closed tight. Other than that, it looked as it usually did, plain, unadorned, and a clone to all of the others in the house.

Without really thinking, Nora reached out and knocked.

Aubrey chuckled darkly and grabbed the doorknob.

"Wait!" Nora said defensively, reaching out and touching her friend on the arm. "You can't just walk in."

Aubrey laughed. "Why not?"

"Somebody could be home?"

Aubrey turned the knob and pushed the door open. "Like whom?"

As the wide panel of wood slowly swung inward, the two women both leaned in. Nora was already planning her apologies and the excuses she'd need to make to Daniel for barging in like this, when her thoughts suddenly came crashing down around her as she got a look at what was inside the apartment.

The room before them was the exact room Nora had seen previously… only now, it was empty. Not only was it vacant, but there was a gray layer of dust over every perceivable flat surface, like the room had been left abandoned for quite some time.

"No one's been 'home' here in, like forever. Not since they cleared the kid's stuff out of here," Aubrey said. "The place now has a bit of a reputation in town. Kids think it's a spook house. Why do you think the rent is so low? And why do you think it's taken The J's so long to rent it?" A tiny laugh. "Shit, we were all surprised when you took the place next door."

As it turned out, the person who rented #3 ended up leaving after only a month. Nora had come home from her job—yes, she nailed that interview—as they were moving their stuff out. She'd spoken with them briefly, and they told her that they kept hearing strange noises in the apartment late at night, so they decided to leave.

Since then, the place has remained empty.

At some point, Jordan just stopped listing it in the newspapers and with the rental placement services because he had a fairly good idea of how it would go (and how short any tenant's stay would be). The continual back-n-forth was just a giant pain in the butt, so, he wrote off any potential loss of revenue from not renting the room as 'not worth pursuing' and forgot all about it. He ended up telling everyone that he was going to use the space as storage or as an art space, but somehow that never happened.

As for Nora… Nora ended up staying in Number 4 for another year or so, almost happy that things had turned out the way they had. After all, she liked the neighbor she had in Number 3, the one who had been there when she first moved in. The thought of someone else living in the apartment, well… it just made her feel really sad.

Oddly, after Nora had seen the apartment empty, she'd not heard anything further from Number 3, not even a repeat of the conversation between Daniel and his mother. Sometimes though, as she'd went by the apartment door, she would swear that she could see something staring back at her from within the darkness between the open door and the jamb.

Something… or someone staring out.

Nora ended up meeting someone at her new job. They got married a short time afterward and she left the Victorian. A few years later, there was a child, and the three of them lived together in a small house down by the seashore. Nora finally found someone who would love her every bit as much as she loved them.

After getting her degree at the local college, Aubrey moved away to work for an aerospace firm in the next state over. About a month after that, she heard that Josh had a heart attack while at work and passed away soon after. Doctors said it was from stress. Jordan, of course, was devastated and ended up selling the Victorian, leaving his garden to the new owners who let it fall to ruin from neglect. He ended up catching COVID and dying in a sterile hospital room. There was no one left in his life to mourn him, and when he passed, he did so alone.

And for all anybody can say… Daniel—or rather, Daniel's spirit—remains there in the apartment at the top of the stairs atop the old gray and black Victorian on San Salvador Street to this day.

THE ATTESTANT

This is another one of those stories that is based on something that actually happened. And while admittedly somewhat grim, I think the piece is important as it also takes a look at how we as a society view death, and the thought processes that might be inherent in someone who finds themselves in this admittedly tough situation.

"Shit!" Gordon Robinson exclaimed as one of the forks he was putting into the dishwasher slipped from his grasp. The utensil bounced between the dish racks and fell with a clatter to the bottom of the appliance, down near the rotating sprinkler blade. "God damn it."

He reached into the machine through the large front door and slid the wire rack out so he could retrieve the runaway implement. Bending down, he snatched up the fork, a single kernel of corn still speared upon one of its tines, and gently eased the rack back in. He set the fork in the small compartment in the door with the rest of the dinnerware.

Gordon had decided to do the dishes despite feeling like shit. He'd spent most of the day studying for this 'Understanding Management Information Systems' class he was taking at the local college, and, well… he just felt like he could really use a distraction, any distraction. After spending so many hours with his nose buried in his books, he figured he needed—no, deserved—a bit of a break. He had this test coming up and he only barely understood the material… which sucked. But he'd also been putting the day-to-day housework off for too long, and things were really beginning to pile up.

Gordon was a Computer Science major at a small college in northernmost Washington state, and he knew that he needed to do well on this test in particular. His grades were not what anyone would ever call 'exemplary,' and his Advisor had so much as told him that he would bomb out of the program unless he brought his grades up. And so, he'd been studying his ass off. Hell, he'd even brought his textbook along with him as he took this break to clean the kitchen a little. Even now, the book lay open on the counter like a spatchcocked chicken.

Gordon turned on the hot water from the faucet and let it run into the sink. The steaming liquid splashed happily over the dirty plates that were still sitting piled in the basin. He played sharpshooter with his thumb over the spigot, jetting off the remaining bits of food left on the porcelain with its power.

Thankfully, he was the only one who lived in the apartment, so there were never that many dishes to do. He'd had roommates in the past, but they'd just never worked out. Over the years, he'd taught himself to use only the things he needed, and to wash them immediately after he was done. It was this spartan practice that usually meant that his house chores never got overwhelming.

He looked over at his textbook.

But that all changed once he'd signed up for this fuckin' class.

Out of nowhere, Gordon's cell phone lying next to his textbook rang abruptly. Its buzzing sent the device skittering across the flat countertop like a nervous beetle. He quickly dried his hands off with a dish rag, then he picked up his phone and looked at the screen, noticing that it was an unfamiliar number. As he answered the call, he silently hoped it wasn't a telemarketer. Or worse, a bill collector.

"Hello?" he said into the phone's mouthpiece.

An older woman's reedy voice responded after first clearing her throat. "Yes, hello," she said nervously. Her voice trembled and it made her sound elderly. "Is this... is this Gordon Robinson?"

Gordon closed his eyes and grimaced. Damn it! He just hoped he could get rid of them before they tried to sell him something. "It is."

"Oh, thank god," the woman said sounding relieved. "I don't know if you remember me, Mr. Robinson, but... My name is Dora Kincaid." She paused as if expecting him to remember her.

"Okay." Gordon was drawing a blank on the name. "What can I do for you, Ma'am?"

The voice sighed sadly. "You don't remember me."

"I... I'm afraid not."

"Well, you see, my daughter is Bonnie Kincaid. She lives right down the hall from you." She paused again for a sign of recognition. "In Apartment 4D."

"Oh, okay," Gordon replied. He thought about it for another second and the image of a middle-aged woman in a velour track suit came to his mind like an apparition. "Yeah, okay. I think I do remember her. Well, what can I do for you, Mrs. Kincaid?"

Bonnie Kincaid was a middle-aged lady who did indeed live right down the hall from him in 4D. He remembered her being one of the super welcoming ones when he first moved in. One of those too-friendly neighbors who had been extraordinarily nice to him over the time he'd lived here. She'd even invited him over for coffee a few times and they'd become sort of friendly in that 'since we're neighbors, we should probably try to get along' kind of way. He dimly remembered giving her his telephone number in case she ever needed anything. He couldn't remember ever giving it to her mother, though.

"Well, as you may remember, I live over in Barton, near the Costco there, and uh…" She paused as she considered the best way to ask him what she needed to ask. "As you know, it's a two-hour drive just to come out there."

Gordon nodded silently even though he was alone and there was no one else around to see it. "Yeah, it's a haul. But what can I do for you?"

The woman's voice chuckled nervously. They shared a heartbeat of silence. And then, she nervously cleared her throat. "You know, I hate to ask this of you, but…" she drew another audible breath. "Again, Gordon, I just live so far away."

"It's no problem, Mrs. Kincaid. What do you need?" he asked, just wanting her to get to the point so he could get back to the dishes… and his goddam studying.

He heard her light a cigarette over the phone. She breathed out and it sounded like she was already relieved, like some great weight had suddenly been lifted off of her. There was some fumbling on the line, like she was carrying the phone across the room to sit down. Then it got quiet again.

"Well," she finally continued, "I've been trying to get a hold of Bonnie for a few days now, and, well… she doesn't seem to be answering her phone."

Gordon thought it over for a second, furrowing his brow. Nope, he hadn't seen the woman in at least a week or two. It could have even been longer. He simply wasn't sure. Last time he remembered seeing her was when they'd run into one another out by the dumpster when they were both taking out some trash.

"Well, come to think of it, I haven't seen Bonnie in a while either, Ma'am," he explained. "But to be fair, and with all due respect… she doesn't exactly go out a lot as I recall."

"That is true," Mrs. Kincaid sighed, her voice sounding exasperated on the line. "Well, I'm not sure if you know, but…" Her tone now took on a conspiratory tone. "Ever since the divorce from Rob, well…" She paused to cluck her tongue. "Well, she's just been going through a rough patch, you know?"

Gordon smiled to himself.

How quickly gossip betrays even the most solemn of confidences, he thought idly.

"I'm sorry to hear that," he said, and he tried to sound sympathetic.

Truth was, he barely knew the woman. Either of them. Sure, Bonnie was nice and made for an unobtrusive neighbor that he'd shared a cup of coffee with every once in a while, but, other than him nodding his head at her whenever he happened to see her in the hall, they weren't exactly what anyone would call friends.

"Well, I hate to be a bother," the old woman in his ear continued.

Here it comes...

"Would you be a dear and go over and just check up on her. I mean, I pray to God that nothing has happened, but well... you just never know."

Gordon looked at the textbook lying brazenly open on the counter. He knew he still had several hours of hard studying ahead of him. He didn't need something like this to come along and derail him.

"Couldn't you just call the police?" he asked hopefully. "I mean, they do 'welfare' checks on people all the time, don't they?"

Bonnie's mother's voice immediately became flustered. "Oh, my goodness, no. I'm... I'm sure it's nothing. I wouldn't want to bother the police over something like this, something that could easily turn out to be nothing at all."

Oh, but you'll bother me though, Gordon thought snidely.

He looked at the clock. 3:45 PM. The way he figured it, he could sit here and argue with this lady, or he could just bite the bullet and run over to the apartment down the hall and be done with it. It would probably only take a few minutes.

Right?

"Okay," he finally acquiesced. "I'll go down and take a quick look. I can at least knock on the door to see if it looks like she's even at home. If she answers, great. If not... I'll come back and call you. You may have to end up having to call the cops after all. I'm sorry."

"Yes, of course," she replied, and she sounded reassured that he agreed to go. But he'd need to get in... just in case. "There's a door key hidden, taped under the doormat, if she doesn't answer."

Rather than argue the point, Gordon agreed to her request and hung up, after jotting her number down in the margin of his textbook. He'd go ahead and pop down to the lady's apartment and knock on the door. If she didn't answer, he'd come and call her mom back and that would be that. He didn't need to be using any key or going inside.

That… was a job for the cops.

After putting his shoes on, he went out into the hallway, turning to the right. Bonnie Kincaid's apartment was a few doors down, past the stairway that led to the passkey-protected front entrance. As he walked along the thin corridor, he once again thought about his interactions with Bonnie, and how much he knew about her. He knew that she lived alone and that she was retired. And that was about all he could really remember about her.

Again, she was someone he knew, but he didn't know her.

And yet, here he was…

He chuckled softly. He could be such a pushover.

When he finally arrived outside of her place, he knocked on the door and waited for someone to come answer it. The hallway was quiet and a little bit lonely as he stood there waiting. The only thing he could hear coming through the wall was one of the neighbor's television sets. From the sound of the laughter and applause, it sounded like they were watching a game show. He knocked again—louder this time—but still no one came.

He shrugged and glared down at the Welcome mat. It was a large, rubber square with the words 'wipe your paws' printed on the front of it. He sighed as he flipped it over—just like he always knew he would. There, he found a small square of duct tape sticking to its bottom. The outline of a key could be clearly seen beneath the silver. He pulled it off and separated it from the sticky adhesive.

But then, just as he was inserting the key into the lock, he hesitated, suddenly imagining himself opening the door to find Bonnie sitting on the couch, peacefully watching television wearing headphones or some shit. He paused for a second, quickly going over in his head what he might say. 'Your mother called, and she was worried' seemed inadequate, but it did cover what had happened.

But okay… he'd have to go with that, he thought, as he unlocked the door. He turned the doorknob and slowly pushed the door open. The apartment inside had much the same layout as his own: a large living area coupled to a small kitchen with presumably a bedroom and bath in the back. The décor of the place seemed stalled in a time that had long since passed. A gold velour sofa and matching easy chair were gathered like boy scouts before a fire in front of a large, flat screen that had been mounted on the wall. Next to the TV was a decoupage picture of an eagle on a piece of flat, lacquered driftwood. Framed photos of friends, family, and the like were hung sporadically on the other walls like stars suspended in a night sky.

"Hey, Bonnie?" Gordon called out as he cautiously stepped deeper into the living room. He hadn't wanted to shout, but… he wanted her to hear him in case she was in the back bedroom or in the bathroom. "Bonnie?"

The house remained mute.

He shot a quick glance toward the kitchen but saw nothing there that was out of the ordinary. The counters were stacked with an array of storage jars, store-bought vegetables, and opened (and half-closed) bags of chips and cookies. There was a smell of coffee and burnt toast hanging in the air like a dead man. A blender and Vitamix completed the picture.

"Hey, Bonnie?" He slowly walked past the couch and angled his head down the hall. "Bonnie? It's me… Gordon. From down the hall. Your uh… your mother called me, and…"

He stopped before heading any further. For the first time, the idea that this woman might be dead struck him, like a sliver of ice fallen down the back of his pants. He couldn't think of anything worse. Finding someone dead could only suck, right? The thought of it was just creepy. But, with the way things were going, it seemed like the perfect capper to his already screwed up day.

"Hey, Bonnie?"

Gordon took another step, noting the open bathroom door on the left and the closed bedroom on the right further down the hallway. He shot a glance into the bathroom and, predictably, found nothing but, well… the bathroom. He couldn't help but notice the shower curtain due to the bright yellow daffodils and peonies printed on it. He sighed in exasperation as he continued on to the only room left in the house: the bedroom.

Just then, just as he was about to set his hand onto the bedroom door's doorknob, a tangy, sour smell struck him across the nose like a rolled-up newspaper. The odor seeped under the door like bilge water, slowly corrupting his senses. Whatever the odor was, it smelled sweet and sour and bitter and oily all at the same time. There was no way this was going to turn out well, he thought, as he gently pushed the door in front of him open.

The bedroom was dark. The drapes had been pulled closed, allowing no illumination from outside to come through. He could see in the dim light filtering in from the hall that there was a bed and a dresser… a couple of nightstands, but not much else. He quickly checked the bed but saw that the bedding was flat and straight. It appeared as if no one had slept in it for some time.

"Bonnie?" he called out nervously. Despite the fact that his brain was yelling at him not to do it, he reached over and flicked on the overhead light. "Are you in here?"

The bulb in the fixture in the ceiling exploded into a blinding, clinical white light. Gordon took a couple of steps back, squinting and shielding his eyes from the glare with one of his hands. He waited a second for his vision to adjust, then he slowly reopened them.

The room before him was exactly as he'd expected it to be, the same bed, the same dresser, the nightstands, but there was now a messy lived-in aspect to it. Looking around him, he noticed more large piles of clothing and some boxes that were stacked in the corners, but he saw no sign of Bonnie.

He noticed that the sour odor he had been smelling in the hall was stronger here in this room. His stomach suddenly felt greasy, and it rolled over like a sick dog in his belly. He couldn't help it. The scent was cloying, nauseating, like being locked in a room with too many flowers. But, as he began to get more and more used to it, he noticed that the aroma also had an aspect of tainted meat to it.

"Bonnie?" he repeated aloud.

He was just about to give up, to shut the light off and head back to his apartment to call Bonnie's mom back, when his eye caught sight of something on the other side of the room, over by the closet. He narrowed his eyes to try and focus them in the light, and it was then that he saw something odd hanging from the top of the closet door. It looked thin, like it was being drawn taught by some kind of weight. Whatever the thing was, it was extended from the top of the door down to something on the floor.

Gordon took another hesitant step into the room, peering around the side of the bed. As his eyes searched the scene, his brain quickly took snapshots and assembled them like they were jigsaw puzzle pieces of a greater mosaic: a cast-off slipper lying on the floor near a pile of laundry, the hem of a light blue bathrobe, a hand laying palm up on the carpeting. His gaze slowly tracked up and, to his horror, he found himself all too soon staring into an unrecognizable woman's puffy, so red as to be purple, dead face.

Bonnie.

"Oh, shit," Gordon erupted, stumbling a few steps backward in shock. The back of his knees unexpectedly struck the bed, and he sat down heavily onto the mattress, the springs crying out briefly in protest.

Bonnie was lying against the closet door in a sitting position a few feet from him, her legs splayed brazenly out in front of her. Her bloodshot eyes were open, and their pupils were cloudy, almost milky. A blackened and bloated tongue hung out of her opened mouth like a half-eaten piece of liver. Fiery red lines of postmortem lividity were already staining the skin of her extremities. Despite himself, his gaze ended up focusing on the thin blue belt from her robe that was wrapped tightly around her neck like a cable. The thin fabric extended rigidly toward the top of the closet door.

"Shit," he groaned as he quickly got up and walked back down the hall. "Shit, shit, shit, shit, shit, shit—shit!"

When he was back in the living room, he paced back and forth a bit before finally deciding to look around for Bonnie's telephone. He finally found it—a landline, for Christ's sake—sitting on a small table next to the TV. He picked up the receiver, dialed 911, and anxiously waited for someone to answer.

"911, can you state your emergency?" a woman's husky voice said when she'd finally picked up the line. The voice was deep, the kind his dad always called 'a smoker's voice.' It was also distinctly Southern.

"I, uh..." he responded. "I just found my neighbor. I think she's hung herself. I mean, I think she's dead."

The operator double-checked the address with him and asked if he knew the identity of the suspected deceased. He said he did, and he gave her Bonnie's name. The operator said she'd send a patrol car to the location as quickly as possible.

"It won't be long. But I'm gonna have to ask you to stay there though, okay, Sugah? Please..." she paused. "Just until the officers arrive."

"Should I at least get her down?"

"No," the voice on the other end instructed emphatically. "You... shouldn't touch a thing. Just wait until the officers arrive."

After he'd agreed to keep his hands to himself and hung up, Gordon decided to do his waiting in the living room, at least until his heart rate decided to slow itself down. Let the cops sort it out, he thought to himself. That's the smart thing to do. They said to not touch anything, and that was exactly what he was going to do.

But, then again, he didn't really know for sure that Bonnie was dead, now did he? Sure, he'd seen her lying there, and she definitely looked like shit, but he never actually checked her. Maybe she was just injured and was still alive. And he'd just left her there.

"Damn it," he said resignedly, and his voice sounded hollow within the confines of the vacant living room. Lamentably, he went back down the hall toward the bedroom.

Back to where Bonnie lay.

Once he'd gotten back to the bedroom, Gordon sat back down on the edge of the bed. Again, he looked at where Bonnie was sitting on the floor against the closet door. He couldn't help himself. He'd never been this close to a dead person before. And she was a friend… sort of. She was at least someone he knew. And now, here she was, sitting there with her legs akimbo, very clearly dead. Hung herself, for Christ's sake.

He sighed sadly. He'd never understood people's desire to do something like this, to kill themselves. Maybe it was his own sense of privilege or whatever, but he'd never faced anything so overwhelming in Life that the only solution available to him was to go and off himself. Maybe he would, given time, but… Right now, it all seemed, well, sorta short-sighted and counterproductive. You had to give things a chance to get better, before giving up on them. At least that's what he believed.

He shook his head and distracted himself by letting his gaze float around Bonnie's cluttered bedroom. The place was a bit of a dump he finally decided: unkempt and seemingly in a state of perpetual chaos. From all appearances, housekeeping wasn't exactly the woman's strong suit. The bedroom looked more like a garage sale had exploded within its walls than anything else. There were piles of clothes that looked like they needed to be folded—or washed—strewn about. Other half-finished chores had been left abandoned on the tops of her furniture or left stacked on the floor.

He shook his head again in dismay. Noticing one of the photographs on the dresser, Gordon got up and walked over to look at it. Taking the picture frame in his hands, he saw a younger, and visibly happier, Bonnie sitting on a park bench with a man. Good looking and sort of debonair, the man had a hand up in greeting, smiling at whoever it was that was taking the photo. Bonnie was sitting next to him, smiling, and looking so happy as to almost burst. Gordon gently set the photo back where he'd gotten it and reluctantly wandered back to the bed.

As he continued to look around the room, he wondered if this was how we all ended up. If this was all that was left after a person died: some old artifacts, a few clothes, and a random pile of totems like pictures and tchotchkes from county fairs and visits to amusement parks whose only purpose was to spark memories.

"We're nothing," he sadly whispered to himself, "without our memories."

He'd read that someplace. Oddly, he couldn't remember where.

There was a half-empty glass of water on the nightstand and Gordon wondered how long-ago Bonnie had put it there. Did she take one last sip before deciding to wrap her bathrobe belt around her neck and sitting down to die? And if so, why? So, she wouldn't be thirsty on the trip to the Afterlife? One last drink before heading off into that good night; to wherever one goes when they're dead? Once again, he shook his head sadly. It was all too convoluted and alien for him to put together in any way that made sense.

Despite his misgivings, he slowly let his eyes drift back to Bonnie. Now that he'd gotten over the initial shock of finding her like this, he was able to objectively document what he was seeing… in case the cops questioned him about it when they got there.

Bonnie stared up at him, her eyes gawking impossibly large, her face as immobile as statuary. He noticed that her eyelids had fallen over her eyes like window shades and they gave her the appearance of being half-asleep… or sublimely stoned. Her complexion was pale and sallow, all the blood having now been drained from her face by gravity. Her blackened tongue still filled her mouth, its mass resembling a decomposing slug resting on her lower lip. Her hair was wet, like she'd just gotten out of the shower, strands of black laying pasted to her face like seaweed.

As Gordon continued to stare at her, his mind wandered. How excited her parents must have been when they found out they were pregnant with a new baby. How that must have filled them both with such love. Then, once she was born, how her parents must have doted on her. How much they must have loved her. He idly wondered what her sixteenth birthday was like. Her first prom date? Her first kiss?

He turned his head away and his eyes came to rest on another of Bonnie's photos. This one was hanging by a nail from the wall. The crucified photo was of Bonnie and the same man that was in a few of the other photos he'd seen around the house. She was wearing a beautiful white wedding dress and smiling like her face was going to come apart at the jaw. The man, that same attractive Italian with the dark piercing eyes—Rob, undoubtedly—held her tightly to him at the waist. Both of their faces… so happy, so full of hope.

Gordon knew from talking to Bonnie over coffee that the marriage had only lasted about six years before the bloom fully—and finally—fell from the rose. Far too short for them to have had children, thank the Lord. See, as it turned out, Bonnie's husband was a guy who was far more interested in the thrill of the chase than in sticking with anything over the long haul. Sadly, he was like a predator whose only interest was running his prey to the ground.

Him actually ever eating what he'd caught, well… that was another story.

So, the divorce happened, and Bonnie never really managed to pull it together after that. She said she'd worked a job or two, but that proved to be too much for her, too much stress, so she'd taken her retirement early. These days, as far as Gordon could tell from what he'd seen around him, her life pretty much consisted of puttering around her small unkempt home and watching television.

Gordon stared into the carpeting and shook his head.

"You know," he finally said out loud, "You could have come and talked to me." He looked back toward his neighbor's constipated-looking face. "Rather than do this?"

Predictably, Bonnie had little to say in her own defense.

Gordon suddenly noticed that a fly had come into the room. The insect hovered and circled over Bonnie's body like a vulture, floating downward in a lazy corkscrew pattern. For some reason, the idea that it might land on Bonnie deeply offended him, so he jumped up from the bed to swat it away. He was on his way back to sit on the bed when there was a sudden loud knock at the front door.

"Police!" a man's deep voice informed loudly. "Mr. Robinson? Mr. Robinson, are you in there?"

Gordon nearly jumped out of his skin in surprise at the sound. He looked over at Bonnie's inert form and snickered in embarrassment.

"Okay, that scared me," he said and immediately caught himself, feeling like an ass for talking to a dead person.

Bonnie remained oblivious to the humor in the situation.

Gordon started to go and answer the door but stopped himself. For a second, he thought about covering Bonnie's exposed legs up, but remembered the 911 operator telling him not to touch anything, so he didn't.

Looking back at her from the doorway, he once again shook his head sadly. He could never be sure what had led her to take her own life like this, but he guessed that she must have had her reasons. Whether it was from the loss of love or the crushing weight of her own loneliness, it was clear that she'd had enough of the world, and she'd decided to do something about it. Maybe she was sick?

He'd heard a man on television once say that life was like a movie, and we can't really blame someone for walking out of the picture early. In a weird way, that made some sense to him. He looked over one last time and smiled warmly at Bonnie.

"It was nice to have known you, Bonnie Kincaid," he sighed. "I just wish I could have done more to help."

And when Bonnie once again failed to give him any kind of response, he left the bedroom and went down the hall to let the cops in. When he was gone from the room, the fly returned, alighting onto Bonnie's cheek, and wringing its hands in anticipation of what was to come.

ALIAS: SMITH AND JONES

As I believe I've previously stated, I've been reading a lot of 'tough guy' fiction from the Sixties for some reason. Novels featuring the likes of Nick Carter, Matt Helm, or Mac Bolan: The Executioner. It's great stuff and I wholeheartedly recommend you seeking some of it out. Me being me, though, I started thinking about how you never see these guys out in the world doing, y'know... regular people things. They're always 'on the case' or 'at the gun range' or some shit. This all led me to the idea of these folks trying to simply live their lives in their off-hours. Y'know, like shopping for clothes, or I don't know... returning an item to Costco. How do they go out for an evening, say, on a date? I mean, how do you meet prospective sexual partners outside of all the requisite murdering and skullduggery? Anyway, long story short (too late!), this train of thought ultimately led me to the idea of 'online dating' sites (because that's just how my brain works), and the rest of the story came together pretty quickly after that. Oh, and if you remember where the title of this comes from, then congratulations! You're officially old.

The night was cold in the city, temperatures down into the low thirties, when the sharply dressed man came in through the front door of the posh, Michelin-starred restaurant called Donelli's. He was tall, darkly handsome, and built in the powerful way that men who used their bodies in their occupations were. It wasn't hard to see the cut of his athletic frame beneath the tailored black suit he wore. His slacks were dark, and freshly pressed, with a pair of expensive matching loafers. A white, button up shirt open at the neck completed the outfit. He looked well-manicured, but casual; like he could have easily been a CEO on vacation.

Coming into the restaurant's front entrance, his cold eyes immediately began assessing the room: scanning the tables, their chairs, and the eatery's occupants. Within the span of a few eyeblinks, he'd sketched out the layout of the place: where the tables were, where the bathrooms were stashed, the kitchen… and most importantly, where all the exits were located should the need to leave suddenly present itself. Like a camera, his mind documented who, and what, was in the room… and where. He'd learned the advantages of doing such things very early in his career. Protecting himself had once been instinct. Now, it was habit.

The Maître d' approached and greeted him with a polite smile. "Good evening, Sir," he said congenially, a polite smile appearing on his face like a mirage. "Welcome to The Mont Clair. Table for one?"

The Maître d' was an older white man wearing what appeared to be the hotel's de rigueur uniform: black slacks and shoes, white chef's coat with black piping accentuating the edges of the tunic. His hair was a steely gray and cropped short, like he'd once been in the military and had never changed his hairstyle. He wore an old pair of black frame eyeglasses; the kind people used to call 'Buddy Holly frames' once upon a time.

"I have a reservation for two. I called yesterday afternoon," the man said. "Smith is the name. Jonathan Smith."

The Maître d' went over to a podium that served as a makeshift desk. Behind him, potted ferns surrounded the waiting area and gave the foyer an exotic appearance. He pulled a large leather-bound book out of a drawer, plopping it onto the flat of the stand like it was heavy with both weight and import. He then carefully opened the thick cover revealing pages with columns of names on them written in a variety of hands. He quickly thumbed through the first few pages until he got to one with today's date on it. His eyes scanned the contents of the page like an accountant.

"Smith, you say?"

"Yes. Jonathan Smith."

The name was a fake one of course. Another one of the lessons he'd learned early on: never give anyone your real name. Ever. Protect that shit like you were Batman. Even the people who hired him knew him by a non de plume. Which made sense. In this perilous line of work, letting people on either side of the equation know too much just wasn't a good idea. Good people—usually the ones you cared about—ended up getting themselves dead like that.

As he waited, Smith absentmindedly adjusted how his jacket hung on his frame. He paid particular attention to something under his arm, something hidden beneath the layers of his suit coat. Something heavy. He sighed. Yeah, he thought, it was simply better for all concerned if he played everything as close to the vest as possible.

"Ah," the Maître d' finally said as he grabbed for two menus, "Yes, Mr. Smith. Has the other member in your party arrived?"

"No. Not as of yet."

The older man smiled congenially. "Would you like to wait at the bar, or shall I take you directly to your table?"

Smith thought about it for a second, and then asked to be taken to the table. He didn't drink, so he had no interest in going into the bar when he could just as easily get himself comfortable while he waited for his date to arrive. It was kind of a power move—to already be sitting when your guest arrived so that they understood that they were coming to your table—but what the heck? Any advantage was good advantage, yeah?

As he followed the Maître d' through the restaurant, he grinned to himself, surprised that he was actually feeling a little nervous about the night ahead. This was a different kind of nervous though. This wasn't 'first night jitters' like he'd had when he'd lost his virginity to that prostitute in TJ. Nor was it the 'lost in a whirlpool' feeling he'd felt in Sarajevo with Natalia. This was something different. This was something novel. But it did feel weird…

He chuckled and shook his head. How was it that he could walk into a room of deadly Cartel members and get into a shoot-out and not even have his blood pressure rise. But get him around women—especially strong, competent ones who he suspected were in the same trade as he—and he suddenly turned into the same dopey kid who'd been scared to steal his first kiss.

Frankly, it was embarrassing.

He sat down at the table that the Maître d' directed him toward, and he got himself comfortable. The older gentleman quickly returned to his podium as another party had just come in and were patiently waiting in the Reception Area. Smith let his gaze drift around the room again. Reflexively, he continued to catalog his environment.

An elderly Asian couple sat in front of the large window that faced the street outside. They were both hunched over a sizable bowl of soup. Steam rose like ghosts from the broth's oily surface. Nearby, two men in their forties wearing business suits were talking to one another animatedly. Their ties were both undone, a signal to the world that they were now officially off the clock. Across the room, a young couple was sitting so close together that Smith idly wondered if they might be in the same seat. He could overhear them giggling and talking to their waiter about how it was their first night out after having a baby, and golly, were they ever happy to be out amongst adults. There were two women who were very clearly on a date from the way they kept using any excuse to touch one another's hands and forearms. Near the front of the restaurant, near the foyer, sat a man who was alone and reading a book while he quietly ate.

Perceiving no threat, Smith allowed himself to relax, even if it was only a little. He smirked as he noticed how he was nervously adjusting the silverware setting in front of him. Look at him... on a date. No one he worked with in the Organization would have ever believed it, even if they'd happened to walk in right now and see him sitting here for themselves. Then again, he idly thought, if they walked in right now, they'd only see him sitting here all by himself. He checked his watch and was surprised to discover that it was still early.

She'll show... don't get weird.

He was aware of his reputation in the Organization as that of a loner, someone who didn't truck much with the company of other people. What he thought of, in his own way, as being professional. He did his job—and always delivered—and never left a mess for anybody to clean up. He was proud of that. In a life too full of abuse, conscription, and death... being 'detail oriented' wasn't the worst of things to be found guilty of. At least, it was something he could control.

The front door abruptly opened, and Smith heard someone enter. He looked up, expecting to see some kind of version of the woman he'd been talking to online, but saw only someone else going out the door. He shook his head once again in disbelief. He still couldn't believe he was going through with this. Online dating was the last thing he thought he'd ever be doing, especially considering what it was that he did for a living.

But an associate of his recently told him about this new website, Social Path, during a reconnaissance run in Venezuela. He said it was a hookup site, like Tinder or Grindr, but it was made for people in, as he put it, 'our line of work.' He said it was made specifically for people who demanded anonymity, but also weren't afforded the luxury of a lot of time. That it was all about the person—again, the professional— being given a safe space in which to take a break from their admittedly stressful job of surreptitiously murdering people; being able to let his or her proverbial hair down, as it were.

And the site's rules were fairly simple: no real names, no discussion of past, present, or future assignments, no long-term relationships, and no weapons allowed anywhere near the encounter. And it was exclusive. He'd only been shown the member's listings that the site's algorithm had picked for him once he'd undergone their rigorous background check.

He shook his head again and chuckled at the thought. He remembered his Handler—the guy who gave him all of his assignments—asking him about it. 'Did you sign up for some fuckin' dating app?' he'd asked. 'I got a call from some dame about it. I figured it was Louie or Sam fuckin' around, but it turned out to be legit.' They'd both had quite the laugh over it.

Smith remembers feeling like an idiot, like a kid who'd been caught jerking off in the bathroom at school. 'Why not just go to a fuckin' whore?' his guy had asked—and understandably so. But Smith had done that. For years. It was just that, now… he wanted to have something in actual common with the person he happened to be fucking.

Like a connection, as weird as that sounded.

Even if that connection was that they both killed people for a living.

Suddenly, the front door opened again, and Smith raised his gaze to see who it was. He half-expected it to be another customer either coming in or going out, but he checked, nonetheless. A cold gust of wind came spilling into the restaurant through the entryway, its icy tendrils making the wide fronds of the ferns in the Waiting Area dance like bedsheets drying on the line. Then, out of the darkening twilight outside, this woman strolled in.

She was tall—maybe five foot ten—tan, and stunningly beautiful with short-cropped platinum blonde hair and a fiery gaze. For some reason, he thought she looked European, maybe Swedish. The haircut was severe, and it probably would have looked too stark on anyone else, but she wore with an aplomb that was sexy and sort of dangerous looking all at the same time.

She had on a sleeveless, turquoise-colored blouse, and sleek black trousers. The way the colors played off her tanned skin made her appear all the more attractive. She came strolling into the restaurant like a snake climbing into a baby's crib. Pulling off a pair of black Ray-Bans and folding them up, she nonchalantly slid one of the stems of the sunglasses into the front of her blouse and let them hang between her ample breasts.

"Bingo," Smith whispered low so that nobody sitting around him could hear.

He watched her with delight as she scanned the room much like he had when he first came in, like a predator. Her intense eyes finally fell on him, and the spark of recognition lit up her face. She quickly said something to the Maître d', and they both looked over toward Smith's table. He saw her wave the host away and walk—stalk, more like—in his direction.

Smith smiled at her warmly, getting to his feet to properly greet her. He remembered the photo she'd sent him and reading her short, undoubtedly fabricated, bio. The picture was a pale imitation of the real thing. He blinked his eyes in disbelief. She somehow became more and more beautiful with every step she took in his direction.

He took a moment and let his eyes slowly wander as he took in the whole package. Long, tapered runner's legs were evident even through the loose-fitting pants. Her torso displayed a deceivingly buffed musculature as well. She looked fit, like she did some kind of aerobics or cardio program, but then... when you looked closer, you noticed that there was real muscle there. Every time she moved her arms, it looked like she had snakes hidden beneath the skin of her forearms.

And her face... lush, full lips, and cheekbones so sharp that you could cut yourself on them gave her an almost regal affect. Forest green eyes glared out from beneath her wide forehead, their countenance like that of a hunter.

She walked right up to him and extended her hand across the table.

"Smith?" she asked, and her voice was the sound of silken ribbon suddenly being drawn taut.

Smith started to get up as he nodded. "Guilty, as charged." He smiled at her all friendly-like. "And you're, um... Judy?"

"Judy Jones, yes." She nodded and smirked. "No need to get up."

The woman walked around to the other side of the table and sat down without waiting for him to do the gentlemanly thing and pull out her chair. He stood there awkwardly for a second before finally seating himself. Once they were both settled, she picked up the serviette and pulled it apart, setting the silverware down to one side of her plate and laying the woven napkin across her lap.

The woman—Judy—looked across the table at him and smiled. Not bad, she silently thought. Handsome, muscular, dresses well, competent looking... what's not to like? And besides, who really cared? She was here to potentially fuck this guy... not to get into any kind of a relationship with him. She nodded to herself, deciding right away that unless he said something stupid and fucked this whole deal up, she was definitely going to sleep with him.

She'd been on the Social Path app for about a month now and, miraculously, it seemed to be working out for her. She hadn't met too many creeps and it was nice not to have to pretend to be someone else all the time, to be able to be honest—sort of—with someone who knew exactly who she was. And what.

She saw him smile at her, and it made her feel good inside, which felt odd. She rarely felt anything anymore, much less something this close to good. Her life had been swayed by far too much darkness for that, way too much death.

She blinked a few times to clear such thoughts from her head. Tonight, it wasn't about any of that, though, right? Tonight was about indulging herself and giving her body exactly the kind of attention she knew it so desperately needed.

"So," Smith said. He'd started to obsessively smooth out the tablecloth and he made himself stop. It was a tic of his that he knew came out when he got nervous. He grinned again and shook his head slightly. Him… nervous. It was crazy, man. "Did you have any trouble finding parking?"

She smiled at the attempt at normalcy. "No, but I know my way around this town pretty well." She winked at him. And then, she looked away, saying softly, "I know pretty much all of the good spots."

To Smith, the way she said it, it was the sexiest damned thing he could have imagined.

"That's good." He shrugged. "I guess I lucked out. I got a spot right around the corner."

How cute, she thought to herself, 'small talk.' "Have you ordered yet?"

He shook his head. "I wanted to wait for you." He paused, then chuckled. "Frankly, I'm sort of surprised you actually showed."

She laughed and shook her head. "Why? Wasn't I the one who said that I thought we should finally meet?" She waved his suggestion out of existence with one finely boned hand. "Silly boy."

Their waiter appeared at the side of the table. He was a Black kid in his late twenties with his hair cropped tight to the crown of his head. Predictably, he was dressed in the same hotel uniform as the Maître d' had been. He cleared his throat so as to not interrupt or intrude on their conversation.

"Evening, folks," the kid said warmly. He held a small spiral-bound notebook in one hand and a yellow golf pencil in the other. "My name's Marc and I'll be your server for the evening. Can I get you folks a little something to drink?"

Smith looked over to the gorgeous woman sitting across from him. He raised his eyebrows as if to ask her the same question. She ignored him, looking the waiter directly in the eye, and smiling. The kid suddenly looked like he'd gone weak in the knees.

"Yeah, hi," she purred. "I'll take a Lagavulin. A double." She glanced over. "You?"

"I'll uh… have the same."

Once they'd placed their orders with the waiter—her: a rib-eye and a loaded baked potato, him: half a roasted chicken, mashed potatoes, and a peas-and-carrots side—and they were alone, they returned to their conversation.

"So," she finally asked, looking at him wryly, "how long have you been on Social Path?"

He shook his head and pursed his lips as if in thought. Then, he just decided to be honest. After all, that was what he'd come here for. "You're actually my first."

She sat up in her chair a little, looking genuinely surprised. Her brow furrowed in sudden suspicion. "Really?"

He held up three fingers on one hand. "Scout's honor."

"I doubt very much you were ever a boy scout." She giggled a little. "But that surprises me… a good-looking guy like you." She paused as the waiter came back, bringing them their drinks. When he was gone, she took a sip from her glass and looked up at him seductively over its rim. "Well, here's hoping you win that merit badge, big boy."

The waiter suddenly returned, momentarily interrupting as he set a basket of breadsticks down between the two of them. Smith was grateful for the momentary respite. His mind was going a mile a minute, its engine being jet-fueled by his rapidly growing interest mixing intoxicatedly with his arousal. It was like someone had given this woman a handbook on how to get him going, and she was playing it by the numbers, right down the middle. It was like she couldn't help but push all of his buttons.

She raised her glass. "A toast! To adoring—albeit transitory—friends."

He grinned and touched the rim of his glass to hers. "Here! Here!"

They laughed together and continued to stare at one another as they drank from their glasses. It was clear to both that they were feeling the beginnings of an attraction, each one already imagining how the night might possibly end. It felt good knowing that they could go back to their lives—and lethal occupations—tomorrow.

Tonight, it was about something… else.

They talked for a bit as they waited for their food to arrive; fabricated chit-chat, mostly, but they were both only too happy to listen. Each gave the other their prepared biographies like it was the required thing. Both of them knew that the stories were, for the most part, woven out of whole cloth, but they were both only too happy to play along with the charade.

Smith chalked it up to it all being a part of the dance of seduction they'd both seemingly agreed to. He took another sip from his drink and felt the warm liquid pleasurably burn its way down his throat. Slowly but surely, he felt the cords of his nerves begin unwinding like clock springs, his reflexes hesitantly coming off 'high alert.'

Then, just as he was about to say something about the weather, the waiter returned with their meals. He had the plates on a large round tray which he held flat with one hand over his shoulder. With his free hand, he grabbed and flipped open an X-shaped stand and gently placed the heavy tray down onto it. He immediately set the first plate in front of her, and then did the same for him.

"Can I get you folks anything else?" the waiter asked pleasantly.

The blonde woman said nothing. She just picked up her knife and fork and started cutting pieces from the broiled slab of steak in front of her. "No, thank you," she finally responded. "I think we're good."

When the waiter had left, Smith smiled at the woman as he watched her hungrily stuff a piece of bloody meat into her mouth. "Hungry?"

She laughed as she wiped at the corners of her smile with her napkin. "Sorry," she said apologetically.

He chuckled, picking up his own utensils. "No, it's… It's fine."

She set her napkin back into her lap. "I know we're not supposed to talk about it, but…" She hesitated, but then forged ahead; like she'd decided to break the first of their mutually agreed upon rules on a whim. "I spent the day at the shooting range and hadn't had a chance to eat yet today. I'm actually starving."

He grinned and made a mental note of how quickly—and easily—it was for her to break the dating site's cardinal rule. He smiled as he took a bite of his chicken and quietly decided to let it go. "So, uh… did you have any trouble finding the restaurant?"

"No. It's funny. I actually come here a lot," she said over a mouthful of food. "I mean, I try to come whenever I'm in the City."

"Oh?" he replied. "How often is that?"

Now, it was her turn to grin. "I thought we weren't supposed to discuss that sort of thing."

He chuckled and took another bite of his chicken. "Touché. But you broke the rule first when you mentioned going to the gun range." He paused and smiled, staring intently into the enchanted forest in her eyes.

"Look," she replied, setting her knife and fork down. "I know…

I know we're not supposed to talk about our real selves here, but… where's the fun in that? I don't want to have to lie to you." She picked her fork back up, poked her baked potato with it, and snickered naughtily. "And, who knows if I'll want to fuck you after dinner if you're made-up shit is boring."

"Well, okay," he chuckled, impressed—and a little turned on—by her brazenness. After a second, he rejoined her in eating. "I'm game if you are."

Once they were done with their meal, the couple sat back in their chairs. Both had eaten their fill and wanted to loosen their respective belts. He was usually someone who ate sparingly, but there was something about this woman that made him want to consume as much as he could get his hands on; take as big a bite out of Life as humanly possible.

"So, I'm in Boston," Judy continued with what she'd been saying. She kept her voice low so only he was able to hear. "And I'm at the Boston Public Library. And again… I have paper on this guy. He owed my client a lot of money and had for a really long time. Anyway, he'd hidden himself somewhere in Bates Hall and thought no one would dare try for him if he were there. Not with all those potential witnesses hangin' around."

"Busy place. Lotta eyes," he responded as he dragged a last bit of bread through the oily remnants on his plate. "So, what'd you do?"

She laughed and it sounded like bells on the wind to his eager ears. He watched lustily as she ran her hand across her short paper-white hair. Then, she continued to speak. "I used my feminine wiles, of course, and lured him into one of the bathrooms."

"Where you…?" he asked, feeling like he already knew the answer.

"Well, I did have a metal tactical pen in my purse, so…"

He grinned, immediately putting the pieces together, grateful that she'd broken that bit of ice. "But, back to what you said about just coming here from the range…" he asked. "I'm curious… What are you using?"

She smiled broadly, feeling sort of naughty for talking about it. "Walther P99."

He squinted his eyes a bit as he tried to recall the gun's specifics. "Forty cal?"

She nodded happily, stuffing a last bit of bread into her mouth. "Got it in one."

"That's quite an instrument for someone your size."

She laughed. "I used to use something bigger, but I didn't think it really suited my style. Nobody likes a girl with a bigger gun than theirs." She smiled coyly. "You?"

Smith still felt a little weird regarding talking about this stuff out in the open. After all, hadn't they been told specifically that giving out any information about their careers went against Social Path's guidelines and they both faced being permanently banned from using the site. He looked around the restaurant suspiciously. But since they were here, and they were alone and unsupervised, he didn't see the harm.

"Beretta 92F as a primary."

She smiled at him knowingly. It was a good gun; reliable and hit like a spinning back kick from an elephant. "Respectable."

"And a Glock 26 as a backup."

He smiled at himself, not really sure why he'd told her that last bit. The one would've been sufficient. He figured it was fine, but... he reminded himself to not be so forthcoming in the future. At least he hadn't mentioned the two Kerambit knives he always kept on him. A part of his brain—the part that had kept him alive for so long—made a note to not tell this woman too much.

Now, with the last of the prescribed barriers of their conversation torn asunder, they both grinned at one another, each already imagining how pleasurably the evening was going to end. She took another sip from her drink and licked her lips seductively. He smiled and felt the most important part of his anatomy stir and begin to take active notice.

He was just about to suggest that they leave and go someplace more intimate, when... the front door to the restaurant was suddenly thrown open and three large men came striding in. They were all wearing rubber Halloween masks and heavy coats. One of them, the one who seemed to be calling the shots, had on a Ronald Reagan mask and a black leather baseball jacket.

There was a sudden commotion from the kitchen, and the staff all came stumbling out into the dining room. They came through the set of double doors that the servers used to move food between the preparation area and the dining room in a haphazard rush. Two more big men—one wearing a zombie mask, and the other who had on something that looked like it was from The Creature from the Black Lagoon—came out after them, wearing the same dark clothes as the others. The Gillman cradled something long and heavy beneath a worn trench coat.

"All right everybody," President Reagan shouted from the door. "This is a robbery! Nobody gets cute and nobody'll get hurt."

The guy in a Frankenstein mask who was standing near him took over giving the instructions. "Set your wallets, cash, and valuables onto the table in front of you. We'll be by to pick them up." He paused. "And don't fuckin' try anything! We don't want to hurt anybody, but we will if you press us!"

Jonathan looked across the table at his date and leaned forward slightly in his chair. He raised his eyebrows as he gazed at her in questioning anticipation. The stunning blonde woman across the table looked back and grinned wickedly.

Then, she winked at him.

"What d'ya think?" he whispered, trying not to visibly move his lips. His first instinct was to just hand over whatever these guys wanted and to not cause a fuss. It just seemed easier that way. He'd maybe lose a few hundred bucks and a pretty good wallet in the deal, but none of that was worth anybody getting inadvertently shot. Or worse, them being stopped and questioned by the cops for intervening. He continued to stare at her intently. "How do you want to play this?"

She grinned like a viper and the light in her eyes danced like campfire flame. "Three in front. Another two behind. I'm armed. I assume you are as well."

He grinned at her darkly; another rule broken. "Always."

"Well?" she asked him as she raised her eyebrows.

"Well, I did just get this wallet and I, uh... do sort of like it."

She turned her head and gave the place another quick once-over.

"We'll probably get our memberships to Social Path revoked for this should we do anything, well..." he said, but then paused, "...too ostentatious."

She smiled and winked at him. "We could, uh... say it was foreplay."

The musclebound Gillman came over to their table and angrily glared down at them. "You two," the big man shouted menacingly. "Cut the chatter or you're gonna get got."

His masked cohorts had by now fanned out across the restaurant and were busy collecting the multitude of wallets, billfolds, and jewelry that had been set onto each guest's respective tabletops. The monster squad all looked over at the sound of their partner's raised voice.

"Any trouble over there?" asked Ronald Reagan in the baseball jacket.

"Naw," the Gillman replied confidently. His gaze suddenly centered on the striking blonde woman. "These two just need to shut the fuck up and get with the program." He glared at them, moving the thing he had hidden under his trench as punctuation. "Wallets! Purse! Whatever you have! On the fucking table! Now!"

Judy grinned over at Jonathan malevolently. She gently took her napkin from her lap and wiped her mouth. She crumpled it in her hand

and set it to one side of her plate. Then, she casually looked up at the large, growling man standing in front of her.

"No."

"Listen up, you Cunt!" the Creature shouted. He took an aggressive step toward her. "I will fucking end you..."

Judy laughed involuntarily. "Cunt?" She looked over at Jonathan incredulously. "You heard it, right? He said it... and you heard it." She shook her head. "Cunt." A pause. "Cunt?" She looked directly at her dinner companion and grinned.

Jonathan chuckled and shook his head in dismay. "Now you've gone and done it..."

"Shut up!" the Gillman roared, and he reared his hand back to smack this mouthy blonde in the yap. He'd show this bitch, show her what happened when someone—especially some bougie broad—got lippy with him!

Judy was up on her feet before Jonathan was even aware she was moving. As she turned her body toward the big guy, Jonathan saw her palm her steak knife, holding the blade back against her forearm in an icepick grip. The Gillman's arm came down, hurtling toward her, but Judy seemed unfazed. It was like she expected it all along and things were playing out exactly as she'd imagined.

She deftly ducked under the haymaker like she had all the time in the world. Popping up on his blind side, she used her right hand—the one that held the knife—to stab upward, burying the knife deep into the spot where his thigh met his crotch. From his reaction, and the volume of his abrupt high-pitched screams, she must have pinned the meat of his dick to his leg. Blood blossomed and soaked the front of the big guy's pants, spreading like black oil down his legs.

Jonathan couldn't help but wince as he imagined the pain of the wound. Anticipating what this injured dope's partners' reaction would be, Jonathan flipped the table with all of its contents onto its side to use as an impromptu shield against the onslaught of bullets that he knew was coming. Plates and dinnerware leapt up from the table like jackrabbits and momentarily hung there before crashing to the floor.

As the table came up and over, Jonathan noticed the girl snatch one of the heavy porcelain dinner plates out of the air and hurled it like a Frisbee at the guy in the zombie mask. The plate sailed across the room, striking him squarely in the front of the neck, and crushing his windpipe like a soda can. The man feverishly started clutching at his neck, but it was of little use. His throat was already flooding with blood, drowning his lungs in a deluge of crimson. He staggered, then toppled to the ground like timber.

After that, pandemonium erupted in the room as customers and staff alike all screamed and scattered, diving behind anything they thought was strong enough to protect them against the ensuing fire fight.

Almost immediately, the trio at the front of the restaurant started shooting at the overturned table as they slowly started moving forward. Keeping his head down, Jonathan watched their bullets strike the empty table and wall directly behind them. Furniture was obliterated and the large glass window exploded into bits of glass that fell out onto the street like diamonds.

Jonathan drew his Beretta from its holster and blindly pointed it above the table's edge. He fired at the trio without looking and smiled when he heard one of his bullets strike something solid. The wet sound of the round's impact pleased him to no end. He peeked out in time to see Frankenstein falling back into a sitting position and slamming into the Maître d's podium. Blood blossomed like a corsage in the middle of his chest. The leather-bound reservation book hit the floor next to him with a sharp sound that blended in with the chorus of gunshots.

By now, Judy had pulled her P99 from God knows where and was also shooting toward the front of the building. Jonathan saw the Wolfman take four rounds in the middle of the chest with perfect grouping. Her last bullets caught him as he bounced off a table, striking him in the face, just under his nose. The slug corkscrewed his expression, his rubber canine face seemingly made of putty.

Despite all the carnage going on around them, the couple did what they could to not hit any bystanders. Unfortunately, that was of little concern to the late president. Reagan fired three rounds wildly and all of them struck the guy who had, up until a moment ago, been minding his own business, silently reading his book. His body was kicked back across his table, blood splashing across the tablecloth like paint. Plates and glasses crashed noisily to the floor.

Jonathan and Judy both ducked back behind the table.

"Cops will undoubtedly be here in a minute," Jonathan said as he deftly reloaded the nine-millimeter. "I think it's ill-advised for either of us to be here when they arrive. I don't think being carted downtown and interrogated is high on either of our To Do Lists. So, sadly…" He grinned at her impishly. "I suspect that our time together has come to a rather unfortunate end."

"Well, shit…" Judy replied disappointedly as she also quickly reloaded her firearm. "That's really too bad." When she was ready, she blindly sent two more rounds toward the front of the restaurant. The bullets hit the glass door with a rapid crunching sound. "And to think, I was just beginning to enjoy myself."

Jonathan grinned as he reached out and took her hand. He gently kissed its back before reluctantly letting it go. "I know this is gonna sound weird given the circumstances, but… I'd like to see you again."

Before Judy could answer, the zombie, the guy she'd hit in the throat with the plate, roused and started to clumsily get to his feet. She unceremoniously shot him, the bullet going in at the collarbone and continuing on through the rest of his pronounced girth. The slug finally exited his back, blowing a good portion of his insides across the floor like spilled spaghetti.

She shrugged as she grinned over at him like a little girl. "I'd like that."

Suddenly, Ronald Reagan was back, talking shit.

"I'm gonna fucking murder the both of you!" he screamed, and he fired twice more at the table.

The bullets hit the protective wood with a short series of loud pocking sounds. The table was thin, and it had taken a beating already. It wouldn't stand up to too much more of this. They needed to act.

"But first…" Jonathan said with a wink. "We should probably deal with this fucking guy."

She nodded and returned his wink seductively.

"Come out, you mother fuckers!" the ex-president shouted.

In response, the couple suddenly popped up from behind the table like twin Jack in the Box, setting free a targeted swarm of heavy bullets that flew across the restaurant like angry bees. After that, silence fell like a drape over the room, and everyone that was left alive held their breath in anticipation of what might come next.

There was a groan from the floor and Reagan slowly tottered to his feet.

Suddenly, two rounds—one fired by Jonathan, the other by his date—cut the silence, striking the President in the middle of his rumpled forehead. Dime-sized holes opened up on either side of his skull, just under the eyes. The velocity of their impact rocked his head back and he reacted like he'd been kicked by a mule. His arms went stiff, and his legs gave out as he crumpled to the floor. Dark blood immediately began pooling beneath his head.

Almost immediately, the sounds of approaching police sirens filled the air.

The couple carefully crawled out from behind the overturned table. The restaurant around them was in chaos. Tables had been pushed over and there was bits of food and glass strewn everywhere. After a minute of inactivity, the other patrons hesitantly poked their heads up from their hiding places to see if the coast was clear, tears streaming down many of their cheeks.

Judy stepped closer to Jonathan as she dusted herself off. Carefully, she slid her arm around his waist. Their eyes met and the next thing either of them knew, they were kissing; deeply, passionately. Her body felt like a sculpture beneath his hands as she pressed up against his chest firmly. He held her tightly, savoring the moment for the perfect thing that it was.

"Be seeing you, Mr. Smith," she whispered seductively into his still-open mouth.

He grinned as he reluctantly let her go, taking a small step back, relishing the taste of her on his tongue. "I look forward to it, Miss Jones."

Somewhere along the way, she'd made her gun disappear like she was dealing 3-Card Monty. One second the weapon was in her hand, and the next... it was gone. It was an impressive piece of legerdemain.

With a deep sigh, she started gathering up the rest of her things. "Well, gee... that just sounds downright ominous when you say it like that."

He smiled. "Care to try me..."

Now it was her turn to chuckle. "Oh, absolutely. We still have plenty we need to talk about, you and me. I mean, we were just getting acquainted. However,..."

Jonathan took a quick look around the restaurant and suddenly noticed how badly shot up the place was. With tables overturned and as many holes as there were in the walls, the cleanup on this was going to be expensive. Reaching into his jacket pocket, he pulled out a billfold and peeled off several hundred-dollar bills and set them onto one of the other tables. He noticed the Maître d' as he was starting to get up from beneath one of the overturned plants by the door. He caught his eye, pointed to the cash on the table, and mouthed the words 'for damages.'

Judy was already scanning the room, presumably looking for an exit.

"The way out is either through the kitchen or through a side door back by the bathrooms," he said to her almost casually. "I don't think we should leave together."

"Okay then, looks like I might need to powder my nose," she replied as she started heading for the hallway that led to the bathrooms. She turned her head as she went, blowing him a kiss. "We'll talk soon?"

As he quickly strode toward the kitchen doors, he winked at her. "Oh, you can count on it."

A few seconds later, they were both outside standing on the sidewalk in the cool night air on separate sides of the building. A crowd was quickly gathering around the restaurant's front door, having heard the gunshots, and seen the shattering glass. Jonathan caught sight of Judy's back in the throng of people down the street. He watched her as she disappeared into the bloodstream of the bustling city.

A moment later, he was gone as well.

KIRU

The sword was an important part of my growing up. It started when I first saw Toshiro Mifune being a badass in Hiroshi Inagaki's Samurai Trilogy. Then I read Eiji Yoshikawa's legendary book, MUSASHI, and I was hooked from that moment on. As a result, I threw myself into things like Kendo, Kenjutsu, and the 'quick-draw' art of Iado. Later, when I discovered the world of Filipino Martial Arts, I returned to it. It goes without saying that I dearly love this formidable piece of hardware. The strength of it. The power. The precision. I've talked about it in other stories, but this piece really speaks to my love of that particular weapon, and for all things martial arts. The format of this story is called a Sijjin, and it is a story form that I first developed in the pages of Carpe Noctem (as well as in other collections) in which a quote fuels the narrative and subsequent quotes are used for context, as a palate cleanser, and to further 'flavor' the overall story.

Well, you'll see...

"If you know the way broadly you will see it in everything."
~ *Miyamoto Musashi*

The morning sun rose slowly over the peaks of Takachiho-cho—otherwise known as the Takachiho Gorge—in the northernmost part of the island of Japan. Deep within the valley, an ancient structure, referred to by the locals as the Isonokami Shrine, brooded stoically. The shrine had seen much in its many years, a silent witness to the passing of centuries.

Locals will tell you that the temple, known by many as the Shrine of Swords, is rumored to have been in existence since as early as 91 B.C. Others will tell you that the structure wasn't actually built until well into the Second or even the Third Centuries. Not that its true date of construction mattered. The simple, yet grandiose structure had stood longer than most could fathom, sitting regally atop its verdant mountain, and looking out over the wonderous landscape like a monarch.

I had come to this valley to perform an ancient and time-honored demonstration for a group of some of the country's most skilled swordsmen. The ritual, known as Tameshigiri, was a test by which one could best judge the lethality of a given blade. And of the swordsman. Once called "test cutting," the examination showed not only the strength of the swordsman's arm, but also the depths of his focus and expertise.

Popularized in the 17th Century, the examination was born of a gruesome parentage. Originally, only the best swordsmen in the land were asked to perform it, to test the swords of the monarch. The reason for this was so that the swordsman's skill would not be questioned in determining how well the sword cut.

The materials used for the target varied: wara (rice straw), goza (the top layer of tatami mats), bamboo, and then later, slender steel sheets. Early on, in feudal times, it was also common practice to use cadavers (often stacked one on top of the other to increase the difficulty) or even the bodies of convicted criminals. Practitioners referred to the practice as Shito (sword testing) or Shizan. During the Sino-Japanese War, Japanese officers routinely tested their blades on the bodies of captured Allied soldiers and Chinese civilians. There were even reports of competitions to see which swordsman could decapitate one hundred people in the fastest time.

The test itself involved a series of very precise cuts (the downward diagonal Kesa-giri, the upward diagonal Kiri-age or Gyaku-kesa, the horizontal Yoko or Tsuihei, and the straight downward Jodan-giri, Happonme, Makko-giri, Shinchoku-giri, or Dottan-giri) performed in an exacting fashion, each motion precisely executed with the utmost calm, and subsequently judged with a keen eye toward both form and function.

Many were called to perform Tameshigiri.
Many more failed.

"You can only fight the way you practice."
~ *Miyamoto Musashi*

I enter the austere shrine to find a crowd of onlookers already gathered there. The building itself is open, with high, airy ceilings and broad support beams. Tatami screens line the room's four walls. All are sitting in precise rows in what is known as seiza: legs tucked discreetly beneath them, hands folded in their laps. Many of these kendo-ka have come from miles away to watch this demonstration, and to learn from it. Others are local monks and martial art aficionados who have flown in from all over the world to see it performed. All realize how lucky they are to be here.

I catch a ghost of my reflection in one of the windows on a far wall, recognizing myself wearing the prescribed hakama pant, Montsuki Haori kimono, tabi socks, and seta sandals as is the prescribed custom. My hair is drawn up into a traditional topknot and oiled to shine like polished onyx. I am the perfect picture of the model samurai.

Walking slowly out into the middle of the cavernous auditorium, I draw my sword from its *saya* (or scabbard) at my hip. The burnished metal glimmers, the light glinting off the blade's sharpened edge and sculpted hardware like star fire. Approaching the target—the rolled bamboo mat set over a thin, upright post—I feel myself letting the rest of the world fall away: the people, the clamor, even the regal building rising up around me. All that remains is my focus centered on the intricately woven pattern of the tatami before me. Drawing in a cool cleansing breath, I wait for the perfect moment to present itself before I strike, allowing my thoughts to drift to a familiar place of quiet and comfort.

"If you think only of hitting, springing, striking, or touching the enemy, you will not be able actually to cut him. More than anything, you must be thinking of carrying your movement through to cutting him."

~ *Miyamoto Musashi*

In the span of my next few heartbeats, I think back over the long road I've traveled in order to get to this moment. The hours of training. The pain. The overwhelming drive toward perfection. How many hours had I suffered? How many relationships had I allowed to drift away solely because of my desire to be perfect in this, my execution of these time-honored techniques?

The sound of my heart beats incessantly within the cavernous halls of my ears, drowning out everything as I remember my first sword: a worn, but still polished and cared for, red oak bokken. It was a gift from my grandfather who'd carved it back when he was but a child, and he'd diligently looked after it over the long ensuing decades. One could still see, if one knew where—and how—to look, the imprint of his hands on the worn, wooden Tsuka (or handle). And over the years, as I'd grown into my adulthood, the marks of my hands soon usurped his until the weapon became well and truly mine.

To me, the sword—and later, all bladed weapons—was everything: teacher, disciplinarian, task master, implement of my discomfort and of my pain. But it was also so much more... The weapon remained my only friend, and sole companion, as I grew to maturity; a metaphor for my ever-improving abilities. The moment, the memory, expands within me, blood pounding like a Taiko drum louder and louder in my brain.

The time has come for me to act.

The moment has come for me to strike.

"A thousand days of training to develop, ten thousand days of training to polish. You must examine all of this well."

~ *Miyamoto Musashi*

I take a step forward, pressing my right foot firmly into the tatami mat that lays over the floor. The musculature of my back goes tense, my sword arm flexing powerfully from the cruel weight in my hand. The sword, a katana forged by the genius Muramasa in 1563, has been in my family for generations and it is an instrument that signifies the import and honor of this life.

A pause lay heavy over the room, like a pronouncement of death.

And then...

My kiai shatters the silence. And, with an expulsion of breath, I slash the weapon in a variation of the Syo Hatto technique. The first slash is an upward lateral slice going from left to right. The razor-sharp edge of the blade kisses the mat, and in that micro-instant, I see its cutting edge move through the individual strands of bamboo like a hot knife through butter. The blade hangs a bit as it catches on the dried bamboo at the target's core, but my strength and will powers it through.

The target is surgically bisected and the large, uppermost portion of it begins to fall away toward the mat-covered floor. As it drops, my next cut, a downward slash from right to left, cuts the piece in half, pulling it out of the grip of gravity. The blow is followed by a final quick, downward cut which separates what's left into two neatly divided bits. Upon the technique's completion, I cease all movement, freezing myself into ice, poised in a perfect pose.

Afterward, the room remains respectfully silent, save for the echo of my battle cry as its tone evaporates like fog within the confined, cathedral-like space. And as my objective mind reclaims my body, returning me to reality, the sound of muted appreciation caresses my ear like a lover. And for the moment, I am content.

"A bullet from a gun does not make a distinction between practice and combat. You are training to be one and the same way in your life."
~ Miyamoto Musashi

WILLOW, WEEP FOR ME

I took a poll online recently and asked folks what story of mine they would be interested in seeing a little more of. The overwhelming answer—"Clown Town"—sort of surprised me. I was always of the opinion that the story was a kind of one-off, but I kicked some ideas around for a little bit and finally came up with the story you see below. Part of the problem of getting back into the swing of things was trying to refamiliarize myself with the terminology of the world. Because, yes… all of the 'lingo' is real. I spent months researching '40s jazz talk, 'reefer culture,' circus vocabulary, and hanging out with some pretty disreputable clowns to learn all about it. But, if you don't know that, it's easy to mistake it for gibberish. I assure you, though, it's all legit.

With this tale, I wanted to tell a different story than the original, one that looked at an idea that was smaller in scope, something a bit more intimate. I finally decided to take a look at what it was to be an Artist. And maybe writing a love letter to Jazz while I was at it. It is my hope that I was successful and able to recapture this particular bit of lightning in a bottle. So, join me if you please, by taking my hand for a trip back to the city of clowns, back to the city of Sarkasa.

The blood-orange sun had only just started setting over the city of Sarkasa when Willow de Troubadour got off of the #12 bus on the way to her appointment. The overhead neon lights were only just starting to come on in the Clip Joints, Chow Huts, and Downtown Wagons that ran along Midway Boulevard.

The green-haired Auguste girl gingerly stepped from the front door of the bus down onto the cement curb, looking around wide-eyed at her surroundings. The air was mouthwateringly rich with the smell of candied apples and freshly popped corn, the odors so ubiquitous that you swore you could taste them both every time you took a breath. Streamers and deflated balloons littered the walkways along the thoroughfare like dropped pocket change. High in the sky, searchlights traced windshield wiper patterns across a rapidly darkening bank of clouds.

It had been hot out today, so hot that every silly clown along the avenue worried about their hodgey-podgey running down their faces and ruining their shows. Every one of them Joeys what were working along the B, especially during that hottest part of the afternoon, had taken what refuge they could find in the cooler shadows beneath the awnings and windows of the wagons and tents. The relief from the sweltering heat was minor and short-lived, but any port in a storm, eh? Word on the street had it that it was going to be even hotter out tonight. At least that's what the weathermen on the gogglebox were saying, if you can believe them Rubber Noses.

Willow had come to the fabled city just a week or so ago in pursuit of a dream. See, Willow was a singer. And a darn good one, if you believed the Rodeos and Bumpkins in her hometown. She'd come to Sarkasa from her parent's farm out in the agrarian wilds of Brahma, near what was known among the riffraff as Long-Haul Town. She'd grown up singing in church and had been told for as long as she could remember that she should one day come to Sarkasa to cast her lot in 'the business of show.' She knew—she just knew—that her destiny was to be one of them professional singers like you saw in the picture shows.

No one in her small burg ever thought she'd actually do it, of course; to actually leave. But she'd surprised them all by putting an egg in her shoe and beating it on her eighteenth birthday. She still remembered with great remorse though how her parents had both cried when she told them she was leaving the homestead and coming to the city to lift her voice in song. But a dream was a dream... and Willow knew down deep in her heart that she was meant for something more than just growing up on a ranch and ultimately marrying the captain of her high school juggling team.

Just like her mama had.

Nope, not her. She was bound for other—better—things... like the stage. She grinned broadly as she strolled down the busy sidewalk toward her destination, lost in her own thoughts.

Because she knew deep down in her heart that she was meant for something more than what the status quo were; much more. She knew down to the depths of her soul that she was meant to help people with the gift she'd been given. Hadn't she'd seen for herself how her singing could make people forget about their bad days or their soul-sucking jobs and failed relationships? She knew beyond a doubt how much her singing helped people.

And how much it had helped her to grow up and be her own clown. How it had given her an identity. So, it seemed only natural for her to one day come to the place where she would be able to help the most people, right?

She'd found out the hard way though that things here in Sarkasa were way more expensive than she'd thought they'd be... or had planned for them to be. Right off the bat, she'd had to spend most of the money in her savings just to get herself into an apartment. And her place was definitely not The Hilton. She knew she would manage, but... that initial outlay of ducats really hurt, and it made her have to make some minor adjustments to her overall plan.

The first thing she'd done right after she'd gotten herself settled was to start looking for a job. She'd approach Marceau's, the infamous nightclub what reigned supreme here in Sarkasa, first thing. Even a hillbilly Auguste from the farmlands like her knew that Marceau's was the Top Shelf joint. The place was legendary. And the way she had it figured, if anyone could appreciate what she did with a tune, it was them. After all, they'd seen the best. They was culchured, y'know?

Unfortunately, the manager, an elegant-looking man by the name of Gentleman Jacques, told her that they weren't hiring and probably wouldn't be for some time. She still remembered he'd acted all haughty, saying, 'This is Marceau's, m'dear. And everyone who's anyone wants to play Marceau's.' She remembered how his callous words had stung her pride, and she'd cried all the way back to her new place.

Once she'd finally gotten over the initial heartbreak, she'd picked up a newspaper on her way home from the grocery. The way she had it figured, she'd look for a job waitressing, or something for the short-term, while she continued to look for a singing gig. And as luck would have it, she'd seen that another nightclub—a tiny little jazz spot called Gonzalo's—had an advert hidden at the bottom of the page what said they were looking to hire a singer. Well, they were hiring a waitress, really. But she'd heard from a Front Bender on the street that the staff at Gonzalo's were often given stage time during the night to sing along with the club's band. And stage time was stage time, y'know? Being out there in front of the people... honing your craft. At least, that's what she'd been told by all the books she'd read about 'making it' in this business.

And besides, how else was someone gonna hear her and her gift?

The good thing was... that the scuttlebutt on the street said that Gonzalo's was nice. Not 'highbrow nice' like Marceau's, for sure... but the joint wasn't dirty or finky and it had no pretensions as to what it was: a small jazz club where a Joey could come in quick and wet his whistle, hear a few good old-time tunes, and not be bothered by the glitz and glamour of them other places.

It was, in a few words, what it was... and that was a-okay.

Not every place in town had to be the Taj Mahal, right?

She'd telephoned the joint from the payphone in the hall and inquired as to whether the spot was still open. Some guy what went by the name of Knick Knack answered. He said he was the manager, and he told her to come in before they opened for the night, so's he could give her a look-see. She remembered dancing for joy in the empty hallway as she hung up the phone and ran back to her apartment to change.

Willow navigated her way passed all manner of Cirkies, Rubber Men, even a few slack-jawed Forty-Milers as she strolled down the sawdust and tan bark strewn walkway of the Boulevard. Out on the windblown street, Keystone Paddies, Delivery Carts, and assorted Pie Wagons moved like snails along the obsidian asphalt, all slowly making their way to their respective destinations. It occurred to her that they were like the blood cells of the city's industrial arterial system, each takin' care of some important bit of business that kept the whole city alive. Bums and businessmen, Ringmasters and Boss Hostlers, all rubbed shoulders along the crowded thoroughfare. It was what made Sarkasa always seem so vibrant and alive.

Willow was dressed down in a pair of loose-fitting silk pants and a plain dark purple Rayon shirt. As a result, most of the Yahoos what saw her walk by didn't think to give a second look, much less a hoot. Her fluorescent green hair was done up nice with a great big yellow and teal bow, but nothing else about her let them know who she was: an entertainer. She giggled at the thought and clutched the gown and shoes which lay secured in the vinyl overnight bag she had tightly slung over one arm. Even with the rhubarb and traffic noise coming from the street, she could still hear the crisp taffeta of her dress crinkle as she crushed it to her chest.

She smiled broadly to herself with delight.

At the corner, she turned left and proceeded down Trapeze Road. She took a second and looked up to once again marvel at the gleaming high rises that rose up like the legs of giants around her. As she rounded the corner, she squinted against the setting sun's glare coming off the panes of glass and struts of steel.

There was a robust Italian man in a green velvet suit working the sidewalk. He had a small monkey in an outfit that matched his own, and an impossibly old barrel organ which his arm cranked with a fervor. He was playing a song Willow instantly recognized from her childhood: "Someone to Watch Over Me." Even as sped up and jolly as he was playing it, the melody still sounded as fine as summer wine to her homesick ears.

The monkey held a tiny tambourine in one paw, and he was joyfully slapping it against the flat of his butt, keeping time with his master's music. Willow had seen them on the boulevard before, so she waved to them both. The man dipped his cap politely as she passed by. He smiled, acknowledging her for having tossed a coin into the basket at his feet. The monkey hooted joyfully and bowed to Willow like a proper gentleman.

She continued on down the street, checking each business' address against the one she'd memorized. Passing Poppers, the gourmet popcorn store, she saw the number she was searching for, and grinned in delight. She quickly checked her watch and found that she was not only on time, but she was also a few minutes early.

The large façade out in front of Gonzalo's loomed over the street like a dozing gargoyle. The letters of their logo were in a loose cursive, and the giant G had a skewer through it, like a martini olive. Finally seeing the place in all its glory made Willow feel a little giddy and light-headed. Like, here she was... out here in Sarkasa, really doin' it: going to auditions, hopefully landing gigs. She was sure that this was the first step toward her manifesting her dream. She couldn't wait to write about all of it, tell them every little thing, when she sent her letter home.

As if on cue, the sign's purple neon lights came on with a stutter, and the illumination splashed out onto the street out front in a dark wine color. Willow hugged her garment bag a little tighter to her chest as she approached the club's front door. She couldn't help but feel excited as she thought about the opportunity that lay ahead.

Using her hand to shade her eyes from the overhead lights, she peered inside the building through its shaded glass. The lobby was dark with only some soft white lights running along the walls. She hesitantly knocked on the metal frame—first softly, then again louder— and waited for someone to come so that she could be let inside.

A young lady suddenly appeared like a ghost out of the darkness in the lobby. She smiled warmly as she pushed on the bar that unlocked the door. She then held it open for Willow as she came inside. The smell of soda pop and warm funnel cake came flooding out of the opened door immediately, making Willow's mouth water, and reminding her of home.

The gal at the door was a cute Whiteface dressed in a yellow button-up shirt with black accents and an oversized floral tie. Her bright orange hair was Shirley Temple curly, and it had the look of being perpetually unbrushed. A small top hat with a single yellow flower sat atop her head like the ghost of a good idea. Her makeup was simple: bone white with only a small red heart at the tip of her nose; subtle rather than something more ostentatious.

"Hey, Doll," the pumpkin-haired girl said in greeting. Her voice was high and reedy like a piccolo. "You Willow?" She let go of the door once Willow was inside of the club, and it closed behind them with the hiss of a snake.

"Yeah," Willow replied. "I hope I'm not too early."

"Naw, you're fine."

"I was told to talk to someone... named Knick Knack?"

"Yup," the orange-tressed girl replied with a nod. "I'm Daisy. Knick Knack is my pops. I'll take you in to see him. Did you bring everything you need? Do you need a place to get changed?"

Willow nodded and held up her garment bag like evidence. "That'd be great."

"Okay, cool," Daisy said, as they started walking across the lobby. It was clear by the way she didn't wait, that she meant for Willow to follow her, so she did. "You ever been to Gonzalo's before?"

Willow shook her head. "No, but I'm sorta new in town. I only got here a little bit ago."

Daisy nodded sagely.

The two of them casually crossed the lobby of the club, and Daisy led the way through a side door. Willow noticed that it opened onto the backstage area behind the main part of the club. Empty save for the lighting rigs and racks of audio equipment, the space had an expectant feel to it, like the calm that came just before some big storm rolled in. Daisy walked over to a door along the nearest wall and held it open for Willow to see inside the club.

"It ain't much, but we like it just fine," Daisy offered proudly.

Willow leaned in passed Daisy and took in the empty nightclub. The joint was a large rectangle in shape, like a shoebox. It was a little on the small side as nightclubs went, but it had been nicely decorated in a palette of purples, pinks, and black. Classy, y'know? The owner— Knick Knack, Daisy's father apparently—had clearly sunk a lot of ducats into the place; selecting the motif, redesigning to maximize the space, and picking out the appealing color scheme. While it may not have been Marceau's, the club was lovely and, by all accounts, remained moderately successful; slowly becoming its own thing over the years. Several times, Knick Knack had used the phrase, 'an option for those what simply love music,' when they'd talked on the phone.

"We had a girl named Georgia singing here for a while, but she called in sick way too many times, so Daddy had to give her the bum's rush," Daisy continued saying as they walked back across the backstage area towards a small room along the back wall. "It's a Tuesday night, so… it shouldn't be too busy; especially this early. We should be able to run through a song or two with you." She paused. "Who knows? If Daddy likes you, he may even ask you to start tonight."

"Oh wow," Willow replied as she nodded appreciatively, lifting her garment bag from her arm by the exposed clothes hanger hooks. She let the rest of the bag fall, its weight pulling the clothing inside straight, as she switched the weight from one hand to the other. "That'd be swell."

By this time, they'd arrived at the door Willow assumed was the Dressing Room. Daisy patted Willow's arm gently, like a sibling might. "You can get changed in here, Honey. I'll talk to Daddy, and we'll see what we can do. When you're done, come on inside. I'll keep an eye out for you."

"Um, thanks a lot, Daisy," Willow said warmly, and she reflexively hugged the girl close in gratitude.

"No problem," Daisy replied with a surprised chuckle as she walked away. "Just make sure you sing good."

Willow smiled to herself, and said that she'd try, as she watched the orange-haired girl head back toward the Showroom door. When she'd disappeared inside and Willow found herself once again alone, she went into the Dressing Room to get into her outfit, closing the door carefully behind her.

As it turned out, the phrase 'Dressing Room' was a bit of lingo that made what was in reality a storage closet seem fancy. The room barely had enough space in which to turn a pirouette. Boxes of assorted gimmicks like juggler's pins, hoops, cap guns, and a box of extra rubber noses were stacked against the far wall like Jenga blocks. The room had a smell of pancake makeup and of sawdust. But to Willow, it smelled of only one thing: Show Business.

Willow carefully hung her bag up on an exposed nail and pulled open the zipper. The slide made a soft buzzing sound, like a bee caught between a closed windowpane and its screen. Inside of the bag waited a bright aquamarine evening dress that was blindingly bright, even in the dim light. It had a large teal and yellow bow tie sewn onto the front of it with purple and pink accents running along the dress' ruffled edge.

First, though, she reached into the bottom of the bag, and pulled out a pair of black patent-leather 'baby doll' shoes, their polished surface glimmered like opals in the half-light. After slipping them onto her feet, she retrieved the dress, and quickly stripped out of her 'street clothes.'

Willow got dressed quickly, finalizing her look by checking her reflection in a small mirror she'd discovered tacked to the side wall. She was just fixing the bow on top of her head when another girl suddenly opened the door and surprised her.

She was a happy-looking Auguste in a turned-up boater's cap and patchwork overalls. Her face makeup was simple with only some Clown White on the upper lids of her eyes and around her generous mouth. Red accent lines and freckles punctuated the cheeks framing her bulbous red nose. She looked like one of those clowns that always appeared to be smiling.

"Oh hey, kid," the girl said brightly. "Hope I didn't scare ya? Didn't mean to. I'm Sunshine. Daisy says you're here for the crooner's gig?"

Willow nodded, laughing nervously. She'd never heard it put that way: 'crooner's gig.' "Yes, I am." She giggled to herself as she paused to check her reflection one last time in the tiny mirror. "Daisy said I should get changed in here and meet her inside the club."

"Cool beans," the little smiling clown said. She looked passed Willow, into the back of the small closet. "I just need to grab a few candles for the sittin' booths along the wall. They're right there behind you."

Willow quicky zipped her garment bag up after tucking her street clothes safely back inside. She left it hanging on the wall for when she was done and needed to change back into her street drag. Stepping out of the way, Willow made room so that Sunshine could get the candles.

"Sorry," she apologized as she stepped outside.

As Willow waited there, still adjusting her clothing, a woman wearing all black suddenly appeared out of the shadows. Slowly, she approached. Her makeup was sparse, with ephemeral vertical lines that ran like dark slashes across her eyes. A black dot topped the tip of her nose, and her lips were wide and painted a dark onyx. She was quite pretty, Willow thought... for a Scary.

"Hey, Eckles, how ya doin'?" Sunshine greeted her warmly, but then again, that was apparently the way she greeted everybody.

"Ladies," the dark woman said as she walked by them, her voice was low and scratched raw from smoking.

Out of nowhere, Willow suddenly thought she smelled patchouli and cloves on the air.

Without saying much of anything further, Eckles ambled past the two girls, and on toward a big walk-in cooler that was near the loading dock at the very back of the building. Once there, she hurried inside and effortlessly grabbed a new keg of beer by its handle, hauling it out into the light. Willow had never met a Scary before, but she heard they were just like any other clown... except their sense of humor tended to be a lot darker; a by-product of their hard lives growing up in Geartown. Willow remembered hearing the rumor that they weren't to be entirely trusted. Willow watched as a silent Eckles effortlessly carried the heavy metal barrel back the way she'd come.

Suddenly, from inside the club, some music started playing. Its sound was rich and joyful. Willow was able to make out the opening lines to Coltrane's "A Love Supreme" and figured the band must have taken the stage and were starting to warm up. Willow silently offered up a quick prayer to Barnum and Bailey that Knick Knack liked her enough to let her sing tonight.

Maybe even get the gig for permanent.

"Sorry," Willow finally said to Sunshine. "I should really go find Daisy and Knick Knack."

Sunshine laughed and patted her on the shoulder. "Oh, go on ahead girl! You knock 'em dead!"

Willow smiled and hugged Sunshine, feeling suddenly grateful to her for some reason. As she did, she remembered the old show business axiom: 'never wrinkle the dress,' so she was careful. The two girls smiled at one another awkwardly, then separated. Without saying anything further, Willow headed toward the door that led to the Showroom.

Inside... it took Willow a second to really take in all of the grandeur of the main room, and to let her eyes adjust to the low light. She'd gotten a glimpse before, but now that she was standing in the center of it, she was impressed. The little girl within her who'd aspired to be a singer silently gasped and felt giddy as she looked out over the nearly empty nightclub. She'd worked hard, become good at what she did, and felt like she deserved this job. She just had to convince this Knick Knack guy.

But if she could only land this gig, she'd finally be on the path to being noticed by the types of people who could really help her career. She shook her head to clear it and pinched herself on the arm for good luck, just like she always did whenever she was about to sing in front of people. It was a habit she'd picked up from her grandmother when singing in church.

'You go on out and sing your heart out, baby,' she'd said. 'And if

it ever feels like you're in a dream, just pinch yourself on the arm...
to make sure it's all real.' Willow had dutifully performed the gesture
ever since.

As she walked across the dance floor, she noticed that the interior
walls of the club were painted black with wide vertical purple and pink
stripes that rose up and disappeared into the shadows of the ceiling.
There was a long bar at the back of the room on the left side. Small
wooden stools were lined up regimentally along its length. Booths
dominated the wall on the right, and there were a few more at the back
of the club. A couple of dozen small cocktail tables and chairs filled
in the center. Willow took it all in as she moved across the polished
parquet floor, pausing momentarily to take in the small stage that was
to her left.

Willow noticed a man standing over by the bar who, by the look of
him, could only have been Knick Knack. He was an older Whiteface who
had on a neatly pressed black tuxedo that looked like it was expensive
and tailor-made. He was leaning against the bar, a dark purple drink in
his hand, talking to a girl Willow recognized as Daisy.

Willow adjusted her course, strolling across the open dance floor.
She approached the two of them sheepishly. Daisy's face lit up the
moment she saw Willow approaching. Knick Knack turned lazily, his
face—painted bone white with high, red eyebrows, simple lips, and a
small dot on the tip of his nose—looked suspicious when he saw her
standing there.

"You da crooner?" he said, trying to be polite and professional.

It had been a day of headaches for him, firing people, chasing down
supply orders, and now hiring a new singer. It could drive a man to
drink. Despite himself, Knick Knack sighed aloud.

Daisy looked up at her father with a look of supreme self-satisfaction.
"I was just telling Daddy about you and how talented you were." She
wiggled her painted-on eyebrows up and down at Willow for emphasis.

Knick Knack grinned as he took a sip of his purple drink. "Well,
look... I can't guarantee nothin', but the band's already warming up if'n
you want to go up and show us all a bit of what you got."

Willow smiled broadly, her heart suddenly pounding like a
jackhammer within the birdcage of her chest. "Oh, geez, really?! Like,
right now?"

Knick Knack casually shrugged with indifference as he drained his
glass and motioned to Eckles for another. "Sure. Go 'head. We're not
open yet, and, even if we were, it's a slow night. And who knows, maybe
you'll be something worth listening to for a change." He laughed for

some reason, setting his empty glass down onto the bar as he walked off wordlessly, heading for the bathrooms at the back of the hall.

When he was far enough away, Willow reached out, doing her best to not start crying, and put her arms around Daisy. Once again, she hugged her tightly. And then, when she was done, she hugged her again.

"Oh, thank you! Thank you!" she exclaimed. A blush of excitement colored her cheeks as she finally let Daisy go. Willow straightened the other girl's clothing as she tried to regain her composure. "I'm sorry. I'm just so happy... and so grateful to you for having put in a good word for me."

Daisy smiled and waved her concerns away. "Well, I'm only betting that you're great, and I never lose a bet. I just know you're gonna wow Daddy. And wait until you meet the band! Now, you go up there and have fun, okay kid?"

Willow grinned at her excitedly, shaking her head up and down like one of those dogs you see in the back window of cars. She took her first few steps toward the stage slowly but gained speed as she went along. She had to hold herself back so that she didn't start running toward the stage abruptly. Her stomach was all aflutter and, for a second, she felt like she might barf up butterflies if she wasn't careful.

The band assembled onstage was a quintet led by a Contra-Auguste on a battered, old upright bass. He was a tall redhead in a red plaid coat, and he had a bucktoothed smile. A Rodeo clown sat at an old upright piano wearing a pair of dark dungaree overalls and a red cowboy hat. The rest of the band was made up of a bright-faced Auguste who was perched behind a turret of Ludwig drums, another Whiteface on a battered ES-175 hollow body guitar, and a boyish-looking Auguste kid who sat holding a sax nearby. The combo was just finishing up the Coltrane tune when Willow cautiously approached the front of the stage.

"Hey, boys," she said, raising her voice once the music had finally stopped.

She did what she could to keep the tone of her voice steady so as to appear casual, to make it seem like she did this all the time, and was a pro. The nervous tremor in her voice remained however, and it made it sound like she was standing on a vibrating mat instead.

"Hey," the boys responded in unison. A few of them took advantage of the interruption to light their cigarettes, wet their whistle, and sort through their piles of gathered sheet music.

"I, uh..." Willow began. She cleared her throat and pinched her arm again before continuing. When she felt centered, she smiled and said, "My name's Willow. Knick Knack said it would be okay for me to come sing a few songs with yas to see if I can pass mustah."

The tall guy with the upright bass smiled toothily at her. "Sounds cool, toots. I'm Shorty." The rest of the band all silently nodded their agreement of the idea. "What d'ya wanna sing?"

Willow was momentarily dumbfounded, all the muscles in her jaw going momentarily slack. She'd always dreamt of this moment, of singing in front of a great band at a great nightspot, but now that the moment was here, she was at a loss as to what exactly it was that she wanted to sing. When she was a kid, she'd imagined every iota of what she thought this experience would be like—the lighting, the dress, the feeling of the microphone in her hand—but for some reason, she'd never actually picked the song she'd sing first. Sure, she'd imagined singing a dozen different songs, but she'd never actually decided on any one that best showed what she could do. For her, in the moment, the imagining of it was enough. But now that the time was actually here... her brain scrambled to offer up an acceptable answer.

The Rodeo stubbed the butt of his cigarette out in an ashtray, Then, he leaned back on his piano bench and looked her in the eye. "Look, Sweetheart... how's about we just start with somethin', and you can let us know what you want to do from there, okey-doke?"

Willow smiled and pretended to straighten the press of her dress. Her brain rapidly sifted through her repertoire. Thinking. Thinking. Then, it came to her.

"How about 'Someone to Watch Over Me?'"

"Yeah, baby," the Whiteface on the guitar said as he, and all the others, started rifling through their sheet music to find the tune.

"But I like to sing it slow," she said. "Like at quarter-tempo, please."

The tall bass player set his sheet music on a stand that was in front of him, and he grinned down at Willow. "You got it, Darlin'." He pointed to a spot on the floor in the middle of the stage and said, "You stand up here... in front of the microphone. Look out over where the audience would be and let it fly, kid. Let us know when you're ready."

Willow smiled at him gratefully. She quickly climbed up onto the stage and did as she was told. The instant the tips of her fingers touched the shiny surface of the microphone, a bright spotlight came on and pinned her to the spot where she stood. The glare was blinding and uncomfortably warm and it, well... it felt fantastic.

She nodded to Shorty, closing her eyes as the introduction to the song began, the band playing it to absolute perfection. Willow felt the hairs on her arm all stand up on their ends. She took in a breath, and as she let it out, she began to sing.

"There's a saying old, says that love is blind," she intoned, keeping her eyes closed against the brilliance of the spotlight.

Like slipping her tired body into a hot, sudsy bath, she felt herself being immersed in the warm tones of the music. And as she continued to sing, she felt transported—like she always did whenever she performed—to the secret world of pure expression that she kept locked away in her heart. She felt an unbridled elation as her soul suddenly took flight, soaring into her own private world of never-ending joy.

The song was a standard, an ode to loss and to a soul-crushing loneliness, a melody of want and of an almost desperate need for something better. It was a song her momma used to sing as she shucked peas while standing at the sink. Willow remembered sitting at the kitchen table doing her homework and listening to her and thinking that her mother had the voice of an absolute angel.

Willow finally opened her eyes and looked out over the empty club, the echo of her voice coming back to her like a small fragile bird. She felt her throat tighten and she had to stop herself from crying. She glanced over and saw the sax player staring at her, his eyes wide, a smile splitting his face. He nodded to her warmly and mouthed something that looked like, 'Outta sight.' She closed her eyes and once again let herself be swept away by the melody.

"Won't you tell him please," she sang, feeling the ghostly presence of her mother watching over her, encouraging her, "to put on some speed..."

As the song reached its crescendo, the final trills of the piano echoed across the room, the old upright's tone ringing out like fine China. Willow took a breath, feeling afraid to open her eyes and see the reaction of the band. When she finally did though, she was surprised to see them all smiling and nodding agreeably.

"That was really fine," the guitar player said, and all the other men onstage nodded their heads in agreement. "Wanna do another?"

Willow nodded her head sheepishly, feeling the same rush of excitement she always felt when she found someone who liked her voice. "I heard you playing Coltrane earlier. Do you boys know Johnny Hartman, "My One and Only Love?" she asked shyly.

The boys in the band all laughed.

"Know it?" the kid horn player said chuckling. He nodded his head in the tall bass player's direction. "Shorty here played on that record, Doll."

Without any further prompting, the band struck up the song, the kid's sax replicating Coltrane's deep, plaintive tones perfectly. They kept the tempo slow, just how she liked it, and she settled herself once again into the headspace of the song. As the horn player reached the end of the instrumental opening, Willow hesitantly stepped up to the microphone and drew breath. When the time came, she slowly closed her eyes and let her voice do the rest.

"The very thought of you, makes my heart sing," she sang out infusing the words with a heartbroken sentimentalism. "Like an April breeze, on the wings of Spring..."

This was one of her dad's favorites. She remembered how he used to sing it to Mama late at night as they sat before the evening's fire. He even sang it at their twenty-fifth wedding anniversary party a few months before Willow left the farm. It was a love song, a song of dedication and of promise, and it was one of Willow's favorites. The band behind her played the tune flawlessly, and hearing them, it inspired her to sing her heart out.

"The touch of your hand is like Heaven," she sang plaintively, feeling real tears wet her eyes. "A heaven I've never known."

The song finally wound down to its end and Willow noticed that the band were all nodding their heads once again. Shorty gave her an 'okay' sign with his index finger and thumb. She felt her cheeks blush and grow warm, and she giggled to herself in embarrassment.

"Boys," said Shorty, once the music had stopped, "I think we may have just found ourselves somethin' very, very special."

"Hey, Sweetie," the guitar player said. "Want to try something else?"

Willow grinned giddily as she shuffled her feet beneath her. "Sure!"

The Rodeo got up from his piano and came over to her with a handful of sheet music. He held the stack in front of her and pointed to the first page. "Know this?"

Willow looked where he was pointing and saw the words, 'Cry Me a River' at the top of the page. Her eyes widened, her mascara cracking with joy. She looked at the Rodeo and smiled. "Know it? Man, I love this song."

The guitar player clapped his hands as he looked around the stage at his pals. "Well, then... whats say we go ahead, and do it?"

Once again, Willow took her place in front of the microphone and waited for the band to cue her in. The strings of the hollow-body guitar rang out like those of a harp, clear and true. Shorty played along in a slow walking bass line. Finally, the Rodeo nodded to her, and she sang out forlornly.

"Now, you say you're lonely. You cry the whole night through…"

Willow was suddenly struck by the raw emotion of the song in a way she'd never been before. The sadness, the resigned loneliness… it all washed over her in a cold, bracing wave. She felt more tears come to sting her eyes and she gripped the microphone with both hands to keep herself upright. Feeling properly moored now, she abandoned herself to the depths of the song's despair.

"I cried a river…" she sang and felt each and every word strike her down deep in her heart. "…over you."

Finally, the song ended, and the band let the final notes from their instruments ring out over the empty club like the peal of a church's bells. After that, silence settled back over the vacant dance floor like a morning's dew. The band all looked at one another, and then, they looked into the darkness toward the bar.

By now, Knick Knack had come back from the bathroom and had retaken his stool at the bar. He casually held another one of his purple drinks in his hand and he was looking up at the stage approvingly, nodding his head. Through the blazing lights, Willow noticed Daisy standing next to her father, her eyes glimmering in the darkness like an expectant mother.

"Well, hot dang," Shorty finally said, breaking the fragile silence.

Willow saw Knick Knack drink his drink down in a single gulp. Then he set the empty glass on the bar and started walking slowly across the dance floor toward the front of the stage. When he got there, he stopped and motioned with his finger for Willow to bend over to talk. He also motioned for Shorty to come as well. The tall Auguste leaned his upright bass against the Rodeo's piano and they both came over.

"That sure was mighty fine there, Girlie" Knick Knack said. "Daisy said you could sing, but, as Shorty just said… hot dang!"

Shorty nodded his head in agreement. "Yeah, that was really somethin,' babe. A total gas, man."

Willow felt her head go light, like a balloon suddenly set free to drift and bobble its way into the stratosphere. She wrung her hands like they were a dish rag and tried not to cry.

"We're in agreement, then," Kick Knack said with managerial authority. "You start tonight, kid."

Willow grinned broadly, barely able to control her excitement. "Tonight? Well, sure! Thank you!" She felt her face get hot and redden. "Thank you so much!"

Knick Knack quickly waved her gratitude away like it was a

bothersome horse fly. "It's not a gimme spot, kiddo. You're gonna have to earn it by doing some bar-backing and picking up tables, but..." he grinned as he walked away, heading back to his place at the bar. "From the sounds of what I just heard, I doubt any of that is gonna be a problem."

Willow grinned like a jack-o-lantern, still fighting hard to hold back her tears. She felt Shorty's fraternal hand suddenly land on her shoulder, and she felt herself losing the tussle.

"Come with me," Knick Knack said to Willow.

Shorty returned to his spot with the band and there were high-fives all around. Willow quickly ran to the stairs and came down from the stage. She hurried to catch up.

When they'd gotten back to Knick Knack's spot at the bar, Eckles the Scary bartender approached and quietly said something to him. Willow saw him nod and he turned back to face her.

"Okay, kid... we open the doors in fifteen," he said. "I'm gonna need you to go fetch a bucket or two of ice from the maker in the back for Eckles here. Dat sound, okay? And be careful... we don't want you to mess up your pretty party dress. You'll go on with the band an hour or so after we open. Until then, help out where you can, okay?"

Willow nodded, looking out over the empty club, wanting to remember the moment. She hugged herself and was already starting to think of what she'd say in her letter back home. Then, she glanced back to the band. The boys were all back at their instruments, ignoring her now as if she'd never existed. They immediately started playing an old Ike Quebec song she recognized as "Willow, Weep for Me," and she smiled. Reminding herself to thank each of them, she quietly left the showroom to find a bucket to fetch that ice.

MAN'S BEST FRIEND

*C*runch!
   Crunch!

The sun hung in the sky overhead like a magistrate passing sentence, its fiery eye glaring down upon the desert, judging everything in its sight. There was little flora or fauna on the lonely stretch of road, just some Cottontop Barrel, Grizzly Bear Pricklypear, and Silver Cholla cactus all trying to stay alive in the oppressive heat. Whatever color there was, it was because of the Desert Trumpet, Wavyleaf Desert Paintbrush, and other low-lying flowering plants. The vista was as beautiful as it was intimidating.

Crunch!
Crunch!

Steven Walker plodded along, doing what he would do every minute of his life if he had his way about it, putting one foot in front of the other, clicking off the miles. To earn his livelihood, Steven worked as a lawyer in a big glass office downtown and he was successful at it. But his real passion, his reason for living, was running.

He'd been bitten by the bug back when he was just getting out of high school. His dad had taken him out for the day, and they'd covered mile after mile, grinding away at the track at the local community college. The run had almost killed him, softening his legs into cataplexy, but... he'd gotten out there the very next day he was able, pushing through the leg cramps and ignoring the pains stabbing into his side. Soon, he was not only keeping up with his dad, he was lapping him.

Crunch!
Crunch!

A rapid snuffling could be heard to his right. Ghost, his Thai Ridgeback who he'd had since the dog was a puppy, ran alongside him joyfully. Periodically, the dog would stop to sniff at something or take a leak, but he'd quickly catch up, clinging to Steven's side like a shadow.

The pair were out in the foothills around a small town called Furnace, near the California / Nevada border. The land was arid and desolate, the hills strewn like pebbles at the feet of the mountain range above. Steven had read up on the area, finding that it was as barren as it was, due to the regular and rampant flooding that happened when the snows on the mountaintops melted and sent their runoff downhill. This overflow made for a lot of flash flooding, which caused deep fissures and box canyons to be formed. Most were shallow slashes in the stone, not particularly deep or dangerous. Others though, could be deep pockets in the rock, some as deep as thirty feet.

Crunch!

Crunch!

Ghost ran up ahead, eagerly sniffing out whatever small mammals and lizards he could find. His light coat shimmered in the sun, the mask of his face a dark counterpoint to the rest of his coloring. As the dog pawed at the soft sand, Steven admired the way the thick cords of muscle in his back bunched together like steel cabling under the blanket of his bristly fur.

Steven slowed and took a drink from the small tube coming out of his camo-colored Osprey Duro 8 backpack. The liquid was warm and a little brackish, but the water tasted like wine to his parched tongue. Stowing the drinking tube away, he wiped his hands on his green shirt. Wet circles spotted the material obscuring the words, Frog Hollow Day Camp, which were printed there. The rest of his running outfit was his usual: Norda 001 running shoes, dark blue Neoprene shorts, and his lucky "U.S.S. SULACO" baseball cap.

Ghost scampered across the loose dirt and sand, a look of pure elation lighting up his face. Steven had gotten the dog as a puppy and spent an arm and a leg getting him trained and keeping him healthy. And at seventy pounds and measuring roughly two feet high at the shoulders, one thing for sure... that boy was healthy.

Crunch!

Crunch!

Steven continued running, his legs burning in that way that made him feel so goddam alive. He'd been moving on pure adrenaline for the last ten miles or so, and he knew he had at least another ten to go before he could turn around to head back to the car. Wiping his brow with the back of his hand, he focused on the road ahead.

Crunch!

Crunch!

Man, he needed this run though, he thought. The office had him up to his ass in alligators, and that had been the case for the last six months or so. His casework was piling up, and well… he found it harder and harder to give a shit. Christ, he saw more of his secretary Sheila than he did his own girlfriend. These days, all he wanted to do, all he thought about doing, was being alone, out on a trail like this, planting one foot after the other.

Crunch!

Crunch!

They bore left and headed up into the foothills, the ground becoming firmer and easier to run on. Foliage became more prevalent, trees more noticeable. Steven leaned forward as the difficulty of the trail increased, bringing his strength and agility to bear. His breath came in short, labored gasps, but it felt good. He could feel his heart pounding in his chest like a kickdrum, pumping blood and oxygen to his muscles. Apathetic, Ghost wandered off the trail to sniff at a bush.

"Ghost!" Steven called as he slowly came to a stop. "Come!"

The dog raised its broad head and looked toward his master. Ghost's ears were up, and his eyes shimmered like opals in the day's sunlight. Thick muscles protruded from his forelegs, as he came bounding over a bush, galumphing up to Steven's side.

"Good, boy," he said as he patted the dog's wide forehead. "Sit."

Ghost looked up at him happily and sat down at his feet, his tongue lolling from his mouth like a wet piece of meat. His long tail whipped back and forth like a riding crop, slapping the backs of Steven's legs painfully.

Steven reached into a little pocket on his backpack strap and pulled out a treat for the dog. The plug of material was oily to the touch and was supposedly made of crickets. Steven smelled it and blanched.

"Christ, boy," he chuckled as he fed the treat to Ghost. The dog gobbled the morsel up eagerly. "How do you stomach these things?"

When he'd swallowed the treat, Ghost licked his lips, and then absentmindedly started licking his balls.

"Then again," Steven mused, "you're not exactly the connoisseur, are ya boy?"

Ghost looked up at him adoringly, his tail beating out a rhythm on the sandy ground. His eyes projected a single-minded, intensely powerful, adoration that made Steven shake his head. He wished the people in his life looked at him the way this damn dog did.

Steven reached up to another pocket on the strap of his backpack. Inside, he found a small compass with his fingers, a gift from his dad.

Without a thought, he flipped it open. He'd been taught how to use one back when he was a scout, and using it just became his habit. And even though his phone had a GPS on it, he always made sure to leave it in the car. There was nothing he hated more than getting a text or call from the office while he was out on the trail. And besides, he still had the emergency beacon on his Apple watch which was stowed in a small pocket in the front of the pack.

After some brief calculations, he put the compass back where he'd gotten it. Zipping the pocket back up, and patting his hands together, he clicked his tongue, and Ghost came bounding over.

"You ready for some hills, kid?" he asked the dog.

Ghost continued staring up at him like he was Jesus Christ.

The two of them took off up the trail, heading into the foothills. They passed more Silver Cholla cactus and Desert Trumpet. They even saw some Mojave Yucca along the way, their branches reaching up pleadingly to a dry sky. Overhead, the sun bore down on them, pressing everything under its fiery eye flat with its heat.

Suddenly, Ghost stopped in his tracks, poised with one of his front legs curled under him, pointing. Steven stumbled to a stop, nearly tripping over him. The dog's hackles were raised, his head was down, and his ears were pressed flat over his skull, as his eyes focused intently on something in the brush. Steven patted the top of the dog's head to calm him.

"Easy boy," he said softly.

Ghost growled a low and menacing response.

Then, from out of the brush, a ball of fur came rushing out. Whatever the thing was, it was small and darkly colored, its mouth a buzzsaw of sharp, snarling teeth. Ghost bolted for the animal immediately. His broad head went for the creature's abdomen, and as his teeth bore down, the animal wrapped itself around his head. For a second, he looked like he was wearing a furry hat.

Steven quickly moved forward to split the two apart, but the dog and whatever this animal was, plowed into Steven's knees bowing his legs painfully. Before he knew it, Steven was falling. His legs buckled painfully backward, and for some reason, he thought of flamingos.

The next thing he knew, he and Ghost and whatever this thing with the fur and teeth was, were all tumbling down the side of the hill. Somewhere along the line, Steven felt his backpack rip open, and most of its contents scattered after him like ducklings chasing their mother. He also lost his hat, which pissed him off.

Somewhere in the middle of all the commotion, Steven's legs got entangled with the dog's and, since Ghost had this thing in his teeth, they all came plummeting down the hill like a loosened snowball, gathering bits of brush and dirt in their wake like satellites.

And then, they were airborne.

Tumbling end over end, the three of them hit the ground with great force, rolling like a boulder. Time slowed… and Steven was able to catch sight of Ghost's face. He noticed how terrified the dog looked as they spiraled in the air. For a second, Steven thought that he looked exactly like he had when he was a puppy, with those big, scared eyes.

He also got a look at the creature that had attacked them.

Shit, he thought to himself, is that a fuckin' badger?

And then, they were all thrown into the air again. This time, though, when they landed, they blew through a clump of brush, and they hit a cactus, sharp needles poking into their flesh. Suddenly, the ground disappeared from beneath them once again.

Steven tried to roll so that he'd land on his back, but it proved difficult with the added weight. He managed to push Ghost away from him as they fell, but that meant that he landed on his feet. Regrettably, his already compromised knees couldn't take the pressure and he felt them and his ankle blow. Striking the ground with a lot more force than he'd expected, Steven had the air kicked from his lungs.

Off in the distance, he heard Ghost yelp as he landed like a ton of bricks on the ground a few yards away. Once the rocks and soft dirt from their fall settled around them, silence returned to the landscape. Ghost whimpered and Steven heard him attempting to crawl closer.

Steven quickly did a 'systems check' and scanned himself for anything seriously wrong. His knees hurt like hell, but they seemed intact. His ankle… well, that was another matter. It didn't take a genius to see that it was badly broken, maybe even a compound fracture, as blood stained his socks from the inside.

He managed to drag himself over to a large boulder that was near the sheer wall of the hole. Once he'd gotten himself settled, Steven looked around and appraised the situation they were in. They were in a hole, that much was for sure. A deep one. From the looks of it, it was at least twenty feet deep, with sheer dirt walls that looked powdery to the touch.

Once again, he remembered something he'd read back when he was looking into running here, about how the area was inundated with flash flooding in the spring, causing deep washed-out fissures in the ground. The book warned against hikers getting caught in them—especially during run-off season. There were reports of people being trapped, and a sudden wall of water coming along and causing them to drown in the middle of a desert.

He let his gaze drift around him as he tried to think of anything else other than his ankle. He definitely was in some kind of small, box canyon, essentially a hole in the ground. Dirt walls rose up around him and there were several boulders littered about. He stared up into the blue sky above, and watched a small, puffy cloud float by.

Then, he looked down at his legs.

His knees were swollen, and the toes on his right leg were pointing in the wrong direction. That was the biggest concern. One thing was for sure... he wasn't climbing his way out of here. Shit, he silently wondered if he'd ever run again... or even walk.

He leaned back and tried to catch his breath as the pain in his leg grew more and more pronounced. A sudden cold chill ran down the length of his body as shock took ahold of his system and overrode everything. Looking around for Ghost, he saw only the badger's lifeless body a few feet away. The animal's eyes were open wide amidst the black and white canvas of its agonized face. The animal's back appeared to have been broken in the fall. Steven must have landed right on top of the poor bastard and crushed him.

Good. Fucker.

Suddenly, he heard Ghost whine from nearby. The cry was not so much based in pain, as it was a groan—if dogs were capable of such a thing. Steven listened and heard the sound of footsteps. Then, Ghost came limping around one of the bigger rocks.

"Hey, boy," Steven said soothingly. "You hurt?"

Ghost came up and nuzzled his head against Steven's arm. He leaned his weight against him, licking the side of his neck. The dog did that when he was scared and needed comforting. Steven pet him, but also did a quick search of the dog's body. From the looks of it, nothing was broken. The poor kid just had the wind kicked out of him in the fall.

Steven checked his leg again, crying out as he tried to move the limb to at least look correct. Swelling had already started around his ankle, bloating it to almost monstrous proportions. And the color had gone a distinct shade of purple. He felt Ghost lay down next to him, setting his broad head across the thigh of Steven's good leg.

Steven closed his eyes as he tried to get on top of the pain.

Soon, he drifted off and slept, grateful for the respite.

Some time passed. Steven was not sure exactly how long, but from the look of the shadows on the ground, it had been a while. He groaned and noticed that Ghost was no longer by his side. He gazed lazily around the hole they were in but saw nothing.

It was then that he noticed motion in his periphery. Repositioning a little despite the pain, he saw Ghost dragging the dead badger's body to the other side of the hole, maybe fifteen or twenty feet away. At first, Steven thought that the dog had just gotten hungry and had decided to eat the dead animal. But then, Steven noticed that he was doing whatever it could to move it, but not touch it. Instead, he used his nose to push the dirt beneath the creature, using it to move the corpse of the creature where he wanted it. When it was as far away as it could be, the dog walked lazily over to his master.

Steven pulled his Osprey pack off and took stock of what he had left. Inside, all that there was, were three granola bars, a few more of Ghost's cricket treats, and a water bottle three-quarters of the way full. Sadly, the water bladder built into the pack had burst, another casualty of the fall. Other than that, there was nothing. He knew he'd packed light, but he'd also lost a lot when the backpack ripped.

He shook his head forlornly. They were only going out for the afternoon. Now, he wished he'd packed a few more things, like food, more water, maybe some bandages... a splint.

Steven broke one of the granola bars in half and ate it with a gulp of water. He gave a cricket treat to Ghost, and then carefully poured a swallow or two into his mouth. He spilled more of it than he would have liked to, but... at least they'd be okay for a little while.

"We'll be fine, boy," Steven said comfortingly. "Someone will come."

Ghost lay in the shade provided by the sheer sides of the hole they found themselves in, his head hot and his demeanor impatient. He'd eaten everything The Man had for him, drunken from his canteen, but the maddening pain in his head would not go away. He loved The Man and was troubled at the thought of not being there to care for him when He needed him.

Ghost moved his gaze across the ground, letting it finally settle on The Man who was leaning up against a rock, his head back, as he did what he could to get comfortable. Ghost knew that The Man was hurt; hurt bad. He also knew how deeply he loved him and would do anything to protect him. That was why he'd attacked the badger so fervently. He did it to protect The Man.

The dog watched passively as a large bird suddenly came into view, circling in the sky over the hole. The bird slowly spiraled to the ground, ultimately landing near the body of the dead badger. The great bird's eyes never left Ghost as it warily took hold of the corpse in its talons.

With a great beating of its wings, it lifted off, carrying the dead body with it. Soon, the two of them disappeared over the edge of the hole.

The dog remained unfazed, setting his great head onto his front paws. He sighed and small bits of dirt flew up from the ground with his breath. Looking over, he saw the Man still asleep, his head back and snoring. Ghost slowly let his eyelids droop until they closed.

If only this pain in his head would go away...

The next few days passed, it was impossible to tell how many, but they proved Steven to be a liar. No one came to rescue them. No one came to save them. And, after a while, Steven started to suspect that no one was going to come. Their stock of granola bars and treats was now depleted. The water bottle empty and lying a few feet away from them.

"Surely someone's out there looking," Steven said to Ghost who was laying in the shade across the flat dirt from him. "I mean, Sheila would have missed us by now and sent someone out to look for us, right?"

Ghost deemed not to reply. He just lowered his head and closed his eyes.

The color of Steven's leg was starting to concern him, due to it having deepened, going from reddish blue to purple black. The good news was that the pain had dulled to a constant roar, but at least it was something he could deal with. The bad was that there were now red lines of infection radiating upward from the ankle, moving up his shin and calf. The way Steven had it figured, if he didn't do something, or if someone didn't find them soon, he was sure to lose the leg to gangrene.

He looked around the deep hole and its sheer walls and felt the embers of panic start to catch at the periphery of his consciousness. Letting his head fall back to rest on the rock, and not having anything better to do, he drifted off.

It was still early in the morning as Steven strolled lazily down the beach in Aptos, California. He was back at the beach house he'd rented last summer. He'd taken a stroll that first day and had repeated the ritual every day since, just as soon as he woke up.

This stretch of beach was about two miles of uninterrupted sand. There didn't used to be an easy way down to the shore, but a workable trail had been formed by decades of people traipsing down the hill face to get to the sand. Now, the path was scored smooth and there was litter all along it.

Steven ambled down the shoreline, his feet splashing in the low tide. Overhead, seagulls wheeled in the sky like fighter planes, their screeches cutting through the air like fingernails on a chalkboard. His mind was elsewhere as he walked. He was troubled by a case he was working on at work—a contract negotiation that wasn't going particularly well—and no matter what he did to clear his mind, the details of the case kept popping up.

He'd just about decided to text Sheila and have her set up a meeting with his client when his right foot suddenly sank into the sand. His foot went into a hole nearly to his shin, water soaking his pantleg and shoe. The change in elevation brought Steven down to one knee, like he was praying.

"Shit," he said.

But as hard as he might, it was impossible for Steven to pull his leg out. The sand had encircled his foot and it wasn't so much as pulling on it, as simply holding it there. He put his hands onto the ground, sand immediately coating his palms, until he was in a push-up position. Pulling back, he was surprised when the leg refused to move.

Suddenly, he felt something pinch his leg, right on the calf. Then, it did it again. It wasn't anything big, maybe a crab or something. But with his foot submerged like it was, it caused him some concern. He pulled at the leg again. Nothing. Not an inch. Again. Nada.

"God damn it," he grunted.

Then, he felt something gently tugging. It wasn't much at first. Soon though, it was incessant, like a heartbeat. Steven pulled against the sand with every bit of his strength, but his foot wasn't going anywhere.

"Shit," he sighed.

He looked down the beach to see if there was anyone who might be able to help him. To his surprise, he saw a circus clown coming toward him. Steven blinked his eyes a couple of times, but no... there was definitely a circus clown coming down the beach. The clown had on a blousy, red work shirt, and a pair of denim overalls.

In his hands, he held a monkey.

And in his hand, the monkey held a gun.

Steven awoke from his dream with a start, and he was disappointed, but not surprised, to find himself back in the hole. He was still leaning up against the boulder, night having fallen over the mountain. There was a chill in the air as the sun slowly slid behind the foothills, a harvest moon rising majestically to take its place in the sky.

Suddenly, something brushed up against Steven's leg, his ankle squawking out in pain. He looked down to see Ghost, laying prone next to his injured leg and looking up at him intensely. Steven noticed that there was a smear of dark fluid on the dog's lips, like he'd been sticking his nose into something. Or licking.

Ghost lifted his broad head and sniffed at Steven's shattered ankle.

He pressed the tip of his black snout against a spot where blood had seeped through his sock, savoring the aroma like he did when Steven was frying up onions. The dog's sad eyes slowly drifted up to his master's. There, in the wet orbs, Steven saw his own fearful face reflected back at him.

He rested his head against the stone and did what he could to get himself comfortable again. This was a mess. He needed to do something, anything, if they were going to get out of this. Otherwise, well…

Abruptly, Ghost licked the skin on Steven's leg, just above where the injury was. Steven sat up, groaning with pain, and gently pushed the dog away with his other foot.

"What the fuck? C'mon, boy… give me a break, okay?" Steven glared at the dog like he had just insulted his mother.

Ghost grumbled and got up, walking across the ground to the other side of the hole. He looked over his shoulder at Steven, his eyes glared at the man darkly. Finally, Ghost turned circles to find his spot, then he laid down, his eyes remaining fixed on Steven.

Time passed. Who knows how long? It might have been minutes; it might have been days. Steven's leg had gotten a lot worse during that time. The blood around his injury had dried to an inky black. His entire foot was bloated like something out of a cartoon. He'd had to piss a couple of times, and that proved both a painful and embarrassing endeavor. Now, he had pee all over the front of his pants and he'd had to abandon his underwear (a painful proposition until he figured out to rip the sides and pull them straight out of his shorts) due to them being soiled.

Across the hole from him, he saw Ghost. The dog wasn't doing well. He was panting a lot, like he was hot, and his muzzle was always wet. Normally, he was a friendly, attentive pooch. Over the last few days, he'd gone sullen, and seemed constantly irritated and pissed off.

It stood to reason. After all, they were starving, and their thirst had become a matter of great concern. For the both of them. He knew that if they didn't find water soon, it would be bad.

It was then, out of nowhere, that he remembered the Apple watch. He quickly dug it out of his pack, only to discover he had no bars. That was okay, he knew the Emergency Beacon would still work. It was one of the things he'd specifically asked the guy at the Apple Store about, did the beacon work anywhere? He'd been assured it would by the emo-looking kid who sold it to him, anywhere in the world. Christ, what an idiot he was for forgetting the damn thing. He opened the app and hit the button. The screen flashed and a message came on saying that local Fire & Rescue had been notified and that help was on the way.

"See that, boy," he said to Ghost proudly. "I think I just saved our asses."

Ghost just lay there, his head on top of his front paws, staring at him. The dog's eyes looked glassy, and he kept blinking them. Finally, it seemed like he'd grown tired, and he closed his eyes again.

In time, clouds slowly gathered in the sky overhead. Far off, a peal of thunder rumbled like God himself was up in Heaven moving furniture. Not too long after, Steven felt the first drops of rain on his skin. Soon, they were being showered by a deluge of crisp rainwater. Steven quickly set out anything he could find in his pack that would hold liquid, so they'd have something to drink.

Ghost got up and wandered to the middle of the hole, staring up into the sky and looking confused. His jaws were open, and he was letting the rainwater run off his face and into his mouth. The dog's throat convulsed as he tried to swallow, and it looked like he was having trouble getting it down. He managed to appease his thirst, but it took him a while. Soon enough though, both man and dog's thirsts were mollified, and they were content to lay under the downpour, letting the water wash away the days of sweat and dirt.

Ghost rested his broad head on his paws, happy to let the rainwater flow over him. It was cool and it helped calm the fever that had been running through his body for the last few days. His right ear hurt in the place where the badger had bit him, but he'd not felt right since. His head was pounding, and he had a thirst that was driving him mad. Not even the rain had been sufficient to quell his body's need.

The dog shifted and eyed the man. The dog closed his eyes and grinned, remembering the taste of his blood the night before. That little bit, taken during those few attempts at simply tasting the substance laid out before him, had ignited a fire deep within his brain, a growing need—no matter how repulsive the act might have once seemed.

The dog's reddened eyes focused on the man again, his vision centering on the exposed wound. In spite of all the rainwater running over him and the heat, Ghost tried to sleep, to no avail. After a moment, he sniffed the air clandestinely, savoring the smell of the leg's infection. The dog instinctively knew that it wouldn't be long before the man was unable to keep him from investigating it further.

And so, being patient, Ghost settled in to wait.

More time slipped away...

Steven awoke feeling weak and dizzy with fever. He knew his leg was getting infected, but there wasn't exactly a whole lot he could do about it. He leaned his head against the rock again and silently wondered what was taking Fire & Rescue so long to find him. He couldn't be sure of how long ago he'd hit the beacon, but he was sure it wasn't that long ago.

Steven suddenly heard a sound from overhead, like newspapers being rustled by a particularly strong wind. He looked up to the rim of the hole and saw a large bird perched there. He wasn't sure what kind of bird it was—a scavenger undoubtedly—but it was big, and it had a beak on it that looked like it was made for tearing flesh. For now, though, it seemed content to simply sit and stare at Steven and Ghost in their predicament.

Then, from across the hole, Steven noticed Ghost. The dog was standing in the sun, his head hanging down like it weighed a thousand pounds. There were strings of drool, like syrupy ropes, hanging from his jowls. His red eyes blazed angrily. Steven noticed a mark on the side of the dog's throat. It was red and swollen, dirt clinging to the flesh in muddy clumps. It was a wonder he hadn't noticed it before.

"Uh, hey boy" Steven said, and his voice trembled despite him not wanting it to. "Something wrong?"

The dog growled as it slowly approached. Inquisitively, he sniffed at the wound on Steven's leg. Steven did what he could to draw his crippled leg back, but any movement caused Ghost to growl more aggressively. Steven even tried to slide his butt over, but every time he put pressure on the leg, it shrieked out in agony.

Ghost sniffed at the ankle once again. Steven reflexively pulled his leg away when the dog took a nip at the edges of the wound, pain going through him like an electrical current. Licking his chops, the dog inched closer.

"Ghost?" Steven asked and his fear was evident in his voice. For the first time he got a glimpse of the dog's eyes up close. The animal's irises swam in a pool of blistering red blood, islands in a sea of spoiling crimson. "Bad dog."

By now, Ghost's nose was pressed against the purple skin at the ankle. His lips were curled up on his jaw, like window shades revealing an array of knives. His growl intensified as his jaws slowly opened. A tongue like a wet slug lolled over the animal's large, ivory teeth.

"Ghoooost?"

The vulture that was observing all of this from the edge of the hole took flight when the first of the man's screams shook the air. The bird had sensed something dying as it flew over the desert landscape, so it came down to investigate. Seeing the man and the dog trapped in the ground, it knew—better than it knew anything in the world—that these creatures were doomed, and it was only a matter of time before they succumbed to the environment, and the bird would feed.

Lazily, the vulture circled in the sky, waiting for the dog to finish.

SALAMAT!

As always, the first (and most) of my thanks goes where it will forever go: to my incredible wife, Cat. She has been, in a few words, an absolute godsend and she's been there for me more than anyone else in the world. I will love you forever.

Next, thank you to my kids. You make me so proud. It's been such an honor watching you grow into such fine and caring people.

And, of course, so much love and gratitude go to my bestest buddy, Ripley. You saved me when I most needed it. And it's been my distinct pleasure to watch your Light as it's come on to shine brighter and brighter every day. Soon, it will illuminate the world. "I gooper, gooper wuv you!"

#ilostmyheartonLV426

Gratitude and appreciation go out to those adventurous souls who took the time to look this book over back when it was all just raw text: Heather Strbiak, Frank Thomas, and Christopher Burch. By telling me what worked (and what didn't), you folks helped me out in ways you'll never, ever know. Thank you!

Also, a big thank you to David Niall Wilson and all the fine folks at Crossroad Press for supporting me and for having faith in The Work.

To my mom... I miss you still, each and every day.

Much love to my four-legged pals, Rocko and Freyja. They get it.

Also, all honor and respect go to Lee Jun Fan. Your inspiration continues to support and guide me to this day. I am trying...

All praise to Crom.

Until next time...

~ Thom Carnell
Bellingham, WA

ABOUT THE AUTHOR

Thom Carnell. As a journalist, his interviews and profiles can be found in *Carpe Noctem Magazine* (for which he served as Head Writer and Creative Consultant), *Fangoria Magazine*, Dread Central.com and Twitchfilm.com. Carnell's fiction has been featured in *Carpe Noctem 20*, the Pill Hill Press anthology *Bloody Carnival*, *Swank Magazine*, in his novel *No Flesh Shall Be Spared*, *No Flesh Shall Be Spared: Don't Look Back*, and in his short story collections *Moonlight Serenades* and *A String of Pearls*.

www.thomcarnell.com

Curious about other Crossroad Press books?
Stop by our site:
http://store.crossroadpress.com
We offer quality writing
in digital, audio, and print formats.

www.ingramcontent.com/pod-product-compliance
Lightning Source LLC
Chambersburg PA
CBHW030249200626
46816CB00002BA/570